ACKNOWLEDGEMENTS

To those who stand up

1

TYPICALLY, THE ROOM was dark, he liked to work that way. Kenny's silhouetted, bulky and stressfully straight profile stared blankly at the computer screen. Light reflected in his black puddle eyes and off his high shiny forehead. Shadows whizzed, and colours striped his puffy face. Absolute concentration. Even when acknowledging Hanna's presence, he didn't look up, just reached for his half-eaten medicinal cookie with a "Hi, bro" and continued. Hanna fell into a leather easy chair and picked up the note he left for her. The note stuck out from the manuscript - all it said was. 'over to you, Mac, done all I can. You know why it has to be this way. XX'. She threw a look over her shoulder at his desk. He was gone. Gone without telling her. Was she being ignored or considered? She could never tell with him. But there were questions nagging she could not figure at all. It seemed he knew something might happen. Life had got that way with him, almost expected disaster. The snarling black dog pursued him almost from the beginning. Had those demons finally consumed him? She still didn't know. People thought him dead before and were wrong. Was it wrong now to think finally he'd been caught, savaged? The evidence leaned that way, but no body had been found. He lingered. The sweet smell of fresh cooked 'Mary Janes' lingered too. She shivered with chill realisation poignant, then stood, taking the manuscript and the file of personal papers and left. On her way out, at the bottom of the stairs, she stopped to look at the job he'd done on the car he loved. She shook her head in acknowledgement of the skill of the man, ran her hand the length of his treasure and her finger traced over the word painted on the front right guard panel, "Javelin". Strangely it was on stands, wheels not touching the ground. She thought that was an odd thing to do if he was never coming back. Was he really gone, left her forever? Or was he close by watching her, same as all the other times, hiding in shadows waiting for the right moment to walk back into her life? Grief tore at her. "Bastard, I just don't believe you. I can look after myself. You might've been cursed, brother, but I wouldn't let that curse get me. You didn't have to do this to protect me. It can't stop now. It's not right, not fair. This car is clearly a clue. But what you meant to do and what happened could be two different things. The car on stands is a clue that you intend to return, and I should look after the place, but you might have told me. I can handle the truth. You know I can."

She vowed, in spite of her first thoughts, that she'd finish what he'd begun. His final statement on stuff that really mattered to him. She owed him that. If dead, he'd rest in peace, knowing she would respect his wishes. If not, then he'd return. His story being finally finished had kept him away from the black dog demons that corroded his life like rust on old steel. He persisted, and it kept his mind on other people's problems rather than his own. OK, they were creations, but it didn't matter. Their lives were real to him. It was finished, and she held it tucked under her arm on her way out. It would be published.

Mark waited in his car. They were due at a fundraiser where her string quartet was to play. She locked the front door and turned to go, almost bumping into a tattooed, toothless local identity with his eyes on the footpath, hungry for treats and clearly in need of more basics than someone else's cigarette butts. You have to be opportunistic living on the streets, a roach, a coin, and even the odd 10 dollar note caught up in a grill or wire fence pleading for rescue. She moved to dodge the vagrant while nodding hello, but he propped and shot an odd look in her direction. She didn't shrink from the rich marinade of long-cultivated aromas that made up his aura, she looked directly at him, a greeting in her eye.

"S'cuse missus didn't think it could be you. Me and him in there, we sometimes have coffee here on the step. Is he home? I know he goes away sometimes."

"Sorry, sir. He's gone away for a while, but I'll be calling in from time to time. Guess you live close by?"

"You might say that, missus. We met a while ago under the bridge at Southbank. He liked the music I played. Wolvie's the name."

"Wolvie?"

"Just like Wolverine, see my sideboards."

He turned his head to display his resemblance to Hugh Jackman.

"Of course, Wolvie. Hanna."

He nodded acknowledgement, stepped around her and shuffled on his way. Hanna watched him wondering, then realising she had to go, took time to look up at the window for a moment. With one more wistful glance, she turned and stepped into the car. "Let's go, Mark." Then suddenly thought, "sideboards? Did he say 'sideboards'?"

2

"**KENNY, MY BOY,** you're so lucky! Father Korne rang to say you've been awarded a scholarship to their boarding school in Mansfield. And if you still want to become a priest, you can go on to Sydney when you finish school. You do want to become a priest, don't you?"

"But Mum…."

Kenny was concentrating on the two-shilling piece memento of pre-decimal days, flipping over his fingers somewhat awkwardly. It fell onto the Laminex table where he and his mother were sitting. He stood the coin on its edge for a moment before his little sister bumped the table, chasing Turner, their dog, through the house. Their father named Turner on the day he stepped in its droppings - a reference to what it did to good food. Mother ignored the sport, impossible to catch every misdemeanour in the happening. Anyway, she was concentrating on the matter at hand.

"Father said you're the best altar boy in the parish. Your responses are so clear, and you know all the ceremonies, Mass, Benediction, Weddings, Funerals and Baptisms. Your specialty is the Latin mass they say for the oldies."

He avoided eye contact by continuing to stare at the coin and smiled to himself at the mention of the nutty priest who presided at mass like it was all about him and his juvenile theatrics. Father McMahon made the sign of the cross with a conductor's flourish and poured portions of wine and water with manic attention. When he turned to face the congregation, some were quietly amused by the ballet dancer's pirouette, chasuble lifting like a cabaret dancer's skirt. Kenny always thought it best to get out of his altar boy tunic and leave quickly after each assignment. He felt uneasy, especially when he was the only altar boy on duty.

"But Mum, I'm only 14. I really want to be a magician, wave my cape and make people disappear."

"You'll have the best teachers. You're so lucky," she repeated.

"Yes, Mum." She wasn't listening. That meant something, everything.

He had a vision there and then. Life became a suspended animation. He hung on to the edge of a cliff by his fingernails, terrified of falling, black abyss beneath him. His mother and the robed priest stood above him, hands extended and light beams radiating from their eyes. He gasped and let go. At that moment, he was back in the kitchen. Her lips were moving, but he heard nothing more. He focussed on her hair. It was short, already white at only 40, a sign of wear and tear. Light bounced off the edge of a gold tooth filling that distinguished her smile or intensified rage when she was upset. There might be an upside to getting out, he thought. After all, a scholarship would help them. There was never any money, never enough anyway. How often had he hidden with his kid sister under the bed when arguments raged about its scarcity. He could see also how important this was to his mother. God took up a lot of her mind space. Blind Freddy could see how pleased she'd be sacrificing a child to religion. Such generosity would be enough to balance the ledger in God's eyes. She was not going to listen to Kenny's lame objections. She was giving him up, his fate sealed in her eyes, his heart broken, and her salvation assured.

"Oh dear, gas has gone out. Kenny put this 50 cent piece in the meter, would you?"

The meter was a feature of the pocket handkerchief-sized bathroom furnished with a chip heater, bath, towel rack and small cabinet with a mirror for the door. It was an event of interest when the gasman came to empty the meter. Sometimes he gave coins back to Kenny's mother. When Kenny offered her heads or tails for the rebate, she'd never take the chance. She knew how clever he was with magic.

His dad was no help, looking up from the paint pot he was burning off, ready for the next job. "Do what your mother wants, son," was all he got.

Kenny bent down to look directly at his father in his eyes.

"Why do you always give in to what she wants, Dad? What about what I want? Why does she want this so much anyway? I just don't get it."

His father stood so that he could look down at Kenny.

"Why can't you do something she asks? Is that so hard?"

That cut. He was desperate for support. There'd be none here. He turned and stomped off. Frank didn't know why the air was always thick between them. He wished it wasn't like that. His son was a closed book beyond his reach. He'd given up trying. So other things came to matter more. He'd never really force the issue with Kenny. Soft? Maybe. More likely, he respected the space his son staked out and allowed him to have it. Anyway, he had enough to do looking for work. Suddenly, fire! He forgot about the smoking paint pot that rolled into the outdoor dunny door setting it on fire. Lucky a rubber garden hose was handy.

"Damn Kenny, look what you've made me do now."

Frank was a handyman long before 'Hire a Hubby'. Much of his work - a bit of maintenance painting, plastering, or small carpentry jobs - were for elderly or infirm, almost exclusively penny-wise customers. He was a soft touch, even if that meant tough times at home. His customers loved him. They had good reason. A born philanthropist and spontaneous entertainer generous with his time and his pricing. His drinking mates in the local pub were a captive audience. The poor buggers relied on his good cheer, especially when needing someone to sell tickets for the chook raffle every Friday night. He was a gifted spruiker, and the Children's Hospital was their agreed cause. Frank was a man who loved to be loved. Yet there was not much tangible love in his life. Bonnie was forever grateful he stood up for her in the biggest crisis of her life. Still, she never really showed much affection for him. She was dutiful surely, but that was it. Frank bore his cross and was still able to look at her as the girl of his dreams. She knew he did and was forever puzzled he could. And Kenny was distant. He could not figure out why. Too smart for his own good. Always challenged his father's homespun, philosophising like children should be seen and not heard, like the system is fixed against the little man, like striving for money is not the meaning of life, like St Kilda will win a premiership. The breaking point for Kenny came as a 10-year-old. One afternoon he ran home from the park complaining to his father that other kids wouldn't let him play with them.

"You can't make someone like you, son. Sometimes you're better off to walk away."

Kenny stormed off sulking because his father was supposed, in his eyes, to march back to the playground and resolve the conflict.

Kenny didn't forget that betrayal for months. It helped distance them. Frank was a good man. Nobody knew how true that was except his wife. Kenny was his son in almost every way. All but one. Bonnie was 17 when she fell from grace into the arms of her first boyfriend, who shall remain a nameless cad. This cad exited stage right, leaving best friend Frank Burgess to salvage Bonnie's honour. Kenny was never told, there was no need. He had a father, that was all that mattered. A cursed child blessed by fate, and he had no idea.

Kenny wrongly sensed they both wanted him gone, if for different reasons. She was happy, Kenny was crushed. His father appeared to be indifferent, and off to boarding school he would go. But he would never be a priest, his secret resolution. He would be on the lookout for his own path and to hell with everybody else. He never saw his father's tears.

3

AS A 15-YEAR-OLD STUDENT, Kenny moved among the elite. His memory was close to photographic, and his analytical skills exceptional. Latin, history, science and mathematics intrigued him. He was fascinated by big names of history: Jesus, Augustus, Aquinas, Luther, Pythagoras, Napoleon, Nelson, Genghis Khan, what they achieved, and how they managed their followers and treated enemies. He threw himself into his studies because he was naturally curious on the one hand and awkward with people on the other unable to go along with things just to be part of the crowd. Most boarders were sons of graziers, the rural elite. He belonged to no clique. But he was no patsy. It was a brave boy who would challenge him on the playing fields or intellectually in the classroom.

"Always stand your ground, son. Bend the knee to nobody. But you must respect everyone once. After that, take no prisoners. You might cop a few knocks along the way, but you'll stand tall in any company free of obligation to anybody."

This was the best advice he ever took from his father, written on the front page of his religious daily missal. The irony didn't escape him, especially when he re-read it in his senior year.

The library became his refuge, even if it was only a spare classroom and most of the books were rescues. There was no official librarian. Teachers were rostered on library duty when they weren't in the classroom. Their attendance was casual. He actually preferred his own company largely because people kept looking at him as alien, a self-feeding cycle. Something else he couldn't see. Few students used the library. Government grants for such facilities didn't reach that room. There was one important, exceptional connection. Kenny had a friend, a jackaroo's son Charlie Sweeney. They first literally bumped into each other in the quadrangle when going for a mark in a game of kick to kick football. Both fell to the ground and sat up, staring at each other for an awkward moment. A twinkle in Charlie's eye captured Kenny's interest. He smiled, and Charlie laughed. They reached out to help each other up, and that was it from then on.

Charlie shared Kenny's intelligence but was gregarious, front and centre of all gatherings, and a natural leader. He was of the big country, Northern Territory, raised on a huge cattle and camel station south of Alice Springs. Charlie and three friends from the same country, all indigenous, were offered further education at boarding schools in Victoria, South Australia and New South Wales. The philosophy of the station's owners was to invest in a future through education. Charlie chose Victoria. He was well up to it, his strength was being able to look at issues from a viewpoint born of country. Even sons of farmers would be in awe of his ability with farm animals. It didn't matter, horses, cows, sheep, chickens and pets. His presence always calmed them. They'd just follow him. Neither was he intimidated by obvious differences to other boys. He'd seen all variations of white people's behaviour at home on the station. He and Kenny didn't need to see each other's colour, they instinctively connected. They didn't need meaningless conversation, happy to share study time or athletic skills. Charlie was impressed by his friend's smarts and often, in his absence, spoke up for him when other boys thought Kenny too distant. Kenny admired Charlie's ability to adapt to his new environment with courage and energy mixed with a wonderful humility.

Both excelled at sports and studies. Kenny bowled off spin for the school's first eleven, able to analyse a batsman's strengths and weaknesses. He could set up strokes likely to get him a result, listen to opponents with his eyes and read thoughts in behaviour. Patience, observation, and persistence were his special skills. Teammates loved what he did, but he remained aloof to them, not superior, annoyingly blank. He never forgot how they treated him in the beginning. Like his father advised, everyone got one chance.

Charlie was brilliant in the field, with explosive speed and great eye/hand coordination. He was a prolific batsman. It all started one afternoon when the first eleven players were practising in the nets. Kenny and Charlie were shanghaied by the older boys to stand far out to field the big hits. Kenny threw in a couple of hand stinging returns to the team captain, big Gerald Bourke. He responded after the third ball slammed into him by dragging the younger boy to the crease and daring him to bowl to the team's best batsman. Charlie egged Kenny on.

"Go on, Kenny, show him what you've got."

Other team members mimicked Charlie, sneering.

"Go on, Kenny, show him what you've got, wanker!"

Most didn't know who the two youngsters were. Year 12s ignored Year 10s on principle and even despised them for being younger. It was the natural order of things. Kenny and Charlie were watching this batsman, Chook Fowler, belt the ball all over the place. Apparently, though he had some talent, he got preferential treatment, his uncle was the school principal. None of the older boys could see just how intently Kenny had been watching. Smiling at Charlie, he accepted the challenge. Bourke smirked, tossed him the ball, and winked at Chook with a coded message that read: "smack him to hell." Kenny rolled the ball from hand to hand, measured his steps and floated a whirring leg break outside the line of leg stump. Fowler misjudged the spin and was bowled. He stood at the crease, embarrassed at what the junior had done, picked up the ball and threw it back. His captain frowned menacingly at him and turned to Kenny in a warning tone.

"OK smart alec, try that again."

This time Kenny threw up a ball that looked like the previous one but in line with the stumps, whirring viciously like the other. Top-spin this time and again, he deceived the batsman. He went forward, anticipating off spin when he should have gone back. He was bowled a second time between bat and pad. Kenny and Charlie were allowed to walk off, but as they did, the next bowler was walloped, and the ball came flying in Kenny's direction, head high. It would've knocked him out, but for Charlie's quick reflexes and one-handed catch. His hand stung like crazy, but he'd never show it. Both boys were invited to the next practice session, all sins forgiven. Those who'd snubbed and mimicked became instant wannabe friends. Such is the way of bullies.

The pair's new credentials carried over into the football season. They had become minor celebrities. Kenny played in the centre, a position from which he could influence key moments, usually feeding off Sweeney's ability to find the ball. They called the pair 'two-up' as in 'odds' and 'evens' because they could attract a crowd. It was a gang of two setting standards of performance in the classroom and in the sporting arena that others couldn't match. They could easily live not being loved but being well respected. That's how it was for the duration. They were not rural aristocracy, so they would never be truly accepted. But Kenny's and Charlie's skills were always going to be tapped for the kudos they could bring to the nobs.

4

CHARLIE COULD DRAW KENNY into pranks and protests, helping stir the pot. He was instinctively suspicious of authority figures, something Kenny admired. The boarding school was a hotbed of crisis at the time. Priests who managed the school hadn't attended to social changes sweeping long-held traditions and mores aside. Catholics were threatened with eternal damnation if they didn't attend mass on Sunday, used contraception, ate meat on a Friday or didn't abstain from food and drink after midnight before taking communion. Their autocratic theocentric ways were long out of step. Strange men, although some were gifted teachers and great coaches. Some, to their eternal shame, were unable to find a healthy way to sublimate sexual energy. They were the ones who preyed on young boys grooming them, sharing them, and finding easy opportunities to abuse them. Charlie Sweeney alerted Kenny to these dangers in the dormitory not long after they'd become friends. They formulated a strategy to protect anyone close by staging disruptions when they sensed a predator was nearby. Spontaneous pillow fights could break out at such moments, or coughing fits needing attention. Even farting competitions worked a treat because the culprit is always hard to identify in a room of twenty. This has been the case since the first offspring turned thirteen. Disruption is a teenage art form. Kenny and Charlie guarded the vulnerable as best they could, at least in their own dorm.

The worst of the pack was the school principal. A 5' 6" pear-shaped man with clammy skin in his mid-forties. He was impeccably groomed and glided rather than walked, right shoulder slightly tilted, tailored cassock. The tell-tale signal of eccentricity was a clumsy comb-over of sandy strands on the left of his head swept across his over-exposed cranium. Chronic balding denial. His eyes were a piercing arctic blue a little too close to a hooked nose nobody dared notice. A menacing sneer on his thin lips was never far away. He iced people with his ability to stare them out and ruled by fear with his alto voice. Staff called him 'Glider', never to his face, of course. Kenny didn't like him, didn't trust him and made sure he was never an easy target for bullying or grooming from him or any of the other sick, corrupt bastards.

Dormitory at midnight was the time boys feared most. When Glider was scheduled for night patrol, he found a pretext for examining beds, nightdress, lockers etc., and always found a reason to punish someone by standing him in a dark corridor outside his own cell away in another wing. Helpless victims stood alone sometimes for an hour, shivering with cold and fear listening to sounds of flagellation coming from the priest's cell and dreading what might happen next. Fears well-founded.

By Kenny's senior year, two of his classmates, twins Adrian and Graham (Guggie because of his stutter), Cripps had been relentlessly pursued and abused for three years. Kenny and Charlie were in another dorm, unable to protect them. They were gentle and unobtrusive compliant souls. Small for their age, they became isolated, fear-struck, shattered innocents trapped in a loop of terror. It was impossible for them to see how to end the incredible pain and filth eating at them. Who could they tell, who would believe? They needed something they didn't have, some kind of defiance. But there was no defiance in them. They had nothing, were nothing. A pervasive spiritual gangrene was destroying them inch by inch, night by night. Their parents, Kevin and Margaret, had no idea why the boys were reluctant to return to school after the Christmas holidays thinking they loved being home on the farm with them and their animal pets. One good harvest that could go close to clearing debt was inevitably followed by years of drought, sending finances spiralling back into debt. Good harvest for them usually meant the same for all farmers, and prices for crops would plunge. In times of drought, seed prices soared with no guarantee of a good crop. Farmers and graziers always get caught on the wrong side of conditions. Boarding school was the only choice available, a gateway to options for lives of comfort and security. The twins did, in fact, love farm life. For one thing, they could sleep without fear. Their favourite house dogs Rafferty and Rules slept beside their beds. They tended chickens, drenched sheep and in the season, banded lambs. Driving the tractor and Land Rover were other favourite ways to crisscross hundreds of acres, gathering fallen dead tree branches for firewood and counting animals. They would often return to the homestead with a hessian bag of fresh field mushrooms.

"You paid the right price for those mushrooms, boys, hey. Leave them on the bench, and we'll have them with lamb chops tonight."

They had fresh milk every day and their mum Margaret owned the country kitchen, producing familiar delights on the huge wood-fired stove. Country woman through and through staunch Christian ethic, hard-working both indoors and in the fields amongst sheep and cattle never intimidated by either. Woe betide the red-bellied black that crossed her path. The boys had seen her pick up an unfortunate snake by the tail and crack its body like a whip. She'd brook no danger to her family or treasured farm animals. On one end of a cross-cut saw, she could almost lift her slightly built but wiry husband off his feet when pulling the saw towards her. He'd resisted the idea of chain saws but secretly hoped his wife would tire of the hard work. She never did. The boys learned early on to obey her and to relish the taste of poached black snake. Their dad did get a chance on Sunday mornings. His specialty was frying eggs on the stovetop and toasting thick slices of homemade bread with the fire door open. Sunday was the day his wife liked to prepare herself for presentation at the solemn Sabbath service. The home was the boys' haven. It gave them space to breathe in safety while hushing the terror that awaited them at school.

St Valerian's school was a stunning property nestled below the Victorian Alps alongside the snow-fed Howqua river. A square mile of Australian highland virgin bush mixed with grazing paddocks, playing fields, dairy and poultry animals, plus a large vegetable garden. Groups of students did much of the manual work on designated afternoons. 1930's depression labour had been cheap, and the brickwork was breath-taking in scope and ornate in design – beautifully crafted windows, arched walkways and a copper-domed clock tower above it all creating a monastic theme. Three storeys, three semi-circular wings joined by covered walkways enclosing the clock tower hub for the campus, the source of its energy reaching, tolling, waiting. Its bells roused cassocks to prayer every morning and signalled with finality the end of every day, announcing dark, dangerous nights. It tolled an austere silence and secrets never meant to see the light of day. The original plan for the teaching order of monastics was to service the moral needs of a broad parish, 'education' for children of believers delivered by men steeped in a medieval commitment to a holy apostolate. A nice concept but easily corrupted.

Easter was the last official camping weekend of an exhausted summer, and the weather in eastern Victoria usually accommodated. From Yea to Mt Buller, suburban-weary Victorians dragged out 14' x 12' canvas tents with annexes or the best in pop-up camper trailers and headed out of town to favourite holiday sites. It might be among towering eucalypts along the Goulburn river or Eildon Weir at Bonnie Doon caravan park. They fished for leatherjackets casting hopefully into secret holes where brown or rainbow trout hid as if knowing they were being targeted. Others travelled further around to Jamieson, while others still headed higher into the mountains. On the other side of Port Phillip Bay, west coast beaches drew thousands. Winter would be long and cold. Easter signalled its approach.

Easter Sunday, also in Autumn, was the greatest celebration in Christendom. A triumphant carpenter's son shaking off his shroud and mortality rose to ignite a new religious mania. His intentions were pure, and it was no surprise history would expose his naivety. His humanitarian philanthropic obsessions were hijacked and moulded into a political system institutionalising elitism and exploitation, sacrifice of innocence and innocents. More practically, Easter signalled the end of the Lenten fast jettisoning restraint, completion of soul-cleansing penance and a celebration of body and spirit. Sunday was the perfect day for parental visits. Students at St Valerian's who fasted for 40 days were keen beyond measure to see parents and siblings. Fathers, of course, would much prefer camping with friends, but being good Catholic parents, they knew about sacrifice and abstinence.

So it was this Easter. Blankets spread on freshly cut lawns of the inner enclosure with feasts for everyone. The warm autumn sun filtered through huge palm fronds bouncing off darting children, doting grandparents and fussing mothers providing for their "Oh look how you've grown" young men.

Adrian and Guggie hiding as they often did, looked down from a battlement window, heads squeezed together, tears in their eyes, desperate unhappiness clawing at them with the force of gravity. Their toiling farmer parents, preoccupied with harvesting duties, would not be visiting. Below them was a scene of apparent peace and harmony. Priests circulated from one family group to another, exchanging pleasantries with parents and youngsters tasting the bountiful generosity of each family, unaware of a wicked irony in the pleasures spread before them. But the twins knew what others could never suspect. Black habits. Terrible frightening folding and lifting black habits. What secrets they covered, moving silently with deadly purpose along rows of beds every night, culling, caressing and smirking, whispering and sweating, promising and threatening.

With composed, desperate purpose, they climbed the spiral staircase. They held hands, standing on the highest window ledge facing each other in the narrow space just below the cluster of bells. One telling act, an act that would free them, cleanse them, and release them from the terrible nightmare. Without a word, they launched their pathetic souls on a flight to heaven. Stricken angels, wings unseen, eyes peeled back, streaming tears whipped away in a deadly rush, hair whistling vertical, and hands clenched. Sweet life snuffed in a sickening, muffled implosion.

Kenny had no visitors while Charlie had gone home to help with a muster. His job was to direct cars to public areas. He sensed something wrong in the preceding days. The twins had not been seen outside meal times. They sat quietly at the table, toying with their food. It was good food, too, because students recently had won a fierce battle with priests about "disgusting meals." Kenny remembered with satisfaction the orchestrated full-scale riot one fateful Sunday lunchtime. Like a scene from slapstick movies often played for their entertainment on a Saturday night, boys hurled trays of food, crockery and chairs around the refectory. Supervising staff ran for cover, abandoning the field of battle. With their blood fully up, boarders ran riot around campus, breaking every single window before they were sated. There were threatened recriminations, but none came. Meals improved immediately.

Still, Kenny couldn't quite grasp how desperately sad his classmates were. He knew about predatory midnight prowling. Everyone did. As an older boy, he understood clearly what was going on but didn't know what he could do to stop it. His only strategy was to strengthen his maturing body with a vigorous commitment to sports and assume an aggressive demeanour to intimidate cowardly priests. Last plank of his strategy alongside Charlie was to be vigilant in his own dormitory. Self-preservation is fundamental, more primal than an impulse to protect others. But this seminal moment in his life crystallised something. Anger mixed with impotence on seeing such raw evil. It was just wrong. Where he thought were the protectors, champions?

Looking up from his gate post position, he saw two hollow, gaunt white faces on the parapet of the bell tower and gasped with horror. He knew immediately what was about to happen. Too late for action. He made an impulsive sign of the cross, felt a tear blur his vision and ran as fast as he could, arms pumping, gravel shooting everywhere from his flying boots to where he knew they would hit in just a few seconds. He saw them leap and stared aghast at their free-fall fruit bat spread arms and legs. The violence of that sickening simultaneous 'thwack' of the beautiful young bodies on concrete was a sound he'd never heard and one he'd not forget for the rest of his cursed life. Kenny was beside them in a second, even before shocked visitors could react. He knelt beside their crumpled corpses, the last heat of life steaming from pooling blood. He kissed them a promise that he'd make things better - somehow.

While others milled in confusion, he stood up and walked inside directly to the principal's office, vaulting three steps at a time to the top floor. The priest showed his back, straining to see from his window what all the commotion outside was about. Kenny leapt onto the executive desk one metre closer to his target. He crouched ominously, hissing a guttural growl that spun the principal around. Too late. With every ounce of strength Kenny could summon in mid-flight, he sunk his right boot into that startled face flinging the hapless pervert backwards with enough force to send shattered glass across the room. Glider's face burst like a ripened melon. He slumped, his blood mixing with that of the twins from Kenny's boot and sounds of confusion outside.

Nobody saw Kenny enter, and nobody saw him leave. At that moment, he couldn't have cared anyway. The creep Glider would never again prowl on another innocent ever. He must've known that lying crumpled amongst glass and his own blood, death rattle in his throat and a look of absolute hatred on the last face he'd ever see.

Police came with forensic teams and counsellors roping off the crime scene. Kenny was found kneeling beside the victims, deeply contemplative, and shoulders sagged. It took little time to establish what occurred upstairs, and detectives had no trouble getting Kenny to go with them.

"I am Detective Sergeant Laurie Ashwood, Kenny. I have to ask you about what happened here today."

Kenny stood but said nothing. His eyes gave nothing to the officer.

"Kenny, it was you who attacked the Principal in his office upstairs, was it not?"

"Yes, I did that."

"Then you will have to come to the station for a formal interview during which charges will be laid. Do you understand?"

"Yes, I do."

Two uniformed officers led Kenny to an unmarked car directing him into the back seat, sheltering his head to make access easier as they always do. The driver in plain clothes took off to Mansfield 20 minutes away. A divisional van escorted the car. A large contingent of detectives and uniformed police spent the rest of the day and much of the night collecting statements and finalising evidence about two suicides and a death.

Formalities of interviewing and charging Kenny were swift. During the whole process, he was silent, offering nothing in defence of his actions, nothing at all. In the station cells, he took no visitors and spoke to no one. His transfer to Melbourne followed, where he was held until the inevitable trial. He allowed one visitor during that time, his sister Hanna two years his junior. Even then, neither spoke, just sat together in silent collusion. Each time she left the cell, his only words were, "Thanks, Mac." They'd always been close. Alone, he sat, paced, thought, and grieved all day and every night. Sometimes he wept. But he said nothing. A maelstrom raged outside and went global. Thousands of victims of abuse by clergy began to surface with horrid stories. Floodgates were smashed open, and Kenny was hailed far and wide for his actions. He heard none of it, read no papers, saw no television, received no mail. He was no hero. Two of his classmates were dead because he hadn't acted, not because he did. That's what mattered to him. He failed, and the consequences were dire. He definitely wasn't looking for an acquittal. He wanted punishment. Given his confession, with no premeditation, the prosecution did not push for a murder conviction. It was a very short trial – for manslaughter.

"Would the defendant stand. How do you plead?"

Kenny stood hands crossed in front. A pregnant hush rippled, anticipation thick.

"Guilty, your honour."

Judge Alistair McCabe, high bony cheeks, grey whiskered chin, banged and banged his gavel to quieten a near riotous crowd. No justice was done this day. Guilty, yes, Kenny was. Remorseful? Not a bit. He didn't have a 'sorry' in him. But there was a crushing sense of guilt, disabling guilt that he'd not acted soon enough, guilt that would haunt him. His tears were for the twins, who appeared to Kenny as a ghostly mist above the judge's head. A glance at his parents ricocheted like a jagged spear straight through his heart, telling him they were in a state of total emotional collapse, lives upended and their moral compass spinning out of control. His father wrapped a hopelessly vulnerable arm around his mother's waist, leading her convulsing body out of the court. He looked away, caught dismay on his one friend's puzzled face. There's something about friendship that transcends words. One glance and each knew everything that wasn't said. He didn't care about jail. He deserved it for what he didn't do. He murdered his classmates by not acting. He'd been as weak as anybody and deserved punishment. But he learned something about how sinister evil can be. How it comes dressed in sheep's clothing and sucks at life for gratification. How it leaves only the shell of humanity behind it like an Indian mynah tearing at the soft underbelly of a cicada pinned to the ground under stiletto toes. He was gutted with an aching impotence on the one hand and a crystal-clear picture on the other. Henceforth he'd dread what came with sleep. Only terror in faces and the horrific sound of flesh on concrete. The gurgling death rattle of life seeping from the priest's eyes over and over every night. Every day a slice at a time, his life would diminish. No respite, no succour. Dead man walking.

5

TWO HOURS AFTER THE TRIAL, Kenny's remand cell door opened, and a guard summoned him forward. This seemed a bit odd to Kenny, questions in his eyes as he stood up.

"You have a visitor, son, follow me."

He did as he was bidden, blinking to adjust his eyes in the brightly lit bowels of the Melbourne remand centre corridor, keeping up with the heavily built, long-striding and uniformed guard. He was led to an interview room at the ground floor level. A crumpled suit sitting at the table stood and motioned Kenny to a chair.

"Kenny, I'm Rupert Crawley. We have a proposition for you."

Kenny looked over this official, who clearly hated being in a suit. Nothing looked in place. Tie askew crushed black leather shoes screaming for a polish, crumpled pants and a jacket never going to be done up over a significant paunch. He looked entirely authentic to Kenny, almost likeable except for the misaligned nicotine-yellowed teeth. That image immediately erased the picture Kenny was building. Here was a story waiting to be told right in front of him.

"Wait a minute Mr Crawley you might have the wrong person. I've been convicted of manslaughter and am waiting for transfer to prison."

"Yes, Kenny, I know all that, but in rare conditions like yours, if you accept, I'm empowered to enrol you in a diversion program. You see, many people would think you really did the world a favour. You saved lives in imminent danger of violation before they'd really begun. Your action shone light where there was darkness. The law is the law, of course, but you're no criminal, son. If you are willing, you might just be able to serve your time and your country at the same time."

Kenny Burgess disappeared that day, and nobody noticed.

The media had a field day with the story. Kenny was hailed heroic for avenging evil. Kenny was gone. Media-driven outrage erupted nationwide. How could a brave young man be convicted of murder when it was clearly justifiable homicide. Kenny was gone. Oxygen was sucked from the issue because he was gone, and nobody knew how or where. The media was cleverly steered towards the big issue. St Valerian's closed. Stories of bastardising, sexual abuse and mismanagement broke in a crashing tidal wave. The religious order fielded predictable denials. In the meantime, their most astute minds were working out how to protect its crown jewels in accumulated wealth in real estate and how to show repentance, accept minimum damage to its reputation and pay as little as it had to in compensation to aggrieved parties. Then one morning, the television news was all over a collapse of a holding dam in a Brazilian iron ore mine. Kenny and dozens of broken families were forgotten amongst exploited workers buried in mud.

A grieving couple from nearby Yarra Valley abandoned their farm and disappeared into the shadows of the big city of Melbourne. They'd never be noticed by churchgoers at St Patrick's Cathedral, where they often stood at the spear-shaped perimeter iron fence tattered, ashen, hollow-eyed and completely broken. She was tall, bent, and skinny. He was shorter but also bowed and trembling. Both of them were forgotten thereafter, never to be noticed.

6

"ROBERT STEPHEN DANIELS Graduate RAAF Fast Jet Programme 1995"

Hanna held the unrolled certificate in her hands, questions all over her face. She'd no idea what was happening, no sign of anything untoward in the name and address on the package until something dropped out of the tube. A plane ticket in the name of Mac Burgess for a flight to Perth. There was only one person ever in her life who called her 'Mac'. From her time as a toddler, she was known for repeating ad nauseam, "me mack Mummy, me mack Kenny, me mack Daddy". It was 'Mac' on the ticket. A shockwave, tears of relief in her eyes and a wry smile underneath. She thought, "that bastard, I knew he'd do something. He's alive. Why has he waited 10 years before showing me what he's done?" He was in Perth and wanted to see her. She could hardly breathe.

A stubborn belief sustained her, he would reach out when he could. If he was alive, she knew he would. Never once in all those intervening years did she allow herself to doubt he was alive somewhere though fighter jet pilot was a bit of a surprise. And his alias Robert Stephen Daniels! Where on earth did that come from? She dreamt of this moment. She'd see him in two days, two wide-awake nights alive with excitement and nervous anticipation.

Not only had Kenny survived multi-tiered intense training, but he shone in the fiercely competitive environment, becoming top of his class of twelve. He'd been stationed in every major base in the country since graduation and flown every plane in the airforce hangar: Macchi trainers, twin-engined executive Beechcraft, Boeing 727's used for ferrying politicians and diplomats, Blackhawk helicopters, F4 Phantoms, F-111s and the latest addition, FA-18 Hornets. A glittering career was laid before him, and he gave his best in return.

Hanna picked up her bag, set alarms, and headed for the street where her concierge Graham had an airport shuttle waiting. Graham was an established identity career veteran firefighter and conscripted participant in that pointless Vietnam war who was vigilantly protective of 'his' residents. The Rialto tower stood head and shoulders over every other nearby skyscraper, and Graham's role was an important one. Kenny was in Perth, and she'd see him this same day. Long lost brother, big brother and hero. Four hours to Perth miracle of flight sipping coffee at 37,000ft and screaming along at 1000km/h. Not in the slightest fatigued, Hanna hurried through exit corridors into the terminal, scanning every direction. She couldn't miss the stand-out RAAF uniform. He was older for sure but unmistakably him despite the Raybans, arms in the air, broad grin all over his face. She rushed, flinging herself into the heaviest embrace, each heaving with emotion. Without a word, he scooped up her bag, and they strode out of the terminal with eyes only for each other, Raybans pocketed.

That evening they sat on the beach at Scarborough. The huge dinner plate iridescent orange sun sliding into the Indian ocean and a bottle of Lagavulin single malt between them. They drank from paper cups and shared a Montecristo number 7 still in its cellophane wrapper, pretending to be smokers and drinkers. An odd couple to passers-by.

"What are those guys doing in the shallows, Mac, do you know?" he asked.

"I do. Uncle Tommy, who, as you know, lived over here after WWII, used to come down here and abuse newly arrived Vietnamese boat people for taking too many abalone. He reckoned they were raping his resources. They are still allowed to take two per person per day. He never objected to swarms of locals who gathered on the banks of the Swan River every night, filling their buckets with some of the millions of prawns brought in on a high tide. Funny bloke Tommy. But it's all over now, nothing left to take. Where are you posted?"

"Wait a minute. I have to see what they've got."

With that, Kenny jumped to his feet and strode squeakingly to the shore break shaking sand from his booty. She watched him talk to a gatherer of shallow bred abalone. The encounter must've gone well because he had one in his hand when sitting again beside her.

"Tyndall at the moment, squadron of F111s. Got to keep an eye on the Indonesians. Plenty of room up there for training flights, ground-hugging radar etc. It'll be interesting for a while. Then in three months, I'm off to the States. Have to do some more hours in a F/A-18 Hornet. Got to take one back to the States for a refurb. Still under warranty."

"I don't really get it sitting on top of a supersonic bomb. Not too good for my vertigo, hey?"

"Heh heh. Pass your cup. I'll wager you're not much slower on the Kwaka 900 you keep in a cage. You still have it, I presume. At least it's on the ground. When you get a chance, you should come to Darwin. We can do a couple of rides together. No speed limit on the Stuart Highway should be fun. As soon as I get my latest schedule, I'll let you know when I have a few days off. Hope you can make it. It's a long ride, so I'll understand if you don't."

"Wait a minute, how do you know all that?"

"I've had a few days off now and then. Some of my training was out of Sale less than two hours on my Honda Valkyrie. I wasn't able to tell you what happened, and even now, they don't know I'm bringing you in. But I do admit to keeping an eye on you much as I could. You do matter, Mac. I was also able to track down Mum, and I've visited Dad's grave in Cairns.

Must get to see her now that I'm kind of on the grid. How did they end up going to Queensland?"

"She's not seen you since the trial. She was broken, gave up on God and everything. Made Dad pull up stumps and move to Queensland. Dad tried to console her, but there was no hope. He was upset at not seeing you, and he was hellishly proud of what you did. He took your disappearance hard and seemed to lose any sense of meaning in his life. He hit the drink hard and died two years ago. Kenny, Mum told me something that I reckon you need to know. She got herself into trouble with her first boyfriend. He scarpered when she got pregnant, and Dad stepped in, offering to marry her and raise her baby. That baby was you, and he treated you like you were his. She never knew how to tell you, and he didn't want her to. Pretty good man, don't you think?"

The pause was long. She could see tears forcing their way to his chiselled frozen cheeks. Kenny was stunned. So Mac continued.

"None of us had any idea what happened to you. You just vanished. I just believed you were OK against all logic. As for riding, I still ride a new version of the one you saw. You'll not squeeze out of this one, big brother. I will make the time."

She was prattling. Kenny was shell shocked. But he forced himself to go with the flow.

"Remember Cooper and the Korams? You were our mascot and scout. You were never afraid then to climb those huge Cyprus pines around the corner near the park. You scoped the neighbourhood and warned us if the Luptons were nearby. We won a few scraps because of you. If you've got vertigo, it must be recent." A long pause.

"He did that for Mum?"

"Yep."

Another heavily pregnant pause.

"I know he tried with me, but I felt there was something missing. How wrong can a person be? I'm so damned stupid. The bastard child fated for exclusion. An outcast. And I can't make it up with him. That's so wrong. No wonder Mum wanted me to be a priest, sacrifice for her sin. It's funny, you know, my only thought was for our dad, not my dad. I never cared who the hell he was. What a stuff up, hey!"

They went back to their memories. Brothers in adventures and tribal battles always had each other's back and often shared beatings and shiners. Hanna was the only girl allowed in the gang, but to Kenny, she was a brother just the same. Souls fused in triumphs and defeats. Only one rule, nobody was allowed to call her Mac. She was Hanna to them and to everyone. Nobody argued.

"Yeah, childhood was good for us. Listen, Mac, after I leave for the States, it'll be a while before I see you. But remember this every time you see a streak of high-altitude condensation, it might be me looking down towards you."

"Yeah, here's to you. I'll be looking. And as for the ride, just give me a couple of days' notice. Can't wait."

They got to their feet, shook off clinging sand, picked up their shoes, left the abalone and headed for the hire car. Kenny took her back to the airport and the 'Red Eye' back to Melbourne.

7

HANNA SAT STARING at her reflection, pondering her own story. Two years her brother's junior, she was as gifted as Kenny, no slouch. She didn't stand aloof like him. She sailed through Law at Melbourne University and cemented her place in the Melbourne establishment as an outstanding practitioner in Contract Law. Thanks to her mother's insistence on lessons as a youngster, she was an accomplished pianist. On her own initiative, she expanded her interest to four instruments and, while at university, joined a blues and rock'n roll band and, oddly, a string quartet. Her image was smiling, warm with memories of uni life. The violinist was Libbi, a rabbi's daughter doing fine arts. She later joined the Melbourne Symphony Orchestra. Sandra was a divorcee returning to study sociology. She played the viola. And the double bassist was Rob, a butcher's son paying his own way through medicine with an ambition to become a surgeon. They used to laugh with him about that, bit of a step up. She loved to step into those forums when she had time. Even had thoughts of ditching the law practice one day to pursue her love of music professionally. Her reflection stayed mute. It knew the whole story, especially about the bold little girl chasing after her big brother calling, "wait for me, wait for me."

Sounds of lowering and locking of landing gear interrupted her reverie. When the plane dropped the last ten feet to the tarmac for a hard landing, the hostess quipped over the intercom system, "I'll speak to the captain about that one, hey." Hanna wondered how she could sound so casual before realising they really know what they're doing. Their risks were real, and odds are strange things. Sounding casual is clearly a way of shelving unspoken fear. She was home safe.

The fog of uncertainty she had lived with for so long finally cleared. She bounded up the entrance steps to her building, cheerily hailing concierge Graham with an impulsive hug as she passed. That gesture made his day. Old man great imagination. She'd found her brother, and life was good. A fifteen-second high-speed ride to the 44th floor made her think of the air hostess for just a second. She was home safe but a long way off the ground.

Picking up Kenny's fast jet graduation certificate, she stared in wonderment. She knew straight away it'd hang on her studio wall in pride of place.

The studio was at the heart of her apartment, with stunning wrap-around views from docklands, port facilities and Port Phillip to the Dandenong Ranges. She was tidy, her instruments neatly racked and manuscripts arranged in glass-fronted shelving. Her favourite reading chair was positioned under a suspended light back to the windows, minimalist otherwise. Parquet flooring was heavily insulated beneath. She didn't need neighbour's disruption caused by her music practice. Her meditative moments were supported by a high-quality surround sound system embracing the whole apartment. Its control centre was flanked by a CD stacker tower bristling, almost vibrating with great music just waiting to burst into her space like a Japanese cherry tree budded, ready for spring and one more chance to colour a dreary world. Picking up the remote, she selected something suiting her mood. A Mendelsohn violin concerto would lift her higher than the building with its soaring crescendos. Kicking off her shoes and abandoning the idea of unpacking, she gave herself a tour of her musical family. She loved her piano, a gift from an Austrian businessman client who had heard her play at the Green Door in Melbourne's jazz district. She alerted him to the financial dangers of dealing with a particularly shonky development group, and he was grateful.

The Stingl baby grand made in Vienna in the 1930s had mysteriously found its way to Melbourne. After a long hibernation in a Toorak townhouse, its tenure came to an end when its owner died. As it happens, the family didn't want to keep it and off to a warehouse it went. Luckily its new owner was tuner/collector septuagenarian and eccentric Theo Slots. His workshop was largely invisible in the claustrophobic laneways of inner Richmond. It was the best thing that could've happened to such a classic. He restored the piano to near perfect condition, carefully dismantling, refurbishing and rebuilding every element, hammers, felt pads, strings, soundboard, everything. Once rebuilt and re-lacquered to finish the job, it was added to a special list he kept for just the right person to come along. Theo saved it from decay, and his effort would not go unrewarded by sending it to the wrong customer. Cohen, the Austrian businessman, understood and even welcomed Theo's demands before presenting it to Hanna. She loved the way her new companion spoke with a voice like no other, almost as if knowing her love of the music she drew from it. She glided past, running her hand lovingly across its lid. Her deep affection for and personification of her instruments extended to her pet guitar 'Max', a collectable Maton steel-stringed acoustic. 'Philomena' flute, in her case on the music shelves, was a generic orphan she found at Camberwell market one Sunday morning on a self-indulgent amble. She always felt a bit like the pied piper with Philomena in hand. It was a recreational interest. Lastly, Mac loved to play 'Chancellor' in her university string quartet group. Since her first year of studies, they had been together, and her skill with the cello belonged in the mix of excellence that the group enjoyed. 'Chancellor' cello stood in a corner on his own rack, waiting for her attention. He thrived in her embrace, always giving his best. He yearned for opportunities to work in cleverly structured harmonies with his cousins of the stringed instrument kind. His voice added velvet to the quartet, and why not, given how he was bowed and how Mac's left hand worked his neck with familiarity, firmness and sublime skill. He shivered at the prospect waiting impatiently for his turn in the orchestra of her world tucked firmly between her athletic thighs.

Her mother's ambitions of squeezing a piano out of a tight domestic budget signalled a devotion to her daughter's intellectual growth, but that's not the whole story. Hanna's childhood piano teacher Miss Rhonda Goodhand was a rare find, one of a lifetime. No mindless rigid disciplinarian repetitive routines for her student. For her, it was all about the love of melody, of harmony, of the dynamics of building complexity out of simple ingredients. That was real music-making drawing it from the instrument almost like seduction. She was the perfect choice for Hanna, intellectually compatible like a date palmed oasis waiting for a thirsty camel. Every lesson intensified Hanna's love of music, and her playing blossomed under such care. Goodhand did not mind her interest in other instruments, she encouraged it. She watched Hanna become the skilled shepherd for a small flock tended with care, firm discipline underwritten by respect.

She picked up Kenny's certificate, and her mind turned to him. He had a life to lead. Hanna was comfortable with that. She was used to getting by without him since he went off to boarding school. She hoped, though, from this point, they would talk more even if they didn't see each other. As for herself, she was comfortable throwing herself into work and music. There was her motorbike, escape-from-pressure machine. It demanded physical skill and stamina, quick reflexes, and clear-headed concentration. No problem for her. When moved, she rode alone, with determination and athletic skill. Whistling slipstream and leaning into the wind, she rode close to the limits allowed by conditions, the bike and the law. The young woman in tight-fitting leathers, helmet under her arm, striding into a roadhouse, auburn hair cropped short of her shoulders, was noticed. Bikers have always attracted attention from the curious. Mac shared many a coffee with those who used to be or wanted to be riders of freedom machines like hers. She was polite, informative and welcoming of that kind of attention. She was a listener rather than a talker, a true believer that if you are not listening, then you are not learning. Never on a mission to convince anybody of anything. She didn't need to. Her life was richly diverse with work, books, business, music and riding. There was little need for anything else. Hers was a full dance card.

8

AT UNIVERSITY, PREDICTABLE and transient collisions were driven mostly by temporary chemical imbalance and curiosity. Still, these were never enough to distract Hanna from her chosen path. By the time she began full-time work as a lawyer, there were enough complications in her life without adding more. But she never closed off options, nor had she sworn to celibacy. It was a rare skill being able to tend to the wild beast of a biological imperative without being consumed by it. In her case, intellect was the ultimate control centre of her complex life. Emotions were welcome mostly, but she was aware they could be cruel, unforgiving masters if given too much leeway. Emotions were most useful in the crafting of composition, harmony and counterpoint. Keen observation taught her that. Her schooling took place in a Catholic girls' school where she learned about those things teenage girls think and obsess about. She loved music more than most but couldn't understand the mindless screaming and swooning over inane lyrics of famous bands like Abba, Bee Gees, Bay City Rollers, Michael Jackson, Little Patti and others. Then too many girls chased after boys and older men in a manic search for meaning. She saw many acquaintances swing wildly from ecstasy to depression in that search. Nobody handles rejection and confusion easily. Hanna did her best to stick to her theory that sometimes the best move is not to play. She was a watchful bystander taking it all in but keeping her distance, concentrating on the things that mattered to her. Anyway, she'd run with boys as a youngster and knew their ways. 'Their minds are so free of complexity', she remembered: 'food, frolic and freedom, paramount.'

Mark Joseph, colleague and business partner, proved worthy of some interest. Mark's wife Samantha succumbed at 34 to ovarian cancer after gifting him two girls, Maggie and Emily, still very young.

They were everything to him. It never matters that you know the end game of a disease like cancer. At least there is a relief for the sufferer when the end does come. Family can be ripped apart with the grieving and the disrupted dynamics of raising children. No different for Mark. He was tossed around like an autumn leaf in a windstorm stabilising his distressed daughters managing all the minutiae of domestic demands grasping for an elusive sense of meaning, finding energy to think of work giving up entirely on his own grieving. He was pretty much a complete mess. To his credit, the girls didn't see it. He was successful on that front.

Fortunately, too, his mother stepped into the breach. She Jeanine, earth mother and grandmother, was dedicated to her only grandchildren. Widowed for more than a decade, she took control of the timber wholesale business that Mal, her husband, had built. She brought a refreshing energy to what had been, for Mal, more a pleasant way of spending time helping customers get the best deals for their jobs and making sure his workers had everything they needed to handle timber in all its variations. The business was successful if old school, ultimately taking up a whole street of factories with carefully acquired stocks of imported and local timbers. Mal spent much of his time on the road visiting sawmills all over the country, looking for treasured packs of blackwood, blackbutt, mountain ash, structural pine, rare cedar and imported Oregon. Back in Dandenong, where he established the business in the 50s, he was able to buy part of an industrial estate building on each block as he needed more space. A heavy smoker and a sucker for junk food, he paid the price.

Jeanine was smart enough to respect her husband's style of management. Still, she systematically introduced new technologies that brought many of their traditional practices across the borders of pre-Second world war times. Her qualifications were in computer languages and business systems. Married life never slowed her interest in education or business. By the time son Mark needed her help, she was able to manage the timber business mostly from her laptop and phone. Luckily for the girls, grandma was willing to be a primary carer. They'd learn much from her.

His wife's mother, Louisa, was a little different. She was happy to help when she could but not often. Her part-time job as a hostess in a suburban poker machine venue made that difficult. On days off, she liked to spend time alone except when she needed to visit her husband in full-time care with early-onset dementia. She had her own cross to bear.

Hanna worked for a large firm for three years after graduation, knowing eventually she'd hang out her own shingle. When she did so, an associate was needed. She found Mark Joseph at a national conference in Sydney on the ethics of law and business. He impressed her with his presentation that nobody else seemed to like. His thesis was that law is an instrument of service, and the practitioner was professionally bound to service above everything. She found him alone in the dining hall. His appearance was curious to her. Nothing of the slick city lawyer about him, more like comfortably crumpled. He seemed to be distracted, poring over what looked like school reports. She sat down to discover enough about him to realise he meant what he said in the presentation. Before long, they formed a business partnership called 'Burgess and Joseph'.

Hanna poked her head into Mark's office.

"Do you have a moment? Need your help."

"Sure, here or in the rec room?"

"Rec room Mark, bring your coffee mug."

"Meet you there in 15. Need to finish this agenda."

"15 it is."

She was waiting. Mark nodded and went straight to the cappuccino machine for a double-shot long black.

"What is it, boss?"

"Oh please, no bosses, remember." She took a deep breath, about to say something important. He sat frozen, wondering what it might be. "You may not know I have a brother, my only sibling. Haven't seen him for 10 years for reasons that can wait for another time. Don't let me off on that story. You didn't see me last Thursday because I was on a flight to Perth. The ticket arrived in the mail. Crazy weekend is all I can say. I have one more chance to see my brother before he disappears again." She paused. "You are gaping."

He was absorbed by the surge of information, unprepared but empowered by it.

"I need three weeks. My question is ... would you keep an eye on my files for that long? I want to take this opportunity while the architects are at least six weeks out from their next presentation on that big job in Oakleigh."

Mark sipped coffee while keeping eye contact. A mysterious brother? Clearly important to her. She was asking a favour. He liked that. And the aura! She positively glowed. He'd never seen that before. Maybe he mused, she's always like this, and I haven't noticed. He jolted back to the moment.

"Hanna, you have a few credits with me given the chaos of the last twelve months. Your brother has reappeared. You are clearly excited. That's huge. Of course, I'll keep things going. Don't think of work for a minute."

He looked at her differently. Something vulnerable, an emotion he'd not seen before. Instantly reality imposed. He couldn't allow his mind to wander that path. Two reasons. He had to stay focused on his girls. But the thought was like a drop of fine red wine on a clean white shirt. It would be hard to remove. So, suitably awkward in the saying, he reminded her why she deserved consideration just to keep the atmosphere on a clearly understood basis. He didn't want her to think he might have any other motivation. Echoes of good advice from somewhere. 'Bad idea to mix business and pleasure, son.' And, funnily, he gave no thought about her brother and why he might've been absent for so long.

"Thanks, Mark. We'll sit down when I come home. It's a great story, and I'd like to share it with you."

"Deal."

Back came that warm feeling momentarily side-lined like a boomerang thrown on a wide arc. She was going to open something of her personal life to him. The following shot of guilt was the boomerang striking him on the head. He was thinking of himself, not the girls. Did Hanna notice his beaded brow, his flushed cheeks? Not possible. No way. Her mind was totally on her brother. He could not see her face once she turned to leave the room.

9

KENNY AND HANNA spoke as soon as he knew his timetable, and she had a week to prepare herself for a marathon ride. The bike would get new tyres, fresh fluids, and a chain tension check. She'd travel light. No choice really. She had two panniers and a top box, room only for essentials, real essentials. Then the night before leaving, she spread maps and plotted a route to get her to Tennant Creek, where they agreed to meet. Departure day 6am. Kawasaki exhaust echoed through inner-city canyons. She was on her way, unaffected by the morning chill and heavy July sky. The ring road was the quickest route to the Calder Highway though tradesman traffic was always manic at that time of day with drivers using phones to organise jobs. It's a hazardous thing to be amongst all that on a motorbike. Hanna was wide-eyed and cautious, allowing room for any unexpected intrusion into her space. By the time she whipped past Calder Raceway, she'd pretty much left crazy traffic behind. At 8:30 am, she glided into Bendigo, ready for breakfast and a welcome stretch of the body, tired backside and frozen fingers. Even young bodies will stiffen after two hours in the saddle. She targeted Nuriootpa for the day, expecting to get there by early evening. Sunset shadows and stirring nocturnal critters are perilous for riders. Stupidity and bravery can be confused especially mixed with fatigue. Her choice of accommodation was a picturesque caravan and cabin park nestled between virgin bushland and local sporting facilities. Kookaburra hurrahs and squawking squadrons of rosellas put the tired evening to rest. After a short walk to the town centre for dinner at the Maple Leaf Chinese restaurant, Hanna hit the hay early.

The second day having greeted early morning visitors grazing nonchalantly in the park grounds, she packed her bike. Only when she ignited the engine did the kangaroos think it wise to move into the shadows. She breezed through Barossa with its beautiful mix of architectural vineyard plantings and lush Australian eucalypt stands on well-kept winding roads. Once through Peterborough, where the last train stands as a museum to another time, she burst into open country broadacre farming. Troops of emus the only spectators, plus a few willy willy wind tunnels. Port Augusta came into view as she scooted off the plateau gateway to the Stuart Highway. When she reached that turn-off, she knew it was only two more hours to Woomera, her next destination. Bikes can be quick, but the historic exhibits she expected to see at Woomera were about real speed, jets and rockets from Australia's early space-age industry.

She'd never seen an outback dusk, but with an ice-cold Cooper's in hand sitting on the hotel decking, she was gob-smacked at the splendour. A brilliant orange horizon leached through shades of ice blue space to an all-black sky. And as she watched, pinpoint stars multiplied to innumerable right before her eyes. She had no words for it all and withdrew reluctantly to her room in a building that once housed space scientists. She slept in a silence only the outback can offer.

The day after, Coober Pedy was her target. She was looking forward to a night in one of the famous underground motels. Stories about opal mining and escapees from civilisation abound in Coober Pedy. Still, Hanna would have to save a closer look at the place till on her way home. On her approach into town, she did notice some of the one million mullock heaps that jealously guard the entrances to every hole miners have dug over the years in a single-minded search for the magically-coloured frozen silicon, opal. She thought, gurgling down the main street in shadows of a spent day past an array of red dusted vintage 4WDS, mostly utes that should have been tethered to rails, 'Wow, this is wild west country for sure.' She chose one of the town's motels, promising a sense of being entombed in the absolute blackness of underground. Rooms are boring-machine gouges into hillsides, walls sparkling in artificial light. They are comfortably warm all year round. When Hanna flicked off the lights, she was pressed into her mattress by the weight of darkness impossible to know and a silence barely disturbed by distant, faint sounds trickling down the air vents. Only an alarm can signal morning in those rooms. When hers beeped, Hanna got herself ready to leave and emerged from her tomb pleased and relieved. Coffee mug on the spread-out map in the courtyard, her focus shifted. Alice Springs would be a hard day's ride close to 700kms beyond Coober Pedy. Topping up the fuel tank on her way out of 'Dodge', she noticed the fuel pump registered two litres more than the designated capacity of the bike's tank. There's only one explanation, and an indifferent cashier looked blankly when Hanna informed her of the anomaly. Larrikins everywhere.

Late morning tea at Eridunda roadhouse, close to the fuel limit for her bike, became a necessary stop for stiffness relief. Caravan traffic seemed to come out of nowhere; she'd barely noticed the nomads to this point. Maybe, she thought, something magic happens when one crosses into the Northern Territory. Eridunda was busy with them. Only three hours more to Alice, she'd broken the back of this day's ride. By mid-afternoon, she cruised into Alice Springs, where comfortable accommodation abounds. Anticipation at seeing Kenny was peaking, but she shelved the emotion while taking a hot refreshing shower hanging her leathers to air on the balcony. She dressed in the obligatory casual T-shirt, shorts and thongs and headed out for a pleasant meal at famous Monte's indoor, outdoor steak house. She over estimated her appetite and found it impossible to finish the monster rib-eye. It's hard to walk away from a great steak, but she had to. Two glasses of a Wolf Blass shiraz capped off the pleasure of the meal, and she headed back to her hotel room with a huge smile on her face at the thought of seeing Kenny the next day. These elements evoked a weird dream that night. She walked a long, long corridor with innumerable doors, opening one at a time and asking "Kenny?" at each. Not her most restful sleep. Joyfully he was just 24 hours away.

From Alice, Tennant Creek is a relatively easy run. Hanna didn't hurry the last 500kms. The first fuel stop and early lunch was at Aileron Roadhouse, where she met Eddie, the wedge-tail eagle with a steel hip, an untamed eye and able still to strut around his huge enclosure. She took time to climb the hill behind the roadhouse and stand in awe at the giant metal sculpture of an indigenous warrior, Anmatjere Man. People think the outback is totally flat. Standing two hundred feet above the roadhouse, it was clear to her that it really isn't so. She'd seen mountain ranges, gorges and sand dunes and the more she saw, the more she was entranced by it all.

Four in the afternoon is always a good time to finish a day's ride, and when Hanna rolled into the motel carpark just next to a BP servo, Kenny's bike was there. She grinned widely through the full-face helmet when she saw Kenny had a photo of their dad airbrushed onto his bike's petrol tank. She'd say nothing. Stiff with fatigue, she lifted herself off the bike, stretched and by the time she stood up, he was there banging on her helmet.

"Always were good to your word, Mac. Here you are. Come here, sis."

"Great to see you, brother and thanks for meeting me here. I'm really going to enjoy formation flying with the three of us from here to Darwin once I get feeling back in my rear end."

"Nice one, Mac. You must be exhausted. See the photo? He's with me a lot more now."

"Great idea. You're together for the first time."

"Here's a key to your room number four. Go shower and relax. I'll look after everything else. Come to my room next to yours soon as you've freshened up. We'll get our bearings for the evening and grab some serenity after the madness of a long hot ride."

Mac had no idea Kenny had been on the road as long as she had. Didn't know his connection with Charlie Sweeney and the Anunga People's cattle station half a day's ride southwest of Alice Springs. Kenny needed to see Charlie again to bring him into his tent, as it were. Their connection meant much to him. It was a planned surprise. Charlie had no idea why the owners of Curtin Springs Station, his remote neighbours, invited him to visit. They offered a pretext about managing a mob of camels to be sorted. Charlie was well known for his skill, especially with troublesome bulls, so he readily accepted the call for help. Curtin Springs Station kitchen served meals to its workers and was also open for tourists coming from and going to Uluru. So, there would've been at least a dozen couples at lunch in the al fresco dining area on this day. Charlie was with Peter Patricks, station manager, on their way to a quick lunch before inspecting their camel herd. He gave his lunch order at the kitchen window and turned to join the manager, who was talking to a tall leather-clad bike rider with very short cut hair and dark glasses. Charlie stopped in his tracks, stunned by the moment of recognition. "Impossible," he thought, and a lump the size of a cricket ball nearly choked him.

"Kenny Burgess – how the bloody hell can this be! Come here, brother!"

Kenny spun around to face the charging maniac. The impact sent them both to the ground in a mad flailing wrestle, guffawing crazily.

A mirror image of their first meeting. All eyes were on them, but they were oblivious. Kenny was first to come to his senses.

"Charlie, can you come for a walk? Got a few things to tell you that these people don't need to hear. Don't worry about your lunch. Won't take long."

They went out to one of the house paddocks where station horses were lazing in the shade of an old man Boab tree.

"I looked at you leaving the courtroom. That was the last I saw of you, usher's hand on your shoulder, tears in your eyes. What a miscarriage of justice. And don't forget, such stories are legion where I come from."

"Yeah, you'd know. Point is, Charlie, I didn't go to prison. Someone chucked a lifeline, and I was sent into the RAAF. You're looking at a dinky die, fully-fledged jet pilot. One thing, though. I must ask you to not tell anyone. To the rest of the world, I'm Robert Steven Daniels. I'm on the way to meet my sister at Tennant Creek. Couldn't miss the chance to catch up with you. Now tell me, what's station life like for you?"

"First of all, I'm so proud of you, brother. You're a hero to hundreds, and I'm so glad you got a chance to show what you really can do. Remember those idiots at school when I said, 'show them what you've got?' Well, you've really done that. Yeah, out here, a million acres is a big operation. We have our own airstrip, three Robinson helicopters and one fixed-wing aircraft, a twin-engine Cessna. Would you believe I, too, have a licence? How weird is that? Engineering is big here, and a workshop like the one you can see over there has all the toys. Our main herd is Brahman beef, but we run a large mob of camels, all wild. We've worked out a deal with Arab Sheiks to develop racing camels. The sport is huge over there with big money for the right animals. Lesser quality animals go off to the abattoirs. Four of us local boys got our schooling in the big smoke. We're all back here now with engineering, business management and flying qualifications. Another part of what we do is to find young boys and girls to follow the same program. Kind of future-proofing our business. C'mon, lunch will be ready. Let's eat."

Kicking dust as they walked back to the dining area, their chat was about how they might keep in touch. Lunch was a blur, they were on a high oblivious to the bush kitchen tucker. Then Charlie saw Kenny to his bike and left him with an offer to think about.

"When you finish the RAAF career, remember we always need good pilots, and I'd love to see more of you. Just keep us in mind when making decisions. One thing, if you're interested in making money, you better do it before you come out here. A lot different to living in the city."

Kenny shook his head, smiled at his friend, slipped into his helmet and threw a leg over the low-slung saddle. They understood each other as if the intervening years had never happened. There was no need to tell him he'd already bought a little factory in Richmond, inner Melbourne and intended to turn it into a residence when time and opportunity availed.

"Charlie, don't be surprised if I turn up one day looking to give a hand. Great seeing you buddy. Cheers."

With that, he lit up the powerful beast, slapped the visor and eased away from Charlie, the pumps and parked caravans and onto the road towards Alice Springs, a high wave as he left.

Tennant Creek, renowned for its unique hospitality, gave Kenny and Hanna a taste of it on their walk to the shopping strip, the locals welcoming. Their pub meal was a traveller's surprise, the biggest Parma in the outback. Impossible to eat it all. They didn't care with so much to talk about food was incidental. A quiet night in the pub mattered not. They were absorbed, soaked in the pleasure of seeing each other. Before walking back to the motel, they did as riders should always do before riding together. They worked out a strategy. Like riding only in daylight, agreeing on speed limits, how long each stretch should be before stopping, meal breaks and traffic management. All important issues for safe riding. They decided it was ok to ride at first light but not before and always with a keen awareness of wildlife movements. Two hours per stretch or close to was smart as well. The road between Tennant Creek and Daly Waters was pretty much a straight run, and they'd be happy to give the bikes a bit of a squirt when safe. Kenny offered to lead because he knew the road but noticed a particular look when he suggested that one and encouraged Hanna to take over whenever she wanted. He'd booked a cabin at Daly Waters on his way down and bought two tickets for the pub's Beef and Barra smorgasbord and floor show with Chilly Pepper NT celebrity comic. He didn't warn her he had volunteered her for a couple of songs during the floor show. The publican could make that suggestion while he headed for cover.

"Look at the paddock next to the pub, Mac. They tell me 250 people turn up here every night of every week, and this is one of the remotest places in Australia. Go figure. After we get through our steak and fish, we won't be looking for another meal till we get to Katherine tomorrow afternoon."

"You've done your homework, brother. I'll enjoy this night."

She didn't interpret his smile. They did enjoy the balmy temperature, a full house, congenial atmosphere, lots of laughter with the floor show, and western blues music, the full package. Kenny's plan to get his sister on stage was a hit. Chilli Pepper completed his set with an announcement.

"She's on her way to Darwin, folks, and we can't let her go before she shows us how they do it in the big smoke. Please Welcome Miss Hanna Burgess."

The applause was polite. In her T-shirt, shorts and thongs having no idea of Kenny's plot, she reluctantly weaved her way across the dining area to the stage, embarrassed. She sat at the piano, hesitated for a moment and offered a thought to the crowd.

"This is for every couple here tonight, it's called 'The Nearness of You.'"

A perfect choice. Her voice was as husky as Nora Jones's, and they ate it up. Grey Nomads held back tears, each one clutching their partner's hand. They called for more, so Hanna unleased a version of Elton John's classic 'I'm still standin''. The joint was jumping. Chilli jumped back on the stage to wish her good riding, suggesting she hurry back to Daly Waters. Hanna returned to their table and punched Kenny's arm for good measure. The house roared approval.

The next morning they were up at first light into their leathers, taking a brisk walk around the small village to get any stiffness out of their bodies before mounting their 'steeds' and slipping out of town. It would be a comfortable day with breakfast at Mataranka roadhouse and an extended break for a swim in their thermal pools. Refreshed, then just two hours to Katherine, where Kenny allowed enough time to check-in at the 'resort' before heading out of town. He wanted to show Hanna the splendour of Katherine Gorge, to take her on one of the cruises that included crocodile spotting and an evening meal on the water. Shoulder to shoulder, equals, brother and sister, swapping memories and filling information gaps. The inconvenience of immense distances paled against the pleasure they found in each other. Funny thing, Kenny's sleep was restful while they were together. Hanna was his rock, it seemed. She didn't know that. It could become a burden for her if she did, so Kenny kept his demons to himself. Ever since the twins' horrible deaths, he'd been pursued by night demons. The demons blamed him for those deaths and immersed his stricken mind with the images and smells of that terrible event. Sleep had become a replaying loop of that day. And making it more intense was the unresolved relationship with his father. In those dreams, he would see his father ahead of him and just beyond reach. He'd try to catch up, he wanted to talk to him, but he could never catch up. Dreams don't always come with happy endings. Kenny knew this in spades. With Hanna close by, the pain eased, and the dreams temporarily dimmed.

Big breakfast was a treat the next morning, and they tucked into the cereals and scrambled eggs on toast. The pressure was off now, they were within a day's ride of Darwin. They had time for a walk to the train station to mingle with the curious locals who gathered to see the Ghan leave on its way back to Alice Springs.

Darwin was their next goal and final destination. Formation riding on the long straight stretches slinging through rare bends, they were acutely aware of each other and totally at ease. Kenny's next treat was a detour into Litchfield National Park. They were there by mid-morning with time for a loop of the park and a refreshing swim at Florence Falls. Stripped of their leathers down to shorts and T-shirts, they were a striking pair. Other swimmers wrongly assumed they were watching honeymooners. This was a different ecstasy. Later, dried off and relaxed back in riding gear, it was mid-afternoon when they cruised past the 'pond', mooring harbour on the outskirts of Darwin. Kenny led her to The Mantra Hotel on the esplanade, where he'd booked a suite for three nights. For two days, they wouldn't move able to unpack and get laundry done, they'd settle in like other holidaymakers. There was still so much catching up to do, one with stories of planes, speed and close calls, the other full of yarns of university days, gigs with like-minded musicians, student pranks and the constant stress of assessments. He teased her about long hair idealists looking for organic loving, and she teased him about women in uniform. They laughed at each other's exploits on cruisy walks around town, hours spent in coffee shops and watching tourists. Then while strolling on the wharf, watching what the sun does at sunset out beyond the ocean, Kenny dared ask.

"I take it you still live alone, Mac?" She nodded. "We're tarred with the same brush. What is that?" he asked.

"I think Mum's experience as a youngster looked after by the nuns at Abbotsford convent informed her attitude towards relationships. She admired women who were happily celibate, and while she fell victim to our dad's persistence and had us two, she always talked about other ways of living. She never told me I needed a boyfriend or a man and always suggested, 'Hanna, walk your own path.' I think she was spot on. What about you?"

"A bit different for me. She was determined to give me to the Church. I was such a pretty little boy, a chunky shock of curly white hair and a great altar boy, I'm told. Never understood what was going on with her. Enough of me. There is a biological thing going on, though. Aren't you supposed to shiver before the sound of the ticking clock? Sorry if I'm out of line, you'll work it out. Yeah, what about me? I can hardly abide anybody in my personal space or my living space, let alone actually live with somebody full time. To be truthful, I'd be a handful for anyone to put up with, don't you think? The obvious presence of mental demons would be problematic for most partners, I reckon."

"Could be." She replied. "I seem to remember a few events in that boarding school. You don't take bullshit from anyone, do you? As for depression, it's clearly ugly for you to deal with. But brother, however you manage, remember I much prefer having you around than not. We have unfinished business. Maybe you need a butterfly in your life, one person who sees it all and doesn't care, keeps your mind on beautiful things."

"That'd be nice. On that other thing, without respect, we're nothing, Mac. You give everybody one chance and only one. When people show disrespect, you owe them nothing, nothing but contempt or at least indifference. Our father wrote me that advice, and it's come in handy."

It was time to go. The next morning before the temperature got scary, they rode together as far as Katherine, close to the RAAF base at Tyndall. It would be an enduring memory for him sitting on his bike beside the road at Katherine, watching Mac ride into the distance on her way back to Melbourne, the one person in the world with whom it all felt right. He'd shadowed her as far as his turn-off to Tyndall on a mission to get back to base before his leave expired. Above him, a spectre loomed while he waved Mac into the distance. 'This night, you are mine', it hissed before vanishing. He quickly turned his mind to his scheduled heavy workload of surveillance in an F-111 squadron and enough hours in the Hornet to master its ways.

10

F/A-18 HORNET ALL CLASS. After the F-111, it was like driving an F-1 race car compared to a truck, with a whole new sense of limitless power and manoeuvrability. Squadron Leader Robert Daniels and colleague Coby Levey were off to the States on a huge assignment. They picked up rides at Richmond RAAF base in New South Wales, waved goodbye to Oz from 40,000 ft over Sydney and made a fuel stop in Auckland, New Zealand. A refuelling tanker met them over Hawaii, filled their tanks and left them to complete their mission touching ground at Edwards Air Force Base, California, just three hours later. Their flight was an exercise in tight formation, meaning each could watch the other for early signs of fatigue. Their mission was to represent the RAAF for two years at the U.S. testing facility in Arizona headquarters for the F/A-18 McDonnell Douglas Super Hornets program. Australia was buying 72 of the single-seater Hornets and was recently scheduled for 24 of the two-seater larger models. Both men would spearhead the training of Australian pilots back home. That was the plan. They had been rookies together and graduated one and two from the fast jet program. Coby was as close to a friend as Kenny ever had since Charlie Sweeny.

"Good morning pilots. I'm Colonel Buck Francis, United States Air Force and commander of this training facility for shaking down prototypes of aircraft under contract for the Air Force. For the newcomers, Squadron Leaders Robert Daniels and Coby Levey just arrived from Australia, welcome to the Hornets' program. We also welcome our Canadian neighbours, Captains Bill Carlson and Pierre Monty and German friends representing NATO Squadron Leaders Gerhard Schultz and Werner Kauffman. You'll be in the simulator for a bit to familiarise yourself with the new aircraft your national air forces are acquiring over the next several years. The differences between the

Hornet and Super Hornet are significant. You have manuals in front of you today, and information sessions will run every morning on their contents. You will be climbing all over the aircraft in the afternoons and will learn every inch and feature of the Super Hornet like it's an extension of your own body. For today you will adjourn to the mess hall and prepare a five-minute summary on the career of one of your new associates, which you will share with us tomorrow morning in this place. Thank you, gentlemen, see you tomorrow."

On schedule the next morning, Kenny walked into his first wasp nest.

"Good morning, gentlemen and staff. Bobby Daniels. I took the opportunity we were offered yesterday to meet with Werner Kauffman sitting there. He tells me he's from a Hamburg family steeped in Air Force culture that began with his grandfather, who flew with the Red Baron. Say no more. Werner's father flew for the Luftwaffe in the second world war and Lufthansa until he retired. Werner's older brother Otto was one of the first German pilots to fly the infamous Lockheed F-104 Starfighter and sadly was the 70th of 116 German pilots who lost their lives trying to fly that death trap dubbed 'the widow-maker'. In all, they lost 275 Starfighters out of the 915 they bought. The rest were sold on to other countries. Like the rest of us, Werner learned his craft behind the controls of the very successful fighter, the F-4 Phantom. He is still a single man, and outside of flying, he loves to race his Porsche Carrera in amateur competition. That's all I have learned so far."

Buck Francis jumped to the podium.

"Squadron Leader Daniels, you've touched on a very sensitive issue. A very complex issue. I suggest you look at all sides of the story before insinuating that anything untoward takes place in the development and sale of American aircraft. Don't think for one minute, any of you, that we'd risk your lives in unproven aircraft now or ever in the past."

Kenny lit a short fuse on his first outing. Not everybody in the room agreed with the commander. They'd all heard about the Starfighter as a dog of an aeroplane though not aware of the full story. There was significant empathy for Werner Kauffman's part in the story.

The room was suddenly rocked by the shock wave of a low flying jet. The sound of two screaming turbines followed. Everyone leaned to the windows but too late, the aircraft was already out of sight. Kenny didn't lean, did not move, knew it was too late. The class was declared over for the morning, and to give Commander Francis credit, he joined in the ring of sympathy for Werner's brother's story. He also needed to gauge what impact the information might have on the others.

Back in his office Buck Francis and his two off-siders hunkered down.

"Sir, send that Aussie home. He'll be trouble."

"Tom, you might be right, but it's not that easy. He comes with rave reviews as a pilot, and we don't want to upset the RAAF. They're buying over 70 Hornets and 24 Super Hornets."

"Sir, the Starfighter was no dog! We used them in Vietnam, so they were in service for a long time. We don't have to take the bullshit outsiders try to lay on us. Goddammit, where would any of them be without cover from the U.S.?"

"Do your own research. All I can tell you is that the U.S. Air Force changed its order of Starfighters from 1000 to 150 based on three months of trials. I don't know anymore. There are conflicting stories about why that happened."

"It's not our fault they can't fly the planes they willingly buy from us. We don't force them to buy. It's probably all human error."

"Whatever, Tom. Just keep your mind on the job we have today. Let's get these fliers up to speed on the Hornet."

Tom was not convinced. Such is the mind of a patriot!

The visitors gathered in the canteen, getting around Werner and talking about the "widowmaker" Starfighter. Kenny didn't stay. He knew what he'd done and thought he might be better catching some fresh air.

The Canadian boys added their bit. Pierre Monty stepped in. "It's not talked about too much, but our Air Force lost 110 planes in crashes and 39 pilots lost, worst stats of any plane ever. NATO command told our government they had a great Air Force and were hand-picked to acquire the Starfighter for a specific strategic potential to deliver nuclear bombs against Russia if the need arose. Our politicians bought 269 as a result of all that. We don't know how it works, but it's a fact. The stats are horrific."

Bill Carlson joined in. "I, for one, am going to look at the Hornet very carefully while we're here. I'd hate a repeat of the Starfighter fiasco, whoever is responsible. I know the families of some of the Canadian pilots who died in that thing. They were not bad pilots. They were fine pilots. I can tell you that for sure."

The feeling was unanimous.

Coby found his partner out near the airstrip sitting on the grass under the wings of a Phantom.

"Bobby, you ok? You look worried."

"Coby, this Starfighter thing we've just learned about. You know it's not insane or improbable that a bad design can be built. There have been others like our own Nomad, for example. But what kind of system allows a death trap to be mass-produced when they know what'll happen to the pilots who fly it? I have a huge problem with that. We are pawns in a big game, and it's not right. Look, the Hornet's a different story. It's a mighty good plane, I love it. But those young men who believed it was right to follow orders to fly the Starfighter lost their lives on a lie told to them by people they trusted. I'm shivering with anger at this moment, anger and impotence. I've had this feeling before and don't like it one bit. I'm diminished by these damn negatives, Cobes they're adding up."

"We can't change the past, Bobby, and we can't let the past poison us now."

"You're right, we might be ok. But that's no guarantee. You have to wonder who's being exploited today by the same bastards who engineered that other disaster and made billions of dollars doing it. Do you think 'Good' outweighs 'Evil' in the world, Cobes?"

"There's no Nobel prize for guessing the answer to that one, hey."

"Huh, what a story that is. Alfred Nobel invented dynamite in the mid-1800s. How many people have been killed by that stuff, and now they award a 'Nobel' peace prize every year? Someone's laughing at us."

"OK, the world is nuts, but if you let it get to you, all meaning to life comes into question, and that is one slippery slope, old friend. Don't walk that path. Come on, let's go to the base club for a few beers."

"Yeah, that might help. I'm up for it."

Kenny's casual agreement belied the inner truth. He knew he was on that slippery path. The faces of the twins, Glider bleeding all over him, the father he ignored, hundreds of Starfighter pilots dead for no good reason. Disappointments 'haunted all my dreams.'

11

"**MORNING MARK**" called Hanna. "You get the message I left?"

"Marie gave it to me first thing. Must be time for a few stories. When do you want to do it?"

"Immediately, of course, but there are jobs to do first. Let's get all that done today. Maybe we can book a round of golf at Keysborough for tomorrow morning, followed by a quick lunch in the clubhouse. The walk will be therapeutic for me, too, after so many days on the bike. Would seven be too early for you with the kids and all?"

"Actually, that'd be fine. Mum's taken the girls to the beach house on the island for two nights. Listen, that package you sent me from Darwin is exquisite. Four F111's in formation. How'd you know my interest in military aircraft? Some people hate going to work, but I never know what the next surprise is going to be working with you. Thank you very much."

"I don't snoop on your computer usage, but some things you can't hide. Glad you like the photo and will understand more after we talk. So yes, let's hit off at seven tomorrow. Oh, and just a teaser. That plane with 'Javelin' written under the pilot canopy is my brother's ride at the moment."

She was gone leaving Mark's face rigid with surprise. Who would've thought? Hanna picked up the basics of golf while at university and, as a contract lawyer, did a lot of business on the golf course. She teed off from the same spot as the men seeking no advantage. Like the best of casual players, she could knock a drive over 200 metres, even straight, when her sweet stroke was on. One can't be perfect at everything, and it's acceptable to show only sporadic genius on the golf course, a game rightly known as the great leveller. She made no enemies here.

A crystal morning crisp, clean air after overnight showers. The greens might turn and be a bit slow. Neither Hanna nor Mark would be aware of those nuances lining up at the first tee looking down 400 metres of a 75 metre-wide unmissable fairway into a morning sun that shimmered off the dew. What a contrast they were. Hanna was crisp and stylish, and Mark, as usual, was crumpled. Her clubs were the latest and best. His set was a mix of discards. Hanna released a new ball from its cute little box. Mark picked a well-used one rescued from deep in the one pocket of his raggedy bag. Mark watched her step up to the tee and address the ball. With her swing imitating the best qualities of a professional, she smacked it left into trees. He didn't notice the trajectory, he was transfixed by her posture. Shaking his head back to the game, it was his turn. Hanna stepped to the rear of the zone and watched him bend effortlessly to place his ball and stand motionless while obviously imagining the perfect line his ball would take. His swing, she thought, was smooth enough, and she watched the ball head well right. He shook his head, thinking, 'how the hell do you miss a fairway that wide? Was this a portent?' Their recovery shots were reputation savers coming to rest just short of the green. Hers had skipped into a bunker, his on the apron. They both were happy with a bogey for the first. And so, over the course of the morning, when their paths crossed, Hanna shared as much about her brother as was appropriate. She chatted about their childhood, his RAAF enlistment and his assignment in the U.S. Mark was fascinated, knowing it's not often one gets close to fighter pilots. They're people who get to play in the world's most expensive toys. He told Hanna he'd been to a couple of Formula One Grand Prix events in Melbourne and was overawed by flyovers of the F-111s, making the racing cars look like toys in comparison. Walking off the last green, Hanna presented him with a RAAF cap signed by 'Javelin'. He loved the gesture saying he would be more than happy to meet her brother one day.

12

COLONEL FRANCIS RAN a tight organisation, and as promised, after several weeks in the simulators, it all got real for Kenny's squad.

Every day the fliers were in gruelling aerobatic drills, mock dog fights, precision arms practice sessions and air to air refuelling exercises. All were ace pilots, and learning curves were steep. Super Hornets were a revelation, impressive from every point of view. They were incredibly fast, acrobatically manoeuvrable, managed by fly by wire technology, and armed with the deadliest of weapons called by the soft word 'payload.'

"OK, gentlemen, it's time for our Aussie friends to show us how to refuel air to air. Your rides are ready, and you'll rendezvous with your tanker at assigned coordinates. As you know, we're using two-seater aircraft, and I'll be behind you, Bob. Tom will be behind Coby. You've simulated this procedure hundreds of times and in real life back in your own airspace, so let's see the precision we're looking for. Good luck lads."

There are simulations and the real thing where you can't take a fall, press a button and reset. The exercise Kenny and Coby were testing was a simultaneous refuelling one on either side of the tanker and well above stalling speed. Once a pilot raises the receiver nozzle on the nose of his aircraft, he has to watch the wide-mouthed cone on a delivery hose right onto the nozzle. The pilot makes all adjustments with this system, no automation with this manoeuvre. This isn't easy because the hose from the tanker is flexible and can move around as it approaches the target. It is much more complex than it might look, given turbulence, handling, and communications between planes. In this case, there was also a supervision factor, an instructor right behind.

Everything was going well, settling in the cockpit, flight checks, ignition, taxiing and clearance for take-off. Fighter jets look magnificent when they begin to move effortlessly in the climb to altitude and banking in formation to begin the approach to the KC-135 tanker waiting on them at 25,000ft on a level trajectory and constant speed of 300mph.

"Pilot, you are in the envelope. Raise your nozzle and prepare for the drogue."

"Affirmative nozzle ready when you are."

A formal inquiry would be held into the reasons for the fuel hose disconnecting from the tanker. The fact is it set off a chain reaction with devastating results. When breaking free from its mounting, one end snaked directly into the air intake of Kenny's port engine. The plane was out of control for the second it took Kenny to call 'eject, eject!'. A metal spike mounted behind both seats shot through the canopy shattering it. Both seats were catapulted into space at the same moment the jet exploded, sending shrapnel in every direction. Chaos. Kenny's jet should've been horizontal for the ejection manoeuvre, but it wasn't. His seat shot past the rear of Coby's plane, and the exhaust damaged its parachute housing. Buck Francis hit Coby's rear fins, killing him immediately. Coby had only seconds to get safely away from the tanker before he and his co-pilot ejected. His jet spiralled earthwards to its doom. Both pilots survived. Kenny's parachute activated, but one of the three blooms failed. The hard landing caused him serious injury, but he survived.

Kenny opened his eyes two days later, regaining consciousness. He was so heavily sedated he didn't know where he was. He couldn't move, his body in traction. Both legs were plastered from the hip to the heel. He did recognise one face, Coby, who had sat by Kenny's bed since they brought him in.

"Bobby, Bobby, it's me Coby. Can you hear me?"

"Cobes where am I? Something happened, what?"

"Man, you're so lucky to be alive."

"I don't have a strong sense of good luck from here. What do you mean?"

"The refuelling hose flew straight into the port intake and blew engine and plane to shit. Your reflexes saved you. A microsecond later, and you would have been totalled. Your plane rolled violently as you hit the button, that's how I got involved. Buck's seat took out the tail of my jet on its way past. The shit has really hit the fan back at base. Investigators are all over the place. Everyone's heading for cover. Two $70m jets crashed, it's a real mess."

"And Buck, where is he?"

"Sorry mate. Buck is dead. His seat took out the fins of my jet."

"Oh, shit I've killed him, oh no!"

His mind shot back to the last time lives were lost within his reach. He couldn't roll over or cover his face, he was rigid.

"Nothing to do with you, mate. It was the idiots in the tanker. Something stuffed up there, not with you. But you never know how it'll work out. You and I are at the bottom of the pecking order though I can't see how the facts can be twisted."

Kenny didn't hear a word after, 'Buck is dead.' Coby should've noticed the eyes frozen, glazed, gone. But he continued trying to bring Kenny into the picture. He needn't have bothered. Kenny was elsewhere, blaming himself for another disastrous death.

Recovery was slow but never complete. His body geometry was askew. A whole year in rehab got him walking again, kind of, more like a shuffle than a walk. He would never be fit enough to get back to the program, and his mental state took a battering. Teetered on the abyss, obsessed by all that is not good, he could easily have gone under a dozen times. But he didn't. No longer fully capable, he left the Air Force working intensively on recovery. A job came up with a chopper charter company in Houston managed by two ex-Vietnam war veterans. He liked the job servicing offshore rigs with supplies and staff transfer services. He liked the owners too. Kindred souls and it was hard for them to find kindred souls. Heroes they might have been for the mortal risks they faced in battle. Still, public opinion soured against the war while they were away, and it was tough being treated more like lepers than heroes when they came home. When they saw Kenny's application for a job damaged by his military service, a bond formed immediately. He needed help, and they needed good fliers who preferably understood their mindset. Kenny was a perfect fit. It was a bit like putting together a tight fighting unit built on that special bond only soldiers can have. Kenny was welcomed, and he understood why. They assigned him short flights knowing he was still in recovery. Nobody gets out of the war machine alive. They also knew how hazardous life can be with prescription pain killers involved. The arrangement worked for a while but could not last. Kenny's curse struck again. Six months later, Alec Dennis and Doc Magoo were closed down by their banks, victims of escalating interest rates and a cyclic downturn in business called 'The Global Financial Crisis.' But it was how it happened that crushed them. Officials arrived without warning demanding everybody leave the premises within an hour. His sense of self-preservation sharpened on the battlefield. Alec got to his radio to warn Doc and Kenny, who were in the air between Houston and the gulf having left base 30 minutes before the crisis hit. He gave them instructions to head for Barksdale Airforce Base, North Carolina, 240 miles away, where they would enjoy a friendly reception. Alec had one hour to call in favours to make his helicopters disappear and retrieve a promise of enough money to prevent a chain reaction. He was still holding the microphone when a hand reached over his shoulder and flicked off the transmission.

"Sir, you have to leave."

Alec could do no more from his office. It's smart to have a backup on every mission. He had a radio at the hotel where he lived. By the time his helicopters reached the Barksdale base, the deal was done. His birds would find haven in the belly of a Globemaster being sent to the Charleston base, a forest where trees could not be seen. Kenny and Doc would be offered a ride on that plane and part ways in Charleston. Doc could return to Houston in a staff car. Military precision was a beautiful thing, Kenny thought as events unfolded. He wondered where in the world those two helicopters would be headed. He stopped wondering because it didn't matter. By the time the banks worked out that they'd been played, it'd be too late, no trace. They'd taken everything from the partners, but the cost would be two aircraft. Meantime, Alec and Doc settled much of their debt to suppliers. Their convincing display of bravado in the wind-up of their business was deceptive. They were totally ruined. Had risked their lives in war and accepted their wounds. But it was too much to be treated as outcasts and murderers on their return home. They were struck, it was not supposed to be like that. Their aeronautic business was the only thing saving them. Now it was ripped out of their hands, and they had nothing left but the smell of failure all over them. No property, no income, nowhere to live, and for the first and only time, no plan B. Under the bridges of Houston and in deserted factories, what they had was the company of people like themselves, people who knew what they knew felt. People without hope together in a spiral to the bottom, grasping hopelessly along the descent at anything that might slow the slide to oblivion.

As for Kenny, Charleston would do for a while. He contacted the hotel in Houston where he stayed and had management send his belongings across. It wasn't much, but memorabilia from his time in the military was important to him, and he was glad to have it back. Anyway, the banks were not chasing him. He was safe on that minor score. No safety on the big issues, though dragged into another disaster. He might have followed Alec and Doc into the world of the homeless and was only a step away from doing that. But he was not driving the bus into the wall this time and had enough residual self-preservation to save himself. While deciding on his next move, he took a job in security, cruising industrial areas of Charleston and dropping cards in padlocks at every stop, not exactly a mind-stretching job. It wouldn't hold his interest for long, and he made plans to head back to Australia. It was time to go home.

13

KENNY TOOK HIS TIME getting back to Australia, lured by easy access to sedation in the east. Two years slipped by. Time lost in a fog of dull ecstasy sharing crumpled filthy space with other addicts, broken lives from every nation spiralling towards hell. The tall, athletic military mien was diminished. He was older and stooped, having spent long enough in Indian and Thai boltholes soaking spirits and bad company, losing weeks at a time in an opium haze. He didn't know how he found himself in a cheap hotel on the edge of Mumbai. There were flashes of ex-military types from the UK, crowded trains, bush tracks, dangerously overcrowded ferries and moonlit still waters. India, the most honestly corrupt country in the universe, embraced him as it did outcasts from anywhere. But here, he was jolted back to a wider consciousness. He'd accepted deals of hashish from a young man, legs only to the knees, who made his way on the putrid seething streets of Colaba on an Indian version of a skateboard. Kenny met Sukra every second day at a coffee 'shop' small table with a couple of milk crates for seats where they conducted their trade.

Awaking from another two day dreaming thanks to the black tar, he took stock, realising that being numb to pain only treated the symptoms. He watched Sukra with growing interest as he scooted around, always smiling or humming to himself, totally free of pessimism. 'Damn it,' he thought to himself ', this kid makes me look pathetic.' Even with opium or hashish, his dreams were the same as they'd always been. Same faces, same sounds. Two years of dodging hadn't worked. He needed another way to deal with the terror always snapping at his vulnerable soul. Two days later, he was on a plane headed for Melbourne.

14

ONE NIGHT IN EARLY WINTER 2010, in the Melbourne suburb of Mt Waverley, Hanna dined in her favourite restaurant with three colleagues who helped her seal a sizeable development deal within that shopping precinct. They enjoyed wines chosen by their host Pierre and allowed him to design a meal to complement the aged Eden Valley delights. In none of her visits had she ever looked at the menu, and Pierre never disappointed her. They rose at the end of the evening she said goodbye to her colleagues and then turned for a quick chat with her host.

"Lovely meal again, Pierre. Thank you very much. My colleagues loved it."

"Of course, Hanna. You bring out the best I can offer every time."

"I've called a taxi, so had better wait outside."

"No need, the drivers know to call me when they are close. Would you like to finish with a taste of the most magnificent port I've blended in a barrel your equally magnificent brother gave me a long time ago?"

"What? My brother? How do you know him?"

"My nephew Basha is in the Airforce. He did much of his training at the base in Sale, where he met your brother. They were my guests every time they came to Melbourne. Your brother is a gentleman Hanna. I see him regularly still, and he's seen you here a couple of times in the last twelve months since he's been home. Oh damn, I'm sorry. You didn't know. I don't get it. He talks about you every time I see him."

"That's all too weird, Pierre. He's not been to see me yet. I wonder what he's up to. I will have that port but just a small one."

She didn't show Pierre how annoyed she was, but she knew there had to be a reason. He'd show up when he was ready. She knew that.

Pierre poured three small glasses, and they sat at what he called the captain's table.

"There are three glasses, Pierre?"

"There are three of us to toast."

She knew in an instant, the instant before the unfamiliar figure of her brother stepped out of the kitchen. She leapt, and he caught her. They didn't speak, they hugged, both weeping and her pummelling his chest at the same time. Pierre headed for the kitchen. Earlier that evening, Kenny meant to speak to his sister but was thwarted when she left her building as he arrived. He followed her taxi to Mt Waverley and saw her enter his friend's restaurant. Slipping around the back, he was able to arrange a surprise with Pierre's help. Now his two friends were together for the first time in eight years, with much water under the bridge. Twenty minutes later, Pierre could see they'd settled into conversation. Hanna had questions, but she was smart enough not to push the pace. Kenny would tell her everything in his own time. Pierre suggested they might like to stay in the unit above the restaurant. They were welcome to anything from the bar. They rose from the table, threw their arms around their host and said goodnight, promising frequent returns and left. Kenny ushered his sister to what looked like an old Holden station wagon parked in the lane behind the restaurant. Looks can deceive, as she soon realised. Clearly, he'd been busy with rehabilitation. The smile and cheeky look out of the corner of his left eye said it all, and she began to feel comfortable.

"Where are we going?"

"Your place, of course. Love to see what you've done. I scoped it for a while and saw you coming and going. Been hard not to grab you as you walked past sometimes."

"Get out, I could smack you one, you know."

"Oh, mack me Mac, haha."

"Concierge, no less, you've picked a nice part of town Mac. Impressive. The guy gave me a bit of a look, so he's on the job. That's good too."

"The lifts get to the top deck in just 25 seconds. 15 seconds to my floor. I like the concept of a flat deck above all the hoo-ha."

"Yeah, the top end of town is a long way from what's going on at ground level, hey? You know, Mac, ever since boarding school, I can't get the issue of how powerless we can be when told all the time how lucky we are while being systematically betrayed and exploited. There's something very wrong about how our world works. I can't do much about that, but I've had this story running around in my head for a while. It's about some old, sick guys who pull off a major heist on the banks and give the money to the poor. A bit like levelling the playing field."

"Robin Hood has been done to death, Ken, there has to be a twist."

"Oh, there are twists, alright."

"Then write the damn thing. If it's any good, I'll help you get it published and promoted."

"Hmmm yeah, won't write itself, will it. How hard can it be, right?"

"OK, you're staying the night. There's plenty of room, and you don't have to rush off, do you?"

"If you've got the makings, I'll bring breakfast in bed, how's that?"

"Deal, brother, you'll love what you see from here in the morning along the bay on one side and the Dandenongs on the other. I usually have cereal, fruit, toast and tea for breakfast, so don't go silly."

"OK, sunrise together. See you then."

It'd been an action-packed day. Both were ready for sleep. No nightmares this night. Kenny was home, really home, with his sister kind of home. And yet even then! Morning stripped him of comfort. His feet hit the floor, and his head spun. Through gritted teeth and a thumping headache, he got himself dressed.

"Kenny, that's a funny way to take in the view. Like coffee?"

Kenny climbed clumsily back over the balcony rail and into the room. Hanna was watching in the wall mirror. She breathed. She also noticed the beads of sweat on his forehead. He didn't speak, sat at the table, cupped his hands around the mug and sipped.

"Thanks, Mac, I need meds, so I'm off. We'll talk later."

For the first time, she saw past her rose-coloured memories of her big strong brother. The man lumbering off-kilter to the door was but a shadow. He shared nothing of the incident she witnessed. She knew she'd have to keep an eye on him. He'd frightened her this morning.

"OK big brother. Hurry back."

The door sailed shut, her words just squeezing through before it did.

While his left hand clicked the car open, Kenny leaned on the roof with his right elbow glancing up at the 44th floor in time to see his sister pull back from view. She'd not said a word about his deteriorated physique, she saw him for what was real. He was comforted in that thought. He smiled to himself with some satisfaction, too, that the car would've been smashed had he let go of the balcony rail. He liked the car.

His life was somewhat diminished, but he had not been completely stupid. Income from courier work for a local seafood wholesaler supplemented the residue of his insurance pay-out from the fateful American adventure. Those short flights to Tasmania and King Island he could easily manage. Most of the other cash reserves went into a renovation of his new home, a worn-out farrier's workshop in Westbank Terrace in Richmond just above the serpentine Yarra. With time on his hands, he'd completed a renovation he could comfortably call home. Secure, comfortable, flexible room to accommodate his beloved restored 1974 HZ wagon all tricked up. Like the car, his pad was a far cry from the state that it was in when he bought it so long ago. Sadly the bike was surrendered to necessity. Too hard on the back. It was snapped up by an ex-detective who wanted something strong and reliable to ride the highways of the nation in a search for tranquillity. Kenny could understand his need. He used the cash to set up access to a medium-sized light aircraft for his new venture.

15

"HELLO MARK, BAD TIME?"

"Not at all Hanna, what is it?"

"Sunday morning, blue sky wondering what you and the girls are doing."

"We're thinking about a walk at Safety Beach Dromana and an early lunch of fish and chips. There's nothing like sea air, a paddle, and a romp on the sand to soak up the energy of two youngsters. You should see them on the beach, pair of butterflies floating from one object of curiosity to another. They define 'carefree'. It's good for a worn and tattered soul to be in their orbit. You looking for something to do?" He crossed his fingers.

"If you'd like the company, I could do with fresh air and playtime with the girls."

"OK, meet us in Dromana, just where the main drag begins. Let's say an hour's time?"

"Great, see you there."

This was a first for Mark, but he was comfortable because his daughters knew Hanna well enough to enjoy her company. Her reasons for calling didn't matter, she'd confide if she felt it right. This feeling of connection pleased him and disturbed him at the same time.

Hanna knew a little about Dromana. In recent times she loved to let the bike have its head on the winding climb to Arthur's Seat, slipping under cable car lines four times on the way. The view across Port Phillip to the city was worth any amount of effort on a clear day. The road led to a smorgasbord of hilltops past Alpaca farms, vineyards and orchards that identify Red Hill. Below the viewing platform, Dromana sat at one end of a kilometre stretch of golden beach where shops serviced visitors and locals with the usual pizzas, fish 'n chips and pub food. The pier sliced about 200 metres into the crystal waters of the bay. There were always hopeful anglers dangling legs over the sides, waiting for the occasional garfish or flathead to commit suicide. Heading towards the northern end, candy-striped beach boxes separated the beach from the walking track. Two more kilometres along the beach, tucked into a half-moon ring of cliffs, was the protected zone known as Safety Beach. Clifftop holiday houses overlooked the whole scene way back to the cable car end. Who needs St Moritz? This place is spectacular. Then Mark wondered if he'd said he was standing on station pier gazing across the bay, would she have met him just the same? Not sure. Didn't matter.

Hanna recognized Mark's Subaru Outlook wagon next to the amenities block 900metres from the shopping strip. Her Kawasaki idled into position beside his car, and immediately the two girls appeared from the long grass squealing for Hanna to let them sit on her bike. She loved that kind of welcome and happily slung the would-be speed freaks over the saddle while she loaded her gear into the back of their car. Mark beamed at the scene. Maybe there was an element of surrogacy about Hanna's attention to his girls, but he didn't mind. The four of them headed off along the foreshore, paddling in ripples, the kids harvesting little shells, wondering about the occasional lumps of clear jelly rolling around on the water's edge. The pier loomed as they approached that end of the beach, and the girls raced to be first to check out the optimistic anglers. Mark and Hanna took their time while keeping a careful eye on the children.

"This is nice, Hanna but unusual. Let me guess. You're worried about the big commercial/residential development our Chinese friends want to do on Blackburn Rd?" He hoped this was not even close.

"That's true but not the reason for today. No work today, just clearing the head. My brother turned up yesterday and stayed at my place last night. He's my brother, and I love him dearly, but he's not too good."

She filled in details about Kenny's changed life.

"He had everything going for him until the accident, he barely survived. Now he's living on his wits and has a vague ambition to become a writer. It might be a way to expunge demons, but it's fanciful to think a good story will accomplish any real change. I hope he knows that. Don't get me wrong, I'm keen to see his take on whatever swims around in his head."

"It's a miracle for someone to survive what happened. You're so lucky to still have him."

"I know. He was my big protector in the neighbourhood, shared all his secrets and showed me how to do stuff most girls wouldn't do. I tell you, I'm not a bad shot with a shanghai, so look out." He was more interested in a lasso than a shanghai, but there was no hurry. Might never happen.

They scooped up the girls and crossed to the shops. Fresh flake, a few scallops, and potato cakes would hit the spot for lunch. There was always room in the covered picnic facilities, so that's where they sat for the next hour, teasing gulls with scraps soaking in the wider view of activity on Port Phillip. Soda soft drink burping and giggling punctuated the walk back to the car. It was time to head home. Mark loaded his girls in the back seat while Hanna geared up for her ride. He was none the wiser about her motivation, but he felt brightened by her presence.

"We'll race you home, Hanna."

"Yes Hanna, Daddy drives fast."

Visor down, Hanna nodded to her young friends and slid out of their day, Kenny still on her mind. It was Sunday. She had a gig with her blues brothers at The Green Door later and wanted to spend an hour or so on the piano before meeting them. No thought of Mark, no room. She was blind to herself. Mark wasn't. While his daughters dozed in the back seat amid the obvious signs of having been to the beach, his mind massaged the moment. A glance in the rear-view mirror at the top part of his handsome dishevelled head and smiling Irish blue eyes reassured him. Hanna was only human. It was fate she dropped into his life. His eyes laughed at him.

16

KENNY SPENT THE REST of that morning in a profound sleep, helped by his little blue friends. He recalled the great line that reality is an illusion brought on by the lack of good drugs. He had good drugs. Needed them. Refreshed after a late afternoon breakfast, he turned to his research, writing and reading table littered with documents, scraps for notes, lists of names and maps he was studying for locations in the story. The computer screen lit up, and he clicked up the document already started. There it was, page one. He read it again, seeing necessary changes every time. He wondered if it would ever be right enough for him. He settled on the title "Zero Downside", meaning there is only one way on, and that's up.

1   INTERIOR OF STUDY OF RON BEAUMONT   MID-MORNING
Ron is sitting at his desk on which is scattered several pieces that identify him as an FBI agent, recently appointed. He picks up and opens the case folder in front of him, consisting mostly of newspaper clippings with large headlines.
- *Major armoured van heist*
- *Outlaws take fortune from Wells Fargo*
- *FBI still baffled by heist*
- *MARDI GRAS BANDITS arrested*
- *Local wives die in crash horror*
- *Local charter firm goes under*

His notes:
Jose Maria Orlando, helicopter pilot
Matthew Jesse James, socialite banker with AIDS
Ed Royston, Used Car Network and $24m in debt
Crime scene photos and maps
The door opens, and his girlfriend enters

LESLEY MASON:
It's time, Hon. We best get going
Ron closes the file, reaches for her hand, and they move to the door.

2   NATIONAL CEMETERY   LATE MORNING
Standing with just a few friends and acquaintances. Lesley is seated with Ron at her shoulder. It is the military funeral service for her grandfather (John Lee Calhoun). Ed Royston is in the group. John Lee's former commander speaks. The girl sobs.

RETIRED GENERAL
Real heroes are humble men.
They are ordinary men who succeed in extraordinary situations.
My friend here was such a man.
A great gentleman, natural leader, gifted pilot, hero and steadfast friend.

His call sign was 'GOD' from the JC in his name.
His prowess at search and rescue was such that any call for 'GOD' became the acknowledged distress call from any downed aviator.

Sadly, our nation never re-paid this man well enough.
For the disease likely caused by the chemicals in
Vietnam. A disease that took both he and his lifelong
friend and business partner, Captain Jose Maria Orlando.

John Lee's life was marked by great business success and terrible personal tragedy when his wife and daughter were lost. A lesser man would have been broken, but John Lee rose through intense distress and focused his energies on his business and raising his beautiful granddaughter.

The later loss of the business he built with Jose Marie took a toll on both men.
Colonel John Lee Calhoun was a fighter to the finish.
While the last years could have been more comfortable for him, he was never without the grace and quiet charm that set him apart.
I asked him recently what epitaph he would prefer.

He said, "I have learned to be free."

Goodbye, dear friend. We miss you and will continue to for a long time.

The military guard gives the rifle salute, the flag is folded and presented to Lesley. She accepts the flag. A very frail Ed Royston approaches the woman and embraces her.

ED ROYSTON

I've only known him for 18 months. He treated me like a brother. He loved you dearly.

LESLEY MASON

Thanks Ed. He felt the same about you and the others. Such a shame you boys didn't get together years ago. That might have been too much fun.

Ed smiles and looks up at a flight of military helicopters passing overhead in salute to the fallen veteran.

17

KENNY CONNECTED a brass school bell to his front door. Its ringing roused him, noting it was after midnight. That surprised him. He'd written the first scene enough times he forgot time altogether. Only one person knew his address, and he knew what she wanted even before he opened the door. He saved the latest changes and closed the file.

"Hello, brother had to see you, and you know why. So tell me you're going to be OK?"

The embrace was warm, she clung a bit longer than she might have.

"Mac, I know what it looks like and have to admit to some pretty dark moments since things went pear-shaped. But I have you nearby, and I'm going nowhere. In the end, the world will go to hell in a handbasket no matter what good people do. It's no good standing in front of something you can't stop. It's going to happen regardless. That's why I've decided to have a bit of fun writing. It's one way of dropping on the enemy. I can't do it the other way, hey, besides, there aren't enough bombs. And if it could be done, the same bastards would be making billions out of it. No use, I'll just stick idealism in my pocket and treasure it. Better writers than I will ever be have plenty to say about our essentially corrupt nature, and the world has not changed. I am doing this project to put precise words to some worrying ideas. My own reasons will suffice."

"Clearly, you've taken your medicine for the day. That's good, good for everyone. Hmmm. Time for a tour. Come on, show me what you've done."

He did, first of all, strolling around the bottom floor, which was exclusively a workshop, studio and garage. Tell-tale signs of activity sawdust drills templates and partly-constructed pieces. No doors except the garage door and front door. Steps to the first floor led from inside the front door up to the living space with kitchen and utilities. He retained red brick walls sand-blasted and varnished. Mac gasped at a framed photo of her in graduation kit. She had no idea how he got hold of it, but she loved the tacit message. Steel and timber defined his décor crafted and welded polished and clear varnished oak, cedar and blackwood benches, tables and shelves. Light came from small halogens suspended from a wire grid covering the whole zone. He'd kept the smithy's double-bricked fire-pit, a huge cowling above it that took hot air in a roundabout way to the rest of the building on its way to the roof and to the atmosphere. A huge stack of cut wood showed he was ready for winter. Natural light flooded from a double-glazed steel-framed window with four sections running the full length of the building. It was night, so the only light came from nearby street lamps. More steps led to a mezzanine. There were no doors anywhere except for one. Essential and minimalist furnishing, most of it crafted in the workshop. His bedroom was spacious under an industrial steel-framed raked profile roof. Two roofing iron sheets had been replaced with a large paned clear skylight visible with the touch of a button sliding the timber cover panels aside. Kenny hit the button, and a brilliant half-moon stared at them.

"Not just a pretty face, brother, you all over. Love it. Now I'm satisfied on all fronts, I will leave you to it and talk more tomorrow. Remember, anything, anywhere, anytime."

They hugged, and he whispered something that made her shiver.

Kenny fell back into bed luxuriating in its acreage and was asleep in a minute but not before last thoughts took him back to the script and how he might handle a flashback to begin the story proper. This story didn't yet have a life of its own, and he knew it was up to him to get the momentum going. Then all he needed to do was wait for it to reveal itself. He smiled in that moment you can never catch, the one between being awake and being asleep. For that moment, he forgot he was terrified of sleep.

Off to King Island in the morning with fresh scallops for dinner with a bit of luck. His ride would be prepped and waiting for him at Moorabbin airport by 5am, so was the nap he slipped into. Waiting for him as well were the four silently howling faces of the dead, screaming jets, a horrible sense of falling and disabling fear part of almost every night. And every morning, he would 'fly' out of bed and 'rush' into a cold shower to chase the images away. Then cup in hand, he took himself out into the neighbourhood lit only by street lights and bedrooms of other early risers. Ten minutes and he was ready for the day. Ten more minutes and Javelin could be seen easing onto the street on its way to Moorabbin.

18

KENNY SWUNG THE CARGOMASTER onto the main runway at Moorabbin. The morning horizon presented an imminent sunrise that would sneak colour and depth into a grey two-dimensional landscape. His right hand on the throttle slid forward, and the whirring propeller immediately let him know it had him covered. An empty cargo bay meant his 675 horses hurtled to take-off in just 550 metres. Nothing like the 70,000 lb thrust of a Super Hornet, but good enough for the job. He was at a cruising altitude of 5,000ft and already over Port Phillip in ten minutes heading for King Island. An odd thought took hold, and spontaneously he altered course to take a look at Wilsons Promontory. The coastline was rugged, revealing a number of inlets with relatively shallow water and pristine white beaches. He swooped for a closer look and, when satisfied, regained altitude and set a course directly for his destination. If he ever had to disappear, this could be the place. Then back to the job at hand. A cargo of seafood and cheeses made famous by that tiny paradise waited for him. King Island airstrip was not long but comfortable enough for this plane to wash off its landing speed without the perimeter fence rushing up at him. His contact Johnny Farrell was waiting in his van, ready to unload 16 polystyrene 30 litre freeze packs of precious Tasmanian seafood delicacies. Johnny also filled Kenny's request for two 1.5-kilogram wheels of world-famous King Island brie. Business done, a smile on his face, and a calm blue sky to the north, Kenny headed for home. Little Billy from Sahara Seafoods would be waiting, then he'd be free for the rest of the day. He clarified some ideas about his script in the air, such as the backstories for the main characters and how they amused themselves waiting for treatment. He was keen to get home. His demons were silent, keeping their distance, and he liked that. He was home by 4pm. Look out, Hemingway, here comes Burgess!

3   FLASHBACK- HOLY CROSS HOSPITAL HOUSTON   AFTERNOON

Matt is standing at the nurse's station, where coffee and refreshment are available for patients receiving treatment. He waits for the sound of a helicopter overhead to pass before he speaks.

SENIOR NURSE:

I don't care if you were the greatest banker since Midas!

You don't come in here with your airs and graces, demanding donuts with your coffee. This is not a hotel. Just be content with cookies and dates.

MATTHEW JAMES:

Ah! Dates! My favourite!

With some animation and a flourish of a wrist, he takes the date between two fingers and holds it in the direction of the nurse.

Would you like one?

SENIOR NURSE:

That's cute, darl (*grinning*), but I know I'm not your type.

Raucous laughter erupts from the three men, John Lee, Ed Royston and José Maria, seated at a table. Two are playing checkers, the other watching. José Maria is on a drip. They are waiting for Matt to arrive. Matt turns away from the nurse, a broad smile on his face. He moves to join his friends.

JOHN LEE:

Still your move, Ed … before Matt's grand entrance.

ED ROYSTON:

You want to concede? You're cornered.

JOHN LEE:

Talking about being cornered. You promised weeks ago you'd find a car for Lesley. No wonder you lost your money in car yards.

You're too damn slow to look after customers.

ED ROYSTON:

OK, I'll take that one on the chin. At least I didn't mislay a business that had 20 helicopters under charter like you and your Latin pal.

He grins, looking at John Lee and José Maria

MATTHEW JAMES:

Am I the only clean skin here? I didn't lose anything.

JOSÉ MARIA:

Hmmm, not so sure about that. You did lose that plum job just before retiring.

JOHN LEE:

Fellers. Let's not get personal. The eighties did us all in

José and I got done when the banks foreclosed on loans after the crash of '87, and Ed got caught up in the same mayhem. Yep, we're all losers. I concede the game, Ed.

ED ROYSTON:

And yes, I've found a car for Les. Genuine low mileage.

JOHN LEE:

Genuine?

ED ROYSTON:

Trust me. Come on Matt, set 'em up. It's your turn to bite the dust.

Matt and Ed re-arrange the checkers and start a game.

You know Matt, when you finally get around to paying the $3.50 you owe me, I'll turn it into a million.

MATTHEW JAMES:

Opening a small purse that shows he has little enough money.

Next time, Ed. Maybe I'll win it back today.

ED ROYSTON:

Come on, it's only a few bucks.

MATTHEW JAMES:

Embarrassed

I know. But I simply don't have it today.

ED ROYSTON:

Come on!

JOHN LEE:

Steady Ed. He said he'll fix you up. What do you want him to do? Rob a bank for it? It's just a game we are playing.

ED ROYSTON:

Guess so. Sorry Matt. I get a bit prickly sometimes. Your move first.

Matt acknowledges the apology with a nod. The game progresses, Matt loses.

19

KENNY FOLDED DOWN the screen, satisfied with his introduction of four key characters about to reveal evils that befell them. He wanted them to not disappear under the weight of perceived failure but find the strength to strike back. They had nothing to lose, old and dying. He had no idea as yet how they would do that. His major difficulty was going to be finding a way to maintain a measured, detached mindset. It was a story, not autobiography. So far, so good. There was something else on his mind. Hunger. Hunger that knew of the fresh scallops waiting for attention. He had to respond. So off to the kitchen to marinate a handful in garlic, pepper, soy and a touch of chilli. He seared them in a hot pan, wiped with butter and set the scallops on a plate of rocket salad. He had thoughtfully chilled a bottle of Eden Valley Riesling and picked up a continental breadstick from his favourite baker Doug, at Dougie's Kitchen.

The food was good, his story was moving, drugs were working, he felt good. Impulsively he picked up a wheel of King Island brie minus the thick wedge which he hacked off. He threw it onto the passenger seat of the javelin, hit the remote and guided the missile through the narrow Richmond lanes and off to Mt Waverley. He wouldn't trouble Pierre with unnecessary company, just leave the cheese and go home. He parked in the lane behind the restaurant and snuck in the back door. A wink and a nod to Pierre's chef Tom and he was off before he could be seen and suffocated in gratitude. It was getting late, and he yearned for bed, not so much for sleep. He loved gazing at the universe under that delightful window, reverse gravity drawing his mind to infinity. It'd been a full day.

Old habits stick. Kenny woke early every day, a reflex embedded in armed forces training and one he cared not to kick. "Best part of the day," he would say to himself, sitting on the front doorstep, coffee in hand, after a brisk warming shuffle around the neighbourhood, sucking up stale city air marinated in the moisture of early morning. He turned his mind to other things when the phone demanded attention. Ignoring its summons, he dragged himself vertical and headed to the workshop, where an unfinished table frame whispered for his attention. The smell of fresh shavings and sawdust drew him like Sirens did to Ulysses. He couldn't resist. But unlike Ulysses, he didn't have to be lashed to a mast for safety. He embraced the call. It would be two hours of sanding and varnishing blackwood boards he had braced, glued and clamped. Two hours of sweet meditation and creation following his hands all over the job.

Then unpredictably, he stopped, dropped the brush he was using on the final coat of marine grade estapol into turps, wiped his hands clean and headed straight to the computer. He was being called. Inspiration was like that. You don't know when it would strike, you just know it would.

4   CORNER OF HOSPICE DAY ROOM   LATE AFTERNOON
John Lee and José Maria are seated in the lounge while the other two play their game of checkers

JOHN LEE:
You seem a little melancholy
JOSÉ MARIA:
Have you forgotten?
JOHN LEE:
How could I?
ED ROYSTON:
Hears the two men talking and turns to his playing partner
Cause for celebration, boys? Love anniversaries.
JOSÉ MARIA:
No, Ed. We lost our women in a plane crash, 15 years today.
ED ROYSTON:
Aghast at his own stupid assessment
Damn! Sorry boys. Didn't know.
JOSÉ MARIA:
No way you could, Ed. It's ok
JOHN LEE:
Maintenance systems should get the highest priority when lives are at stake.

You gotta ask yourself what really matters.

I can tell you that we, the people, do not matter when we bump into big systems.

MATTHEW JAMES:

Sounds like we've all taken hits

ED ROYSTON

The world is on its way to hell.

MATTHEW JAMES:

Well, boys, my grandpa did his bit. The banking system of the day shivered at the mention of Jesse James. And you know, it would be something to have his guts.

JOSÉ MARIA:

Yeah! He robbed them, and you ran them.

ED ROYSTON:

Or …

MATTHEW JAMES

Enough, enough! I get the message. Anyway, my ancestry is not proven.

Grandma died a single woman. She changed her name to James before my Pa was born.

ED ROYSTON:

How come the bank shafted you, Matt?

MATTHEW JAMES:

I was VP of Customer Services with a few months to go before retirement and a substantial pension. I was relying on that money.

5   FLASHBACK TWO YEARS   VP OFFICE AT BANK - MORNING

A comfortable wood-panelled office with a view across the central business area of Houston. Matt is sitting at his desk looking at his personal credit card and other bills he's struggling to keep up with. There's a knock at the door and his secretary of many years enters.

SECRETARY:

Good morning Mr James, your coffee.

She places the coffee on the desk and cannot help but see the concern on his face.

How long have we known each other?

MATTHEW JAMES:

Through most of my failed affairs, Magda, and too long at this place.

SECRETARY:

Yes! And I still don't understand how you can live so far beyond your VP pay.

MATTHEW JAMES:

Style is so expensive these days, Magda.

SECRETARY:

You have to get a handle on your affairs. Oh! Your doctor wants you to ring, and the CEO will see you at 9:30.

MATTHEW JAMES:

Thanks. You are the best.

But I retire in a couple of months, and my pension will see me right.

Magda leaves his office. Matt looks at the phone and hesitates before calling his doctor. While afraid of the likely news, he hopes he might be spared. He makes the call.

It's Matthew James returning Doctor Living's call.

DOCTOR'S RECEPTIONIST:

One moment sir, I'll put you through.

DOCTOR LIVING:

Matthew. Thanks for the call. I was wondering if you'd stop by, I'd like to discuss the test results.

MATTHEW JAMES:

Not usually given to acts of courage, he mounts the strength to say

Give it to me now, and give it straight. Seeing you will not change the facts.

DOCTOR LIVING:

You should come in, Matthew

MATTHEW JAMES:

Arnold, do me the courtesy, please.

DOCTOR LIVING:

OK. The results are positive. Sorry, Matthew, but you have full-blown AIDS.

MATTHEW JAMES:

He didn't hear any of the following conversation about what it meant, likely outcome etc. He would get to all that in time. For now, he was in shock, and while the doctor was still talking, he put the phone back in its cradle. He's in shock and oblivious to everything. His secretary enters.

SECRETARY:

Mr James. Are you all right? It's 9:25, you're expected upstairs.

MATTHEW JAMES:

He tries to gather his wits, pacing
Er….Er… I think so. What did you say?

SECRETARY:

You have to go upstairs. He is waiting. Are you sure you are OK?

MATTHEW JAMES:

Oh, yes Magda, I'm fine.

He makes his way slowly to the elevator for the ride to the 45th floor. He gets out and heads for the office of the CEO.

CEO SECRETARY:

Good morning Mr James. Please go through. Mr Moldrich is waiting.

He walks through

MOLDRICH:

Good morning James. Take a seat. This won't take long.

SECRETARY:

Would you like coffee, gentlemen?

MOLDRICH:

No. Won't have time for that. Now Mr James, to the point.

When we bought the bank six months ago, we promised everyone would be protected. That is something we have proudly honoured.

MATTHEW JAMES:

Yes

MOLDRICH:

What we are doing in the meantime is reviewing the operations of the bank and the number of divisions. It has become clear that some rationalisation is necessary.

MATTHEW JAMES:

He hears the word 'rationalisation' and snaps back from wherever he's been.

Rationalisation?

MOLDRICH:

Yes. Sadly, your division is to be combined with Corporate Planning, and I have to say there will be no place for you after the implementation next week.

MATTHEW JAMES:

But I have three months to retirement. Without a contract, I have no pension.

MOLDRICH:

That is true. You will be paid for outstanding leave and a small separation amount, and that's all we can offer. You know the pension is dependent on reaching 65. Your office will be needed by the end of this week and if there is anything I can do to help, just call.

He rises and invites Matthew to the door.

Miss Hendricks, would you ask Mr James to sign those papers before he goes. Thank you.

6   FLASHFORWARD TO THE HOSPICE

The men have listened to Matt's story

MATTHEW JAMES:

Guess that's it. I was out, broke and terminally ill. Had to start mortgage broking to make ends meet. Guess I had a bad day

JOHN LEE:

They don't get much worse than that.

MATTHEW JAMES:

No, they don't. Of course, so-called friends deserted me.

It was a different life. Strangely I've come to look forward to treatment and our little group. I don't even mind it when it gets a bit pesky. The only thing I am immune to now is bad news. What about you and José?

JOSÉ MARIA:

My story is the same as John Lee's

We met flying Hueys in 'nam. He was my commander, and I was…

JOHN LEE:

… a pain in the ass. Always partying, disruptive, insubordinate…

JOSÉ MARIA:

Enough with the compliments. I love you too. Anyway, we had a small accident that sprayed us with agent orange, which resulted in us being here, as well as giving John Lee a new lower leg and me the loss of some vital organs. They let us go with thanks, and we set up a helicopter charter outfit

You may have heard of 2GEE AIR. We named it after our call signs, God and Gladys.

ED ROYSTON:

God and Gladys.

MATTHEW JAMES:

I knew a fellow who liked to be called Barbara, but he was a sailor, not a pilot.

JOHN LEE:

No doubt. But Gladys, after José's middle name Maria,
Me GOD, because of my initials JC.

ED ROYSTON:

Why do Latinos do that with middle names for their menfolk?

JOSÉ MARIA:

Beats me. Made my mother happy, but she didn't have to go to my elementary school. Do you want the story, or are we going to fuss over names?

ED ROYSTON:

Keep your shirt on. We want the story, of course.

JOHN LEE:

2GEE was a great outfit. Huge fun servicing the oil industry here and overseas. Banks loved us. We listened to their advice and spent on acquisitions just as interest rates spiked, then it hit the fan globally. The crash of '87. All businesses suffered, cash flow was one-way, and collateral values dropped. We didn't have enough, and the banks shut us down.

MATTHEW JAMES:

My bank was part of the consortium that closed down that Texas jewel.

JOSÉ MARIA:

We lost the lot. Worst of all, we had 150 families dependent on us, and the crunch for them was worse.

JOHN LEE:

We let down a lot of good people.

ED ROYSTON:

What about Lesley's mum, John Lee?

JOHN LEE:

Our daughter, Stephanie, took the plane crash and death of our wives real hard. She married a no-hoper who was always in trouble with the law, and when he left her, it all became too much. We lost her, and I raised their daughter.

ED ROYSTON:

Hell. My story dishes up honey compared to all that, and I thought I had it tough. So, what have you two been doing since?

JOSÉ MARIA:

I fix electronic equipment, and John Lee works part-time, running the furnace in a crematorium. What's your story, Ed?

MATTHEW JAMES:

You were Ed Royston Fine Cars. Car lots all over the country. What happened, Ed?

ED ROYSTON:

Abandoned baby.

Succession of foster parents.

Child labouring in a chrome plating shop. Foster father's care resulted in my current condition.

No real education.

Learned how to fix odometers for car dealers.

Lived on my wits.

Never married.

Saved my money and started a car yard.

Like you boys, the banks threw money at me to expand.

Then closed me down. Left me with nothing.

I'm now back on my wits, fixing odometers.

I've not spoken about it since.

Until now, with you lot of misfits.

For once, I fit in, what a laugh.

Remember the line.

'It's not personal, it's just business'?

Well, it sure was personal to me.

The four men are all seated, looking at one another. Ed is calming down from telling his story. Matt is the first to speak.

MATTHEW JAMES:

I guess you had a bad day.

There is a silent moment of tension. Simultaneously they burst into laughter.

JOHN LEE:

Time turns tragedy to comedy. How strange is that!

More raucous laughter. They return to their checkers.

The stories had Kenny glued to the screen. Kind of cathartic moment pouring out all that venom, all that hurt to people just following their dreams, inexplicably cut down and betrayed by the very system they believed in. Alec's and Doc's faces floated past. The beast within awoke and flashed the red curtain over his eyes. He grabbed the monitor, raised it over his head, and was ready to smash it to the ground when he paused at the sight of Hanna's photo on the wall, sucked air and quietly put it down like a naughty child caught in the act of mischief.

He walked to windows facing the Terrace, stretched arms high palms on the glass and pressed his forehead against the window, nudging it repeatedly. He wished the glass was not there and he could quieten the beast once and for all, permanently. Bloodshot manic eyes stared back at him from the other side of the glass. Time for medication. He dragged himself over to the oasis and stood motionless at the kitchen bench, a glass of water in one hand, pacifiers in the other, mind racing.

"Breathe deep, in....., out....., in....., out...... Turn your scar into a star, boys. You must find a way to even the score. Just be careful, don't take them head-on. You can't win that way. You'll have to be smart, smarter than them. Find their weaknesses, exploit them. But know this. You'll have a moment of success. Maybe. If you're very lucky. But don't think for a minute the world will change. No, that can't happen. Don't stand in front of something you can't stop. Duck, cover, feint, use their momentum against them, and you just might be left standing alone and free for the moment it takes. Granddaughter has a wayward father, that could be something."

These thoughts helped the chemicals lower the blood pressure, and the beast, subdued for the moment, crept back into its cave. But it didn't slumber. It never did, but it did make strategic retreats from time to time without complacency, always ready to pounce.

20

"HI, MAC. IF I BRING fresh Tassie salmon and whip up something nice, are you interested?"

"Like I said, brother, anytime. I've just got in and thinking about dinner. Your idea sounds good to me. Do you mind sitting around a while afterwards? I'm working on a piano piece. Oh, you have my entry card for the garage. You'll find my spot, 44/2. Hate to see the javelin blunted by idiots in the street."

"You don't know how good that idea is right now. See you shortly. Meant to thank you for the card. Inner-city parking is crazy, as you know."

Hanna didn't mind Kenny in the kitchen because he cleaned as he went and was particular about washing dishes. Not a bad cook either, like herself. Their parents always encouraged them to have a go, and she recalled the clouds of flour when Kenny made scones on a Sunday afternoon, her helping shape and paint the tops with egg. Not every attempt was successful, but that's how you learn. Mostly it was fun. She watched him from across the room then the phone rang. It was Mark's older girl, Maggie. Mac put her on speaker.

"Hello Hanna, this is Maggie Joseph speaking, how are you?"

"Lovely to hear from you, Maggie. Have you had your dinner?"

"I have. Daddy and Emily are washing up. It's her turn. Do you like broccoli, Hanna?"

"Broccoli is green, isn't it? I like it if you smash it up and put butter and salt and pepper on it, what about you?"

"Yuk, I can't even look at it, it's green. I'd like to smash it."

Whispering

"I have to have some, but luckily Alice likes it. Don't tell Daddy."

"Your secret is safe with me, Maggie. I used to have a dog, and he shared my dinner. Why are dogs always hungry?"

"So they can poo a lot, that's what Daddy says."

"All right, Maggie, it's nice talking to you, but I must go. Dinner is ready, and I'm hungry. Lucky it's not broccoli, hey. Bye now."

"Oh, we had fun on your bike. I'm going to ask for one like that for Christmas. Bye, Hanna."

Kenny looked meaningfully across the room.

"One off? Sounds like a regular thing to me, Mac."

"Getting that way. Something about kids, Kenny. They give it to you straight. And given my profession, talks with these girls are refreshing."

"Sounds like she's dreaming big already. How old are they?"

"Maggie is six, and Emily is four."

"We were a dynamic duo, hope they are as well."

They sat down to dine. Hanna found half a bottle of white pinot that went well with the fish and green salad.

"Hmmm, just thinking about those kids, their father and his boss."

"You can think all you want. I do like them but have enough projects for now and enough interests. And I'm not his boss, colleague."

"Guess so. Do they learn music?"

Mac laughed a little nervously, knowing where he was going.

"How's the book going?"

"Oh, I get it. Keep out of it Kenny. Bet they've been here and played around with the piano. Sounds like you have hero status." She glared at him.

"I'll stop there, Mac. The book? Yeah, a funny thing. I started with this idea of impotence and anger that goes with seeing people abused and exploited. I thought, who's weaker than terminally sick old guys. I put four of them together, and almost straight away, they began to take over. I get the feeling I'm just the scribe. Been told that would happen, the sign of a good story. I can be going about my business like flying between Tassie and Melbourne, and these characters start messing with my head. For example, began thinking of them as just retired factory workers or school teachers. At the same time, I was reading the instruments on the Cessna dashboard and realised that two of them would be retired pilots like me. And then I thought about the job I had for a while in Texas, and they became Vietnam vets. I really don't know what they're going to do, but I'm not worried, they'll tell me."

"Have you done enough for me to read, or do I have to wait till it's complete?"

"Yeah, it's a bit early, they're still just learning about one another. I think I know one of them is going to come up with something. Not a plan, mind you, but an idea they can debate. In fact, talking with you has got it going. Good therapy, if nothing else."

'Never outstay your welcome.' Dinner had been comfortable, and they both enjoyed the tap-dancing conversation. He rose to leave. Hanna thought, 'he would be the first to know anyway if there was anything to tell.' She'd always be able to tell him. As yet, there was no need and no deed. The eyes said it all in the farewell hug. Each knew the other, and both loved innocent mischief in their exchanges.

It's funny how you can drive a car, and your mind, bored with the simplicity of the activity, goes missing. Sometimes it dozes, and sometimes it gets busy. It behoves one to be respectful of its capacity. For example, you can forget a name of a place or person, and no matter how hard you try, it just won't come. Kenny did a deal with his brain. He'd explain his difficulty and then ask respectfully for help. When the answer popped into consciousness, sometimes after a day or two, Kenny always thanked his brain for helping. Positive reinforcement is always a good idea. So, on his way home that night, he pondered on his characters. Who, he wondered, would come up with an idea? It was only a short trip from the city to Richmond, but as Javelin came to rest in the garage, Kenny had a flash. It'd be Matthew, the banker, the outsider in some ways. The others had recognisable skills. Matthew was a sad penniless gay banker but could think of something to energise the others. Kenny raced upstairs, flipped the computer to life and watched it all come to him like a gift.

7   MATTHEW JAMES: AT HOME READING   EVENING

Matthew is in his comfortable chair, reading. The TV news plays in the background. A report from Chicago of a payroll heist from an armoured van catches his attention.

TV REPORTER:

She stands in front of a Brinks armoured van in the background.

Four men in balaclavas, armed with automatic weapons today, hijacked the van behind me. Nobody was injured in the attack. The take is estimated at $3M. At this stage, police are not disclosing details except they believe it is the same gang responsible for two similar attacks in the past 12 months. That brings the total take from these heists to $18M.

The security company declined to comment.

TV ANCHOR:

Thank you, Helen. Does this mean we can expect more?

REPORTER:

Police don't seem to be making any headway, so I guess this is not the last we will see of these bandits. Back to you, Jim.

MATTHEW JAMES:

He uses the remote to kill the sound, gets up and goes to a filing cabinet, withdraws a file, and places it on the coffee table. The file has the word SECURITY stamped on it. He opens the folder and finds papers and a videotape. He pours a whisky, leans back in his chair, and takes a couple of slow, thoughtful sips. He reaches for the phone and dials.

Come on, Ed, answer your phone.

Ed does not answer, and it clicks over to the answering machine.

Ed, it's Matt. I hate these machines.

Mimicking.

Your call is important to us, press #1 for poor service or #2 for worse. Doesn't matter. Just be a half-hour early to the Hospice on Friday. Bye now.

He makes another call.

José, it's Matt.

JOSÉ MARIA:

Yes, Matt.

Something wrong?

MATTHEW JAMES:

Not at all. Been doing some thinking about the four of us and was wondering if you and John Lee could get to the Hospice a half-hour early on Friday. There's something I want to run past you.

JOSÉ MARIA:

Sure, Matt. I'm intrigued. Look forward to it.

MATTHEW JAMES:

I've left a message for Ed. Would you ask John Lee?

JOSÉ MARIA:

Sure.

MATTHEW JAMES:

Thanks. Bye.

8　　HOSPICE ROOM　　　　　　　　　　　　**FRIDAY MORNING**

Three of the men are sitting around chatting and drinking coffee. Matt is five minutes late. He walks in.

ED ROYSTON:

Always good for an entrance, Matt.

Matt takes a small bow and joins the men.

JOHN LEE:

Well, Mr Mystery Man, what's this all about?

MATTHEW JAMES:

It was to be about the $3.50 I owe Ed that is now $4.60.

ED ROYSTON:

What!

MATTHEW JAMES:

Don't get me wrong ….

He hands the money to Ed.

It's not the money but what John Lee said when I was a little short of cash.

He turns to John Lee.

You said something that stuck.

JOHN LEE:

I did?

MATTHEW JAMES:

Yes, you did. I want you all to watch this videotape.

JOSÉ MARIA:

Mysterious, what's going on?

MATTHEW JAMES:

Please, indulge me. I'll answer all your questions.

JOHN LEE:

Let it roll, Matt.

Matt puts the tape in the machine. The image that comes up is a promotional video from the Wells Fargo company. The tape relates to the introduction in 1985 of the FARGOSAFE armoured security van. A presenter is standing in front of a vehicle. Matt fast forwards to the piece about the vehicle specifications.

WELLS FARGO PRESENTER:

The FARGOSAFE design is unique, the very best in security technology. Some of the outstanding innovations include armour protection 40% better than the President's limousine. Protection from all commercial and plastic explosives and most armour-piercing rounds. Blast resistant, run-flat tyres. Air filtration against gas attack. Door opening only by remote control from a central base. Multiple GPS real-time tracking. Multiple radio links.

The tape then demonstrates those qualities. He stops the tape.

JOHN LEE:

OK, Matt, what's this all about?

MATTHEW JAMES:

Almost there. Point about the vans is there are lots of them on the road and only ever been three attempts to take one.

They failed because of the exceptional design. They're impregnable.

At the bank I was with, there was a process called the 'garbage run'.

ED ROYSTON:

The what?

MATTHEW JAMES:

The garbage run. That's where the banknotes due for destruction are collected in Houston, Fort Worth and Dallas and taken by one of these vans to Baton Rouge to be burned at the Federal Depository. It used to be done in Dallas, but the Feds moved it as a campaign promise to boost investment in Baton Rouge during a congressional election. The vehicle always used is a FARGOSAFE, camouflaged as a hazardous waste vehicle.

He pauses. He can hardly believe he is about to make the next utterance.

Fellas, I'm not a believer in fate. But it's a heck of a coincidence that here we are, about to see our last Christmas, and our lives have each been destroyed by the banks.

ED ROYSTON:

So?

MATTHEW JAMES:

What if there's a way of evening our score with the banks?

JOHN LEE:

Good grief, Matt. I hope you're not going to say …

MATTHEW JAMES:

Yes, John Lee. Why don't we rob the garbage run!

JOHN LEE:

Have drugs done something to scramble your brain?

MATTHEW JAMES:

John Lee, you're a thoughtful man. Hear me out.

ED ROYSTON:

How much is in the van?

JOSÉ MARIA:

Ease off a second, Ed. Let him speak.

JOHN LEE:

OK, Matt. I'll listen for five minutes before I walk away from this nonsense.

MATTHEW JAMES:

The run varies between $70M and $150M in unmarked, used notes. The money is still the banks' before it gets to Baton Rouge.

Over the years, the banks reduced insurance cover on the money, becoming conditioned to the security.

The run carries only 50% insurance.

The run is as regular as clockwork.

It has never been subjected to threat. Some people in the banks know the time and place of its movement. I am one.

The security in the van is so good, with only two unarmed guards.

It has an escort vehicle.

It travels at night along the same route.

All we have to do is take the van and the money.

JOHN LEE:

I grant you that hurting the banks is attractive, but don't you think that if such a stunt was possible, then younger, healthier, more nimble characters would have a go?

I don't believe that I'm sitting here conspiring about one of the great robberies. Even if we did … what happens if we get caught?

MATTHEW JAMES:

Well … I've sort of thought of that.

Let's say we all agree to do it and get busted. Probably the worst that can happen is we get put away for life on a prison farm with three square a day, our own room, TV, computer and internet, games room, library access, a workshop for hobbies, gardening for fresh food, occasional weekend passes, free medical, dental and optical, free clothing … Do you want me to go on? It's actually not that unattractive.

JOSÉ MARIA:

Are you saying that this secure van has an Achilles Heel?

ED ROYSTON:
A what?
JOHN LEE:
A weakness that hardly anyone knows about.
MATTHEW JAMES:
No. I don't think it has.
JOSÉ MARIA:
Then what's the plan? How can we do this? What's the next move?
MATTHEW JAMES:
I've got no idea.
JOHN LEE:
The next move will be on the checkers board. Matt, you nearly had us in.

21

KENNY SAT BACK and stared. He was getting used to watching things happen before his eyes with his fingers flying. "I knew someone was going to come up with an idea, and he has. I'm with the others now. What happens next? Will they even nibble the bait? Haha, this is really something."

It was time to slide the skylight and take a look at the neighbourhood, the cosmic neighbourhood, the biggest of pictures. Lying there, Kenny mused on the paradox that believing he could see during the daytime was an illusion when in fact, he couldn't really see, not right out. The sun's blinding light, what astronomers call 'light pollution', prevented it. At night the sun slept, and a curtain opened on a view of the infinity of time travel, dimensions impossible to grasp. Of course, he'd seen the night sky more clearly than is possible from the laneways of Richmond. Night flights in a super Hornet at 40,000ft were breathtaking. Trouble was there's a fair bit going on interacting with flight systems in that environment. With those thoughts bubbling in his fading consciousness plus the pleasure of having spent time with his sister and scribing, it'd been a fair kind of day. He hardly noticed the ever-present discomfort of damaged vertebrae and aching knees and ankles. That was the best part, and it wasn't often thus. Then he slept.

Every day started the same, it had to. He loved to leave the night behind. It was always such torture, and the rush of cold water did that in spades. Every morning his body would hardly work if he didn't follow a series of stretches for the damaged parts. It was tough going. The back didn't want to bend or roll from side to side, he had to encourage it. The drills helped, but he still needed chemical help to dull the pain. New distractions in his life also helped to direct his attention away from the crumbling body. Just as therapeutic was a 20 minute walk around the neighbourhood.

The beast within, contained for the moment, was driven by the conviction that it would have its way with this man one day not too far away. Persistence always paid off. Darkness was the ultimate reality clawing at the frail until they succumb, run clean out of resistance, gas tank empty. Kenny could fight this certainty for only so long. Right now, his tank was not empty. In fact, he was getting impetus he never thought possible from his sister and from his obsession with a story that had to be told. Inner beasts were challenged.

Kenny walked out of his apartment after the morning ritual struggle with his broken body. Coffee was on his mind, and he knew of a nice little place on Swan St where he could sit outside under a voluptuous wisteria undisturbed for an hour or so. The owner hated customers who could not put their phones aside, so she built a wire cage shrouding the alfresco zone. People found phones didn't work in that area, not understanding that the mesh prevented microwaves from entering or exiting the enclosure. Kenny liked the idea because special customers realised the place was conducive to idle interaction, conversation, and genteel social behaviour. Contrary to expectations, this coffee spot was very popular. Siobhan, the owner of the business, presented Kenny with his preferred straight-up cappuccino with no frills, no soy, and no decaf.

"G'day, Rob, may I sit a minute?"

"Hi Siobhan, sure you can. Thanks for the coffee."

"My pleasure. Our customers adored the brie you found for us. Know I can find it in specialty delis which I've been doing since I finished the one you brought. I just wanted to tell you thanks."

"You know how it is, I was in the right place at the time. I have another surprise for you."

Reaching into his backpack, he pulled out the book he was reading, something called "Picnic on Vesuvius", warning the capitalist world that it was walking on thin ice, a good antidote for preventing an outbreak of optimism. There was also a notebook and the day's easy crossword. Then he grabbed a chiller bag which he presented to his host.

"I know you have an enticing lunch menu, and I thought perhaps you might be able to use something I picked up where I found the brie."

Siobhan bent over his shoulder and peeked inside to find a complete fillet of fresh frozen Tasmanian Atlantic salmon. As she did, he was taken by the bright colours of a small tattoo on her shoulder of a most beautiful butterfly. He said nothing.

"Nice, Robby, thanks. How much is that?"

"Please, Siobhan, maybe a toastie with coffee one morning. I watch what you do here and like the ambience you have created. My way of saying I notice. Tell me, though, where did you get the idea of the wire cage to confuse microwaves?"

That's not all he noticed, but he didn't have to say. She already knew. Most people found her scarred right arm confronting, a memento of a kitchen fire some years earlier. Kenny saw her totality, humanity, professionalism and liked what he saw. The scarred arm was a trophy, not an impediment.

"I can do better than that young man. You and I will have dinner tonight at that lovely Greek place up the road just near Church Street. Nick does the best lamb in town. I'll be here until six, then I'm yours. Deal? Oh, the wire cage? A customer is a professor of physics who got annoyed with loud phone conversations. He told me about the cage. Good one, hey?"

Kenny was surprised, pleased and informed all at once.

"You flatter me. See you at six, and we'll go walking and dining together."

22

SIOBHAN WENT BACK to work glowing. Kenny sipped coffee and made notes about the phone dead zone. He could use that. Needed research, but he had the rest of the day. He felt a session coming on.

9   TWO WEEKS LATER – SCIENCE MUSEUM   EVENING

Opening of an exhibition at the Science Works Museum. John Lee and José Maria walked through the exhibit space on the way to the display to which they had been invited. They pass a large artificial lightning machine inside a cage. Lots of sparks.

JOHN LEE:
Very pretty machine. Power of nature and all that stuff.

JOSÉ MARIA:
You bet. Put your hand on the cage.

JOHN LEE:
I've trusted you with my life before but never with a zillion volts.

JOSÉ MARIA:
Come on, try it.

John Lee tentatively touches the cage while the lightning machine operates. Just as he touches the cage, someone places their hand on his shoulder. He is startled. Turning around, he sees his granddaughter and her boyfriend.

JOHN LEE:
Lesley! Almost a shock to see you.

They embrace. Breaking apart, she reaches out to her boyfriend to come closer.

Grandpa …. This is Ron.

RON BEAUMONT:
Reaching out to shake hands.
How do you do, Sir.

JOHN LEE:

Pleasure to meet you. Les has told me so much. FBI agent, no less.

RON BEAUMONT:

Well, yes, sir. Just a rookie agent at this stage.

LESLEY MASON:

Turning to José.

Ron and this is Grandpa's closest friend and business partner, José.

RON BEAUMONT:

Great pleasure to meet you, sir.

JOSÉ MARIA:

The pleasure is mutual.

Looking at Lesley.

Good looking fella, Les.

She shrugs, feigning embarrassment.

JOHN LEE:

Ron. Honorifics are nice, but please first names for us.

José nods in agreement.

RON BEAUMONT

Thank you, sir. Les has told me lots of stories about you two. Hope my life is half as colourful. Although, I don't have a nickname that I know of. Not like yours, God and Gladys.

Kenny paused. Creating the FBI man and placing him within the family had been a good idea. It was going to create tension. Kenny didn't know how it would play out, he was just putting the players on the board at this stage. It was fiction, he could do what he liked. And the call signs? They would have to be important, but when and how? He had no idea. Meanwhile, he knew exactly what he was doing in the museum, so he continued.

JOHN LEE:

Don't worry, your associates will look after that when they notice something particular about you. Hope it's one you like. Ours have caused some confusion over the years.

JOSÉ MARIA:

Looking at Ron.

Have you touched the cage? Try it. Gosh knows how many million volts are on the other side, but on this side, you're perfectly safe.

The young man reaches out and smiles when he survives.

JOSÉ MARIA:

The wonders of the natural world. What about you, Lesley?

LESLEY MASON:

I'll take your word for it.

Taking Ron's hand.

C'mon Hon. Let's go ahead. Want you to see one of grandpa's helicopters.

The two older lads fall in behind. José smiles. John Lee does not know why.

10   **HELICOPTER-EXHIBITION**

The group walk up to the exhibition featuring a helicopter that 2GEE AIR donated some years earlier after its sponsorship of the first solo, single-engine helicopter flight to the North Pole. The exhibition contains other memorabilia from the flight.

RON BEAUMONT:

Love the chopper, what a flight that must have been.

JOHN LEE:

Brings back memories.

JOSÉ MARIA:

To think we had enough to be able to donate a perfectly serviceable Jet Ranger without counting the cost. They were the good times. Couldn't do it now.

JOHN LEE:

The Hoff was a good pilot. One of our best.

JOSÉ MARIA:

Spoke to him recently. He retired down in Australia doing charters all over the east. Laughed when he told me some guy down there claims he was the first to do the solo flight.

JOHN LEE:

Those Aussies. They tell good stories. Maybe someone should check that one out.

The museum director calls the gathering together to mark the opening of the new exhibit.

MUSEUM DIRECTOR:

Ladies and gentlemen. Tonight, we celebrate two native sons who believed there were still challenges for aviators.

11   HOME/WORKSHOP OF JOSÉ MARIA   THAT EVENING

John Lee and José Maria enter the room, which is largely taken over by José's electronics repair business. There is a small kitchen. John Lee knows the place and sits at the small table. José busies himself making coffee.

JOHN LEE:

Great night?

JOSÉ MARIA:

He nods agreement.

That heloe looks ready enough to fly away. Coffee?

JOHN LEE:

The usual, please.

JOSÉ MARIA:

What about one of my famous Mexican sandwiches?

JOHN LEE:

Just the coffee, thank you. You and your jalapeno chilli.

*José is placing a mug of water in the microwave. He closes the door, and the light in the oven goes on. He pauses, opens and closes it **again**. He does this several times.*

Is this groundhog day? Just boil the water.

JOSÉ MARIA:

Looks up, his face excited.

I think I've got it.

JOHN LEE:

Got what?

JOSÉ MARIA:

How to bust an armoured van.

JOHN LEE:

What! You've actually been thinking about it?

JOSÉ MARIA:

Yes. The banks took everything. We can give them their own medicine. May not make a difference to world history, but it would still be sweet.

JOHN LEE:

OK. I grant you the idea of demon purging is attractive. But so is the idea of the four of us piloting the space shuttle. Highly unlikely.

He pauses before finishing.

Have you lost your moral and legal compass?

JOSÉ MARIA:

Good grief! How long on the rock and you still don't know that moral and legal should never be confused. They come together only by accident.

JOHN LEE:

You lecturing me?

JOSÉ MARIA:

No! But I know you well enough to see the moral ones bother you the most. Hell! Just consider the morality of what we have endured in the last few years. By the banks, by the government's use of agent orange on us, as well as the other victims. How come they duck for cover when called out over all that? And what about the airline that didn't bother with proper maintenance causing the accident that took our families? Should I continue because I could. Same goes for what Matt and Ed have been through. We are legion, my friend. You know I love you, man, but sometimes you can be a bit stiff. This could be a moment when the moral high ground isn't good enough.

We could swap boots and do a little kick-ass ourselves, leaving the moral high ground to those other bastards for a change. I want to do this thing for all those reasons and for GOD and GLADYS to go into battle one more time. But I won't do it without you. You have to take charge.

JOHN LEE:

You make it hard to say no. But it's still wrong to take someone else's money for personal gain.

JOSÉ MARIA:

So, you'll do it if we don't keep the money?

JOHN LEE:

Long reflective pause and then almost with surprise.

Guess I would.

Give the banks some grief, sure. But I'll join you only if we don't keep the money and nobody gets hurt. Of course, this is all academic without a plan to bust one of these impregnable vans.

JOSÉ MARIA:

Give me your cell phone.

JOHN LEE:

Why?

JOSÉ MARIA:

Trust me. Put your phone in the microwave.

He does so cautiously and closes the door.

Take my phone now, dial your number and watch what does not happen.

A long pause.

JOHN LEE:

Nothing happened. It didn't ring.

JOSÉ MARIA:

Precisely. The oven is like the lightning machine cage. Microwaves cannot get in or out. That's the Achilles heel we needed to find.

23

EXHAUSTED, KENNY STOPPED. His mind was still spinning with possible variations. The plays were in motion. A plan was imminent. He could squeeze no more out of the session, so he stopped. Anyway, there was something else on the agenda, and he needed to prepare. No hiding the fact he had significant physical issues, not to mention the mental health ones. Siobhan, at this point anyway, didn't seem to mind. But he needed a clear mind. Before going out for the evening, he paid a visit to his favourite masseuse, working out of a shop front on Bridge Road, a short walk but not an easy one in his condition. Her name was Rosie built strong enough to make a sumo wince. She also could be gentle, as he discovered.

"Afternoon, Rosie, thank you for making room for me."

"OK, Mr Robert, I like to see you any time."

"Only have half an hour, Rosie. Do you think you can make me loose in that time?"

"You take off clothes, me get ready. Make you loose for sure."

Half an hour in her hands was as much as he needed to have a clear head for the evening. There was no need to drive, everything was within walking distance, even Kenny's walking distance. At 5:55pm, he was at the coffee shop door. Siobhan was just turning out the lights, smiling when she saw him there. Not a good idea having to wait in a dark shop front.

"Hello Rob, this will be nice. Glad you could make it."

Siobhan was not desperate for attention. She decided she could do without relationships, had her share of disappointments. Her business provided as much socialising a person could take. But there was something about the presence of this man that stirred her interest. She was deliberately straightforward, and he passed the test. His reason for accepting was the uncomplicated adult way she treated him as a customer, nothing to do with the delicacies he had donated.

Neither of them was complicated by being too young. Mid-forties both of them and plenty of life experience they'd navigated without twisting their essential goodness out of shape. It was that essential goodness they saw in each other over brief exchanges they'd shared since he had been drinking her coffee. Arm in arm, Kenny walking on the gutter side of the footpath carrying a bottle of red in the other hand. He had not needed to ask what wine Siobhan preferred. They were dining Greek, and a fair bet red would be most suitable. He played it safe with his choice, he didn't want to be ostentatious. The five-year-old Pepperjack would certainly complement the cuisine, hard to beat a big Barossa shiraz.

"Siobhan good eveninK. Tonight is special, I can see that. Come for me, you have quiet table. No noise for you, I know you like it."

"Could feel like a sacrificial goat. Do you bring many victims here?"

"You're onto me, and I was being subtle. What gave it away? The leash and studded collar in my handbag? No? Must have been the skeleton bones scattered around my coffee shop. Damn! You got me. I'm the dreaded Slaughtering Siren of Swan Street."

Laughter dissolved any nerves either felt about a first date. They signalled to Nicholas he should just do his thing. A feast was required, and a feast they would have.

"Do not worry, I know what you like. My wife Sula, she make the vine leaves today, yes. You start with the dolmades, very special. And tonight I justa cook him shoulder of lamb, very slow, you know. I cut it for you, you love it, and the yoghurt, my friend, you will die with a smiling on your face."

Smiling was already on every face within earshot.

"Careful of the garlic Rob. Food is great, but they're always generous with garlic, typical Greek touch."

Kenny's ear was close to her whispering, making his crooked spine tingle. Most disconcerting. He'd not enjoyed that feeling since a particularly friendly nurse whispered sweetly to him in hospital. Not even on a good day could Rosie have this effect.

The wine, the food, and the ambience were too much for differences. They were suffocated. The would-be lovers could only see what they wanted to see in each other. Such is the power of first touch. But the advantage of experience and a very recent thorough massage allowed mental clarity for managing enthusiasm for what inevitably would come next. Could it be a totally meaningless romp to be dismissed within 24 hours for being just that? Electricity between them was as powerful as the lightning machine in his story. He had to decide how many parts selfishness and how many parts generosity made up the recipe. For Siobhan's part, the same questions applied. Qualities she had seen so far delighted her. But the question for her would be about the whole story. What kind of darkness dwells there as well? Was this going to be ascension into blazing ecstasy or a train wreck? She didn't know. Just at that moment, Kenny reached across the table with his serviette, and she let him wipe a small dollop of yoghurt off the corner of her mouth. His closeness and attentiveness sealed it for her. She was a goner, prepared to surf the moment and dance the wave all the way to the beach.

Siobhan insisted on Kenny being her guest, and she paid happily. When they shook hands, Kenny slipped a gratuity slyly into their host's generous Lesbian hand. Nick was proud of his heritage and happy to tell anyone about it. Arm in arm on the way back down Swan St to her own shop was more intimate than the earlier walk. Their bodies moved as one touching all the way from shoulder to knee. They hardly spoke. No need, a special few moments. Arriving at her car parked in front of the shop, Kenny stopped and made a half turn to come face to face. Siobhan accepted the invitation, hoped for it anyway and was ready for an embrace and kiss that could easily have lasted till dawn. It was 11o'clock. Coming up for air Kenny took his chance. A motionless shadow stood in the doorway unseen.

"This night, Siobhan Slaughter Siren of Swan St goes down in my history as top three of all time. Whatever the others were, I don't even know, let alone remember. I don't know what to do next because I want to be able to have coffee with you, drop in the odd lobster or cheese for you, and anticipate the hottest love affair of my life with you. You've opened a door in my heart to a room I didn't know about. Forgive me if you expected more out of this night, but I have to tell you I can't make that step yet. Before you ask, I can tell you the only other woman in my life is a sister I worship. I am completely available and oh so willing, as it turns out."

Her gaze was intense, close, her breath warm on his face.

"On one level, my sweet smelling intended victim, I could carve you up at this moment. Everything raging inside me right now is screaming, 'take him, take him now and bugger tomorrow.' This is not over, young man, not by a long shot. Now out of my sight before I throw you on the ground and have my way with you."

They resumed the embrace until the central locking pinged. She had the remote control in her hand. That sound ended round one. Kenny turned and walked towards Bendigo Street, one hand raised, waving. She watched him fade into the night, the last she would see of him or anything.

Next morning full of warm feelings and the gentle aroma of last evening's garlic, Kenny hurried through his routines and made his way along Westbank Terrace past the old television studio where it became Bendigo Street. He had decided that Siobhan was the genuine article: vivacious, independent, alert, flirtatious and generous. He would pursue what had happened. It was worth the gamble. You never know how things are going to turn out. Then he saw from a hundred metres something happening at the coffee shop. It didn't look good. Police vehicles, crime scene tape, media vehicles, and a hovering helicopter.

"Sir, you can't go here, stand back, please."

"Officer, please. Just tell me, is it Siobhan?"

A suit stepped through the barrier, noticing Kenny's approach, hearing his plea.

"Sir, what's your interest here?"

"Detective, Robert Daniels. Siobhan and I are friends. I saw her to her car at about 11 last night after dining just up the road."

"Then you're the last person to see her alive except for whoever killed her. We will need to talk to you further. Would you mind coming with us back to the station to do that?"

"But she unlocked her car as I walked away. There was no time for …no, of course, I don't mind."

"Car? What sort of car was it?"

"White Subaru Liberty with personalised plates, SCOFF."

The detective asked Kenny to go with a uniformed officer while he alerted his crew about so far unknown details.

Kenny knew about crisis and about extreme emotion. He steeled himself against what he was seeing and hearing and against the spectres that leapt into his mind. He knew how critical it was to remain calm even though his heart lay smashed to pieces on the footpath where he'd stood with her for a few blissful moments. He was ushered into an unmarked car, where he waited for the detective to return.

"Robert, I'm Senior Detective Paul Simpson. Thank you for helping us fill out the scenario. You say you dined together. Where was that?"

"Agape on Swan Street."

"And you walked back to the coffee shop where Siobhan left her car?"

"Correct."

"You saw nothing or nobody to arouse any suspicion?"

"Nothing."

"Sorry for this, but I have to ask. You left on good terms with the deceased?"

"The best of terms."

"Are you a regular customer at the coffee shop?"

"Almost daily for about three months."

"In your visits over recent days, was there anything you might have noticed to arouse any response at all from you, strangers, situations?"

"Some customers show disappointment they can't use their phones or WiFi in the outdoor area. She liked to encourage people to socialise there."

"Did she ban the use of phones?"

"In a way, she enclosed the area in a wire mesh, Faraday's cage. Microwaves cannot penetrate."

"Oh. But nothing else?"

"Not at all."

"Thank you, Robert. I'm fairly sure we'll need to speak again. We have your details and will be in touch. We have a car waiting for you."

"Anything to help."

Kenny deliberately didn't ask for gruesome details, those didn't matter in the sense he was powerless to do anything. He was dropped at his front door and hurried immediately upstairs. He closed out the light completely, lying in the dark for the rest of the day and the whole of the night, holding back all those emotions that dogged his life. Why her, why now? What did she do to deserve this? It was his fault for accepting the invitation to dinner. The beast grabbed the moment and tried driving survival instincts out of his reach, sending images of his father, the twins, the priest, his instructor and of Siobhan swirling him dizzy. The longer he lay there, he would be in danger of being swallowed, claimed finally. Kenny agonised until morning when he made his staggering way to the tabernacle of treats. He had to be clear and stay clear. That was a good sign. He thought back to the balcony scene at Mac's apartment. In his mind, he let go of the railing, imagining terminal velocity heading straight for the roof of his car. He snapped out of the reverie, picked up his phone and booked an hour in the Cessna for that morning. Anger, impotence, over and over, a mantra he could not escape spooling the tension in his head. Revenge on the maniac who had crashed into his life, yes. There's an idea. But no, did that the last time. The result didn't make the world right. There was no point hatching a plan to catch and kill the bastard who took one of the beautiful people and senselessly ended her. There is beauty in the world, and there is ugliness. Kenny swore to himself that ugliness would not get him or define him, but that oath was hollow. He headed for Moorabbin airport with one thought in his head. The twenty-minute drive did nothing to cool him. With steely determination, he walked into the hangar where Josh, the engineer who looked after the Cessna, was making sure the aircraft was ready.

"Here, Josh, catch."

Kenny tossed his keys.

"You'll be here for a while. Do you mind shifting the car into shade while I'm gone? Treat it like it's yours."

Josh was trying to work out Kenny's body language. Had he known what happened in Richmond, he might not have allowed Kenny to fly.

"Sure, Bobby, but there's no sunshine today."

"Yeah, you're right about that."

Josh did what Kenny asked and walked back to the hangar, standing in the doorway, watching the plane turn onto the runway. He paused, car keys twirling in his fingers. He thought there might have been something wrong because the aircraft just sat there motor idling. He glanced up and could see another far out to the north had turned on to final approach. Something had better happen sharply, or it could get ugly. Just then, Kenny gunned the engine, and the plane bolted down the runway and shot into the sky. Josh breathed a sigh of relief. He still couldn't figure out what was wrong with Kenny, but something strange was going on that was for sure. He pocketed the keys. Sitting at the start of the runway, Kenny thought calmly about which route suited him best. A look over his shoulder helped him decide. He thrust the throttle forward.

At 500 ft above Bass Strait, heading into a strong southerly, progress was slow for the empty cargo plane. He reckoned he was about 80 kilometres out when he saw something that changed the course of his life. An overturned yacht floundered in heavy seas, two adults in high-viz life jackets clung to the keel. He switched into automatic, spotted the radio call sign for the Maritime Safety Authority and made the call. He advised he would continue circling the stricken craft until their Challenger jet could take over rescue procedures, calling in helicopters and gathering all relevant data on conditions that the rescue crews would need. A flare gun was attached to the cockpit, and Kenny readied it for use. He figured the jet would be airborne within 15 minutes, and its flight time to his position from the Essendon base would be about 15 minutes. In the meantime, he circled the yacht at about 500 feet so the survivors would know they had been located. That should give them the strength to hold on. When the jet came screaming into view, Kenny slid open the side window and fired a flare in the direction of the yacht. He knew the crew was onto the situation when their plane started circling the yacht at about 1500 ft. It was safe for him to leave the scene. The thought driving him all morning was gone. His purpose evaporated. Fate stepped in, people in distress and a need for action. The beast in his head fell silent, foiled at the death knock. The red mist that clouded his mind cleared. He was rational, knowing he could do nothing for Siobhan. Killing himself out of grief would not be good for the guy who owned the Cessna Cargomaster, so he banked the aircraft in a tight turn, nose headed back to Moorabbin. It would be a quick trip on the stiff southerly now behind him. When Josh saw his plane in the circuit a short time later, he felt guilty for having misjudged Kenny's intentions. Chatter on radios around the hangars informed the involvement of Victor Hugo Bravo, his plane, in the rescue of two sailors in Bass Strait. He was keen to talk to the hero of the moment and was right there when Kenny climbed out of the cockpit. Josh chuckled with surprise when the only thing Kenny said was:

"Thanks for looking after the car Josh. Keys please."

Sliding behind the wheel of the javelin was a sweet pleasure. Home safe demons foiled. Josh did as asked, parked his ride in the shade, and Kenny nodded gratitude in response to the waving engineer. Every sensation felt new. Even heading up Warrigal Road in heavy traffic couldn't shake the nascent optimism. He wondered if this feeling was anything like winning a big lottery. Chance was all around like seemingly trivial decisions were rolls of a cosmic dice bringing consequences impossible to predict. When he stopped at traffic lights and saw an ailing elderly woman on a walker, his mind turned to his characters. He felt a stirring of inspired magma swirling beneath the surface.

Two days later, police came knocking. Paul Simpson sought clarification on a few issues. Kenny dusted a couple of chairs in the workshop where he'd been idling with busy hands.

"Robert, thank you for your help the other morning. We're still chasing the whereabouts of the car. Your information was correct. The post mortem shows your DNA on the victim's face and hands. Was Siobhan your girlfriend?"

"Detective, it was our first night out together. We held hands, and we kissed. I wish I had followed my instincts to bring her here for the rest of the night. At the very least, it would have saved her life."

Internally he'd been cursing himself for the visit to Rosie on that afternoon. Siobhan would still be alive. He was a complete idiot. There was no need to tell the detective.

"Do you think she would've wanted to come with you?"

"I was the one not ready to take that step, a tragic mistake. You have to ask, but I assure you my grief is as intense as any I have ever felt."

"I've done some checking, Kenny. You have killed before."

"As you should. Don't know what you've read or been told, so ask what you need. I will tell you the truth."

"The government took you from jail and sent you to RAAF flight training?"

"They did."

"And that was after you killed a priest."

"Are the facts you have as bare as that, Detective?"

"Did you kill Siobhan O'Rourke?"

"My thoughts about her were extreme. Extreme affection. No, I did not."

"You had means and opportunity but no discernible motive. You know, for what it's worth, every action we take, every decision we make changes history from that moment onwards. Not all have such tragic consequences, but some do. Those are the bare facts, Robert. That's all for now."

"Thank you for that one. Tell me, have funeral arrangements been made?"

"The only family is a twenty-year-old daughter from Sydney. She identified the body as her mother's and collected it from our facility today. I am told there's a private cremation planned in Sydney, where Siobhan came from originally. The daughter is particularly grieved because she didn't get a chance to reconcile with her mother."

Kenny showed the detective to the door.

"You will get the bastard, won't you?"

"Without going into details, yes, we will."

"But the world will continue its path to oblivion, won't it?"

"That's a safe bet, my friend. But we have to stand for something worthwhile, don't you think?"

"Yes, Paul, here's to the best of us."

"That's a toast I would join."

"If the daughter needs to or wants to have a conversation with me, I don't mind if you give her my details."

"Yes, I'll tell her. Oh, by the way, I hear a couple of sailors are pretty happy to have seen you in the sky above them a couple of days ago? Every action we take and consequences, hey Bobby?"

Kenny mused over the detective's words, 'decisions, consequences.' The very subject that occupied his mind for the last few days. But he didn't linger, the consequences of doing so could be sad. You can't see consequences coming every time. Sometimes they'll inspire, and other times crush. It's that damn cosmic dice game again. He had a flash at that moment, ignoring the compliment and headed directly to the computer where he might explore the theme of reconciliation. He was thinking of John Lee's granddaughter and her estranged father.

24

12   LIQUOR STORE   **LATE AFTERNOON**

Ed Royston is on the way home from a trip to Fort Worth. The owner of the store knows him well and what he likes. He is leaning on the counter, reading a newspaper when Ed enters.

LIQUOR STORE OWNER:

Hi Ed. Good trip? Refresh any good cars?

ED ROYSTON:

Refresh, yes. Good, no. Just a regular run to Fort Worth. Am fagged out.

LIQUOR STORE OWNER:

Doesn't get easier as we get older, hey? The usual?

ED ROYSTON:

My insides are playing up with the treatment. Think I should have something really smooth. They tell me not to drink. What the hell. Can I be in more trouble than I'm in? How about some of that Irish cream concoction?

The liquor store owner smiles broadly. He bags a bottle and gets a lottery ticket from a drawer.

LIQUOR STORE OWNER:

Twelve-year-old Jack and your 20-week lottery ticket. That's $54.20. By the way, Ed, have you ever won anything? You've bought hundreds from me over the years. I often wondered. You were the biggest in your industry, money no option, and you bought lottery tickets. Why, Ed?

ED ROYSTON:

It was hard work making money after costs, you know. Guess it was the thought of clearing money without all the effort. I'd probably waste it, but the feeling would be nice, I think. Maybe it's just a habit I can't kick. Bye Ralph.

Several people enter the shop and are browsing.

LIQUOR STORE OWNER:
G'night Ed.
CUSTOMER #1:
To shopkeeper.
Isn't that the guy from TV, the one who sells all those cars?
LIQUOR STORE OWNER:
Yep. One of the biggest. He's had a few problems.
CUSTOMER #1:
God Dammit!

13   HOSPITAL DAY ROOM   **MORNING**
Regular checkers game two weeks later. Ed and Matt are playing.
MATTHEW JAMES:
Your move.
Pause as Ed seems distant.
Your move, Ed!
ED ROYSTON:
Thinking about that armoured van of yours. How much is in it?
MATTHEW JAMES:
Between $70 and $150 million.
ED ROYSTON:
That's a lot of garbage! What a man could do with loot like that. Women, booze boats.
MATTHEW JAMES:
And probably waste the rest. Ha Ha.
ED ROYSTON:
You're certain it's impregnable?
MATTHEW JAMES:
I am, but I'd love to try.
ED ROYSTON:
Me too. What about you, John Lee, José? Wouldn't you like to give it a go? As Matt said, there's no downside if we blow it.
JOHN LEE:
Moving towards the group.
Enough of idle chatter. If you're serious, there might be a way. José believes there is, and I agree. But a job like this needs precision, planning and no clues left behind. Are you prepared to face the consequences of failure? Are you prepared to take orders and follow them to the letter?

MATTHEW JAMES:

You serious?

A pause, then realisation.

You are!

JOHN LEE:

I am.

A pause.

How serious are you and Ed?

A long pause. Moment of truth.

ED ROYSTON:

I'm in.

MATTHEW JAMES:

So am I.

JOHN LEE:

OK! José and I have decided there is a way, and we are prepared to do it on two conditions.

ED ROYSTON:

Yeah …. What are they?

JOHN LEE:

There will be no violence, and we will not keep the money.

Ed and Matt are speechless.

We do this job because we can, and the banks get a wake-up call. If you don't agree, then forget it or do it on your own.

MATTHEW JAMES:

No money? Are you crazy? We could live our last days in luxury. If you are going to burn the money, you might as well let the banks do it.

ED ROYSTON:

You bet. What do we have afterwards if there is no money?

JOSÉ MARIA:

Self-respect and the pleasure of having done it. Tell the world that some things matter more than money.

ED ROYSTON:

C'mon! You're not serious!

JOHN LEE:

Deadly. Take it or leave it.

Long pause.

MATTHEW JAMES:

Ed, it could be a lot of fun.

ED ROYSTON:

I guess. But ....

MATTHEW JAMES:

Ed, say yes. What have you got to lose?

ED ROYSTON:

Reluctantly.

Alright!

MATTHEW JAMES:

I'm in.

JOHN LEE:

Good! From now on, no one is to say anything outside of the group.

ED ROYSTON:

Wait up. Who elected you the leader?

José glares at Ed.

I nominate John Lee as leader. Any dissent?

Silence.

JOHN LEE:

I've formulated an initial plan. No more discussion in this place. We meet at my place tomorrow night, and I will explain everything.

14 JOHN LEE'S LIVING ROOM   **EVENING**

John Lee and José Maria are present. The doorbell rings.

JOHN LEE:

Ed, Matt, come in. Make yourselves at home. Coffee?

Matthew and Ed help themselves.

JOHN LEE:

Let's get to it. The plan is basically simple. From what Matt tells me, the best place to take the van is about 50 miles east of Dallas on the I-20. There's a curve where we would separate any escort vehicle from the money.

Ed will pose as a highway patrol officer in a cruiser. José has figured out a way to isolate all the GPS and communications of the van from its base. Once the van is separated from its escort, José will ram the van from behind into the trailer of a prime mover. Once the van is isolated, we all meet at a safe location where we access the van and take the money.

Any questions?

ED ROYSTON:

Where are we going to get the vehicles we need?

JOHN LEE:

That's where your experience comes in.

MATTHEW JAMES:

What about me?

JOHN LEE:

You get as much current detail as you can on the garbage run so we can pick the date. You also help Ed with the cars.

José and I will get the parts he needs to fit out the trailer to kill the electronics. We will also get essentials for accessing the van.

I will find a safe place to store our gear, scout the actual heist location and get a place for us to take the van to and get into it.

Details of all our needs are on these sheets.

A sequence of visuals shows the preparations the men make.

Ed stealing cars and trucks. John Lee organising an old factory in Houston and casing an abandoned mine site where they will take the armoured van.

José Maria at auction paying cash for rolls of screening wire to make the cage inside the truck trailer.

Ed trying to teach Matt to drive a truck.

José Maria testing radios.

The men constructing a Faraday cage and restraint mechanism to lock the hijacked van in position inside the trailer.

Matt talking to old friends to confirm garbage run details.

Loading the truck with compact people movers and cruiser.

15   DERELICT HOUSTON FACTORY   EVENING

The four men are in the factory where all preparations have been made

JOHN LEE:

Gentlemen. Within our limitations, we've done well.

Based on Matt's information, we'll take the run in four days' time.

Make sure you only bring clothes that we can destroy. Remember, set timers at home to operate lights and TVs so that evenings appear normal. Get some rest and meet here at 6pm on Saturday when we roll north.

16   HOLIDAY INN   HOUSTON   MORNING

Graham Mason, Lesley's estranged father, is on the phone.

GRAHAM MASON:

Look, Hal, I told you I'd be back in Chicago by the end of next week. I'm in Houston to see my daughter. Well …. Yes, I do have a daughter. I haven't seen her for a long time. OK! Yes, I know we have a contract, remember, I retire after the next one, and I'm serious. I'll see you then.

He drinks his coffee and flicks through the telephone directory to find the phone number and address for Lesley Mason. He circles the entry.

17   LESLEY MASON'S APARTMENT   LATE SAME MORNING

She is alone, marking student papers. She gets up to answer a knock at the door.

LESLEY MASON:

Yes ……..

She recoils in shock when she recognises the visitor as her father.

GRAHAM MASON:

Hello, Les. I …. Er, I don't really know what to say, but …..

LESLEY MASON:

The shock subsides, anger kicks in.

HOW DARE YOU!

She slams the door and leans against it, tears welling up. She remains thus while he knocks several more times.

GRAHAM MASON:

Les. I know you can hear me. I am at the Holiday Inn room 345 for the next few days. Please, please ring me.

He starts to walk away. She hesitatingly opens the door and sees the figure of her father down the corridor.

LESLEY MASON:

YOU LEFT ME!

YOU RAN AWAY!

WHAT DID I DO TO DESERVE THAT?

WHAT ARE YOU DOING HERE?

He stops and turns. He's uncertain what he should do. He moves towards the screaming woman. She is wild with anger and confusion.

GRAHAM MASON:

I …. I … You're right. Don't know what I thought would happen. I'd forgotten that you're a grown woman. You were still a little girl in my memory. I…. But I'm still your father.

LESLEY MASON:

Don't pull that one on me. You gave up birth rights long ago. John Lee is my father. He raised me. You never even sent a Christmas card.

GRAHAM MASON:

I'm sorry.

LESLEY MASON:

SORRY!!!

GREAT!!!

You want absolution? See a priest. Don't arrive here as some ghost from the past and expect YOUR LITTLE GIRL to fawn and carry on as though nothing has happened. MY MOTHER KILLED HERSELF PARTLY BECAUSE OF YOU! WHERE WERE YOU WHEN I NEEDED YOU? ALL YOU COULD DO WAS THINK OF YOURSELF! GO AWAY. I WON'T SEE YOU.

GRAHAM MASON:

Les …

LESLEY MASON:

Sobbing

LEAVE ME ALONE! LEAVE ME ALONE!

She retreats, slams the door and bursts into uncontrollable tears. He leaves in a stunned and bewildered condition. She stumbles to the phone and rings John Lee.

Grandpa ….. Grandpa……

JOHN LEE:

Les. Les, what is it? What's happened?

LESLEY MASON:

He's back. My father's back.

JOHN LEE:

What? Slow down, girl. Take a deep breath and tell me.

LESLEY MASON:

He was here. Just now, here. He's at the Holiday Inn. I told him to get out and leave me alone. What am I going to do? Can I come and see you?

JOHN LEE:

Sit tight, I'm on my way.

18   HOLIDAY INN   **LATE EVENING**

Graham Mason is packing his bags. He is expecting the porter. There is a light knock on the door.

GRAHAM MASON:

Just a minute.

He opens the door and is confronted by John Lee, standing there. Pause.

JOHN LEE:

Well, son. Inviting me in?

GRAHAM MASON:

Come in, John Lee. Can I offer you a drink?

JOHN LEE:

This isn't social. Anyway, I'm under doctor's orders. No drinking unless it's a celebration. Is this a celebration?

GRAHAM MASON:

I guess not. What can I do for you?

JOHN LEE:

Well, son, you've left a little girl in a very distressed state today. I hope it wasn't intentional, but it sure has opened a wound that we thought had healed. Les has a good life, a job she loves and a boy who loves her.

GRAHAM MASON:

John Lee …

JOHN LEE:

Do me the courtesy of shutting up. You and I go back some distance. We both know that you were an S.O.B. well before you left. There were times that I would have happily squeezed the last breath out of you. Coming over here tonight, there was a part of me that wanted to do that still. But not anymore.

GRAHAM MASON:

John Lee …

JOHN LEE:

Just listen. This won't take long. I'm indifferent to you. I'm much older and not long to go on this rock.

GRAHAM MASON:

I had no idea.

JOHN LEE:

You do anything more than you did to Les today, and I'll be forced to reconsider my lack of feeling for you.

GRAHAM MASON:

You warning me off?

JOHN LEE:

No. I'm just stating facts. I see you've already made your decision and probably a good one. Before you go, though, I'd like the answer to one question.

GRAHAM MASON:

Only one?

JOHN LEE:

But the truth.

GRAHAM MASON:

The real truth?

JOHN LEE:

Yes. I can only handle the truth.

GRAHAM MASON:

I doubt it. Tall in the saddle like the Duke. Gonna teach the town bad boy a lesson with his 'indifference', good manners and only one question.

I'll answer your damn question, and I don't care if you believe me or not. Remember, you asked for it. I didn't ask for this. But let's be straight. Les is the catalyst for being here. Your daughter, my wife, is the reason. OK. I've done bad things. Regrets, plenty. But I loved your daughter, and I still do.

JOHN LEE:

You what?

GRAHAM MASON:

You listen. I loved your daughter more than you can know. Trouble was I got into serious difficulty trying to maintain the lifestyle she was used to and deserved. But I couldn't compete with you. When I came to you for help with my business, you passed me to your underlings. They told me they had all the sympathy in the world. You treated me like a bank manager. They relayed your message that help was not available. You didn't have the decency to tell me to my face. I turned to gambling, selling small amounts of drugs.

Don't get me wrong. I learned to enjoy the thrills of that lifestyle. I got caught and was dealt with. Your daughter stuck with me. But getting my life and business back needed money. I couldn't ask you again, so I got it where I could. I couldn't even tell my wife about the threats that came. They were in real danger. And she was dealing with the death of her mother. Maybe I was wrong. Maybe it was the coward's way out. I ran. They chased me then, not my family. When I heard she had died, I was ripped apart. But, selfishly, I figured Les was better off with you. I regret that decision. I ended up being dragged into the criminal underworld of Chicago. I'm no saint, and I'm not looking for forgiveness. That would be too much to ask. I've made my final peace with those people. I'm free, and I'm coming back to live in Houston. I'm going back to Chicago now to get rid of my apartment, then I'm coming back. I just hope that, in time, Les can learn to accept my presence. That's as much as I can hope for. I can't make up for the hurt.

JOHN LEE:

Slumped in a chair

I ... I ... am sorry. I had no idea.

GRAHAM MASON:

No, you didn't. None of us can change the past, but maybe the future can be different. That's all I want.

JOHN LEE:

This is the second time in six weeks that I've been told I spend too much time on the moral high horse. Maybe I should take up walking more often.

He gets up and looks out the balcony at the moon. He turns to look at Mason.

I will have that drink. I need it.

Graham Mason pours a drink and hands it to John Lee. They look at each other without the anger and hostility of the years.

Drink? There's a good idea, Kenny thought, flipping the computer closed. He headed for the cookie jar and brewed a coffee, wondering whether or not to bring Hanna into the picture. While he waited the usual 45 minutes it took for the magic to work, he kept his mind busy studying the maps that informed him about Texas. Then he slept. And he dreamed the dreams of the inspired. Some would say chemically-induced and fair enough. Doesn't matter. She came to him in a place of light and vague shapes, holding his head in her hands, and her searching eyes probed his. It was comfortable. Then pictures changed.

He saw his four characters and bit players. Money fell from the sky, and they were running around trying to catch it. A police car came out of nowhere, lights flashing, heading straight for him. He was frozen to the spot, and as it ploughed into him, he woke startled, disoriented. Time to capture and shape. It would be a marathon session. The story was carrying him along. He followed but paused for a moment realising there was no nightmare. This was encouraging.

19   I-20   50 MILES EAST OF DALLAS   VERY LATE EVENING

A moonlit night at the truck parking bay of the side of Interstate 20. The convoy is the prime mover and trailer and a heavy vehicle towing truck. The ramp on the trailer is being lowered. Ed is dressed as a highway patrol officer. He backs the cruiser out and joins the others.

JOHN LEE:
Ed, are you OK?
ED ROYSTON:
Well, I have never stolen as many vehicles before. Think I'm OK.
JOSÉ MARIA:
None of us have Ed.
JOHN LEE:
Remember Ed. Give us the coded call when the armoured van and escort go past. Otherwise, complete radio silence. We don't want loose ends. Monitor the police frequency, and if there's any unusual activity from that side, we abort. No questions asked. You're our eyes and ears. Good luck, and see you at the rendezvous.

The four men join hands in a handshake. Ed climbs into the car and slowly drives back towards Dallas.

JOSÉ MARIA:
This is it! Roosters or feather dusters, that's us after tonight. Remember, Matt, as soon as I say 'GO', hit the release. Now we wait for Ed's call.

20   HWY I-20 JUST BEFORE EXIT 12   LATE EVENING

Ed picked a dark corner of the carpark outside Ida's Truck Stop Café.
ED ROYSTON:
He keeps repeating instructions. Is increasingly nervous.
Give the call. Pull over escort vehicle and delay them five minutes.

Ed, you can bloody do it. Yes, I can.

Checks his watch. 11:40, the armoured van passes, followed by a black Suburban. He has two microphones, one police and one their own.

He picks up the one to advise John Lee of the targets.

Targets at 11:40 at 12 and 55 and 600

Starts the car and pulls into a safe following position behind the Chev Suburban.

Good. Escort vehicle. It's a big haul.

21   HIGHWAY AT TRUCK PARKING BAY

Ed makes his call. A man and woman in a sedan pass the parking bay where José and John Lee are parked.

FEMALE PASSENGER: **SAME TIME**

Looking at the two heavy vehicles parked in the gloom.

Darling. Long haul drivers are getting better since the law changed.

MALE DRIVER:

Sure, Hon. Used be they'd do drugs to stay awake. Now they must stop.

FEMALE PASSENGER:

Those poor guys there. Can't be too comfortable for them.

MALE DRIVER:

Nup. They sleep like babies. Not a care in the world.

22   TRUCK PARKING BAY   **SAME TIME**

John Lee and José Maria monitor the call from Ed, no response.

JOHN LEE:

Out loud to himself.

OK, The van's at exit 12, speed 55mph, and the escort is 600ft behind.

He picks up the radio to call Ed.

Take 2 at 14.

JOSÉ MARIA:

Good! Get 'em, Ed, at exit 14. We'll do the rest.

Both vehicles start up and pull out onto the highway.

ED ROYSTON:

He is increasingly nervous. Perspires.

Exit 14. Go for it!

23   NEAR EXIT 14   A SHORT TIME LATER

Ed is trailing the Suburban and speeds up to overtake. He flashes his lights and gives the siren a 'whoop' to signal the driver. It does not slow or pull over. He repeats the siren. The driver accelerates and pulls away.

ED ROYSTON:

What the heck! STOP!!!

He panics and grabs the wrong radio.

GOD! WHAT DO I DO ....

He realises his mistake and picks up the right one.

What do I do? He's speeding away from me. Almost level with the target. No, he's passing the target.

24   INSIDE ARMOURED VAN   SAME TIME

Driver and his assistant enjoying the night trip, watch the chase.

DRIVER:

Looking in the rear vision mirror.

Check this out Fred. Cops are trying to nail someone.

Suburban draws level and passes armoured van.

SECOND MAN:

GM should be proud of their product. Good speed, good handling.

Both men start laughing.

DRIVER:

Yeh! Go, Suburban.

25   FURTHER UP THE HIGHWAY   SAME TIME

JOHN LEE:

Rapidly assessing the situation.

Has the target changed speed?

ED ROYSTON:

NO! No difference.

JOSÉ MARIA:

Breaking into the conversation.

You've rumbled a stolen car in the wrong place and time.

JOHN LEE:

Chase it at speed until you are 10 miles clear. Then rendezvous.

ED ROYSTON:

OK. Out.

He settles back to enjoy the high-speed chase with full lights and siren. The two vehicles shoot past John Lee and José Maria and head into the distance.

26   HIGHWAY PATROL DISPATCH   **SAME TIME**

Dispatcher at his station, monitoring the fleet of police cruisers. He hears the truncated call from Ed. He doesn't recognise the voice or the message.

DISPATCHER:
Please say again? Please say again?
Silence.
Please identify and repeat message.

DUTY SUPERVISOR:
Entering the radio room after hearing calls over his monitor.
What is it, Frank?

DISPATCHER:
Don't know. Someone taking the lord's name. That's all.

DUTY SUPERVISOR:
Try again. May be one of ours is in trouble. Do a roll call.

DISPATCHER:
All cars. Please confirm location and status.
Dutifully, all cars make their calls. All accounted for.
All cars accounted for, sir.

DUTY SUPERVISOR:
Forget it. Must be a hoax. Damn kids. Too many hi-tech gadgets.

DISPATCHER:
Should I log it in the X file?

DUTY SUPERVISOR:
Log it as a number.

DISPATCHER:
Seven?

DUTY DISPATCHER:
At the seventh hoax radio call this month.

27   **EXIT 14 HWY I-20**

John Lee and José Maria are on the highway, a mile between them. José Maria is going at 45mph as he watches the armoured van pass him.

JOSÉ MARIA:

On the radio.

Passing me.

JOHN LEE:

Checking his speed at exactly 50mph speaks to himself.

Just a few more minutes.

JOSÉ MARIA:

Waits till the van passes behind a curve. He lowers night vision goggles and kills the lights on the truck. He flicks the switch to break the circuit on his brake lights. He speeds up to close the distance between the target and himself. He settles into a close following position behind the target. He picks up the radio.

In position. I can see you both. Get ready.

JOHN LEE:

He reaches down and flicks the switch to disconnect his brake lights. He picks up the radio.

Ready. Matt, are you ready?

MATTHEW JAMES:

Ready.

Speaking to himself as he pulls his balaclava down.

Damn material. It makes my skin itch.

As the armoured van closes on the truck in front and before the driver eases out to pass, José Maria gives the call.

JOSÉ MARIA:

He accelerates as hard as the truck will go.

GO! GO! GO!

The next moments are a cacophony of noise and light. John Lee hits the brakes as Matt, in the back of the trailer, drops the ramp to the road. A shower of sparks erupts, engulfing the van. The van driver takes a split second to react to the events in front of him. He has no knowledge that the lead vehicle is under brakes. He is also unaware of the speeding truck coming up behind him. His only thought is to apply his own brakes to avoid whatever is going on in front of him. José Maria had counted on this and reduces the momentum of the vehicle as he slams into it. The force of the collision propels the armoured van under brakes directly into the bowels of the trailer. As John Lee feels the trembling of the armoured van going into the trailer, he speeds up.

MATTHEW JAMES:
Standing in shock and nailed against the side of the trailer as the van sweeps past, only inches from his face.
BABY IN BED!!! BABY IN BED!!!
JOSÉ MARIA:
CLOSE IT! WE'RE OUT OF HERE!
MATTHEW JAMES:
He hits the switch that closes the ramp in ultra-quick time.

Kenny shivered with satisfaction. The old crocks had become professional. Now what? It was well past midnight. His players could wait until tomorrow to let him know how they meant to secure the money and escape. The pros were on a roll, and the last thing they needed was for Kenny to pull the pin. In spite of their objections, Kenny needed sleep, and after that, he wanted to see his sister. They'd have to wait. They were caught suspended on the page at his mercy for the moment. Flipping the computer closed, he headed to the bathroom to wash his eyes. Screen fatigued, they needed refreshment before Kenny retired. Because his mind was still in overdrive, he didn't even think about sleeping pills, cookies or anything. His doona was calling, and he had no resistance. His dreams morphed into something different. This night he stood on a clifftop in the dark, a thunderous black ocean in front of him. He could see a light shining on three figures in the sky above the ocean. They were the twins with Siobhan between them. He watched them hover for a moment, then soar through the clouds and out of sight. Everything went black.

25

HANNA'S PHONE WENT to message bank. Kenny advised he'd be at Dolly's restaurant in Mordialloc making a delivery of Tasmanian oysters and would love to buy lunch for her if she could make it. And sorry for the hour. He figured the wholesaler was paying for the trip and that spare freight space might as well be put to good use. Josh, his engineer acquaintance at Moorabbin airport, suggested Kenny talk to his sister Sarah chef at Dolly's, about fresh seafood. He did so, and after the success of the first delivery, she became a regular.

Kenny paused over the Yarra on Bridge Road, his morning walk. The phone roused him from his thoughts. Dark thoughts were rising up from the black water surface, urging him to look more closely. Kenny anticipated an approach like this from the resident demons ever since the flight over Bass Strait. He was ready and resisted a whispered urge to drop into the black water.

"Morning Mac, you caught me just looking at the Yarra. Got my message."

"It woke me. Thought you'd be up early, but this is crazy, no?"

"Moorabbin by 5:30, King Island by 8:00, back at Moorabbin by 11:00 and Mordialloc by 12:00. How are you fixed for lunch? My thought is Dolly's."

"Breakfast bullshit meeting with architects in Hardware Lane at 7:00, staff meeting at the office at 9:00, Developers in Collins St 10:30, Dolly's by 12:00, how's that for you?"

"Better than a swim below this bridge. Your offer sounds more interesting. See you there. And thanks, Mac."

Another fine day for flying. A bit on the cool side till the cabin warmed but once through the early morning mist at about 50 metres, the sky opened. He was alert over water, one never knows what might happen, what one might see. Also, his flying time thoughts were happy because his fictional friends flew with him while they were busy with the biggest challenge of their lives. They were all in it together.

On the return trip, he had arranged for the chef from the Terminus hotel in Bairnsdale, young Beau, to be at the airport to pick up the week's seafood order. It added about 40 minutes to the trip, but he had allowed for that. Flying back over Yallourn, he couldn't miss gazing at the enormous open-cut coal mine that was soon to be mothballed. He knew immediately how his bandits were going to finish the job on the armoured van and dump all the vehicles. They'd be pleased with him, he thought. It was like they saw what he saw and told him how they'd use that resource.

Dolly's restaurant stands on the foreshore at Mordialloc. The cuisine is similar to up-market pub food, and seafood is its specialty. Kenny was partly responsible for that with his weekly deliveries from Tasmania, which they picked up at Moorabbin in a refrigerated mini-van. Kenny booked a table on the decking overlooking the Mordialloc beach. Wind can be an issue, but on a calm day, it's comfortable and picturesque. He and Mac arrived almost at the same time, bumping into each other in the carpark.

"A spring in your step, sis, good to see you."

"Like to say the same about you, Kenny, but the best I can do is compliment the suave shuffle. I'm loving these moments, so don't give me grief about it."

They were shown to their table. He poured glasses of chilled water for each of them.

"I recommend the oysters, came in this morning."

"Haha. And for mains, let's have the marinara."

"I've noticed they don't skimp on the prawns, calamari, mussels and whiting pieces. Good choice."

While waiters did their thing, Kenny told Mac about meeting Siobhan in the coffee shop and how they spoke daily for three months, slowly becoming comfortable with each other. Then with some difficulty, he finished the story. His profound sigh told her everything.

"It happens too often, Mac...."

She cut him short.

"Stop right there, brother. None of it was your fault. Get that flaming guilt thing out of your system. Morbid self-pity is not working for you. Your father loved you. The evil priest deserved to die. You didn't kill your classmates. The dodgy jets were before your time. The Hornet thing would have been worse if it wasn't for you. Sounds like Siobhan had rare pleasure in the short time she knew you. Depression is ugly, Kenny. Couldn't be prouder of the way you've managed it so far. OK, it sticks to you, hijacks you, wears you down, and I understand it can overwhelm. Don't let it take you. I want you to stay with me. I love you. Wow! Sorry if that's too much. Life for us is a bit like a butterfly's. So fragile and beautiful a thing fluttering for minutes in a rainforest heaving with dangers that in a second can just sweep it away. You, Kenny, are my personal butterfly, a fragile thing of rare beauty."

"How's the marinara?"

"I know, shut up, Mac. Now you listen to me. I haven't said anything to you yet, but something's happened since that thing over Bass Strait."

"Oh yeah, forgot to mention that. Really, are things that bad for you I need to worry? I mean, you saved two people from a horrible death."

"If you'll be quiet for a moment, I'll tell you. Siobhan was the last straw for me, and you've picked up on that. But you're right, Bass Strait shook me in a good way. Sis, I am going to be around for a good while."

Hanna listened but was not convinced. The Black Dog doesn't give up that easily, and Kenny sounded to her like an addict who claims a total cure after going a couple of days without a hit and needs to convince someone. They grinned. An hour with Hanna was a tonic for Kenny, but she needed him to know how much she wanted him near. The last thing Kenny needed was for her to be burdened.

"How are the girls?"

"Now you're talking. Don't see them much, but they have my number and use it. Mark's amazingly calm given all the claims on him. They're just kids, energetic, curious, demanding, and affectionate. They're all doing well. I know what you're asking and can't tell you any more than the last time. I am comfortable being able to drop in from time to time. Full time? That's Mark's job."

"Hmmm. OK. Let's wait and see."

Hanna had to go back to work. Kenny forced the beast back in its cave, pushed a boulder across the entrance and headed home for another big session with his ailing bandits.

26

HANNA'S PEP TALK stopped Kenny in his tracks. Maybe he was getting ahead of the game. Would have to be on guard just in case. Right now, though, he had an armed robbery to deal with.

28   ARMOURED VAN   **SAME TIME**

The two security men were in shock. The vehicle could not move, no matter how much the driver tried, they were in almost complete darkness.

DRIVER:

WE'VE BEEN HEISTED!!! CALL BASE!!! CALL BASE!! HIT THE EMERGENCY BUTTON!!!

SECOND MAN:

Hitting the GPS emergency button.

TRUCK 34 TO BASE!!! TRUCK 34 TO BASE!!! TRUCK 34 TO BASE!! Only static.

DRIVER:

USE THE CELL PHONE!! I'LL USE MINE!!

SECOND MAN:

NO SIGNAL!! WHAT'S GOING ON??

DRIVER:

I DON'T KNOW!! NO SIGNAL!!

Gradually, the men become a little calmer

DRIVER:

At least we've got the GPS alert. No one can fool that.

SECOND MAN:

They can't get in here either. Can they?

DRIVER:

No way. We're bombproof, and the doors are on remote control.

A man in a balaclava holding a lantern holds up a sign to the windshield.

STAY CALM, AND YOU WILL NOT BE HARMED. *The men sit still, stunned.*

SECOND MAN:

Starting to think we might be on our own.

DRIVER:

Nonsense. These guys know nothing.

SECOND MAN:

Maybe not, but they got this far.

MATTHEW JAMES:

He climbs up the side of the vehicle to seal the exhaust and stall the motor.

Ed was right. Those fumes could take a man before his time.

29   FARGOSAFE CENTRE   SAME TIME

Herman Waterman is the duty monitor. He's drinking coffee and reading comic strips. There are only 11 vehicles to monitor this night. An audible alarm scares him. The main screen flashes EMERGENCY.

HERMAN WATERMAN:

What's the drill? Kill alarm tone… ID the vehicle in distress... No. 34.

Confirm last known location. Exit 14 – I-20 12:05 AM, heading east at 55mph.

Auto check communications.

He presses the right screen icon and waits for the monitor to give him status.

Zero communications. Auto check GPS systems.

He presses the right icon and waits.

Zero GPS. Shit! This isn't a system failure. THIS IS REAL!

Instead of alerting the police, he first rings the FARGOSAFE director.

30   DINNER PARTY IN HIGH RISE APARTMENT   SAME TIME

Group of eight well-dressed and urban sophisticates enjoying brandies and desserts, looking over the lights of Houston. A cell phone rings.

FARGOSAFE DIRECTOR:

Excuses himself and goes to the balcony to answer the phone.

Yes?

HERMAN WATERMAN:

Sir. It's Herman from the centre.

FARGOSAFE DIRECTOR:

Disdainfully.

This better be good, Herman. Some important people are with me now.

HERMAN WATERMAN:

It is, sir. Distress alarm on a $47M garbage run out of Dallas.

FARGOSAFE DIRECTOR:

You have WHAT?

It's probably a system fault. Have you checked?

HENRY WATERMAN:

I've checked everything four times. ZERO!

FARGOSAFE DIRECTOR:

That's not possible. Check again.

HENRY WATERMAN:

Sir, THIS IS REAL!!

FARGOSAFE DIRECTOR:

Becoming unsettled.

Have you told the authorities?

HENRY WATERMAN:

No sir. Thought you should know first.

FARGOSAFE DIRECTOR:

NOTIFY THEM NOW!!! I'M ON THE WAY!!

He slams the phone shut.

Oh no!!

He moans. Then he returns to the dining room. He is ashen, shaken.

WOMAN GUEST:

Laughing

Darling, you look like an awful martini, badly shaken and stirred. Have you lost something?

FARGOSAFE DIRECTOR:

In a monotone.

Probably my job!

30   I-20 NEAR EXIT 14   A SHORT TIME LATER

Scene is a montage of police activity with cars and people racing along the interstate towards exit 14.

31   DIRT ROAD LEADING TO ABANDONED MINE.   SAME NIGHT

Dusty dirt road. The two heavy vehicles and the police cruiser make their way to an abandoned mine site. The wind blows the dust cloud to one side of the road, so the vehicles are easily seen in the moonlight.

32   APARTMENT OF LESLEY AND RON   SAME TIME

Phone rings in a darkened bedroom. Ron stirs and breaks the sleeping embrace with Lesley. She stirs at the sound and buries herself under the pillow. Half asleep, he reaches for and answers the phone.

RON BEAUMONT:

Hello.

PEARCE KELLY – FBI DUTY OFFICER:

Ron. Get to the heliport straight away. An armoured van has just been hit east of Dallas. We don't have many details yet, but a crime scene team is being assembled, you included. The FBI has lead jurisdiction.

RON BEAUMONT:

How much?

PEARCE KELLY:

Guessing at this stage. Could be up to $80M.

RON BEAUMONT:

Hell! On the way.

He replaces the phone.

LESLEY MASON:

Work?

RON BEAUMONT:

Afraid so. I have to hustle. Going to Dallas. Ring you when I find out what's going on.

He dresses quickly, kisses the sleeping woman and leaves.

33   ABANDONED MINE SITE   SAME TIME

The vehicles are inside the deserted mine warehouse. The men are jubilant.

ED ROYSTON:

We did it! We pulled it off!

JOSÉ MARIA:

Not yet. We've got quite a bit of work to do, and get out of here in 45 mins.

JOHN LEE:

Right now, they're just waking up to what we have done. They'll be coming. Celebrations come later. Let's get the cage in position so we can get poor Matt out.

The men pull a frame covered with very fine mesh to the back of the trailer and attach it. They enter through the first flap of mesh before progressing through the second flap of mesh. This crude airlock prevents any signals from getting in or out while giving the men access.

Balaclava time, gentlemen. Remember what you have to do. No talking. This van is equipped with external microphones that we cannot neutralise.

Signalling to Matt, he knocks three times.

The signal to lower the ramp.

They work in silence. Ed starts to drill a hole through the van wall. Takes longer than expected but once drilled, they insert a small metal pipe and pump anaesthetic gas to the interior. The two men inside are asleep within 20 seconds. The four men wait in silence for one minute.

JOHN LEE:

OK, José. Over to you.

JOSÉ MARIA:

You bet. Stand back, boys.

JOHN LEE:

Turns to Ed and Matt.

While José does the cutting, we can start clearing up any evidence of our presence here. Ed, you do the cruiser. Matt, you in the prime mover and I'll do the tow truck. Collect everything into these garbage bags. Make sure to spray solvent over everything. We leave no traces.

The men set about their tasks.

Gentlemen, we are in!

The door falls off after a hefty whack with a heavy hammer.

ED ROYSTON:

Grabbing one of the money sacks

Yeehah! I can't believe it.

JOSÉ MARIA:

Slow down a bit, Ed. Help me tie and gag the men up front.

They blindfold, gag, and cable tie the men. Meanwhile, John Lee and Matt throw money bags out of the van. José Maria and Ed Royston join them as they haul the load through the screen airlock to their getaway cars.

MATTHEW JAMES:

Nine bags. Three per vehicle.

Looking up.

Ed, check the van for a manifest. Should be a slip with a figure.
ED ROYSTON:
Searching through the documents in the car.
EUREKA! I'VE GOT IT!! 47,647,000!!!

JOHN LEE:
Turning to the men with a wide grin.
Not a bad day's work! Don't stop, we've still got plenty to do. Get changed, and put on new gloves. Throw everything in the garbage bags I'm taking with me. You three hit the road, and I'll see you back in Houston. Don't leave any clues when you dump the cars. Bring your gloves and the rest of your clothing to me for disposal.
After jobs are done and high fives all round, Matt and Ed leave in one vehicle.
JOHN LEE:
Walks over to José, who is in his car, and they shake hands
You know, Gladys, we might just pull this mission off.
JOSÉ MARIA:
God shows optimism. Who would have believed that?
John Lee smiles.
Good luck, my friend. See you at home.
José drives away.
JOHN LEE:
Surveys the scene and bends to pick up the wrapper from a fruit bar. He scans the area and then sweeps the area of footprints in the dust.
Good. Leave nothing to chance. No clues.
He climbs the rusty staircase at one end of the building and goes to a large water container. He reaches down and opens a small valve. Water starts to flow slowly into an oversize container several feet below. Light rope and pulleys to the enclosure at the back of the trailer attach the container. He looks at the water flow.
Gravity! Do your thing.
He commands.
I'm out of here!
Hops into his car and drives away.
Water continues to fill the container. When close to full in three hours, its weight will start to pull the enclosure away from the trailer.

As this happens, the signal from the onboard GPS equipment will be re-established with the FARGOSAFE control centre and the location of the van and the men, known.

34   AT ROBBERY SITE ON I-20   ROBBERY +2 HOURS

Approximately 50 miles west of Dallas on I-20. A helicopter lands and disgorges the team of FBI agents. The leader of the group is Special Agent Harry Glover. Ron is part of the four-man team. The highway is cordoned off with a number of local police and highway patrol vehicles in attendance. The local Sheriff approaches Glover as he gets out of the helicopter.

SHERIFF DAWSON:
Approaches the FBI Agent.
I'm Sheriff Dawson.
SPECIAL AGENT GLOVER:
Shakes hands with the sheriff.
Special Agent Glover. What have you got so far?
SHERIFF DAWSON:
Very little. Skid marks, broken plastic from vehicle lamp assemblies.
SPECIAL AGENT GLOVER:
Beaumont, Anderson, Fells. Start looking around, see what you can find.
Looking at the skid marks and the minor amount of debris
What do you think happened, Sheriff?
SHERIFF DAWSON:
Not certain. But it looks like at least two vehicles are involved. See here.
He points to part of the skid marks.
There's a section of a multi-wheel prime mover and trailer braking. There's another set of skid marks behind, probably the armoured van. Normally I'd say the heavy vehicle was under brakes for some reason, and the other vehicle braked as a consequence.
SPECIAL AGENT GLOVER:
I agree.
SHERIFF DAWSON:
What puzzles me is the debris. Look here. The plastic and metal come before the two sets of marks are together.
SPECIAL AGENT GLOVER:

Beaumont! Over here!

He hurries over. His boss looks at him.

What do you make of these tracks and the debris field?

Ron paces up and down a couple of times and returns to where the sheriff and Glover are standing.

RON BEAUMONT:

Not certain, sir, it appears two vehicles have had a collision, and the debris is from the rear of one. Mainly from the rear of the lead vehicle.

SPECIAL AGENT GLOVER:

Looking at the rookie.

Partly right. Yes, it was a collision of two vehicles. However, it's from the collision of the armoured van and a third vehicle.

RON BEAUMONT:

How so, sir?

SPECIAL AGENT GLOVER:

The plastic is polycarbonate. Normally they don't break except under extreme force. It's not used on any normal vehicles. Look at the size of the pieces. They're from vehicle rear assemblies. Something hit the armoured van from behind at speed while another was braking in front. OK, Sheriff, we're looking for two heavy vehicles as well as the armoured van. Find them, and we find the money. At least one of them is damaged at the front.

SHERIFF DAWSON:

Already got roadblocks on a 25 mile perimeter.

SPECIAL AGENT GLOVER:

Whoever they are, they're good. We should have a 50 mile perimeter. Block the I-20 as far as the border. I've a hunch that's the direction. Check anything that moves. Do a 100% check on every truck on the road. There's one out there with front-end damage. Find out if we have witnesses. Can we use your office as a forward command post?

SHERIFF DAWSON:

Be my guest.

SPECIAL AGENT GLOVER:

Come on, men, we're out of here.

35   FARGOSAFE CONTROL CENTRE   **ROBBERY + 4 HOURS**

Suits standing around talking.

DIRECTOR:

Damn it, Peter. How can you possibly blame me? It's not my design.

FARGOSAFE CHAIRMAN: (HAROLD CARTER)

Gerry, you've been responsible for its continuous development for over eight years. Remember? No expense spared? No one knows more about the system than you. Agree?

DIRECTOR:

I do.

HAROLD CARTER:

Good. We have a point of agreement. That being the case, there's either been a breakdown in security, and we have a mole. OR there's is a weakness in the system that's been overlooked. Whichever way it goes, you're responsible. Now, you tell me which one is it?

DIRECTOR:

Terrific! I'm the patsy.

HAROLD CARTER:

Putting his arm around the shoulder of the man.

Gerry… Gerry… Gerry. You know how it works. We have to protect the banks' confidence in our business. It's not personal. It's just business. Your severance will be appropriate to the way we've always felt about you.

At this point in the evening, Kenny could contain himself no longer. He jumped off his chair and did laps around the whole floor.

"Yes, yes, yes, take that, you smarmy bastard. You've passed the buck one time too many. Take your own medicine." He found himself in front of the tabernacle of treasures, selected a cookie and took a break. He shuffled downstairs and sat on the front step. Early evening with constant movement on the street, people heading home or out for the evening. Some nodded in passing. Leaning against the door jamb, he went over events again. His study of Texas geography was serving him well, and the mesh cage idea from Siobhan was brilliant. Should not have thought of her, straight away, he was hit with a guilt bullet. Just in time, the cookie magic took over him from serious grief. Feeling an urgency to continue the wash-up from the robbery, he headed up the stairs to his desk.

36   ABANDONED MINE SITE   ROBBERY +4 HOURS

The water container was now heavy enough to pull the cage away from the rear of the trailer. The GPS signal was able to be seen at base.

37   FARGOSAFE CENTRE   ROBBERY + 4 HOURS

Herman Waterman is sitting at a bank of monitors when a signal from the missing van is received.

HERMAN WATERMAN:

It's back. The van is back online. I've got coordinates about 40 miles from the robbery site.

FBI AGENT:

Where?

HERMAN WATERMAN:

Just a minute. Up on the monitor screen now. Thirty miles east of the hijack site and 13 miles north. The old Silverado mine site.

FBI AGENT:

On cell phone, advising Special Agent Glover.

HAROLD CARTER:

Have we got radio contact?

DIRECTOR:

Moving to the console – as HM talks to the FBI in the background – he clicks a few icons to activate an onboard TV and radio link with the van. He pans the scene that shows a door missing, an empty van and two bound and blindfolded employees.

Trying the open monitoring channel. Can either of the men hear me? Can anyone hear me?

DRIVER:

Garbled sounds through his gag.

DIRECTOR:

Can't understand. Say again!

FBI AGENT:

Nod your head if you understand!

DRIVER:

Nodding his head.

FBI AGENT:

You both OK?

DRIVER AND SECOND MAN:

Both nod their heads.

FBI AGENT:
We're on the way. Don't move.

38   I-20 NEAR TEXAS AND LOUISIANA BORDER   NEAR DAWN

John Lee is driving at the speed limit, heading towards Louisiana before returning to Houston. Ahead he can see the flashing lights of several Highway Patrol vehicles, warning flares on the roadway and a line of traffic. Highway Patrol officers are waving drivers to pull over and stop. He sits nervously, waiting for his turn to be approached. An officer walks up and shines a torch in his face

OFFICER:
Good morning sir. Where are you headed?

JOHN LEE:
Baton Rouge, officer. What are you looking for?

OFFICER:
Shines torch around inside of vehicle. Emotionless stare at older man. The money bags are covered by the garbage bags full of stuff for disposal.
What have you got in the bags?

JOHN LEE:
Please take them. I am sick of cleaning the trash that grandchildren make at my place. They come for a holiday while their mother chases the next crisis in her life, and they leave me with the wreckage. Who'd have kids, hey?

OFFICER:
His attention has shifted to the van next in line.
Yeah, ok, keep your garbage, off you go.

JOHN LEE:
Breathes a huge sigh of relief and pulls away.

39   ABANDONED MINE SITE   BREAKING DAWN

Helicopter lands with FBI team. Area around site secured by sheriff and highway patrol vehicles. FBI team goes inside the main building, where they see a prime mover, trailers, a heavy tow vehicle and a highway patrol cruiser. The rear of the trailer has a ramp and armoured van inside. Armoured van driver colleagues are drinking coffee while talking to a police officer. FBI steps in.

SPECIAL AGENT GLOVER:

Talking to van driver.

From what I know about these vans, there are multiple backups on every system. I gotta tell you now if we find out that any of them have been tampered with, YOU are our prime suspect.

DRIVER:

WHAT! I've just come through one of the worst nights of my life, and you are saying that to me! God, I don't believe this. Where was that patrol car when we were being knocked over just a couple of minutes later?

SPECIAL AGENT GLOVER:

What patrol car?

DRIVER:

The one chasing the speeding Suburban.

RON BEAUMONT:

Sir! I think you should look at this.

SPECIAL AGENT GLOVER:

What have we got?

RON BEAUMONT:

A highway patrol cruiser in the other trailer and really special stuff in the main rig.

SPECIAL AGENT GLOVER:

Turning to Highway Patrolman.

Find out if we know anything about a speeding or stolen Suburban.

HIGHWAY PATROL OFFICER:

Yes sir.

RON BEAUMONT:

The two men walk past the overturned cage and up the ramp.

Look, the whole interior is covered in a fine mesh, the same as the cage on the ground. It was all connected.

SPECIAL AGENT GLOVER:

What does that mean?

RON BEAUMONT:

I'm guessing, but somehow, the wire must suppress radio waves. The overturned barrel of water seems to be a counterweight to break the cage away from the back of the truck.

His mind went back to the Faraday's cage at the museum. The penny drops.

SPECIAL AGENT GLOVER:

Are you saying they led us here?

RON BEAUMONT:

Think I am. Certainly lucky for the crew. It would've taken us a lot longer to find them.

SPECIAL AGENT GLOVER:

Don't know who these guys are, but I'm starting to respect them. This is a professional hit, and the timings haven't given them much room for escape. They know exactly what they're doing. My God! We've just seen one of the great robberies. An impregnable target, taken down with a chicken wire cage and a big bucket of water. All we're missing is the chickens and some feed. Talk about high tech! Doesn't get much better! Get forensics on the case, but I tell you now, it's probably a waste of time. We're out of here!

"Ha Ha, you bastards, and it's not over yet."

Kenny was exhausted, self-medication was wearing off, fatigue snuck up on him. He would retire but nervously, knowing what visitations were likely in his dreams, hoping for something less intense. He loved the calling of the doona at the end of the day. This night he heard it and knew he'd have to go, but he felt the presence of dark forces. The usual agents of torture populated his night, leaving him unprepared for the following day. He should have expected it. Two steps forward, one backwards, he knew. Lucky he didn't need to fly, that would have been hazardous. Meds in the morning brought back enough mental balance for him to research the next phase of the story. The boys escaped with the money, and it looked like John Lee would get rid of the evidence in the crematorium. He needed a way for them to distract the FBI while they got rid of the money. Then he thought about his Cessna cargo plane. Something like that would work, or maybe a helicopter. Yes, that's it. He had two helicopter pilots in the group. He'd need to look at reachable but not too busy airports where they might nick a chopper for a couple of hours. He'd muse over choices for the time being.

27

HANNA HAD SNARED a big fish close to Monash University. Speculator Jet Mathews corporation had invested in a five-hectare site facing the Princes Highway. They picked one property at a time over six years as each came on the market. There were 12 retail shops and a whole street of medium-sized factories in the package. Ronaldo Gray architects worked up the concept offering 200 high rise residential units supporting retail and commercial spaces. Chinese investors through 'Golden Toad' private equity group saw an opportunity to vertically integrate all elements of the build and came on board as the majority partner. Hundreds of contracts were involved. Hanna and Mark were stretched to the limit. Their city office was the hub. They needed to hire four junior legal clerks to manage the mechanics of the processes. 'Golden Toad' had offices in Singapore, so negotiations required many trips. What interested Hanna was how the Chinese wanted to supply work force and materials for the build. Then they expected to sell various elements to lower-tier Chinese investors, especially parents of university age children. She had to represent Australian laws that limited what the Chinese wanted. Vertical integration looks like exploitation of the host, smells like it, and most assuredly is it. The only aspect of the whole deal left for the host was fees for university tuition of Chinese students. Hanna had a dilemma to work through. She couldn't stop the project, but she might be able to limit the damage it could cause. The first win for her was the engagement of Melbourne based firm Ronaldo Gray architects. The Chinese accepted local knowledge of design requirements as a good idea and agreed. After that, they were going to play hard. Hanna's only apparent move was to keep various government departments informed of Toad's decisions. It would be a hazardous testing journey. The local building industry was already under siege, seduced by cheap prices for Chinese manufactured materials like copper wiring, all electrical fittings, copper water piping, cladding, glass, steel and aluminium. The trouble with so many of these products was the way Australian standards of quality documentation could be forged. Copper was not supposed to corrode, sheathing on copper wiring was not supposed to break down, cladding was not supposed to be flammable, and electrical switches were not supposed to crack. Problematic use of cheap materials incurred a heavy price somewhere down the line after culpable corporate entities had evaporated. Bankruptcy was the normal way of exiting the scene of their crimes, leaving footprints in the sand, so to speak and avoiding consequences for unscrupulous behaviour. So common was the practice it had its own name, 'Phoenix'. Hanna and Mark Joseph carried extra costs monitoring these issues.

Kenny picked up. It was Hanna.

"Brother, know you have your own thing going with Tassie seafood but wondered if you could help us out a bit. This 'Golden Toad' mob out of Singapore has a deal going with a chartered Gulfstream G550 fitted out for 12 passengers with all the pleasures of a corporate jet. They want us to share travel overheads with this big development. They've asked us to cover the costs of one of two pilots. Are you up to sharing the cockpit for a two-day trip once a month?"

"The plane's a piece of cake, Mac. I have the endorsement. As long as there are two up-front, I could do it. And since you will be on board Mac, I would love to do it. Count me in. Love flying over big water. By the way, I've found a pretty good Lebanese restaurant on Bridge Road. When you feel like it, we could grab a bite and a glass of wine."

"Thanks. I will let you know in plenty of time for the job, and of course about the restaurant. What about lunch on Sunday? You're going to love this. I could bring the family. Shut up, don't say anything."

"Sounds good Mummy!!!"

Water, he thought. Fishing. Old guys love fishing. I could use this. His morning started to look better.

40   ROADSIDE DINER   MORNING

Ed and Matt have pulled into a diner for breakfast. They are in very high spirits, settling into breakfast. The owner is pouring them coffee. The NBC TODAY show is playing on the overhead TV.

OWNER:

Coffee boys?

MATTHEW JAMES:

Sure thing. Black for both of us.

OWNER:

Where you boys headed?

ED ROYSTON:

We're on holidays. Just looking at the country.

OWNER:

Some guys get it good, hey! We got plenty of country. What would you like?

MATTHEW JAMES:

My good man: eggs over easy, bacon, hash brown, toast, pancakes, juice.

OWNER:

You boys sure have worked up an appetite.

ED ROYSTON:

We sure have.

The diner owner is caught by breaking news on the TODAY show.

TODAY SHOW HOST:

We're receiving breaking news of a major robbery in Texas. Reports suggest that a Fargosafe armoured van carrying $145M from Dallas to Baton Rouge has been hijacked. Details are sketchy, but we do know there have been no injuries to the van crew. Special Agent Glover is on the line near the scene outside Dallas, along with Chairman of Fargosafe, Mr Harold Carter, in Houston. Good morning gentlemen. Thank you for your time. Agent Glover, tell us.

SPECIAL AGENT GLOVER:

Not much as yet, except four men have taken a large amount of cash.

TODAY SHOW HOST:

We understand the money is used and unmarked?

SPECIAL AGENT GLOVER:

I cannot confirm that at this time.

TODAY SHOW HOST:

Is there any connection between this crime and armoured van robberies in Chicago?

SPECIAL AGENT GLOVER:

Too early to tell, but that is one of the possibilities we're looking at. We would ask if anyone travelling on I-20 close to Dallas last night around midnight saw anything unusual to contact the police or FBI.

TODAY SHOW HOST:

Mr Carter. The Fargosafe system is supposed to be impregnable, with the latest security technology, including position tracking. How did this happen?

HAROLD CARTER:

Our system has been hailed as the ultimate in security transfer, and in all the years of operation, this is the first time one has been taken. Does seem this is a one-off event with unique circumstances I cannot go into. It's most unlikely that this could happen again.

TODAY SHOW HOST:

Are you saying there is a design weakness?

HAROLD CARTER:

Not at all. But in light of this event, we will examine every last detail to ensure our system is the best.

TODAY SHOW HOST:

Agent Glover, do you expect an early arrest?

SPECIAL AGENT GLOVER:

The FBI is throwing everything at this case. As soon as we have something to announce, we will let you know as a priority.

TODAY SHOW HOST:

We look forward to that. Thank you, gentlemen, again for your time. That was FBI Special Agent Glover and Harold Carter on the overnight armoured van robbery in Texas that netted approximately $145M.

DINER OWNER:

Some good old boys have been up to mischief overnight. Can't say I mind hearing the banks taking one on the chin for a change.

Laughing.

Just like we always say. Things are always bigger in Texas!

ED ROYSTON:

Turning to Matt.

Those liars. $145M!

MATTHEW JAMES:

It's just the way the bank minimises its losses. All to do with insurance. We've just gone from anonymous outlaws to anonymous celebrities.

Laughing.

Maybe we could sell the movie rights.

ED ROYSTON:

Who would want to see it? Who would believe it?

MATTHEW JAMES:

Where would they find the right old-timers to play the likes of us?

ED ROYSTON:

There are plenty of old stagers with dying careers needing a shot in the arm.

41   FBI OFFICES   TWO DAYS LATER

Special Agent Glover in front of a whiteboard, writing all over, crime scene photos pinned up on the wall and the team assembled.

SPECIAL AGENT GLOVER:

What the hell are we doing? Two days on and not one solid lead. The vehicles were stolen from Houston and the Galveston area. The cage material came from an Oklahoma cash auction sale. The rest of the gear left behind probably came from Louisiana.

We have a couple who saw the vehicles parked by the interstate. We have several witnesses from a diner who saw a parked Highway Patrol cruiser. We have a police recording of a hoax radio call that's probably nothing. We have statements from the van crew. Four men, one with a limp. The underworld contacts have nothing, and we know this is a professional hit.

Let's face it. We have zero, and I'm here to tell you that zero is not an option. The only break we are going to get will come from crims chasing the money like we are. That cash has to show up somewhere.

The Director is barking for a quick resolution. The media is playing havoc with the story. The Governor is up in arms over the bad publicity for Texas, and banks are nervous there is more to come.

Shake the trees. Put the fear of God into every low life criminal and contact on the books. Someone knows. I want these men, and I want them now!

The men get up and move towards the door.

42   HOSPICE   MORNING

The four men are together for regular treatments. It's John Lee's birthday. Lesley and Ron are coming to help celebrate with the men and the nursing staff.

JOSÉ MARIA:

Smiling and raising a glass of soda to the group.

To God and his three apostles.

MATTHEW JAMES:

This isn't the last supper, I hope.

JOHN LEE:

In time. In time. For now, quiet celebration of stage one of our mission.

ED ROYSTON

We did better than good. We did REALLY good. I've never seen so much.

JOSÉ MARIA:

Easy Ed. Even this place could have ears.

MALE NURSE:

Approaching the group.

Don't know what treatments you fellows are having, but they're clearly working. You all look better than I've ever seen you.

MATTHEW JAMES:

Must be you, Adrian. You obviously work out.

ED ROYSTON:

Slow down, Matt.

MATTHEW JAMES:

Slow down? I was just getting started.

MALE NURSE:

It's OK fellas. I get a lot of old flirts in here. Must be the water.

They all laugh. The nurse moves on.

MATTHEW JAMES:

Faking indignancy.

Flirt, maybe … but old? Never! I DON'T DRINK THE WATER!

JOHN LEE:

Settle down. We have to decide how to get rid of you know what. I've been thinking of a fishing expedition. My place at eight tonight.

ED ROYSTON:

Keen to hear more.

God! How we gonna do it from a boat?

As he utters these words, Lesley and Ron approach the group. Ed does not see them. John Lee sees the couple and puts up his hands for Ed to stop. There is a strange look on Ron's face as he processes the similarity of voice and cadence between the voice on the tape and Ed's remark.

LESLEY MASON:

She carries the birthday cake with candles burning.
Happy birthday, Grandpa.

"It's a work of genius, wish I was writing the thing. These guys are doing the lot, as well as acting."

Kenny continued under his breath. The FBI is on the back foot, yet one of their least experienced agents is already on the verge of discovery. The boss's ego is evident and must be used to good effect. Is there a hint that Ed and Matt might grab some of the money? The chase now starts in earnest. The celebration at the hospice would be a good chance for Ron to get a good look at the four patients.

Mid-afternoon, time for a cookie and more work. First, he needed to walk and think and stretch. "Funny," he thought. "I've got the hungries before the cookie even gets out of the jar. Oh well, a falafel roll awaits." It was only a 10 minute walk down Bridge Rd to 'Kanzaman', where his new best friend Bilal specialised in delicious Lebanese offerings. Normally Kenny would head out to see Pierre but had no time for that today. He wanted to get back to the birthday party. It was all about momentum, and the pace had picked up. Falafel crumbs on his lap, he forgot everything else, mind focused completely on the birthday party and related surprises.

JOHN LEE:

Hon! I'd forgotten. You never do.

LESLEY MASON:

A group of nursing staff move towards the light and the cake.
And never will. Here, blow out the candles.

JOHN LEE:

Blows out the candles and looks at his three friends. They know his wish.
Whew! Gets harder every year.

LESLEY MASON:

Nonsense. I've not seen you look this great for ages. What's your wish?

JOHN LEE:

Smiling.

I wished for a fishing trip for me and these three reprobates. Just the thing to perk us up. What do you think?

LESLEY MASON:

Sounds wonderful. Four handsome fellows alone on the sea. No girls?

JOSÉ MARIA:

You're more than welcome. But Ron might not agree with you being alone with four single men.

RON BEAUMONT:

Trying to shake recognition of Ed's voice, feigns mirth.

Reckon she'd be safe with you lot. Be my guest.

LESLEY MASON:

Teasingly.

Darl! Don't be too eager for me to wander. Just might do it. Probably only equal the score for whatever your exploits are when you claim you're chasing bad guys and can't come home.

Touches his face gently.

Were you really in Dallas on that robbery or off with a girlfriend?

RON BEAUMONT:

Darl! Please don't mention my work.

LESLEY MASON:

Tch Tch. Don't be so precious. We're family, and you said that's OK.

RON BEAUMONT:

Embarrassed.

Sorry. I get a little sensitive. They tell us you never know who's listening.

JOSÉ MARIA:

Quite right. You never know who's listening.

LESLEY MASON:

Pause as she takes a knife.

Now, who's for cake?

She cuts and plates up slices. The group mingles, and Ron moves to Ed.

RON BEAUMONT:

Using small talk to glean information.

Ed. Must be tough, driving all over the place working on used cars.

ED ROYSTON:

A little tougher than it used to be. You do what you have to, hey.

RON BEAUMONT:

What sort of area do you cover?

ED ROYSTON:

Houston, Dallas, down to New Orleans. Of course, to Galveston and along the coast. Keeps me out of mischief, but it's only spasmodic these days.

RON BEAUMONT:

You'd know the geography well.

ED ROYSTON:

Every highway and byway. Drive it blind if I had to.

RON BEAUMONT:

Any recent trips? …

JOHN LEE:

Overhearing. Maybe paranoid, given the agent's part in the case.

Ron, Les tells me you're a fisherman. What do you know about deep water fishing in the Gulf?

RON BEAUMONT:

Not a lot, sir. I hear stories about big game, but I like mountain Bass.

JOSÉ MARIA:

Fresh water man!

RON BEAUMONT:

Getting keen, forgetting about Ed.

Yes sir. Nothing quite like a 40 lb bass hitting your lure. A real rush. Trouble is their numbers are not what they used to be.

JOHN LEE:

The way of the world, hey?

RON BEAUMONT:

I guess. But when I get time off, I go to the Ozarks in Missouri. Still, good lake fishing there, if you know the spots. Next trip, Les is coming.

MATTHEW JAMES:

The Ozark Mountains, eh!

RON BEAUMONT:

Why yes.

MATTHEW JAMES:

Reminds me of an old advertisement for hiking boots. "Mountain boots for Mountin' men". Bought 'em, but they never seemed to work.

LESLEY MASON:

Laughing to Matt.

You're sooooo.. wicked.

NURSE:

Mr Orlando and Mr Royston, time for your treatment. You, room 9 and you 8.

MATTHEW JAMES:

Just when the party gets going, someone brings out high-quality drugs!

Everyone laughs.

LESLEY MASON:

Kissing John Lee.

Happy birthday. We'll get going.

JOHN LEE:

Taking her aside.

Les. I'm visiting the graves on Sunday at about 5pm. You know what date it is. Care to meet me there?

LESLEY MASON:

Of course. I'll bring flowers.

Pause.

I love you, Grandpa.

JOHN LEE:

I love you too.

Lesley and Ron walk away. John Lee turns to his confederates.

8:00 tonight, my place. Remember, from now on, not a word in front of them.

43   HOME OF JOHN LEE   **NIGHT**

The four men are sitting around, enjoying a quiet drink. John Lee starts the meeting.

JOHN LEE:

Now, are you all certain you've given me all clothing, gloves, paper and everything else that's evidence?

They nod in agreement.

Good. I'll get rid of it on the weekend. Now, next thing. Les's boyfriend. He's got me worried.

JOSÉ MARIA:

Do you think he knows something?

JOHN LEE:

Well, don't think he knows anything for certain. But he gave me a bad feeling earlier today. Maybe I'm paranoid, but he seemed to focus on Ed.

ED ROYSTON:
Didn't say anything special. Just asking about the used car trade.

JOHN LEE:
I know, but there was something in his tone that made me uneasy. I'm probably overstating things. Nevertheless, we have to be vigilant, give nothing away. I don't want the youngster being caught up in our scheme, even by accident. Nor do I want the honour of being arrested by my granddaughter's boyfriend.

MATTHEW JAMES:
I agree. Keep the kids away from this.

JOHN LEE:
We agree, good. Let's move on. José and I have been working on a plan to get rid of the money.

ED ROYSTON:
Looking at Matt.
Come on Matt. If you won't say it, I will.

JOSÉ MARIA:
Whatever are you talking about?

ED ROYSTON:
Well, while you two were working on the plan, so were we, a different one.

JOHN LEE:
I'm easy-going, Ed, but I know I won't like what you're going to say next.

ED ROYSTON:
I.... I... I mean, we ... agree that getting rid of the money is the right thing to do, and we still support it. But we were thinking that maybe we could keep three or four. Nobody would ever miss it, and it would be nice, just as a memento.

JOHN LEE:
Cut the crap! You want us to keep three or four!? Matt, you agree with him?

MATTHEW JAMES:
W..e...I...I it made sense when Ed and I spoke. But sitting here, it doesn't sound quite the same. But yes, I agreed that keeping some would be good.

JOHN LEE:
Shouting.
GREAT!! BUT LET ME TELL YOU, WE HAVE EACH SACRIFICED A NUMBER OF LIFELONG PRINCIPLES TO GET THIS FAR. WE AGREED NOT TO KEEP THE MONEY AND GAVE OUR WORD OF HONOUR. WE CAN NOT AND WILL NOT SACRIFICE HONOUR. IF WE DON'T HAVE HONOUR, THEN WHAT ARE WE?
Deathly silence greets the men. John Lee pauses and regains composure. He speaks to himself.
Must learn to walk more.
JOSÉ MARIA:
What did you just say?
JOHN LEE:
Nothing, José, just reminding myself of something.
He pauses, looking at each of the men.
You may, in part, be right. If José agrees, then I would support keeping eight.
JOSÉ MARIA:
You what??
He pauses.
Don't know what you're up to, but you have my support.
ED ROYSTON:
That's terrific! That's more than we planned! $8M.
MATTHEW JAMES:
John Lee, you sure?
JOHN LEE:
Never been more certain. We keep $8000 to cover our expenses, including the boat hire. I think that's fair and doesn't compromise us too much.
His eyes narrow.
Think about it. I'm going to the can.
He gets up and leaves the room.
ED ROYSTON:
Chokingly.
$8000 …. $8000!
JOSÉ MARIA:
Fellas. I know each of us can use money. But when we started this thing, it was about making a point. Seems to me, with each of

us looking healthier than we can remember, the whole thing has been hugely worthwhile without the money. We've given ourselves a reason to fight our demons and live better, more exciting lives than before. We've become a sort of family where we had none. We've even proved a point if only to ourselves, that being on the physical road out doesn't make us dumb or useless. I, for one, want to go with the original plan.

Pause.

I've seen John Lee like his is right now only a couple of times before, and I can tell you straight, for him, it's the original plan less $8000, or he will let this thing pull itself apart. Who really wants that, after all we've been through?

Pause. John Lee returns. Matt rises to his feet slowly, Ed and then José Maria do the same.

MATTHEW JAMES:

Solemnly extending a handshake to John Lee.

$8000 seems very fair.

Then with a grin.

Although, with our recently found good health we may have lived to spend the lot.

The other two men extend their hands for a group handshake. Their collective fate is sealed.

JOHN LEE:

Quite calmly.

Now, to the plan. I've booked the boat for up to three days from next Monday afternoon. Assume that suits us all.

They nod.

Good. I would like Ed and José to bring their part of the haul to me on Saturday afternoon. Arrive separately. How does 3pm sound for you, José and 6pm for you, Ed?

They both agree.

Ed, is the van ready and loaded with extra fuel?

ED ROYSTON:

It's been hidden for over two weeks. Still don't know what it's for?

JOHN LEE:

All is about to be made clear. First, we transfer the money to the fishing boat and set sail for three glorious days on the Gulf. Next, we...........

28

KENNY STOPPED. He had to wipe tears from his cheeks. Just to see people, even though they were fictional characters standing up for decency and honour in the face of temptation to be greedy, self-indulgent, and facing imminent death, was too much for him. There was no room for mixed motives, no time for pretending. He felt he'd been alone since childhood, that wasn't new. His characters were standing up challenging the empire of evil, knowing that their action - though successful in many respects – wouldn't be enough to overcome the terrible end-game. This was new for Kenny. Futile action embraced only to demonstrate that such action solely for the benefit of all people is possible.

"Am I totally mad? This is absurd. They should take the money for themselves surely. So they get to feel good about themselves for being altruistic. Isn't that a bizarre kind of selfishness, the worst kind parading as something noble? I need to talk to someone about this."

He was suddenly terrified this story was killing him while saving him at the same time. Certainly, it set him on a dangerous path tonight. He saw the path he was on and veered by turning thoughts from the story. That always worked to keep him from the abyss. A walk would be good, in the city. He'd ride on the tram, take in the lights of Federation Square, maybe sit on a bench by the Yarra at Southbank. Didn't matter, it was getting late. He didn't care and would happily defer going to bed.

Trams stopped at the end of his street. Kenny felt warm inside his RAAF overcoat this crisp night. No one else was waiting for a tram, and when it came, it had only half a dozen passengers. One was a young man right at the front behind the driver. He was in deep conversation with himself while staring at his reflection in the side window, mouthing an attempt to convince an invisible second party things would be alright when he got a job. He promised he'd not had a hit of smack for three months and really wanted to see his son. "Just one last chance, pleeeese". No good talking to him. As he edged past, Kenny exchanged meaningful looks with a pair of Asian students entertained by the performance. They probably had little English. A seat at the rear would be the spot, so he moved where there was space. Bridge Road was Richmond's main street. Chic shopping, central pub, many restaurants and the floodlit town hall. The hall glided silently by, as did a dozen restaurants, a shopping mall, and a big hotel, all the way to Flinders Street in the centre of Melbourne and only a short walk to the Rialto. Within 100 metres of Hanna's tower, Kenny stopped to look up. Lights were out in her apartment, and darkness crashed all over him from a great height flattening him to the footpath. In the next moment, city noises exploded in his head and all around. Honking cars, the crackle of electricity, pedestrian hurryings, voices, flashing lights, trains on rails, the hum of trams and jet aeroplanes descending on their flight path to Tullamarine. Kenny dragged himself upright and clung savagely to a nearby plane tree standing in a line of clones of itself stripped of canopy hungering for spring-time energy. He followed them to the city square. Shortly after, he crossed the Yarra and inched his way down the winding staircase to the riverside precinct. Here he found a gathering of people, probably homeless, settling in for a night out of the weather sort of. Three men and a woman found a 20 litre can and were sitting on makeshift seats, two milk crates, and a rolled-up sleeping bag, enjoying radiant warmth from their fire. He nodded to them, and one about his own age gestured him to join them. It might've been a trap to mug him, but he didn't care. Maybe he had something they needed more than he did. His bravado was rewarded.

"Hey, You lookin'?"

"You could say that. You want fuel for the fire?"

He'd seen a partially destroyed pallet at the bottom of the stairs.

"Nah, mate, we got enough. Got a name?"

"Bobby, you?"

"Yeah, Wolvie, this here is Wayne and Peter over there, and this is Pam."

Nobody spoke, just nodded, all of them curious about the newcomer who didn't quite look like he belonged though they couldn't be sure. His greatcoat could cover anything, and he wore sneakers. He looked clean.

"You camping out tonight?"

"Nah, got noises in my head won't go away, could end up in the river but don't really want to, you know?"

"Hell yeah, welcome to the cellar dwellers, brother. We've all wanted to do that, and those who did were not even noticed. We're the invisible John Does."

"Hey, take a walk in a cemetery, look at the old graves. Doesn't matter who they were, everyone ends up forgotten. All it takes is time."

"Time! Man, do you even know what time is?"

"Some say time is money, some say it flies. What do you say?"

"Try this one, brother. Time is what stops everything from happening at once!"

Kenny staggered back as if struck. An idea impossible to grasp but capable of causing circuit breakers in the brain to trip.

"C'mon, Wolvie pull out your mouth organ, let's give this guy a lift."

"Harpsichord Pete, I keep tellin' you. Here goes."

Kenny saw how surreal this was, down and out, a warm fire, kind of congenial company. Was he joking about 'harpsichord'? Damn good music, Kristofferson's 'Sunday Morning Coming Down'. He wondered why there didn't seem to be drugs on hand, then chastised himself for that judgement. Reasons people have for camping under bridges were legion. He was there after all and seemed to fit in. He was still having trouble with balance and focus, he knew he should try to get home.

"People, thanks for the moment of sanity and especially for the biggest thought I have heard in a long while. Have to go, hope to see you again, all of you and before time collapses, us all."

"You OK buddy?"

Kenny grinned. The others nodded farewell. Climbing the spiral stair was fine. Trees waited for him at street level. He clung to one. Somehow he would have to get home. He was in a mess. "OK, focus. Breathe deep and slow. Close your eyes and let the spinning stop. Breathe deep and slow, focus." This was a mantra he'd often turned to when a spiralling crisis swept him away. It worked, but he'd have to get home where help was at hand. A brave taxi stopped, and he fell into the back seat, having whispered his address. His driver wanted to see his money. "Fair enough," Kenny thought, imagining how he must look and sound. He showed a $50 and somewhat placated, though not entirely, the driver headed towards Richmond. Outside Kenny's door, the driver chirped. "Thank you, sir." His fears were allayed when Kenny suggested he need not give change for the $50. Kenny smiled to himself, knowing the trip involved unnecessary detours. Change from the $50 would have been significantly bigger had the driver taken a more direct, honest route. "Hit for six again, damn it," Kenny whispered, letting himself into his refuge. Exhausted, it was all he could do to get to the meds before crashing into bed, boots and all. Then he slept. A deep, dark, quiet sleep. Stirring at first light, he realised he'd not moved for six hours. A long hot shower would give him life. And just like your tongue seeks out an ulcer in your cheek, his refreshed mind sought out his story, keen to get back to it. But Kenny wouldn't allow it to spoil his shower. The boys could wait for a couple of hours surely. They did, reluctantly.

29

44   RESTAURANT IN HOUSTON   **THAT NIGHT**

Outskirts of Houston, ROB'S Steakhouse, had an increasing reputation for the finest cooking and good fellowship. It welcomed everybody.

RON BEAUMONT:

Holds the door open for Lesley Mason, they are met by the owner.

LESLEY MASON:

Good evening, Rob. Told you we'd be back.

ROB:

Good to see you too, Les, and good evening to you, sir.

LESLEY MASON:

Rob, this is my friend, Ron.

RON BEAUMONT:

Pleasure to meet you.

ROB:

My pleasure Ron. Come in, come in. For you, tonight, the honeymooners' table.

LESLEY MASON:

Oh, thank you, Rob, you're so sweet.

Rob escorts them to their table. They sit.

RON BEAUMONT:

Nice place, those carvings on the wall look genuine. The lanterns are definitely Moorish. Look out for Saladin. Almost a Spanish feel. I look forward to a beautiful rib-eye with all the trimmings. Those photos of cattle, what's the story there?

LESLEY MASON:

It's all about respect for what the animals give. While we enjoy beautiful steaks, we can see where they came from. Rob has a ranch. His cattle live in small herds of about a dozen, like the ones in the photos, and each herd is together for the whole of its life. When time, each group is taken to a special barn where they are anaesthetised by gradual exposure to a sleep-inducing gas that's colourless and odourless. The animals just go to sleep. The carcasses are then processed, and the steak is aged, still on the property, until needed at the restaurant. The best part is that cooking is all done on a charcoal barbeque, nothing exotic. Rob keeps it simple from start to finish. There's only one sauce that he created from tomato, onion, capsicum, salt, pepper and sautéed in a little olive oil. The flavour is spectacular. I think we deserve a bottle of wine, darling, don't you? Have a look at the list. The last time I was here with Grandpa, we had a bottle of Australian red, the best I've ever tasted. Ask Rob if he has a bottle of a Langhorne Creek Shiraz.

RON BEAUMONT:
Rob comes over to take the drinks order.
Rob, Les tells me she had an Australian red last time.

ROB:
Indeed. Her grandfather developed quite a taste for those Aussie reds, not that he's been able to drink much of late. A cousin in Australia keeps me stocked with some of the best. I've shared many a beautiful meal with John Lee Calhoun.
Rob whispers conspiratorially.
Some of the biggest reds in the world come from a place called Barossa. I have one for you. Just give me a moment.
Rob extracts a bottle from a rack at the rear.

RON BEAUMONT:
They toast each other, and Ron broaches a sensitive subject.
To us. Gosh, this is good stuff. Hon, how much do you know about John Lee's friends at the Hospice?

LESLEY MASON:
What an odd question on a romantic date.

RON BEAUMONT:
I know. I just want to understand more about them.

LESLEY MASON:
Whatever for? Is there something I should know?

RON BEAUMONT:
No. Nothing I know of. Just curious.

LESLEY MASON:
You're never just curious, Ron. I've known you for 18 months,

and you're only ever curious about something related to your work. Is that what this is about? One of them is in the crosshairs of your professional interest.

RON BEAUMONT:

No. It's nothing like that.

LESLEY MASON:

Becoming irritable.

If it's nothing like that, what is it like, Ron?

ROB:

Darlings, why don't you leave tonight's choice to me. A selection to die for. Perhaps a rib-eye for you, sir and Lesley, I think, would really appreciate the eye fillet.

RON BEAUMONT:

Sounds good to me. What about you, hon?

LESLEY MASON:

Thank you, Rob. I've never looked at the menu, never been disappointed.

ROB:

Strap yourselves in, heh, heh.

He heads back towards the kitchen.

RON BEAUMONT:

Now, where was I?

LESLEY MASON:

Cuttingly.

You were about to explain your interest in Grandpa's friends.

RON BEAUMONT:

Look, if you're going to behave like this, forget I said anything.

LESLEY MASON:

Nice try, Ron. Turn it back on me. I didn't start whatever's going on here.

RON BEAUMONT:

How can a man win a conversation when emotion gets in the way of reason?

LESLEY MASON:

You start out having a spurious interest in a bunch of old men, and before you know it, it's a conversation about a man winning against a woman. Next, I suppose you'll give one of those great hoary old lines like – the difference between a man and a woman is, you take away honour and imagination from a man, and they're the same.

RON BEAUMONT:

Wow! That's not bad. Where did that come from?

LESLEY MASON:

Damn you, Ron. I love you and know you're working on a tough case.

A long pause and then a sense of realisation crosses her face.

You … you … think Grandpa and his friends are connected to …

RON BEAUMONT:

No, not at all!!

LESLEY MASON:

Gets to her feet, throwing down her serviette, steaming with anger.

How dare you imply such a thing. You better get your act together quickly, buster, or WE might be in trouble. Blankets are in the study. Don't bother to wake me.

She storms out of the restaurant.

ROB:

The scene has attracted attention. Rob approaches Ron.

I suppose the meal for two is out of the question?

RON BEAUMONT:

His eyes follow the woman. He is roused by Rob's voice.

Sorry, Rob, dinner isn't the only thing off the table.

45   FBI OFFICE HOUSTON   AFTERNOON

Ron is walking up the steps leading to the offices of the FBI. He passes through the crowds, rides the elevator and passes through outer offices to the conference room.

SPECIAL AGENT GLOVER:

Gentlemen, Special Agent Montrose, is chief of the profiling task force, and I have asked her to brief us on her conclusions so far.

SPECIAL AGENT MONTROSE:

You've all got copies of notes prepared by my office. These offenders are skilled professionals, probably in the age group 30-45, with skills in sophisticated electronic systems and vehicle handling. The split-second timing needed for ramming the armoured van into the lead trailer would require a degree of skill generally only possessed by stunt drivers or sections of the military. The fact that no one was injured indicates the leadership of the group is tight and focused on the target.

Their knowledge of police procedures and crime scene forensics is very good. Their meticulous attention to detail displays considerable discipline of mind. Violence for its own sake is not part of their make-up. For these people, violence would be the last resort and only then in immediate peril with no alternative. I do not believe these people should be regarded as necessarily dangerous but should be treated with extreme caution. They will have a code of honour. They will be in peak physical condition. They are obsessive and driven individuals. They are likely to be from Texas and, more particularly, from the Dallas area. The fact that all gear used has been sourced from Houston and elsewhere is a blind to cover their true home base. I believe the likely composition of the gang is predominantly ex-military, with skilled drivers brought in for the heist itself. I suggest you start checking the backgrounds of Dallas-based stunt drivers, ex-Delta Force, SEALS and the like who have been discharged within the past two years. Look for at least one who was injured in the line of duty and now limps. I would suggest you focus on those who have left the forces carrying any form of grudge for authority. Any questions?

SPECIAL AGENT GLOVER:

Come on, men. Any questions?

RON BEAUMONT:

Is it possible that these people could be much older than you suggest?

SPECIAL AGENT MONTROSE:

Well, anything is possible. Why, what did you have in mind?

RON BEAUMONT:

Well, I am aware of a group of four men .....

Scene goes to silence as he explains his theory about our four men.

SPECIAL AGENT GLOVER:

Sensitive to the rookie's youth and inexperience but containing his humour was extremely difficult. His colleagues in the room were less concerned about concealing their mirth.

Let me see if I understand you. Four terminally ill old men with little time to live. One is your girlfriend's grandfather. Not only do they have clean sheets, but two are also decorated veterans, and each has distinguished himself in business or commerce. They are linked by a shared game of dime checkers in the hospital while getting treatment. You say that they spontaneously conspire to commit one of the biggest robberies in history. Forget the fact that this heist reeks of practised professionalism and state of the art knowledge. What possible motive could they have? A few bucks for their old age?

He knows that sarcasm is cruel, but he continues.

Maybe we can clean up our case book. Is anyone else in your family or circle of friends involved in terrorism or serial killing?

RON BEAUMONT:

Chastised but undaunted.

No! I'm unaware of anyone else. Couldn't we at least start enquiries in relation to these men?

SPECIAL AGENT MONTROSE:

Thank you, agent Beaumont. I don't for one moment believe you are correct. Still, I am sure that Special Agent Glover, along with me, appreciates the refreshing nature of your observations. At least you had a go.

SPECIAL AGENT GLOVER:

Beaumont, don't take the last remarks as any form of approval for active investigation. If you want to stalk your family, you do it on your own time, not the company's. Do we understand each other?

RON BEAUMONT:

Yes sir!

SPECIAL AGENT GLOVER:

OK. I have assignment sheets for each of you. Focus on the ex-military and find me my outlaws. Beaumont! You liaise with forensics to see if anything can be turned up to help this damned investigation.

30

KENNY STRUGGLED to his feet. Stiff back, sore legs, numb bum, full suite. He had not moved in three hours. The pleasure from his wonderfully refreshing hot shower was now a memory. He needed diversion. To that end, he dressed in old clothes to work on the table. He'd been in jocks and a heavy jumper since the shower. For the rest of the afternoon and into the evening, he became totally absorbed, planing, sanding, drilling, morticing, clamping and gluing. Building furniture was like writing for him. The article in hand often had a mind of its own, and he'd learned to listen to grain and curve, thickness and age. Yet it was more therapy than art though the end product would invariably sit happily in any home. He had one in mind. He picked up the phone, it was Hanna.

"Hi, brother had a sneaky kind of feeling all day we should meet for a bite and a glass of good stuff. What about that place in Bridge Road near your place? Hope their falafel is as good as Pierre's."

"Would you believe same family? Pierre set the benchmark for me, but Bilal is worth a chance. I'll meet you there at seven. And yes, thought of talking to you last night but was distracted in the workshop. Tonight would be great."

Hanna parked her Peugeot 504 at Kenny's place just as he was leaving. They walked arm in arm to the restaurant, him teasing her about the ready-made family and her teasing him about his crazy notion the world might be saved.

"Remember the last guy who had your idea, Kenny. They nailed him to a tree and scattered his fan club."

"OK, ok, but doesn't it make you mad to see what goes on?"

"Nah, not at all. I work in the holy world of property development, a world of saints and virgins."

They giggled at the image.

She filled him in on goings-on in the building game with substandard materials. Kenny shook his head.

"All true, sis, but I've finally worked out why I'm doing this thing and no longer care what the world might think. I know what I think."

"Wow brother. I really like that one. Frees you entirely. It's like a big moat around your castle. How'd you work that out?"

"Dunno took a few kicks in the head, I suppose. I'm a slow learner."

Middle eastern aromas met them at the door of the restaurant. A waitress showed them to a table beside a wall entirely taken up with a mural of mythological creatures at a bacchanalian feast. While absorbing this, the owner Bilal appeared at their table.

"You must be Kenny and you madame, Hanna. I'm under strict instructions from a mutual acquaintance to look after you tonight."

"Bilal, thank you. I'm to use the word 'mezza'. Pierre taught me that one. Don't know what it is, but we'll have it."

"Haha, trust him. OK, sit back. Leave it to me."

"Love the way these people do business. Like they read your mind."

As expected, the meal was delicious and varied, plate after plate of entrée size delicacies. Filo parcels of feta, onion and mint, filo rolls of spicy lamb with onion, capsicum and pine nuts, small grilled lamb sausages and minced lamb on a stick. When they thought it was over, out came grilled prawns, calamari and fingers of Tasmanian salmon in a chickpea covering. They even shared a couple of Lebanese beers.

"You'll laugh, but I'm going to bring the girls and Mark here."

Kenny obliged and laughed. He could see something was happening to his career-obsessed motorcyclist musician sister. She was adding another dimension to her existence, and he loved watching it. Hanna also enjoyed watching his amusement. It was tennish by the time they got back to the Terrace, glad for a walk after a sumptuous meal. She had work to do, and he was champing at the bit to get back to his bank robber friends. He was just a figure in her rear vision mirror, spotlit from a light in the doorway. She wondered how long she'd have him. His optimism was a fabrication clearly transparent. He couldn't hide from her. He was under siege, surrounded, threatened. Doomsday weighed on him. His burden was visible to her. Kenny closed the door and turned to lean against it. He was finding it harder to hide his real mental state from her. A heavy sigh and he realised there'd be no further work. A cookie, half an hour or so in the headphones, maybe Leonard Cohen would cheer him up with 'Hey, That's No Way to Say

Goodbye'!! Siobhan's face would be the last thing he'd see before darkness closed in. Not only her face. Her arms were open to him, beckoning, almost pleading for his embrace, drawing him into the shadows. Then he slept.

31

MORNINGS ARE THE BEST time for optimism. The earlier, the brighter. Still warmed by his sister's closeness and the evening's pleasure, Kenny didn't have a leap left in him but worked through his morning exercises with energy, walked the neighbourhood, brewed coffee and, against his usual routine of writing at night, returned to his wayward friends. There was a new urgency, time to wrap up the adventures of his bandit friends. All they had to do now was distribute the cash, complete the route of investigators and return to the hospice for the last rounds of treatments. He'd then be ready for his final confrontation with the pursuing demons, hell-bent on victory over him. But there were options. He would not go easily into that night.

46   GARAGE OF JOHN LEE   **SATURDAY AFTERNOON**
John Lee is standing in his garage. Six bags of money are in the middle of the floor. He hears a car pull up, Ed's voice calling "hello."
JOHN LEE:
In the garage, Ed. Come around the side entrance.
ED ROYSTON:
Give us a hand with these two bags JL. José's been already?
JOHN LEE:
Indeed, he has. I'll get the third bag for you.
ED ROYSTON:
No need. Couldn't help myself. Had to sort of count it, and when I repacked, I only needed two bags. I put the other bag in the garbage for disposal. Just a minute. I'll get the garbage bag.
JOHN LEE:
He stands there looking at their haul.
Gosh! More than $47M.
ED ROYSTON:
Brings a tear to your eye, but it's only paper going to a good home.

JOHN LEE:
Indeed, it is. Will my $5 padlock protect it for a couple of days?
ED ROYSTON:
Anyone who can only afford a $5 lock can't be hiding much.
They both laugh.
JOHN LEE:
You're still OK for the trip on Monday?
ED ROYSTON:
Sure am.
JOHN LEE:
Get some rest because we are about to have fun giving the money away.
ED ROYSTON:
Great. I was hoping to be part of that. See you at the docks.
JOHN LEE:
Bye Ed.
He follows Ed outside and waves him off. Sun sets.

47   CEMETERY CREMATORIUM   AFTERNOON
John Lee sees Lesley in the distance and waves to attract her attention.
LESLEY MASON:
Hi Grandpa.
JOHN LEE:
Hi, darling.
They embrace and link arms as they stroll.
LESLEY MASON:
You been waiting long?
JOHN LEE:
Been here about an hour. Had to dispose of some garbage first. That's one good thing about this place, clean way to get rid of domestic waste.
LESLEY MASON:
You don't … do you?
JOHN LEE:
Yes, hon. Sorry to shock you, but I can't waste such good burners.
LESLEY MASON:
You're incorrigible. Grandpa, I'm worried about you. Something Ron almost said the night of your birthday.

JOHN LEE:

You're worried about something that was almost said to you?

LESLEY MASON:

It sounds silly, but yes. We were dining at that favourite restaurant of yours.

JOHN LEE:

ROB'S?

LESLEY MASON:

Yes. Rob sends his best wishes.

JOHN LEE:

Lovely fellow. Tells outrageous stories. Hard to believe some of them.

LESLEY MASON:

Well, Ron started asking questions about your little hospital friends. He never actually got started because I lost it there in the middle of the restaurant and created a bit of a scene. He sort of implied that there is a connection between your group and that dreadful robbery outside of Dallas. He slept on the couch that night. Came to his senses.

JOHN LEE:

What an extraordinary association.

LESLEY MASON:

Gave him both barrels. He won't mention it again to me or anyone. He's been so lovely since. Keeps giving me flowers. I must be a bit of a shrew!

JOHN LEE:

Somehow, I don't think so.

Long pause as they walk.

He really is a fine young man. I'd be proud to have him as a son.

LESLEY MASON:

Grandpa! Are you pushing me into wedding Ron?

JOHN LEE:

Heavens no! But the idea of you marrying him would make me very proud. And being present would be a bonus.

LESLEY MASON:

I secretly hope for both of those things.

JOHN LEE:

As far as this other nonsense is concerned, don't pay it any heed. I was young and enthusiastic like him once, and while it sounds patronising from an old fart who is on the way out....

LESLEY MASON:
Grandpa!
JOHN LEE:
It's a fact, dear that neither of us can change. Where was I? Yes. When I was young and … ambitious to carve our place in life, including our work, we sometimes let enthusiasm and ambition colour the way we see things. I don't know what Ron has in mind or why. Doesn't matter a hoot to me. But I'd put it down to youthful exuberance. I know he's a man of honour.
LESLEY MASON:
You are the most adorable and understanding person I've ever known.
She hugs the old man.
They approach the two gravesites next to each other. One is John Lee's wife, and the other his daughter, Lesley's mother. They stop and quietly look down at the markers. She places a small bunch of flowers on each grave.
They are still the best.
JOHN LEE:
Yes, they are. I sometimes wander up here on my own to talk to the girls. Tell them my troubles, what's happening with you, keeping them up to date on when I'll likely be with them. Have to imagine them talking back, but their words are always straight from the shoulder and comforting. And you, my dear, sure have all their fine qualities. You know, I was here the other day to talk to them about your dad.
LESLEY MASON:
You what!?
JOHN LEE:
I did. Needed their advice. Saw him recently, the day he turned up at your apartment. We had a long chat about a lot of things. But mainly about how he and your mum got along and why he left town. Don't know how to say all this, but the ill-feeling that I had for your father is now gone. We've made our peace. He's done things he truly regrets, and I learned that I mistreated him on a bunch of stuff. Didn't know it then, but I helped push your father away.
Tears in the old man's eyes.
Darling Les. I am so sorry for being part of the pain you've had to endure all this time.

LESLEY MASON:

Grandpa, it's not possible!

JOHN LEE:

It is, and I'm profoundly sorry. Listen, your father will always be just that. I know he loves you and regrets the lost years. He lives with the hope maybe he can be some small part of your life again. He will do anything. ... but will not force the issue.

LESLEY MASON:

You're saying I should forgive and let him back in?

JOHN LEE:

Only you can decide. What I'm saying is that maybe you could hear him, listen to what he has to say. It would be a great gift to an old man, and who knows what might happen.

They turn away from the graves and walk the path.

LESLEY MASON:

Anyone but you, Grandpa, and I would say we were going on a guilt trip.

32

KENNY FELT LESLEY WAS lucky. She had the chance to reconcile with her father. He was denied one conversation with his father that would have made all the difference to both their lives. You don't get past something like that easily. Kenny knew it was all his doing. He took his father for granted and didn't look closely enough at the man. He was paying a dear price for that mistake. Now he was toying with the idea of denying his fictional character making a similar mistake. He'd have to come back to it because other events were coming to a head.

48   MARINA AT GALVESTON   **AFTERNOON**

Many pleasure boats moored at the marina. The four men parked cars at the jetty leading to their charter. José Maria and John Lee have selected a high-speed off-shore, six-berth cruiser. $1000 per day. Top speed 45 MPH and fully optioned for a safe time in open water. The men are loading bags, provisions and fishing tackle. The last task is loading the money from John Lee's car.

MATTHEW JAMES:

Think we are all set, John Lee.

JOHN LEE:

All good, crew. Have to make one call, and then we can up anchor.

John Lee goes to the payphone at the entrance of the jetty. He rings and gets the answering machine. This device also records the number calling in.

Les, it's Grandpa. Me and the boys are leaving on our trip. We'll be three days, maybe four. I've given the Coast Guard our intended plan as insurance. We're headed due south for the 26th Parallel east of Brownsville. We'll see you at about 8am on Thursday. Love you.

He returns to the boat, they cast off the ropes and ease out of the marina.

49   SERVICE TOWN   LATE AFTERNOON

Service Town is a backwater sea village 30 miles up the coast from Galveston. A former cannery town neglected rusted buildings except for a café/diner that services the few inhabitants with fuel, food and general goods.

JOSÉ MARIA:

We'll pull up on the blind side of the cannery wharf so we can't be seen from the diner. Matt, get the bow line ready to make fast.

MATTHEW JAMES:

Yes, sir.

Matt scrambles to get ready to tie up. The boat moors, Ed gets up on the wharf and goes into the cannery building. Moments later, he returns, driving a FedEx delivery van.

Nice cover, Ed. Why FedEx?

ED ROYSTON:

Laughing.

'Cause if it's valuable cargo, you only go FedEx.

JOHN LEE:

Climbing onto the wharf.

You men are having too much fun. How about we unload fuel containers first.

They proceed to carry a number of full fuel containers from the van to the boat.

MATTHEW JAMES:

José, why the extra fuel? Haven't we got enough onboard?

JOSÉ MARIA:

We do have plenty, but we are about to do a lot of extra miles, and we don't want to show unaccounted fuel use.

MATTHEW JAMES:

Thinking, thinking, always thinking.

ED ROYSTON:

You bet! We're getting good value from all our taxpayer military training.

JOHN LEE:

Laughing.

Keep that up, and I'll slap you in the brig! OK, the money is in the truck.

They haul the money bags into the back of the van and slam the doors.

Ed, is my carry-all bag in the van?

ED ROYSTON:

Yes, skipper, what's in it?

JOHN LEE:

Just some stuff for our ride later tonight.

Turning to José Maria.

You know the drill from here. Absolute radio silence between us. Monitor the VHF for other traffic. We meet at the agreed coordinates. You wait a maximum of three hours from our expected time of arrival, and if we don't show up for any reason, you leave. I mean it. You leave.

JOSÉ MARIA:

I understand.

JOHN LEE:

Turning to face the group.

I guess that's it.

The four men stand on the wharf, looking at each other.

MATTHEW JAMES:

This really is it?

JOSÉ MARIA:

Yes, it is!

JOHN LEE:

A solemn note enters his voice.

We now do what we set out to do, get rid of the money.

Standing rigid to his full height, he looks at each man in turn.

You are a class act, each one of you. I am proud to be part of this family.

He salutes. José reaches up and gently pulls John Lee's hand down from the salute. He embraces his skipper. Ed and Matt, in turn, join the embrace. Nothing more is said. Ed and John Lee get into the van and drive away. The other two get onto the boat and unhitch the mooring ropes, and motor away.

50   SERVICE TOWN DINER   SAME TIME

John Lee and Ed drive past the diner on their way out of town. John

Lee is driving. He stops and rings Lesley on his cell phone. There is no signal. He looks at the diner.

JOHN LEE:

I'll just be a minute, Ed. Have to ring Les.

ED ROYSTON:

Nothing wrong?

JOHN LEE:

No.

He walks into the diner. There's a payphone in a far corner. He nods to the waitress behind the counter. He has pulled a cap low on his forehead and tries not to look at anyone directly. He dials Lesley Mason's number. The answering machine clicks in.

Les, it's grandpa. Sorry, hon, but would you do me a kindness and go around to my place and put my trash can out. The collection is the day after tomorrow. I forgot. Love you.

He hangs and starts to walk out. The waitress calls to him.

WAITRESS:

Time for coffee?

JOHN LEE:

Hand across his face.

Love to but got to get to New Orleans. There will be a next time, promise.

WAITRESS:

Bye now, you take care out there. I'll hold you to the promise.

John Lee nods as he leaves. Gets in the van, and they leave.

51   LESLEY AND RON'S APARTMENT   SAME TIME

Ron enters the apartment as John Lee hangs up. Ron hears the click of the answering machine and moves to check it. There are two messages. The first one says they are leaving the jetty in Galveston. He listens to the later message and thinks nothing of it until he realises that the displayed caller number is a landline.

RON BEAUMONT:

That's odd. How come a landline number when he's supposed to be at sea? It should be a cell number.

He pauses to think.

John Lee should be well out to sea, but he's calling from somewhere else.

He rings the displayed number.
WAITRESS:
Hello. Service Town Diner. How can I help you?
RON BEAUMONT:
Where did you say you are?
WAITRESS:
Service Town. You know where it is?
RON BEAUMONT:
Somewhere east of Galveston?
WAITRESS:
Well done. This could be the start of something interesting. How can I help you?
RON BEAUMONT:
Someone there just left a message for me. Didn't leave a name.
WAITRESS:
Big outfit like that, they never do.
RON BEAUMONT:
What do you mean?
WAITRESS:
Gee, Honey, FedEx, of course.
RON BEAUMONT:
FedEx?
WAITRESS:
If you keep echoing, we could go on all day.
RON BEAUMONT:
What did he look like?
WAITRESS:
FedEx uniform, tall and a limp. Didn't get his blood group.
RON BEAUMONT:
Do you know where he's headed?
WAITRESS:
Something about New Orleans. Anyway, what's your interest?

RON BEAUMONT:
I'm an FBI agent lady, so don't get sassy with me!
WAITRESS:
Oh Yeah! And I'm the FIRST LADY!
She hangs up.

RON BEAUMONT:

Still holding the handset in his hand.

John Lee as a FedEx driver. A long way from where he should be, doing goodness knows what and going to New Orleans.

Pause.

Sorry, John Lee, but you are up to no good, and I've got to find out.

He goes to his study and pulls out a map of Texas. He searches along the coast for Service Town.

There it is! About 30 miles south of the interstate and about 40 miles east of Galveston. He won't want attention and will sit on the speed limit at best. If I fang it could intercept maybe 20-30 miles this side of Baton Rouge. Ron, you're staking everything on this. Are you up for it? I have to do this.

He leaves in a hurry, jumps in his car and speeds off.

52   ABOUT 30 MILES WEST OF BATON ROUGE   NIGHT

It's after dark, and Ron spots a van in the distance ahead of him. He gets close enough to see it's a FedEx van and closer still to confirm the distinctive silhouette of the driver is John Lee. He settles back to tail the van at a safe distance.

RON BEAUMONT:

Where you going. I know it's something to do with the robbery. But what?

ED ROYSTON:

John Lee, we're really doing a good thing. Love to see it at ground level. You sure those old workers of yours still live in the area?

JOHN LEE:

No. But a lot of the offshore oil industry is supported out of Baton Rouge and down to New Orleans. We used to have a lot of heavy helicopter service work done in Baton Rouge, and our operations base was outside New Orleans. There's a good chance that some of the old crew are still there. I'm just pleased that the rest of you agreed with my request.

ED ROYSTON:

See. We're all sweetness and light when it comes to a good story.

JOHN LEE:

Stop it. You'll make me cry with all your tenderness.

ED ROYSTON:

Laughs.

JOHN LEE:

Long pause. John Lee keeps checking his rear vision mirror.

You know that one of the good things about having 20/20 vision is that when you play hide and seek, you see little things that help you catch others.

ED ROYSTON:

Where did that come from?

JOHN LEE:

I've been watching the lights of that vehicle some way behind us. My guess is that we're being followed.

ED ROYSTON:

We're what!?

JOHN LEE:

Relax. We're being followed. I don't think he knows enough to stop us. Could take a stab at who it is. Let's flush this guy out.

ED ROYSTON:

What are we going to do?

JOHN LEE:

You keep watch on the car. I'm going to indicate and pull over at the next lighted section of the road and stop for a minute. That car will pull over or pass us. If he stops, then we know. If he goes past, we will see him.

He sees an appropriate spot and pulls over to the shoulder. He watches his rear-view mirror. The trailing car's headlights go out, and nothing passes.

ED ROYSTON:

He stopped.

RON BEAUMONT:

Even nature can't be held back for too long.

He kills his lights and pulls over, and stops.

JOHN LEE:

Ed. Open your door and step out to pee nearby.

ED ROYSTON:

Well, I don't have to fake it. Needed a pit stop.

He gets out and does the business.

RON BEAUMONT:

There are two of you. Who's the second man, I wonder?

JOHN LEE:

Let's get out of here, Ed. We have a little extra work to do. Any ideas on how we might lose our tail?

ED ROYSTON:

Not out here on the open road. But when we get to Baton Rouge, follow my directions and ask no questions.

JOHN LEE:

You're in charge.

53   BATON ROUGE   **NIGHT**

John Lee and Ed Royston are driving through Baton Rouge.

JOHN LEE:

Which way now?

ED ROYSTON:

Take the next left go three blocks, and turn right. You will see.

JOHN LEE:

He still with us?

ED ROYSTON:

You bet. After the right turn, you'll see the entrance to the Baton Rouge FedEx Depot.

JOHN LEE:

Haha, hiding a tree in a forest.

ED ROYSTON:

C…O…R…R…E…C…T.

They pull into the FedEx depot with similar vans coming and going. There is also a large back lot of unattended vehicles: the place from which Ed borrowed their van. They mingle with the FedEx traffic and drive out the opposite side of the site to where they came in. Ron stops at the entry to the Depot and looks at all the same vans moving in and out.

RON BEAUMONT:

Damn! Damn! Damn! NO! YOU'RE NOT GETTING AWAY!

He drives into and around the depot site looking for his quarry. John Lee and Ed have long gone.

JOHN LEE:

OK, next stop Coulter Airport. 10 minutes for our ride out of here.

54   COULTER AIRPORT BATON ROUGE   NIGHT

Their van quietly pulls into a darkened area of the airport movement area.

JOHN LEE:

Good. Security here has not improved.

ED ROYSTON:

Actually, non-existent at this time of night.

JOHN LEE:

That about sums it up. Now… where's our ride? Let's get out and check those birds over there.

In the darkness, John Lee points to a row of helicopters. He climbs in and out of several until he gets into an aged Bell-UH1. He sits down and picks up the service paperwork lying on one of the seats.

Think our luck is going to hold, Ed. It's rigged as a workhorse. Has modern GPS equipment. Just had a major overhaul and was cleared to fly.

Looks at the paperwork.

Tanks have even been filled.

ED ROYSTON:

Great! Can we load up and get out of here?

JOHN LEE:

Push the bags out of the van. I'll load up while you ditch the van. Must disable the cockpit recorder as we planned. Take the van back where you found it and be back in 30 minutes.

ED ROYSTON:

Consider it done.

Ed drives away as John Lee loads the aircraft and waits.

33

A NOISE AT THE FRONT DOOR disrupted the flow, it was the bell. This time Kenny had no idea who it might be.

"Detective Simpson. Forgive me. I'm surprised, and I hope pleased."

"Evening Kenny. Sorry, Robert. Could I have a few minutes? There have been developments to share with you."

"Yes, of course, you can, come in. I'll get the kettle going. It's alright, Kenny will do."

They moved up to the living area. Kenny sat the detective in a comfortable chair while he made coffee. Lucky he had a packet of chocolate-coated Jaffa biscuits to offer his guest, he didn't dare open the cookie jar. They sat opposite each other, and the detective started.

"Kenny, we found Siobhan's car and have arrested and charged someone. Thought you might like to know."

"My guess is this was opportunistic, and the guy… I assume the guy needed the car more than he needed to kill to get one. He just didn't care, probably because he was high or needed to get high?"

"Okay, pretty much spot on. We got CCTV footage at a servo. Police at Frankston recognised him and knew where he lived. That's where they found the car. The guy was stupid. He had no idea how to manage what he had done. When police got to the house, there were junkies everywhere, all of them spaced out. Sorry to bring it all back for you, just thought you should know."

"You know, that woman was a jewel. The butterfly tattoo on her shoulder really suited her. She had an aura about her, complex but fragile, just like the tattoo. This event changed history on so many fronts, and I'll grieve for her always even though I knew her for only a short time."

"Been interesting meeting you, Kenny. Thank you."

Paul Simpson walked out of Kenny's life that day, satisfied he'd done a good thing. He didn't see what his visit did to Kenny's day, couldn't see. After he left, Kenny felt like he'd been hit by a bus again. He was in no shape to deal with his delinquent bank robbers. On top of that, he knew with certainty what kind of a night it was going to be.

They came to him in the night, reaching out, weeping, bleeding, their faces stretched like images in warped mirrors but more frightening. Morning could not come soon enough for Kenny, and when it did, he scarpered to the shower, anxious to wash it all out of his system. Sitting on his front doorstep, second coffee of the day in hand, soaking up what warmth there was in the morning, nodding hello to passers-by, he settled enough to respond to fictional friends calling him from upstairs. He was ready for them.

55   SOMEWHERE WEST OF THE MISSISSIPPI DELTA   NIGHT

José and Matt have been going at maximum speed to get to the rendezvous point. Matt is not an experienced sailor and is violently seasick.

JOSÉ MARIA:
How are you down there?

MATTHEW JAMES:
Moaning.
Didn't think I'd ever say it, but … Let me die, please.

JOSÉ MARIA:
Come on, Matt, can't be that bad.

MATTHEW JAMES:
Would you care to swap places? Will we make it on time?

JOSÉ MARIA:
We're doing very well. Will be close, but I'm getting confident.

MATTHEW JAMES:
Lucky you two are experts in search and rescue.

JOSÉ MARIA:
That was a long time ago. But some things you never forget, hey.

MATTHEW JAMES:
Could you please find smooth water?

JOSÉ MARIA:
I'll try.

56   COULTER AIRPORT   BATON ROUGE   NIGHT

John Lee is standing silhouetted against the helicopter as Ed walks towards him. Ed has a fake moustache and fake scar on his face.

JOHN LEE:

You ready, Ed?

ED ROYSTON:

Never been readier. The van is back where it belongs, and I swept it of all trace. Here's my little bag of trash. And yes, I sprayed it as well.

JOHN LEE:

Good man. Why the disguise?

ED ROYSTON:

Put the cab driver off. If they look for someone, it's a fella with scar and mo.

JOHN LEE:

Grinning.

Good thinking, Ed. Now, before we go, there's stuff about safety you need to know. This tether will secure you. If anything goes wrong, this is how you release it. OK?

ED ROYSTON:

Got it. Anything else?

JOHN LEE:

Yes. Put this 'chute on.

ED ROYSTON:

Parachute!?

JOHN LEE:

Yep. Don't worry. Just a precaution we always follow when flying. If we have an emergency with the helicopter, you release the tether, jump from the chopper, count to three and pull this handle hard. The rest happens by itself. I'm wearing one too.

ED ROYSTON:

Just for an emergency?

JOHN LEE:

Emergency only.

ED ROYSTON:

OK then.

JOHN LEE:

Put on these headphones so we can talk to each other.

ED ROYSTON:

All this for a joy ride!

JOHN LEE:

Get in, hook yourself up, and we're gone.

John Lee starts the engines, and slowly they take off into a moonless night.

ED ROYSTON:

You do know how to fly this thing.

JOHN LEE:

Second nature.

ED ROYSTON:

When was the last time?

JOHN LEE:

Thirteen years ago.

ED ROYSTON:

JEEESUS!

Ed grips the aircraft with one hand, saying aloud.

Undo the tether, jump, count to three and pull the handle HARD!

JOHN LEE:

Relax. It's like riding a bike.

ED ROYSTON:

Oh yeh! I got news for you. Bikes only leave the ground in ET!

SECURITY GUARD:

The sound of the helicopter taking off disturbs the slumbering guard on duty. It takes the guard a few moments to realise that all is not right, and he raises the alarm.

ED ROYSTON:

We're low enough to touch the trees.

JOHN LEE:

Flying below radars between here and New Orleans. Trying to stay hidden till we get there.

57   POLICE HEADQUARTERS   BATON ROUGE   NIGHT

Ron Beaumont is exasperated. He's been driving around in circles trying to find the FedEx van. It was useless. He walks into police headquarters and asks to see the officer in charge. He is shown into an outer office. The inner office door opens, and he hears part of a telephone conversation.

OFFICER IN CHARGE:

Don't tell me what you can't do. Tell me something you can do. I don't care. Someone has stolen a helicopter in my jurisdiction, and you tell me it's trying to evade radar detection. You think New Orleans. Can't your goddam toys tell you for sure where it's heading? Call me as soon as you can tell.

Slams the phone.

Damn the FAA. Public servants!!

Looking up as Ron stands in the doorway.

WHAT DO YOU WANT! CAN'T YOU SEE I'M BUSY!

RON BEAUMONT:

Holding up his credentials.

FBI Agent, Ron Beaumont. Think I can help.

OFFICER IN CHARGE:

Well, FBI Agent RON BEAUMONT: Spit it out. Haven't got all day.

RON BEAUMONT:

I'm tracking suspects in the FARGOSAFE job. Tracked them this far tonight but lost them.

OFFICER IN CHARGE:

Tell me something new about the FBI.

RON BEAUMONT:

Based only on a hunch, he says with authority.

My targets are the men in your stolen helicopter. I believe they are transporting the loot to New Orleans.

OFFICER IN CHARGE:

Slumping in his chair and taking a deep breath.

How can I help?

RON BEAUMONT:

Get me to New Orleans, and fast.

OFFICER IN CHARGE:

Picking up the phone.

Chuck, is that evaluation helicopter we've got gassed ready to go? Get it cranked up. I'm sending an FBI Agent out. Do whatever he wants.

A young police officer enters the room.

YES!

YOUNG POLICE OFFICER:

Sir, we've just had a message that the stolen helicopter is circling the suburbs of New Orleans. One report has them throwing money out the door.

OFFICER IN CHARGE:
W…H…A…T!!!

RON BEAUMONT:
Running to the helicopter for his ride to New Orleans. Ron belts up and puts on headphones.
Let's go.

58   AIRSPACE OVER NEW ORLEANS SUBURBS   NIGHT

John Lee is swooping and circling over the worker suburbs of New Orleans. Ed is in the rear, breaking open the bags and tossing bundles of money into the air. Most of the bundles break open into loose notes as they hit wash from the main rotor. John Lee gets constant radio calls from Air Traffic Control that he is in restricted air space and must land immediately.

JOHN LEE:
Laughing in pure delight.
This sort of flying could get me banned for life. Having fun, Ed?

ED ROYSTON:
Never thrown money away like this before. Sooo much fun. About ten more minutes should see the job done. I get tired quickly these days.

JOHN LEE:
You'll be fine, buddy. You're doing just fine.

At a time most people are in bed, the air above New Orleans is filled with money like confetti. There are screams of delight in the streets. House lights flick on, and people stumble outdoors. Swarms of people are picking up money from all kinds of locations.

MINISTER IN CHURCH:
Overnight vigil to raise money for homeless families.
And friends, if you pray hard enough, the Lord will provide. Our homeless families are numbered among the needy and the meek who are meant to inherit the earth. The Lord will not let them down….

YOUNG WOMAN CONGREGATION MEMBER:
Opening the main door, she runs down the aisle. Her hands are full of money.
PASTOR…… PASTOR…. The Lord has answered. It's raining money.

MINISTER IN CHURCH:
He looks up and sees money floating past the windows.
Praise the Lord! …. Praise the Lord!
YOUNG WOMAN IN STREET:
Walking arm in arm with her boyfriend.
If I could have any wish, it would be to have enough money for you to have your teeth straightened the way you want.

YOUNG MAN IN STREET:
Arm in arm with girlfriend. Horrible set of front teeth. Looks up, sees money.
I'm gonna marry you. You're the best wisher around.
BAG LADY WITH TROLLEY:
Dressed in rag clothing and pushing her worldly possessions. Talking to herself and looking down.
Damn world. Came to New Orleans from Mississippi as a good-looking young girl. The streets are paved with gold, they said. Baloney. Look at me.
She pauses as she steps onto an area of pavement covered with money.
Wow! I guess we're off the gold standard.
MAN UNDER CAR:
An elderly man in worn-out overalls is working under a dilapidated car in his driveway.
What a man has to do to make a few dollars. Buy wrecks, fix 'em, sell 'em. No God in my world.
He hears a terrible thud on the roof of the car. He slides out from under the car, stands up and looks at the roof. There in a large indentation is a large bundle of money. He grabs it with both hands and looks skyward.
Sorry Lord. Man, there really is a GOD!
As he speaks, he turns to show the worn-out logo of 2GEEAIR on his back.

59   RON BEAUMONT IN POLICE HELICOPTER   NIGHT
RON BEAUMONT:
Speaking to pilot.
How fast can you go?

PILOT:

We're maxed. Won't take long. This is a special high-speed unit. Sit back and enjoy the ride.

RON BEAUMONT:

Picking up his cell phone, he calls Glover.

Hello sir.

SPECIAL AGENT GLOVER:

Speak up, there's dreadful background noise. What is it?

RON BEAUMONT:

Helicopter, sir. I've tracked the FARGOSAFE money. I've sort of commandeered a police helicopter from Baton Rouge, and I'm heading for New Orleans.

SPECIAL AGENT GLOVER:

Beaumont, what on earth is going on?

RON BEAUMONT:

THE FARGOSAFE MONEY'S IN NEW ORLEANS!!!

SPECIAL AGENT GLOVER:

Where, in New Orleans?

RON BEAUMONT:

ALL OVER IT!!!

SPECIAL AGENT GLOVER:

You certain of this Ron?

RON BEAUMONT:

Two of the gang and all the money. They're throwing it from a helicopter.

SPECIAL AGENT GLOVER:

Ron, you have my complete authority to act as you see fit. I'm ringing New Orleans office for backup. You're the lead officer until I get there. Don't know how you've done this, but well done. Get me my outlaws Ron!

RON BEAUMONT:

Thank you, sir. Yes, sir!

He hangs up, feeling good about himself. He speaks to the pilot.

How much longer?

PILOT:

We have a speed advantage, and we will catch them.

He takes a radio call and relays the message to Ron.

Two local police choppers have been scrambled and are closing in on our target as we speak.

RON BEAUMONT:
Speaking to himself.
Sorry Les, but this time I have to take John Lee down.

60   AIRSPACE OVER NEW ORLEANS SUBURBS   NIGHT
Ed has almost finished throwing money out of the helicopter.
JOHN LEE:
How much longer, Ed?
ED ROYSTON:
That's it, skipper. All gone.
JOHN LEE:
Good, because we've got company. If I'm not mistaken, we've got police helicopters on either side, another coming from the rear.
He checks the radio frequency and starts to get calls from the police for him to land immediately.
It's OK, Ed. They're not allowed to shoot civilian aircraft down just yet.
ED ROYSTON:
If you say so. What do you want me to do?
JOHN LEE:
Make yourself comfortable. We're heading for open water and home.
ED ROYSTON:
What about the police?
JOHN LEE:
Back in Baton Rouge, I trusted you. Now it's your turn to trust me.

61   AIRSPACE OVER DELTA COMPANY   NIGHT
Inside police helicopter.
RON BEAUMONT:
Talking to pilot.
I see what you mean about speed. This baby flies.
PILOT:
Yes, sir. She does.
RON BEAUMONT:
How are the two local choppers going?
PILOT:
Been monitoring them. They know we're on the way and waiting

for us to be vectored to intercept. They're running low on fuel and will have to abandon the chase soon as we meet. That will be a few minutes. We will pick up the target about 30 miles southeast of New Orleans. After that, it's up to you.

RON BEAUMONT:

Good, It's down to me.

PILOT:

See the strobe light up ahead. You can talk directly to the chase choppers.

RON BEAUMONT:

Talking to New Orleans police helicopters.

This is FBI Agent Ron Beaumont. Thank you, gentlemen. Your efforts are much appreciated. Safe journey home.

The two helicopters break off the chase and head for home.

JOHN LEE:

Monitoring the police frequency.

It was Ron. He knows. But maybe the old dogs have a surprise or two yet.

ED ROYSTON:

What was that about Ron?

JOHN LEE:

It was Ron tailing us on the highway. Now he's in the chopper behind us.

ED ROYSTON:

You're right. Two helicopters are flying away. A third is behind us.

RON BEAUMONT:

This is FBI Agent Ron Beaumont. I know it's you, John Lee. Please return to New Orleans and land. You cannot get away. I have orders to do whatever it takes to make you land. Please acknowledge? Please acknowledge?

JOHN LEE:

Speaking to himself.

Sorry Ron. No talking, no way. My winning move is not to play. We'll shake them soon, very, very soon. We're getting within range of the rendezvous point.

He checks a map with current GPS coordinates. He punches in numbers and watches the timer on the display run down from 4 minutes and 50 seconds. Sets his stopwatch to match. He activates the autopilot and places a small package under his seat. He returns to where Ed is standing.

You OK?

ED ROYSTON:

Who's flying this thing?

JOHN LEE:

Relax, autopilot. Now repeat the parachute drill just in case you need it.

ED ROYSTON:

Jump, count to three and pull the handle hard.

JOHN LEE:

Good.

In that instant, the stopwatch sounder activated. He detaches the tether securing Ed to the helicopter and, with a shove, sends him into free space. John Lee follows. The parachutes were military issue and black. The chase helicopter saw nothing of the men escaping.

ED ROYSTON:

Screaming as he realises after a split second, he's in total darkness and rushing towards the ocean.

ONE … PULL THE CHORD!

The canopy blossoms above him.

JOHN LEE:

Opens his parachute. He waits for the sounds of the two helicopters above him to disappear before he yells out to Ed.

ED … ED! CAN YOU HEAR ME?

RON BEAUMONT:

Speaking to pilot.

What's he doing?

PILOT:

I'm not certain, but he's made a lazy turn towards the Florida coast. He changed his heading gently from about 15 minutes ago. He's probably going to Tampa. Must think he can make it. He hasn't got enough fuel for that.

RON BEAUMONT:

Would you contact Tampa and request FBI aerial support from there?

PILOT:

Yes, sir. While I'm at it, our own fuel situation is nearing a point where we have to consider going home. We've got about 10 more minutes.

RON BEAUMONT:
Take us as far as you can.

ED ROYSTON:
Dangling from his parachute as they fall towards the water.
ONLY IN EMERGENCY, YOU SAID!

JOHN LEE:
IT WAS! THE ONLY WAY OUT!

ED ROYSTON:
I MAY NEVER FORGIVE YOU!

JOHN LEE:
I'LL TAKE THAT RISK! ED! WHEN YOU HIT THE WATER, PULL THE HANDLE ON YOUR RIGHT SHOULDER! IT WILL RELEASE THE PARACHUTE CANOPY AND INFLATE YOUR LIFE PRESERVER!

ED ROYSTON:
ONLY IN AN EMERGENCY?

JOHN LEE:
IF YOU DON'T, IT WILL BE!

PILOT:
Sir, we'll have to break off in two minutes.
As he spoke, a huge fireball erupted in front of him. The lead helicopter was no more. To himself.
Un-survivable.

RON BEAUMONT:
Shocked at the scene before him.
What the …

PILOT:
That is a catastrophic failure. Your bad guys are dead, and we're out of here. BRAVO ROMEO TO NEW ORLEANS CONTROL. BE ADVISED THAT ROGUE HELICOPTER IS DOWN. Two occupants … likely no survivors … We're low on fuel and returning to base. Accident coordinates are …

RON BEAUMONT:
To himself.
How on earth am I going to tell her this?

PILOT:
What's that sir?

RON BEAUMONT:
Nothing, nothing at all.

John Lee and Ed hit the water not 50 yards apart.

JOHN LEE:
Ed. You alright?
ED ROYSTON:
If you call bobbing around in the middle of the Gulf on a dark night alright, then I'm alright.
JOHN LEE:
Swimming towards Ed's voice and waving a chemical light tube.
Good, you haven't lost your sense of humour. Now, reach into your vest and activate the chemical light tube.
Pause, waiting for Ed.
Good, Ed. Now, if only the other two could see the both of us.

62   GULF WATERS SOUTH OF THE DELTA   NIGHT
José Maria and Matt have been standing quietly in the rear of the boat with the motor off and listening for signs.
JOSÉ MARIA:
ED! DID I HEAR YOU WONDER WHERE WE ARE?
ED ROYSTON:
WHERE ARE YOU?
JOSÉ MARIA:
ABOUT 100 YARDS AWAY! HOLD TIGHT.
He motors carefully towards the voice.

ED ROYSTON:
Clambering aboard.
Thank you for saving me from being fish food.
MATTHEW JAMES:
In the moment, his sickness vanishes.
Fish would spit you out.
JOHN LEE:
Permission to come aboard?
JOSÉ MARIA:
Permission granted.
JOHN LEE:
Clambering aboard.
Don't you just love GPS?

JOSÉ MARIA:
What a rush. We could not have done better. Almost forgot I am old.
MATTHEW JAMES:
Coffee gentlemen?
ED ROYSTON:
No way! Jack Daniels and plenty of it.
JOHN LEE:
Turning to José Maria.
What do you think, skipper?

JOSÉ MARIA:
After I engage the auto navigation and stoke the motors, I think a bottle each would be about the right measure.
The four men throw their arms around one another tight with an overwhelming sense of achievement.

34

KENNY STOPPED, stretched his fingers, and leaned back in the chair, staring in amazement at what he'd just done. Clearly, his immersion in air force culture had equipped him better than he could've thought. John Lee's brazen and highly skilled flying was embedded in Kenny's subconscious and came to the front just when needed. His phone disturbed the reverie. He leaned over to answer. Hanna.

"Caught me dreaming Mac. You're OK, I take it?"

"Sorry to disturb you but glad you're home. My question is about inspecting the Chinese Gulfstream. They're in town today and tomorrow, and we're flying with them back to Singapore, leaving on Thursday and coming back Monday. I've offered your services for those flights. Hope you're still Ok about the job."

"You're coming?"

"You can't shake me, brother. If you have the time, we can look over the aircraft any time later today. I'll pick you up if you want."

"Caught me at the right time, Mac. I'll be here."

"I'll see you about two this afternoon."

"They're happy for me to do a couple of circuits to check out the plane's quirks?"

"I'll arrange clearance. They want to meet you anyway, even though I've shown them the paperwork you gave me. Thanks for this, brother. See you later."

"Yep, bye."

It was a big moment for Kenny sitting at the controls of a commercial jet. Beside him was the company's chief pilot, another former Air Force flyer formerly of the RAF, Captain James Barry. Clearance had been arranged for a return flight to Phillip Island.

"Robert, no surprises here, so you're welcome to the controls. Keen to know what you think of her. Few little quirks, as in every aircraft, but easily managed. See what you think."

Kenny acknowledged the captain's generosity and slipped immediately into a well-worn routine of pre-flight checks. He'd already completed a walk-round check of the outer surfaces. He followed that up with a thorough check of controls, gauges, fuel and engines. Then, they were off with the blessing of the control tower.

"You haven't forgotten anything, Robert. Smooth as silk. Your high recommendation was well deserved."

"Would be disappointed if you'd not checked, James. I've done enough hours to keep up the endorsements, so I'm quite comfortable. Have to do jobs in civvie street to pay for them but still love adrenalin. I wouldn't take any shortcuts, especially with my sister as a passenger. I'll do this trip with you then you can decide about further adventures. There's a slight pause between asking for acceleration and getting it, the rudder is lightning quick. Still, otherwise, this is a sweet aeroplane."

"Of course. We should be good. Looking forward to the company."

There was one issue lingering in Kenny's mind. People who got close to him were in danger. Siobhan was the last one, and he didn't want his sister to be next. This flying commitment had better turn out safely for her. No way he could sustain anything happening to her. The job had his complete attention, especially for this reason. No way would he roll the dice a second time. He'd tell her this later.

That night Hanna arrived with the architect, his assistant and the business partners. After departure formalities, the party left Melbourne on a direct flight to Singapore. Kenny, ace pilot, was doing what he was trained for, flying. Compared to military missions, this trip was a piece of cake. When he was tired, his companion took over and vice versa. It was a comfortable job. Hanna had done well for her brother, and he was giving her his best.

By the time they returned to Essendon three days later, they were both satisfied and exhausted, each for their own reasons. When Kenny walked through his front door, he headed straight for the cookie jar and then directly to bed.

When Hanna walked into her apartment, she was hijacked by a gang of three, excited to see her. Her visitors were to stay the night, having prepared a little banquet to welcome her home. At another time, Hanna would not have been impressed with the take-over of her personal space. But walking into the warmest of welcomes from people she had come to care about was different. She dropped her bag and gave herself to them - a taste of what family might have been like. At the end of the festivities, when her guests slipped off to bed, Hanna finished reassembling the kitchen, poured herself an aged French cognac and with the balloon in hand, she snuck in to see how they were faring. When she cracked the door open and peeked, the three were in the same bed, open picture book on the floor, Mark pinned in the middle, all fast asleep. Hanna quietly back-stepped to her own space. A thought about pecking order crept in, but she gave it no oxygen, savoured the last sip, set the glass on the bedside table and drifted off to sleep.

Kenny had not wasted downtime sitting as a co-pilot. He had to keep the story's momentum going. Now four of them were together on the boat heading for Galveston, they were about to confront a stressed leading investigator intent on presenting closure to the whole nation on live TV. He need not have worried, they were well prepared. All Kenny had to do was write. He did, having rested his obsession for three days.

35

63   FBI OFFICES – NEW ORLEANS   **MORNING**

The team has assembled.

SPECIAL AGENT GLOVER:

Just look at the news coverage. Somehow, I have to face the TODAY show in an hour, under the Director's personal orders and put some spin on this fiasco. Gentlemen, we have just lost more money than we can dream of, the media is celebrating the re-emergence of Robin Hood at our expense. There are thousands of happy and dishonest people in New Orleans refusing to give back that which is not rightfully theirs. We've seen a $3M helicopter destroyed, we are no closer to being able to prove the identities of the perps, we do not have a single recorded transmission from the helicopter. We've got two dead bad guys scattered in pieces along with any other pieces of evidence in the Gulf of Mexico. HAVE I MISSED ANYTHING?

Long pause.

THIS CASE WILL COST CAREERS, AND IF I GO, SO WILL OTHERS! THE HEADLINES ARE HAILING THESE OUTLAWS AS MODERN-DAY HEROES, AND WE LOOK LIKE BACKWATER HICKS. BEAUMONT, WHY DIDN'T YOU TAKE THE SHOT? YOU WERE IN CHARGE.

RON BEAUMONT:

Sir, that's illegal.

SPECIAL AGENT GLOVER:

I DON'T CARE!!!

RON BEAUMONT:

Sir, may I speak?

SPECIAL AGENT GLOVER:

This better be good, very, very good!

RON BEAUMONT:

We still have the other two on the water somewhere. Why not pull them in and give them the third degree.

SPECIAL AGENT GLOVER:

PULL THEM IN? I DON'T CARE IF YOU PULL OUT THEIR FINGERNAILS! I WANT SOMEONE, AND I DON'T CARE WHO IT IS!!

64   FBI BUILDING NEW ORLEANS   MORNING

Ron decides to ring Lesley to inform her about John Lee.

RON BEAUMONT:

The phone rings several times, and she answers.

Hi, hon.

LESLEY MASON:

Where are you? You didn't come home, been a bit worried.

RON BEAUMONT:

New Orleans. I'll be back later today. Sorry for not calling, but it's been a very hectic night. That's why I'm ringing now.

LESLEY MASON:

You sound so serious, what is it?

RON BEAUMONT:

It's John Lee. We believe he is involved in the robbery, and he's missing after a helicopter accident. The one in the news this morning.

LESLEY MASON:

Don't be silly. That's connected to your robbery. He's out fishing on the Gulf with the others. Hasn't been in a helicopter for years.

RON BEAUMONT:

Even so, we think....

LESLEY MASON:

RON! We've been down this road before, and I thought you'd given up your silly idea. Seems not. Don't say any more, I don't want to hear it. John Lee is fishing, that's all there is to it. You just get your act together and apologise to my grandpa when he gets home. Or else we are finished!

RON BEAUMONT:

OK. I hear you. See you when I get back. One thing, would you keep your answering machine tape for me?

LESLEY MASON:

Is this another stupid trick? If so, it's in very poor taste!

RON BEAUMONT:

Why?

LESLEY MASON:

I don't care why! The tape is now blank! Goodbye!

65   IN THE GULF OF MEXICO   MORNING

The Stingray is speeding to a location on the 26th parallel.

JOSÉ MARIA:

Ed. Can you and Matt empty the remaining fuel from those containers into the tanks?

ED ROYSTON:

Sure thing. Anything else?

JOSÉ MARIA:

Yes. Collect all the empty containers and anything from the chopper ride and bag it up. We'll commit them to a deep-water grave as soon as you're done.

JOHN LEE:

Standing at the helm with José Maria. The other two are working.

Any trouble with radio calls to the Coast Guard regarding positioning?

JOSÉ MARIA:

None at all. Everything is normal.

JOHN LEE:

Shame Ron has been caught up in this. Hope his career is safe.

JOSÉ MARIA:

You can relax on that one. From what we know, he's probably the only one who's had any sort of clue about what's been going on. And he's a rookie.

JOHN LEE:

Wonder how we alerted him. We were pretty methodical. Got me puzzled.

JOSÉ MARIA:

Beats me too. We must have slipped up somewhere. If they had anything concrete, we would've been yanked off the street before now.

JOHN LEE:

Rubbing his chin.

That makes sense.

JOSÉ MARIA:

I was monitoring the VHF for your flight. You didn't answer one call.

JOHN LEE:

Mission rules, hey. Old habits kick in. How did you go with the GPS?

JOSÉ MARIA:

All sorted. Our little black box shows us bobbing on fishing grounds well away from what you were doing.

JOHN LEE:

You're still a gun officer.

JOSÉ MARIA:

Thank you. Now, if the FBI thinks you are dead, they will turn on Matt and me.

JOHN LEE:

How long before we're in a safe position?

JOSÉ MARIA:

Given current speed and conditions, ... I'd say about an hour.

COAST GUARD GALVESTON:

This is Galveston Coast Guard calling motor vessel Stingray... come in.

Galveston Coast Guard calling motor vessel Stingray... please come in.

JOHN LEE:

What do you think?

JOSÉ MARIA:

They're onto us. I'll have to answer.

Picking up the microphone.

Coast Guard Galveston ... this is Stingray.. please go ahead.

COAST GUARD GALVESTON:

Stingray... please report your position and heading.

JOSÉ MARIA:

This is Stingray... position, approximately 250 miles southeast of Galveston... currently drift fishing. You have a problem?

COAST GUARD GALVESTON:

No Stingray... no problem... just doing radio checks on vessels in the area. We've had hoax distress calls... just confirming known boats in the area.

JOSÉ MARIA:

This is Stingray... good idea, Coast Guard. We've heard zero. Can we help?

COAST GUARD GALVESTON:
Coast Guard Galveston... No Stingray, no assistance required. Would you confirm your ETA at Galveston?

JOSÉ MARIA:
This is Stingray.... As advised... approximately early morning, Thursday.

COAST GUARD GALVESTON:
Coast Guard Galveston... thank you, Stingray... Out.

JOSÉ MARIA:
Stingray out.... They'll be waiting.

JOHN LEE:
For sure. That's what we'd do. And they'll send a chopper to casually cruise past at a distance over the next couple of days and see if we are running for Mexico. Let's catch some fish.

JOSÉ MARIA:
We sure will. And they'll be beauties!!

66   FBI OFFICES-HOUSTON   MORNING NEXT DAY

Glover has called a briefing of the team to examine their status on the case.

SPECIAL AGENT GLOVER:
Gentlemen. I apologise for the outburst in New Orleans, but this case is shaping up as the biggest public relations disaster since J. Edgar was discovered wearing a dress at the Plaza Hotel.

Pause

Somehow these criminals have turned the table on authority by becoming celebrated heroes. I realise it's hard to believe, but unless we get our next move right.... You will be getting new leadership.

FBI OFFICER:
They wouldn't fire you!

SPECIAL AGENT GLOVER:
No, not that. But they've already asked what I think of going to Iowa.

Pauses and looks at the men.

While I still can, I'd like to acknowledge our rookie, Ron... Stand up.

Ron stands up... Glover continues.

Your persistence led us to the money. However, two perps... one being John Lee Calhoun and an unknown other, are dead. Two more accomplices are on a boat in the Gulf of Mexico. They're being monitored. We assume something went wrong with their plans. We'll arrest these two on suspicion of the robbery as soon as they dock. We will hold them until they confess. They're old and terminally ill, how hard can it be to crack them?

Pause.

The Director in Washington has agreed for the TODAY show to cover the arrest live. We'll not be informing any other media. You will mention none of this to anyone until after the arrest. Am I clear!!

67   MARINA AT GALVESTON   APPROX. 8:50 am THURSDAY

Stingray is in the harbour, preparing to dock. José Maria and Matt can be seen from the jetty. The jetty has been closed, but the FBI, local police and vehicles are parked nearby. Glover, Ron and other FBI officers are on the jetty, each one wearing distinctive FBI jackets. A television crew and reporter are standing behind the police.

RON BEAUMONT:

Talking to Glover.

The helmsman is José Maria Orlando, and the man on the bow is Matthew Jesse James.

SPECIAL AGENT GLOVER:

Nods acknowledgement. Pause. Matt throws a rope to one of the officers, and the boat is made fast. Glover steps up to the boat. The cameras roll.

68   ROADSIDE DINER   SAME TIME

The same roadside diner where Ed and Matt ate breakfast after the robbery. Three late-middle-aged people are enjoying breakfast at the counter. The TV is on when their attention is turned by the presenter on the TODAY show. The owner moves to turn up the volume.

TODAY SHOW PRESENTER:

We cross now to an exclusive and breaking major story in Galveston, Texas. The FBI have identified the suspects in the Robin Hood Gang or the Mardi Gras Bandits as they're now being called. An arrest is about to happen. We understand that the other two men in the gang were killed in a helicopter crash after their celebrated disposal of the robbery money. We have been asked not to release the names of the victims at this time.

Our reporter on the scene is Jill Anderson from local affiliate KYTX.

Good morning Jill.

JILL ANDERSON:

Good morning America. We are standing on the jetty at the Galveston Marina as the boat you can see, the Stingray is mooring. I'll get a little closer so we can hear what happens next.

SPECIAL AGENT GLOVER:

Are you José Maria Orlando and you, Matthew Jesse James?

JOSÉ MARIA:

That is us.

SPECIAL AGENT GLOVER:

You are under arrest on suspicion of the Dallas FARGOSAFE robbery. Gentlemen, cuff them and read them their rights.

TODAY SHOW PRESENTER:

Jill, can you hear me? They look like elderly men!

JILL ANDERSON:

That's right. They are. Hold on, something else is happening. There are two other old men on the boat… coming out of the cabin. They seem to be… Yes, they are… they're carrying large fish.

SPECIAL AGENT GLOVER:

Who the hell are you two?

JOHN LEE:

John Lee Calhoun, sir and my friend here is Ed Royston.

Looking over to Ron.

Hi Ron.

RON BEAUMONT:

Er… you're supposed to be…. 'mornin John Lee.

JOHN LEE:

What's this all about?

Having trouble climbing out of the boat, extends one of the fish to Glover.

Would you hold this for me? Thank you.

SPECIAL AGENT GLOVER:

Impulsively takes the fish, and the image of him holding a fish beside four old cuffed men is beamed nationwide.

What's going on here?

Suddenly aware of the camera, he turns.

Get rid of that damn camera. I want to know…. Beaumont! What's happening here.

JILL ANDERSON:

From a safe distance with much commotion among the men on the jetty in the background.

I am not quite certain what we have witnessed, but the FBI seems to think at least two old men are the Mardi Gras Bandits. They told us there would only be two. However, it seems that two other elderly men identified as the alleged victims of the helicopter crash are similarly frail but decidedly alive. This is very confusing.

TODAY SHOW PRESENTER:

Grinning.

At least they're chasing bad guys who can't outrun them. Jill, that was a lovely fish the FBI officer was holding.

JILL ANDERSON:

Giggling.

They always get the big fish.

TODAY SHOW PRESENTER:

Laughing.

That was Jill Anderson in Galveston. This is TODAY, back in a moment.

DINER OWNER:

Turning to his customers.

I don't believe it! Two of those good old boys had breakfast here the morning after the robbery! A fine pair of Texas boys.

CUSTOMER #1:

You think they did it?

DINER OWNER:

They had a powerful big appetite. Said they'd had a long night on the road seeing the country.

Pausing.

Hope they did. Giving that money to ordinary folk is the best news since V-Day.

CUSTOMER#2:

Good to see wrinklies doing this sort of stuff. Gives a man reason to think.

I reckon I might go fishing myself… More coffee, please, with a shot!

69   MARINA AT GALVESTON   SAME TIME

The scene is chaos, with Glover screaming at the FBI team in the background. His words are indistinct. The Mardi Gras Bandits have been released and are walking along the jetty to the local police cordon. Lesley breaks through the cordon and rushes to embrace John Lee.

LESLEY MASON:

Crying and burying her face in the old man's chest.

They said you were dead... part of that robbery... I told Ron you were fishing. So glad to have you back safe.

JOHN LEE:

Seems we caused a bit of a ruckus. Dangerous stuff this fishing, if you get receptions like this. Why they picked on us, I'll never know.

JOSÉ MARIA:

Grinning.

At least they let us go when they'd realised they had nothing more than four old men on a fishing trip. If they wanted fish, they only had to ask.

LESLEY MASON:

Grandpa? What am I going to do with this man of mine? ... and his foolish notions about you and robberies?

JOHN LEE:

Honey. Follow your heart and your dreams. The rest just happens. I'm starved, why don't we go somewhere for breakfast. Why don't you ask Ron?

LESLEY MASON:

Looking back at the jetty.

I don't think he's in the mood right now.

Men on the jetty are still yelling and flailing arms.

70   ROYSTON APARTMENT   TWO MONTHS LATER

Ed is reclining in his favourite chair, watching a video. It's the Old Liberty Valance movie with John Wayne, Jimmy Stewart and Lee Marvin.

ED ROYSTON:

Maybe if I watch this enough, John Wayne will eventually get the girl. He keeps making the same mistakes. Great movie. Funny how the Duke lets Jimmy take the credit for the killing. Jimmy even built a political career on his own legend. But there's always someone who knows the truth.

The phone rings. He ignores it at first until its persistence forces him to stop the video and answer it.

Yes. This is Ed Royston. Yes … Yes … Oh no! When? Are you sure? What should I do? Alright.

Ashen faced at the news, he slumps back into his recliner chair. He picks up the phone and rings Matthew. The phone rings.

MATTHEW JAMES:

Hello.

ED ROYSTON:

Thank God you're there.

MATTHEW JAMES:

What is it?

ED ROYSTON:

I've just been given some shocking news.

MATTHEW JAMES:

Are the others OK?

ED ROYSTON:

Far as I know. We're all still alive. It's worse than that. After all this time…

I don't want to tell them just yet. Can you come over? We have to talk.

MATTHEW JAMES:

On the way.

ED ROYSTON:

He hangs up the phone and steadies himself.

71   ROYSTON APARTMENT   THREE HOURS LATER

Ed and Matt are seated at the kitchen table. Half-eaten food, empty glasses and coffee cups are spread around. They've been talking.

MATTHEW JAMES:

Well, that's it. That's what we have to do.

ED ROYSTON:

Do you think they'll hate me for having done this?

MATTHEW JAMES:

Well, I'm one of the Mardi Gras Four, and I don't hate you, why would they?

ED ROYSTON:

If you say so. What about the final party? Is it really the right thing?

MATTHEW JAMES:

Of course, although it will be expensive.

ED ROYSTON:

I don't care about the cost. The least I can do.

Reaching under the sofa, Ed picks up a small tin box and unlocks it. It is stuffed with money.

MATTHEW JAMES:

You rob another bank, or just been holding out on us?

ED ROYSTON:

No … No … It's rainy day money, and the forecast is for a change in the weather. Here, take the lot and do what you have to. I want everyone to remember it.

MATTHEW JAMES:

Let's see. … You and I meet tomorrow to get a few things organised. I get the luxury suite at the Hyatt. Let's say three days from now. I'll ring the boys and Lesley.

ED ROYSTON:

Les?

MATTHEW JAMES:

Yes. She and Ron have a right to know. Can't do any harm now. They're the only family we have.

ED ROYSTON:

What will you tell them?

MATTHEW JAMES:

Just that it's a surprise party sponsored by you. I'll get them there, the rest is up to you.

ED ROYSTON:

OK, my friend. Let's do it.

72   HYATT HOUSTON   NIGHT

Matt and Ed are in the Presidential suite. Laid before them in the dining room is a sumptuous banquet of the finest food the Hyatt kitchen can conjure up. Plenty of liquor is available.

MATTHEW JAMES:

Well, I think this could be the most memorable party I've ever planned.

ED ROYSTON:

This is good. You must have been a stunning host in your prime.

MATTHEW JAMES:

Haughtily and laughing.

Dear man. I am still in my prime.

ED ROYSTON:

Where are the others?

MATTHEW JAMES:

As always, the team will be punctual. I said eight, and at eight, they'll arrive.

With concern.

Are you ready for later?

ED ROYSTON:

I think so.

A cab carrying Lesley and Ron approaches the Hyatt.

LESLEY MASON:

Certain you want to be here?

RON BEAUMONT:

After everything this lot has been through, I wouldn't miss a party they can ill afford in the best hotel suite in the whole of Texas. No, ma'am, I wouldn't miss this for anything.

LESLEY MASON:

You're not going to do anything silly?

RON BEAUMONT:

I've learned it's no fun rushing to ride a wild steer. Only so many times you can be thrown before you decide there are easier ways to kill yourself.

LESLEY MASON:

That is so corny. You've never even been to a rodeo. Although you have taken a few hits, some from me. Glad you've seen the error of your ways.

Knock on the door of the suite.

MATTHEW JAMES:

Goes to open the door.

Ah! José, my dear friend. Welcome to the temporary Casa de Royston.

JOSÉ MARIA:

Looking around.

If this is only the temporary one, I'd like to see the permanent one.
They all laugh.
I'm not game to ask what it costs, or will we be paying on the way out?
MATTHEW JAMES:
Enough. Ed will explain everything in a while. For now, let's have something to eat and a few good drinks.
More knocks at the door.
Ah! The beautiful girl and, may I say, the similarly splendid-to-look-at boyfriend.
LESLEY MASON:
Teasingly slapping Matt on the wrist.
Just remember, he's mine!
MATTHEW JAMES:
Story of my life. Always arrive too late for the best ones. Come in, come in.
They enter and move towards Ed and José Maria. Matt closes the door.
Your grandpa should be here any time now.
LESLEY MASON:
Good.
RON BEAUMONT:
What's the occasion?
JOSÉ MARIA:
I asked the same question.
RON BEAUMONT:
And?
JOSÉ MARIA:
And … don't know. What would you like to drink?
Another knock at the door.
LESLEY MASON:
As Matt moves to the door.
No, Matthew, allow me. It'll be Grandpa.
She opens the door to John Lee. She hugs him.
This is so mysterious. Ed won't tell us why we are here. Do you know?
JOHN LEE:
No hon. I don't.

Reaching out into the hall way he brings a man into view.

I've brought someone with me.

LESLEY MASON:

Looking stunned.

Daddy?

GRAHAM MASON:

Nervously.

Hope you don't mind me being here?

LESLEY MASON:

I.... I....

Looking at John Lee, then her father.

Think it's about time. Our recent phone calls were good, this is better.

She breaks the embrace with her grandpa and moves to hug and lightly kiss the nervous father. She takes his hand and leads him into the room.

EVERYONE! I'd like to introduce my father, Graham Mason.

John Lee stands quietly in the room, looking proud of Lesley. They mingle around introducing themselves. Much handshaking.

JOSÉ MARIA:

Speaks almost as an aside to Ron.

Think we're looking at the reason for the party. Reckon Ed and Matt have engineered this reunion.

RON BEAUMONT:

Good men.

JOSÉ MARIA:

The best.

The party is alive with conversation, eating and drinking. Lesley has her arm around her father's waist.

RON BEAUMONT:

Talking to Matt.

Matt. I need to see the bathroom. Which way?

MATTHEW JAMES:

Pointing.

Through that door, you'll find what you need.

Ron excuses himself and goes into the bathroom.

Some kings live like kings. This bathroom is worth more than our whole apartment.

He finishes, washes his hands and turns to leave. He looks at a second door leading from the bathroom.

What wonders are on the other side of this one?

He opens the door and steps into a palatial bedroom.

How the other half live! Except they're much fewer than half.

He notices a room service trolley covered by a large table cloth.

Must be a cake surprise.

He lifts the cloth to peek. Dropping the cloth, he reels back in horror. He walks back and removes the cloth. Before his eyes is a pile of money.

Oh my God! There is more than a million dollars here.

Pauses while furtively looking around.

This isn't a reunion party! These men are celebrating their haul. NOW I'M PART OF IT! Calm down, Ron … calm down. What do I do?

Pacing in circles around the money.

Don't be too eager. That's it. I won't be eager. I'll sit put. Let the hand play.

Deep breath. He replaces the cloth and re-traces his steps. He emerges from the bathroom.

LESLEY MASON:

Honey, you're back. We almost sent out a search party, Matt kept volunteering, but I stopped him.

MATTHEW JAMES:

I never did, had duty called….

ED ROYSTON:

He takes the floor.

Family. You've all been curious about tonight. True?

They all respond.

Well, Matt and I have had our heads together…. But first, please raise your glasses to Les and her father, Graham. It is wonderful to see them together.

JOHN LEE:

Hear … Hear…

ED ROYSTON:

Next, I have a surprise.

He turns and goes to the bathroom, returning with the covered trolley of money.

MATTHEW JAMES:

Wish I had a fanfare.

ED ROYSTON:

No matter.

He rips the cloth away, revealing the money. Shocked silence descends.

Well, say something!

JOHN LEE:

I should have known. Two bags, not three!

JOSÉ MARIA:

Ed…. What have you done to us?

LESLEY MASON:

Looking around at everyone.

What's going on?

RON BEAUMONT:

It's alright, hon. I know. Gentlemen, I am impounding the money and arresting you for ….

Without getting the words out, they are all stunned by the main door to the suite bursting open and a team of FBI identified men rushing in with drawn side arms. The lead officer is yelling.

FBI OFFICER:

Nobody move… nobody move.

His officers rush to the other rooms and yell CLEAR. CLEAR.

RON BEAUMONT:

Reaching into his coat pocket is seen by the FBI officer.

FBI OFFICER:

STOP OR I'LL SHOOT!

RON BEAUMONT:

Stops his hand movement.

I'M FBI OFFICER RON BEAUMONT! I'M GETTING MY ID!

FBI OFFICER:

I'M SPECIAL AGENT WARREN OF THE CHICAGO TASK FORCE!

Withdraw your hand very slowly.

RON BEAUMONT

Withdraws his ID. The officer lowers his gun.

This is my collar. I've already arrested them for the FARGOSAFE job.

FBI OFFICER:

Arrested THEM. We're not after THEM. We're after him.

Turning to Graham Mason, who is being cuffed by an officer.

RON BEAUMONT:

What's he got to do with it?

FBI OFFICER:

Graham Mason. I have a warrant for your arrest as an accessory to the Chicago armoured van robberies. Read him his rights.

LESLEY MASON:

Daddy, Daddy, is it true?

GRAHAM MASON:

Thought I was clear, but it looks like there's more penance to do.

FBI OFFICER:

We've been following his movements for months. Get him out of here.

LESLEY MASON:

As her father is led from the room.

Don't worry, Daddy. We'll fight this together.

FBI OFFICER:

Take the money as well!

ED ROYSTON:

YOU LEAVE THAT MONEY ALONE. THAT'S OURS!

RON BEAUMONT:

It is not your money at all. It's the property of FARGOSAFE. Be quiet!

FBI OFFICER:

It's robbery money from Chicago!

ED ROYSTON:

STOP!! ....STOP!! It's our money.

Standing between the money and the officers.

It's money I won in the lottery… notified only days ago.

He brandishes the lottery winning ticket and a letter from the Authority.

FBI OFFICER:

Taking the papers and reading them.

You, I take it, are Ed Royston?

FBI OFFICER:

Says here you won $19M after taxes.

Ron snatches the paper and reads it.

ED ROYSTON:

YES, IT DOES!

Calming down a little.

This money is a sample of the win. This party is a celebration to share the win with my family, John Lee, José Maria and Matthew James. We are each $4.75M richer.

RON BEAUMONT:

I don't believe it.

LESLEY MASON:

Turning to Ron and shaking her head.

What was that about riding bulls, Ron?

JOHN LEE:

I am mortified, Ed, for having doubted you.

ED ROYSTON:

Forget it John Lee. Even I slip up now and then.

MATTHEW JAMES:

As FBI officers withdraw, taking Graham Mason with them.

Come on, everyone, this is a real party now.

RON BEAUMONT:

Walking over to John Lee, standing next to the money.

I apologise, John Lee. Thought just I ......

JOSÉ MARIA:

Talking to no one in particular.

Hell of a night! And you know, Graham really is family!

JOHN LEE:

Looking directly into Ron's eyes and with his hand on the younger man's shoulder. He silently acknowledges Ron has been right all along.

RON BEAUMONT:

Sensing what he is being told.

Why?

JOHN LEE:

Y'know, Ron, it's only the question that matters. Pondering the question can take one to dizzy realisations. Any direct answer would only disappoint.

MATTHEW JAMES:

Helping Ed to secure the broken hallway door to the suite.

Ed, have I ever mentioned the treasure of gems being stored at the...?

Just as he says it, there is another knock on the broken door. They all look at each other.

JOSÉ MARIA:

WHAT NOW?!

He opens the door slowly. Standing there is the Hotel manager.

HOTEL MANAGER:

The police gentlemen downstairs said there was some damage here. Might I enquire as to who is going to pay for the repairs?

JOHN LEE, JOSÉ MARIA, ED ROYSTON, MATTHEW JAMES:

They all look at one another and burst out laughing, pointing at one another.

HIM !!!!!!!!

36

"DONE", KENNY THOUGHT. Relationships resolved bureaucracy looking stupid, the elders empowered, romance sustained, fear of dying evaporated, and excellence achieved. It's a royal routine, the unbeatable hand. He sat back, entranced by an achievement he wouldn't have believed possible. And like the feeling of slipping into a hot bath, everything that bothered no longer did. It was a weird feeling. He'd been shackled by demons for so long, and telling this story freed him. At that moment, he was struck by an idea to test this new feeling. First, he would make a call, set up a meeting, and test the waters. He knew Hanna had her hands full, so he'd leave her alone. It was time to disappear again. If things worked out in his new project, he'd return just to tease her. There'd be clues, he knew she would catch on.

"Here we are, Kenny hope you like roughing it a bit. It's basic but clean. When you've unpacked, I'll take you out to the shed where the birds are resting. There's no air traffic control out here, of course. Think it might be a good idea to fly the perimeter and give you an idea of the size of the station and where stock is at this time. Will take you three days. Ben knows where fuel is stored around the station. Have a good time."

"Charlie, appreciate what you're doing. We'll do good."

"Lucky, really. Nathan Striker had been with us for a year, the longest any pilot has lasted, but he had family issues and had to get back to Sydney. Your timing is perfect."

"A year huh? Let's see if we can beat that."

When they met in the 'bird cage' a little later, Charlie introduced Kenny to the other pilot on the station Ben Fiddler, an ex-army air wing pilot and engineer, a young man out for adventure. Charlie sent them off in one of the Robinsons to get a feel for each other's ideas.

"Charlie tells me you fly, civil or military?"

It was hard talking over the noise of the helicopter, but there was no option. "Yes, Ben, mostly fixed-wing, all kinds in the RAAF stable. I've done a few hours in Blackhawks, so trust that'll be enough to get the hang of this machine."

"Yeah, like your style, you'll fit in OK around here. Here, let's see if you remember what it's like."

Kenny assumed control, continuing the course they were on, scooting over the big country at 500 feet, stirring bunches of brahman cattle, big red kangaroos and scrawny camels as they passed. Ben watched closely as Kenny regained familiarity with the eccentricities of this much-maligned Jackaroo machine.

"You've forgotten nothing, Bobby, smooth as silk."

"Thanks, Ben. Yes, think I'll fit in."

At that moment, what they call the 'Jesus' nut on the rear rotor, gave way. That failure is catastrophic for the craft. In the next moment, Kenny cut all power to the engine to minimise the uncontrollable spinning of the fuselage. But nothing could stop the inevitable collision, the earth racing up at them. The craft didn't have doors fitted, so when Kenny shoved Ben, he slid straight out about 50 feet above a clump of thick scrub right on the edge of a precipice. That broke his fall. The young man was severely winded and twisted a knee. When he looked up, he could see nothing of the stricken craft. It shot over the edge of the escarpment and must have spiralled hundreds of metres to the flat country below. The point of impact was visible, smoking remains signalling its position. Ben could do nothing but look. He had to wait for Charlie to figure something was amiss. It took two days for the rescue craft to find him. Wisely he didn't move from his position and survived by staying out of the heat of the day by using the shade of the few boab sentinels along the ridge.

"Charlie, who was this Bobby Daniels? I can tell you he was a hell of a pilot. He fought that spinning thing like you do on a bucking horse. He even had time to throw me out of the thing before it went over the edge. Man, he saved my life."

"Ben, you were the last life he saved, but you were not the first. He was always the best person beside you when things went bad. I loved that man."

Charlie led the team of climbers to edge their way down the precipice, scouring every nook and cranny for Kenny's body. They found no sign. Wild dogs were always a problem for station operators. They accounted for a significant loss of stock, especially animals that had befallen accidents and lost the strength to fight or flee. A gruesome thought, but the remains of a body could be dragged, torn to pieces and carried off by the time it took the rescuers to get to the scene. 'Missing, presumed dead' was all that could be offered. Nobody but Hanna would see the irony. A pack of black dogs!

On reflection, she noticed how he'd been gently prodding her to examine her priorities against possibilities that were right under her nose. Of all the things she was thankful for in her brother's life, it was his consideration for her. She felt all along that he needed her in his diminished condition. The truth was she also benefited enormously from him. Her grief was profound, but her life blossomed at the same time. She had to face the fact he was gone.

Or was he?

PART TWO

LIKE A SKIPPING STONE

"GLAD IT'S STILL WINTER, Sue, because there's not much shade around these parts, and I guess we'll be here for a while."

Old mining of early 20th century harvested half a million tons of fuel for power generation and pumping water to settlements. All new growth eucalypt and acacia were less than a hundred years old, as far as they could see. Sue looks around their campsite just as a rarely seen bilby darted from one clump of wild purple mulla mulla to another and disappears. She smiles in recognition.

"Right, Jack. It is scrubby out here but still beautiful, lots of wildlife and gorgeous wildflowers. Did you see those emus on the way in? And you'll see plenty of lizards and a few snakes too. Do they worry you? We will soon be out of reach of winter, and you'll see the bush come alive."

"Snakes? Beautiful creatures, but I give them plenty of room to work out where to go. Not a good idea to upset them."

"Fair enough, good attitude. Same with people. More dangerous than snakes. Then there's the night sky. It is as good as any in the outback, so when you fall backwards off your chair tonight, you can go to sleep under a cosmic and infinite canopy. Now, would you mind taking the shovel for a walk? We need a long drop. Always the first job when camping. Ground here will be a bit hard so carry a bucket of water with you to help. Never forgot the old bloke who told me about that trick. Legend in his own mind was Lou Whittaker."

"Isn't your name Whittaker?"

"Yep, and the old bloke was my dad. I mean, is my dad."

Kenny let that one pass. First time she had mentioned a connection. If she wanted to add more, then it was up to her. She had turned away and was busy setting up her collection of mini nuggets. The first job might be the long drop, but Sue always took the time to set up a display of her little treasures. She was protective of them, and he wasn't allowed to handle them. And, 'Jack'? He was having a bit of trouble with his new name. Admittedly he couldn't remember his real one, so he endured the uncertainty and discomfort of adopting the name of some poor old ghost from a Freemantle gravestone for a new identity. Sue's idea. Something to do with access to social security payments, but he knew nothing else of her motivation. He happily signed any documents she offered him. New name, new bank account, new licence, unemployed fossicker. He owed her his life, having nursed him back to health after he staggered into her camp, wounded, disoriented, clothes shredded and one arm badly burned. It was the nurse thing. She couldn't help herself when the poor damaged stray crawled into her camp and fell, exhausted at her feet. Even after all this time, she reminded him. He owed her. As another old digger had said, 'No way, son, you think you can eat the grass for nothing?' He was mindful of the extent of her care and didn't need reminding, but it didn't stop her from making the point. She had also shelled out for his personal camping gear, sleeping bag, one-man tent, kit of suitable clothes and a good bushman's hat. He didn't think too much about it because he paid her in kind as he regained strength. They were of practical value to each other.

"OK, Sue, a metre should do. Looks like I'll need the crowbar too. Doesn't matter, plenty of time and not much else to do. What say you get the fire started and a brew on the make while I dig?"

"Good idea, sonny, nothing like it, campfire and billy tea. Think we've still got some fruit cake to go with it. God, I love these little nuggets. When you think about it, they've been sitting in creek beds for eons until I came by and picked 'em up. Each one is a unique shape and exquisite to look at. I'm hypnotised every time. You know, I remember exactly where I found each one of them. We'll never get rich, but then this whole idea of aimless wandering under a big sky is as rich as I ever want to be. It's an interest my old dad hooked me into, dragging me all over the Dargo plains in Victoria as a kid and cherishing the specks we found in the creeks."

"Yeah, Sue, so you've said on the odd occasion."

He kept edging towards the door while she rhapsodised, and when she took a breath, he made his escape adroitly, stepped outside to gather tools and head for a likely spot for their dunny. She was still talking, and he was gone. He didn't mind the job, but she seemed unaware of the pain in his left arm. The skin was still far from healed, and it was three months since she found him crawling, in a near coma and sporting burns that were, thank god, mostly superficial. His arm was a bit different. He'd carry scars, he knew. He was oblivious of the coincidence of this injury with Siobahn's scarred arm back in Richmond and how her injury meant nothing in those few delicious moments, they enjoyed before she was taken from him. He didn't yet remember her or the way she was taken. Mostly he liked Sue's matter-of-factness better than cloying sympathy. He walked twenty metres from the vehicle, picked a spot and began scraping away surface gravel and gently pouring water on the patch, watching it soak in and pouring more until he felt the ground was soft enough to give way under his endeavour. It was slow work, water, wait, dig, but he was determined to find the hole. Almost half an hour later, and he'd only managed half the depth needed when he was summoned for a cuppa. He was already sweating and fighting the lactic acid build-up in his arms. He dropped tools and joined her at the fire, flopped into 'his' camp chair and accepted the mug she offered him. She cheekily ruffled his mop of unkempt mane and ran her gnarly fingers up his neck and through his gingery beard as he accepted the chipped enamel mug of steaming tea.

"Now, now, don't start something you're not going to finish, girl."

They both chuckled at the thought, so unlikely in the circumstances.

"Yeah, sonny, if it wasn't for ten years, you'd be in all sorts of trouble."

"Hells bells," he thought. *"There's fire in the furnace yet."*

Sue read his mind.

"Never forget this, Jack. Older women are the best ones to play with. They don't tell, they don't yell, they don't swell, and they're as grateful as hell."

She rubbed her belly while delivering the line, and there was a genuine sparkle in the telling. His chuckle sounded a bit nervous.

Sue then put her own cup on the ground and eased herself carefully onto her favourite canvas chair, holding her slice of cake, having forgotten to cut one for him. The first sip, and she sighed with pleasure. She was happy to be back in the bush, off the bitumen and away from other travellers. It had been too long for her, all that distance from where she found him to Esperance, where she might have him assessed without attracting attention. She was always going to be happier in the bush. Luckily it turned out Kenny responded quickly to her nursing and soon became a good help around the camp. Didn't seem to mind isolation and the camping. On the way to civilisation, she guided him to her ways of doing things, and she enjoyed his company, such as it was without any memory of what had happened to him. For this reason, she persisted with the idea of going all the way down to Warburton, on to Kalgoorlie and to Esperance. She had worked for years in a clinic in Esperance and decided to call in a couple of favours to have Kenny checked. In all, including slow travel out of the centre, this pilgrimage had taken more than two months. Their stay in Esperance was lengthy because she decided to do something about his identity. Dealing with bureaucracies is never quick and, more often than not, frustrating, but Sue was on a mission and wouldn't be denied. While in the south, there was another job to do in Freemantle before she could think about going bush again. But, as soon as it was all done, she was ready to get away. They headed out of Perth with a vague idea of finding a good spot to prop for a while, a place where she could fossick. She thought somewhere near Kalgoorlie would be good but not near the commercial operations. Impulsively after another full day on the bitumen, she stopped in Coolgardie for a few supplies before heading out of town.

"Have you ever been here before, Jack? Does the wide street and old brick and corrugated iron buildings ring any bells for you?"

"Not even a tinkle, Sue. Why did we stop?"

"I've noticed your partiality for good food, and the fridge is nearly bare. Thought we might visit the butcher and, while we're at it, re-stock the pantry. Then, I think we might find a spot between here and Kalgoorlie. I'm itching to grub around in the dirt in some likely spots out there. OK with you? Look, you've still got some cash in your pocket, why don't you see if you can find a few treats."

They were parked outside the IGA, and he headed in there while she went to the butcher. They parted company, each with an agenda, him wondering how she kept tabs on how much money was in his pocket.

"Any surprises, Jack?"

"Yeah, actually. I thought you might like these different flavoured chupa chups. Also got some chocolate. Only got treats, like you said."

"Chupa chups, hey? They're hard-boiled lollies on a stick, take hours to finish. I think I'll like them."

Kenny wasn't so silly. He hoped she liked them too.

Instead of heading to Kalgoorlie, Sue drove the other way.

"What are you doing? Are we going back to Perth?"

"My nose is itchy. I think we might find a spot a little way along here. Just be patient."

About 10 minutes out of Coolgardie, Sue turned off the road and into the expanse of open country where campers and fossickers could feel welcome, not by people because they were scarce but by the country itself. Kenny's eyes glazed over, and he mused.

"Silly girl," he thought, *"she really thinks she can smell a good place to fossick. It's taken her ten years to collect the few scraps she's got and still doesn't realise it's blind luck, and she hasn't had that much of that."*

So, having found their spot and set up camp, they sat together, Sue took out her first lolly, and Kenny relaxed with his tea. He spoke first, for a change.

"You know how we stopped at that beach in Perth, sat on the sand and watched locals walk out of the water with bags of shellfish, and I said to you they were harvesting abalone? I just realised I don't know how I knew that. It was eerie, like a memory long lost popping back for a moment like a nugget jagged out of clay."

She pulled out the chupa chup and held it in the air while she responded. He hoped she would get the taste for the thing.

"Good, Jack. You're probably right. Amnesia's a funny thing, and you'll probably have more flashes as you heal. You must have taken a whack on the head, whatever happened out there where I found you. Let the healing take its own time. My regret is I'm going to lose you when it all comes back, and you remember who you are and where you came from. Your company and your strength have been so good, though you might not like sleeping in your tent. You know, a girl's got to worry about what the neighbours think."

The chupa went back to its work. He didn't bite because he didn't mind the tent at all. There was so much he couldn't remember. Like when he sat on the Perth beach with his sister, Mac to him, Hanna to the world. Like the jet pilot insignia, he'd worn on his RAAF uniform that day. And the whole saga from altar boy to boarding school nest of paedophiles which he severely disrupted and ended up convicted of killing the worst of them. And the mid-air disaster over the Arizona desert and the lost years on his slow way home to Australia. And the super effort of creating a movie script, and finally, the helicopter accident on his first day at his best friend's cattle station, an incident he was very lucky to survive even if he couldn't remember. No, there was a lot in that mysterious bucket.

They sat for a while, soaking the afternoon sun on their backs and staring at a beautiful scrub country most city people think is monotonous. Kenny's tea had cooled, waiting for cake. It didn't come, so he hauled himself out of the chair and headed back to his chore, smiling at her forgetfulness. They would need a functioning convenience before nightfall, and he wanted to be able to take full advantage of the campfire dinner and a glass of wine.

Sue was tidying up in the van when Kenny's voice alerted her to a crisis. She sighed with the expectation he'd disturbed a western brown or an ants' nest, so she didn't hurry. For a city boy, she guessed he was, he was savvy in the bush. She didn't have to watch him too closely. When she thought about it, she knew she didn't really have a hurry left in her. Standing in the doorway, she could see he was sitting on the edge of the hole, she couldn't tell how deep it was from where she stood. He leaned back, resting on both arms, head sagging with fatigue, staring at his feet, still calling her to hurry. She was first inclined to yell back that the hole had to be finished before light faded. Her second thought was he might need help.

"I'm here, boy, I'm here, don't tell me you've chopped into your feet. What have you done? Show me."

He stopped yelling but didn't move an inch. He'd gathered his senses by the time she spoke, lifted his feet out of the hole, climbed painfully to stand and looked intensely into her eyes and complained.

"I can't get it any deeper. It's too rocky, but it needs to be deeper. My arms are hurting, so you'll have to have a go, I give up."

"Wait on, Jack, I don't mind scratching around in the gravel but buggered if I'm going to attack this rock with a crowbar. I'm too tired now, I'll do it when nature calls me in the morning. Thought you had more stamina. You must be getting soft with all the spoiling."

"OK, Sue, up to you. Just be careful you don't fall in. I'll leave the tools here. Let's eat."

She took a cursory glance at the hole.

"Leave it as it is, it's deep enough anyway."

She turned to go back to the camp, and he followed.

The steak was fresh, the fire hot, and they substituted fresh bread rolls for damper. Bellies full and feet warm, the fire subsided just as the curtain lifted on the most spectacular sky. Kenny was gobsmacked, silent, absorbing the immensity of infinity. Sue stood up, still sucking on the chupa chup she had started earlier and slurped on her bedtime cup of tea. Kenny gritted his teeth at the annoying disruption of his reverie but could see she was about to retire. He said nothing, and she left him to the spectacle.

It was cold that brought his attention back to earth. He stirred the fire to warm himself, threw a couple more logs on the fire and crawled into his tent, a smile on his face he couldn't help enjoying.

Kenny was up at first light to check on the short drop but wasn't tempted to dig. He wanted Sue to continue. First, he walked away from camp, not to the long drop which was for serious business. Better to water the ground cover. He did walk over to the hole he had started and wasn't tempted to dig any more. He was adamant Sue should do her bit for the cause.

"Good boy, Jack, the water's hot, and I'm not. Let's have tea."

"Sure, Sue, but you are going to dig the hole while I make breakfast. My arm's still sore."

"Gee, Jack, you're nagging a bit. But eggs on campfire toast is good enough to get me going. You get started, I won't be long."

Kenny fiddled about, but anyone could see the tension he was feeling. Then came the shout.

"Jack, Jack, you bastard. How could you do this to me? Jack, come here and look. Oh, Jack, I love you, you sly bastard."

He was at the scene in a second, beaming at the revelation. Sue, head down, bum hard against the side of the hole, heaving away, huffing, puffing.

"I can't budge it, Jack, get in here and help."

"No room for two in that dunny, Sue. I'll wait till you've finished."

Sue wriggled herself upright, saw the joke and broke into unrestrained laughter, tears coursing across her dusted cheeks.

"OK, smartypants, help me out of here, and you have a go. It is big, Jack, but no way to know how big."

"Oh, no, you don't, Sue. This is yours. I just found it for you. I have to get back to cooking before the sausages burn. I'll get you a couple of trowels, and you can keep working. Or do you want to stop for a cup of tea?"

"So funny. No way am I getting out of here until I've loosened this bloody thing. God, it is beautiful, Jack and I can't even see all of it yet."

"Oh, well, looks like I'll be eating alone this morning. See you later."

So, he had breakfast, cleaned up around the campfire, chopped some firewood and washed dishes and pan, every move punctuated with a glance towards the frenetic activity going on just a few metres away. Sue was grateful, however, when he turned up with a cup of hot tea. She had not thought about food or anything else for the hours she had been in the hole, alone, with the biggest nugget she had ever seen.

"Thanks, Jack. Look how much I've uncovered, and I still can't tell how big it is."

"Should I start digging another hole, Sue, for when you've finally got that lump out? Maybe there's more to be found."

"Funny bugger. I think one miracle in a lifetime suffices and this, Jack, is one big miracle."

"It's getting late in the day, and I know you're having fun, but do you want a hand. I could tie a rope and pull it out with the car."

"Don't even think about it yet. Go and get dinner ready. We are going to celebrate tonight, that's for sure."

Kenny wasn't disappointed, he couldn't be. He was overjoyed for the pleasure this good woman was getting, covered in clay dust, thrusting and scraping with the trowels. He pretended to mope off but was quite happy to prepare a feast for the evening meal. There would be much to discuss over dinner. It was another two hours before she called him over. The camp oven was on the hot ashes, loaded with veggies and a kilogram pack of chicken thighs Sue had bought in Coolgardie. They had plenty of time to work on the nugget before dinner would be ready.

"Coming, Sue."

She was out of the hole, staring at the miracle. It stared right back at her.

"Jack, Jack, what have you done. I can't believe it could be that easy. All these years, I've worked harder and longer for just a few flecks. How on earth did you find this? I told you my nose was itchy. This is why, don't you see? Look at it just sticking right out of the clay. It's at least fifty ounces, maybe more."

"Yeah, Sue, you found it. I just got the dirt away from it. And don't you tell me it was easy, my arms are still aching. Yours must be aching too now."

They stood looking into the hole, chests heaving with pleasure, arms around each other. Up to this moment, Kenny had struggled to think how he might repay Sue for her kindness to him. She'd saved his life when she might have ignored him. There is no bigger gift. In one instant, he'd resolved the issue in a small way. No idea how big the nugget might be, most of it was still stuck, unseen, but it was certainly the ultimate thrill for Sue. There would be no more reminders about how much it had cost her to have him along.

"Just one question, Sue. What do we do now?"

She was jolted by the question and looked quizzically at him.

"We could fill in the hole and walk away and forever not know any more about it because if we pull this thing out of the ground, our lives might change in ways we couldn't imagine. Yeah, that's what we should do."

She paused and studied his blank expression for one moment only.

"Then again, damn it. Let's take the ride, what do you say?"

"Okay, we'll do it. There, didn't take too long to work out, did it? Now, this is what's going to happen. I'm going to widen the hole, and we are going to try lifting it free. Once we've got it out of the hole and before anything else, we'll carry or drag this lump over to the van and get out your bathroom scales to weigh it. The person whose guess is closest gets to name it. Fair enough?"

That's how the nugget got its name "The Coolgardie Drop" after they had jousted, throwing a few ideas back and forth.

It was a busy afternoon and evening. Sue found energy she never knew she had, toiling with determination and chuckling all the while, increasing her intensity the further she excavated. It took longer than either of them thought. It was clearly much bigger than they expected. It didn't matter to her, imagination had taken over, running wildly through possibilities. The nugget ended up being so big that Kenny had to tie a rope and haul it free of its hold on the ground. They had forgotten about the ebbing of natural light, happy to work in pitch dark if they had to.

Job done, they stood and stared at the nugget for what seemed an age, circling, inspecting, picking at reluctant bits of clay, caressing it and pausing to look at each other and laugh each time. To get it back to the van, Kenny threw a sack on the ground, rolled the nugget onto it, and the pair of them dragged it across the ground to the camp.

"Hey, Sue, what about dinner? Have a look in the pot. Hope you're hungry."

She threw her hands in the air in mock rage at the suggestion she get back in the kitchen.

"Not before we weigh this and then get it under cover. Got to be careful, Jack. Anyway, it's about time I had your cooking. Surely I'm not the only one who can cook."

She smiled at him and stepped inside, returning a moment later with the scales. Job done, and the fire blazing, Kenny opened one of her prized reds, poured it into cups and offered a toast.

"Here's to the Coolgardie Drop and to the woman who dragged it from the earth. Cheers, Sue."

"I know what you're doing, smartie. Cheers to you, the miracle fossicker."

A laugh, a sip. Another sip, and they were ready to attack the contents of the camp oven.

It is doubtful either of them would remember the meal even though it was stunning in its simplicity and flavour. Kenny watched her ecstasy, wondering if her prediction of their lives changing forever would prove right. To top off the meal, out came a bottle of port she kept for cold nights. Later, midnight later, when Kenny fell backwards off his chair, most of the port was gone, and he was an incoherent mess. Sue cleaned up with some enthusiasm stepping over his unconscious body to do so. And then she retrieved his sleeping bag from the tent and covered him carefully. He was too heavy for her to move, and she didn't want to disturb his sleep, very noisy sleep too. She chucked a couple of logs on the fire before sneaking quietly back to her van.

Kenny roused early the next morning before light, dry and sore throat from all the snoring. Alcohol never gives a full night's sleep, just a couple of hours, and every drinker knows about its side effects. No prize without price. He had begun to feel the chill having rolled away from his makeshift blanket. There were a few glowing ashes in the fireplace, and he reached for more fuel. The fire reignited gradually, and he sat close to it, teeth chattering. He crawled over to his tent and came back wearing his jacket. At that moment, he noticed he was alone. Sue, the van, gone. He sucked air staring at the empty camp space, and then let out a long sad sigh with the realisation he had probably been dumped.

The car, van, the nugget and Sue were gone. Kenny turned back to the fire, stretched his hands over it and pondered. *'Often disappointed, never surprised,'* he thought. He knew a bit about human nature and felt right about having paid his debt to Sue, though 44.4 kg of gold included a fair tip, he smiled. He had stayed calm in far more deadly circumstances, so there was no outburst, just calculation. He'd work out what to do next a bit later. In the meantime, he needed to get warm.

"FRIDAY NIGHT, BEST NIGHT of the week, hey. The Chinese developers are quiet, and the girls are off with grandma for the weekend."

Mark kicked off his work shoes and dropped onto the two-seater beside Hanna, who eyed his approach and made room for his next move. He took her attention away from the local evening news she'd been watching, a glass of a Langhorne Creek Malbec cradled in both hands. He sat, leaned back and sagged against her side. She smiled a welcome, released her right hand and began to tease the back of his neck with her fingertips and puffing her breath into his ear. His eyes closed, and he was rendered helpless.

The next minute, Hanna placed her glass on a nearby coffee table, stood up, hooking Mark's chin with a single finger and effortlessly, he rose and followed, a longed-for promise beckoning him in the direction of her bedroom. The television was still on, but the audience was gone. As they stepped into the other room, an announcer read to the world the news that another Robinson helicopter crash in the outback had resulted in the almost certain death of the pilot, Robert Steven Daniels and the miraculous survival of co-pilot, Ben Fiddler, both in the employ of indigenous operated cattle and camel station managed by Charlie Sweeney.

Hanna had already slipped under the doona, white T-shirt, cotton brief knickers and clear intent, her body untouched by another for a long time. She had concluded Mark was worth the effort, and her usual reservations dissolved with the second glass of wine. Her week had been complicated enough. A recreational romp had its appeal, clear the head and get back focus on important stuff later. She could be so practical. As for Mark, wrestling his way clear of his business shirt and stumbling out of his trousers was as much as he could handle. And as he kicked free of all that and stood bare to his briefs, revealing his enthusiasm for what he expected to follow, he stupidly asked, smiling broadly in a self-satisfied kind of way.

"What time is your recital tomorrow? Can't wait to see you play at last. I really envy that cello."

He thought it was a smart thing to say in the circumstances. Why would anyone envy a cello of all things? Her initiative had taken him by surprise, and that is all it took to blow his strict rule about relationships and colleagues. He was nervous and hesitant. That's where the question came from. Bit of a misjudgement.

Hanna looked over her left shoulder to tell him the time he asked for and added.

"On the way, I want to stop off at Kenny's. I think he's gone missing, and I want to check. OK?"

'OK?' As if in the moment, before accepting the ever so ready male, he is going to say no. Maybe later, but not in that instant, you would think. His eyes betrayed him when he should have protected an ambience he had desperately hoped for and could hardly believe had happened. Instead, he reacted on impulse. Not pleased. Tired of hearing about Kenny or Bobby or whatever she called her ever-present pilot brother. The novelty and awe he had initially felt about this elusive adventurer was gone. Too much competition for him. Hated the idea of sharing her now that they had reached this moment. His body language said it all. Too late to backtrack. She saw it instantly. Surging sexual energy morphed into a ripple leaving only mutual fatigue and the odour of disappointment hanging in the room. There would be no crashing surf over writhing, entangled bodies this night. Mark sheepishly gathered his things and headed off to the guest room where he usually slept on stayovers. Hanna sighed heavily before curling foetal and submitting to the second thing she had been looking forward to, sleep.

Mark's last and lingering thought in another bedroom and alone was Hanna's gorgeous body cocooned in her doona. He had been so patient with her while still grieving for his wife, tinge of guilt whenever he thought romantically of her. Then, the moment she decided she was ready to be pursued, he stuffed up. His own fault. And there she was in the next room, warm and snuggling, and he in his monk's cell. He tossed one way and another in frustration and annoyance at his stupidity, got out of bed and tiptoed to her door three times, hand reaching for the doorknob before giving up and forcing himself back to his room, back to his celibate bed and finally, to sleep.

Morning came soon enough. Hanna flipped her eyes open when her nose caught the aroma of brewing coffee. She almost knocked the cup out of Mark's hand as she opened her door.

"Thought this might be a good idea. Good morning."

"You silly boy, but yes, it's the best idea for now."

Once more to the brink only to be turned. Missed it by a few seconds. They padded to the living room, cups in hand, to the full wall window and took in the panorama of Port Phillip and the city landscape 44 floors below.

"Of course, we can stop at Kenny's place. Clearly, I'll have to play catch-up on the importance you two feel for each other. Last night's reaction was automatic and stupid. Don't know where it came from. I do apologise."

"Yeah, did yourself no good at all, hey. They say there are eight kinds of sex, angry, revenge, curious, pity, make-up and whatever else, I don't know. We have danced around each other for a while, and I reckoned it was time to find out a little more about you. Well, I did, and it looks like we still have a few things to sort out. OK with you?"

"What can I say? This is all new to me, widowed, two girls, new job, all of those things with challenges. It's all complex. Don't give up on me yet, I reckon I'll work it out."

"That's enough for our board meeting. Feel like a Lebanese breakfast at Oasis Bakery before we nip across to Richmond?"

"Yes, I do. You shower first because my bedroom's a wreck. Don't ask why."

He couldn't see her smile as she headed to the bathroom. All seemed to be going well, fresh morning clear agenda for the day, when that phone call from Charlie Sweeney out of the blue caught Hanna completely by surprise. Kenny had left Melbourne for a cattle station near Alice Springs, crashed a helicopter and disappeared. The incident was in a remote canyon, and officially his body had been taken by wild dogs or feral pigs, no body was found. Not much room for optimism. She was lightning struck.

"Go, Hanna, you have to find out what happened. Don't worry about work, it'll be covered. Let me know everything when you call."

Mark's sympathy was genuine, sensitivity his great asset. But this time, unlike when Kenny turned up 2 years earlier after 10 years mostly in the RAAF, was different. He couldn't help feeling the fraternal relationship had a pathological element to it. He figured Kenny had too much of a hold on his kid sister. After all, she had a law firm to manage and huge clients to satisfy. He covered for her on two extended occasions and now a third strike. He pushed back the thought it might be a good thing if Kenny died this time. Maybe then she'd be able to focus her attention on the business partnership and, even more importantly, to foster the nascent relationship with him and his two girls. The huge outburst of self-interest and guilt smacked him. While she packed, he booked a flight for her to Alice Springs via Sydney, leaving Melbourne at 2pm.

As for Hanna, there was nothing except a driving compulsion to find out everything she could about the incident, still almost unreasonably clinging to a fragment of hope he might have survived. Mark drove her to the airport but felt he might as well be invisible. Not a word from her all the way, lost in terrible fear of what she might find out when she reached Charlie. Again, Mark had to check rising resentment. Coming to terms with the complexities around him was a bigger job than he thought and likely to be more than he could handle. There are emotions, chemical compounds released into the bloodstream when triggered. They are unpredictable, powerful, and even explosive, and their influence can disappear just as quickly as they flood the system. Then there is the intellect and thought. Thought evolves from observations, learning, and pondering variations and options. Thought is conscious and a guide for considered behaviour. Thought is much more trustworthy than emotion. It can change, of course, but not in a lightning strike usually. Mark was wrestling with emotions, and this was his problem. It is hard to throw a rope over a pigrooting stallion. Better to wait, watch, whisper, and build trust and confidence until the stallion comes to you, quietly, out of conviction it is safe to approach. Mark had intellect, a fine one too. Still, it was suffocated by the swirling emotions of resentment and jealousy eating at his fragile self-assurance.

Last time Hanna saw Alice Springs was on the bike, on her way to Tenant Creek to join Kenny on a ride to Darwin. On this day, she could see the tiny strip of the Stuart Highway from 30,000 feet in air-conditioned comfort. A thin line on the hard open ground stretching from one side of the fuselage window to the other. On the airstrip at Alice, a blast of outback heat hit the line of passengers when they emerged onto the portable steps, the stairway to heaven. It wasn't even summer, but a whole lot warmer than Melbourne. Hanna had not met Charlie Sweeney, so she keenly scoped the waiting throng looking for a sign. She picked him out easily. Tall, slim, strikingly handsome in white shirt distressed denim jeans, desert versatile work boots, Raybans hooked into the shirt pocket, his favourite well-worn Akubra atop his generous jet-black mane. That man was surely Charlie Sweeney. And it was confirmed when they locked eyes. He scooped his hat from its comfortable slouch.

"Hanna, Charlie. I am so sorry."

He was just as sure who amongst the approaching line of passengers was Hanna. They shook hands. He held hers firmly to emphasise his feeling.

"Don't, Charlie. You say you're not sure anyway, so let's hold on to that. The other man survived, Ben, wasn't it? Will we be able to talk to him? Maybe he can tell me something."

The handshake was released. One was as shaken as the other.

"Yes, of course. He's in the local hospital, dehydrated and with a couple of broken bones. He'll tell you exactly what happened."

Emerging from the terminal, it was a short walk to the carpark. Charlie tossed Hanna's bag onto the back seat of the twin-cab station ute, and they headed out of the airport for the drive to town, the first stop the hospital. Charlie led her directly to Ben's room. He was dozing, drip feeder in his arm and sensors to heart monitor stuck to various parts of his chest. He heard them come into the room and pulled himself to a sitting position.

"Hi, Charlie."

"Hello Ben, this is Hanna, Bobby's sister from Melbourne."

Hanna looked quickly at Charlie. "Bobby?" Then she remembered the assumed identity Kenny had used for so long.

"Hello, Ben. How on earth did you survive. Must have been a horrible moment in the chopper?"

"Hanna, I had only just met your brother when we headed off to scope the extent of the station and do a sketchy audit of animal numbers. Charlie had filled me in on his experience, and it wasn't long into the flight I handed control over to him. I can tell you his flying was silky smooth. When the rear rotor shat itself, pardon the language, he didn't flinch. He knew exactly what to do. At the same time as he cut power to the engine, he was scoping the ground, flying towards us while we were in a wild spin. I don't know how he did it, but he snapped my seatbelt and shoved me out of the craft, knowing there was a good chance I would land in scrubby acacia bushes. Just as he did, the chopper shot over the edge of a steep fall of about two hundred metres. The impact happened halfway down, and the craft continued sliding and tumbling to the bottom before exploding. I was knocked almost unconscious by my fall, it was about 3 metres, but I was able to crawl to the edge. All I could see was the fire and smoke. I couldn't see if he was in the wreckage or not. Then I blacked out. My body was too broken to climb down the escarpment. I'm sorry Hanna. His last act was to save my life. I hope he got out of it alive. He might have, though the police say he didn't."

"Thanks, Ben. Hope you heal quickly. I also hope, like you, he survived. But they say it's highly unlikely. Horrible way to go, poor man. Nice to have met you, Ben. I think Charlie's going to take me to the scene this afternoon or tomorrow."

"Tomorrow would be the soonest, Hanna. Got to arrange a few things and make sure the other chopper is available."

On the drive out of Alice, he continued preparing her.

"They know you're coming and will inspect the craft thoroughly before letting me take it out. The plan is to leave at first light. Mornings are cold so wear a jacket. We'll be away overnight because it is so far, and there are a couple of bore water supply systems we are going to check while we are out there. The thing is, camels can do serious damage in their rush to drink. We have to monitor them all the time. I'll bring the sleeping gear and tent and enough stuff for a cooked dinner and breakfast. We need a bit of ballast for the four-seater anyway."

"Poor boy, he's so upset and stressed," she thought as he rattled on. After a while, he settled, he couldn't keep chattering for the 2 hours it would take to get to the homestead. They didn't talk much at all, both hypnotised by the huge sky and a road disappearing in a straight line to the horizon.

Charlie walked with her around the compound to stretch their legs after the long and sometimes bumpy drive. He showed her the chopper they would use, the machinery sheds and the house garden before introducing her to his colleagues in the outdoor dining area at dinner. She was tired and worried, so excused herself with apologies and retired. Homestead accommodation can be surprisingly comfortable. No luxuries but spacious rooms, clean bed and bathroom. Her sleep was anything but restful, and she was so relieved to wake the next morning. As her consciousness emerged from the fog of fear and ghostly images, she realised where she was and curled up for a few moments before rising. Her body ached so badly with grief that she wasn't sure she could face what she was going to see this day. But the aroma of a country kitchen sneakily intruded, and it was a welcoming thing, a warm and embracing thing. She steeled herself, rose, abluted, dressed and followed the wafting invitation to the dining room where other members of the household and work crew were well into their breakfast. Charlie looked up to greet Hanna and introduced her again to his colleagues.

"Don't know what your usual breakfast is, Hanna but suggest you tuck in now because we won't be eating until we set up camp tonight. And take your time, the chopper is packed, fuelled and ready to go."

She was immediately included in the conversation about the chill of the morning, the freshness of home-baked bread, and job lists for the day. All talk about the recovery of remains of the ill-fated helicopter was avoided for the moment, replaced by funny recollections of catching horses, chasing camels and training reluctant dogs to do what they were told. The ambience was welcoming on every level. People moved off as they finished their meal, leaving Hanna and Charlie as the last ones to go.

"OK, Hanna, ready? I know what you're facing today, and we'll deal with it. I suggest you check out some things Kenny would have noticed when he and Ben left the homestead, keep your mind on the positive stuff."

"I'll be all right, Charlie. Nice of you to think of that. Sure, I will tune into the experience of flying in a helicopter. Never done it before."

Hanna was getting a sense of why Charlie and Kenny would've been good friends. Charlie's sensitivity was fermented from clear respect. His attention was not intrusive or overdone. She liked that. He listened with all his senses, especially with his eyes, something else people don't usually do. He had planned the excursion in detail, another tick. She felt comfortable with him. All this was going through her mind while they headed to the chopper. She noticed it had only a two-blade rotor. Minimalist, she thought. Charlie made sure she understood the seatbelt functions, air vents and headset controls while he got the engine started and ran through pre-flight checks. The helicopter faced west on the pad, and as it lifted, Charlie eased it around to face the sunrise. Black landscape, a ring of light across the horizon and an aura above the point at which the sun would pop. Above them was still star shot, but colour was seeping the stars away as the earth rolled its well-worn path towards the sun. They were silent and rightly awed in the presence of majesty, becoming absorbed by infinity, climbing to 2000 tail up and accelerating. Hanna was fully aware of Charlie's light touch on the controls, and she relaxed completely about his competence. However, her mind stayed focused on the day's main objective, the examination of the crash site and the place where her brother disappeared. She took no real pleasure from other aspects of the flight. Mostly she was silent, musing over headlines of Kenny's life, with and without her. Charlie was smart enough to not interfere too much apart from signalling a few significant moments when they overflew small groups of camels, mobs of kangaroo, straggling brahmans and the odd wedge-tailed eagle gracefully soaring its domain. It took two hours to reach their destination. Firstly, Charlie landed at the top of the escarpment. He reached into the rear of the cabin to retrieve a brand new hat he'd selected for Hanna and watched her get it settled on her head. While she stretched her legs, he set up the campsite they would use later in the day.

"Hey, Charlie, thanks for the hat, it's great."

He smiled in recognition but thought he had misjudged when he noticed her standing on the edge, peering towards the crash site, so he stopped what he was doing and joined her.

"Sorry, Hanna, I wanted to show you the miracle of Ben's survival. You can see this deep patch of scrub where he fell. Do you think it possible Kenny actually meant him to land where he did? There would have been a lot going on at the time."

"Can't tell, Charlie. Do you think it's too steep to climb down?"

She hung on to the hat, the updraft was strong.

"It can be done, but I think we'll take the quick way if that's ok with you."

"Sure."

He'd been astute enough to set up the campsite far enough away from the helicopter for it to be safe from turbulence, eased the craft into the air and headed well over the drop to avoid uncomfortable updrafts and descended to the crash site. Looking up from the point of final impact, they could see where the stricken craft hit and slid down the face of the escarpment before finishing where they stood. More recent models of the R22 have an emergency valve to choke fuel supply if there is a danger of a fire, but this older model didn't have it. In this instance, few pilots would have the presence of mind to reach for it. The ensuing fire had melted the fuselage, it was so violent. Hanna picked through the wreckage, looking for any significant sign, but there wasn't any. She then began walking around the site in expanding circles. If he got away, there just might be some sign, a dragging foot mark, signs of having fallen, something. When the idea seemed finally to be futile, she was about five hundred metres out, and she stopped. A small circle of rocks and the remains of a campfire. It could mean nothing or something, she wondered. There was evidence of a rarely used vehicle track. Clearly, to her, people used the area, if only infrequently. Charlie noticed what she was looking at.

"I saw this when I first came in, Hanna, and it made me wonder. Surely if someone was here and found Kenny, they would have made contact. But if this spot was upwind of the site, nothing could be heard or seen from here. The thing is, this fire was fairly recent. Someone has camped here not long ago. The police didn't come this far out, so they made their assessment without it. Can't be sure though."

Hanna was struck dumb and smacked by a feeling Kenny was alive. Where and in what condition? No idea.

"Oh, Charlie, he's alive. He was here. I know it, and I know him. I can go home believing. What I don't know is what happens next. It could be years before I see him again. I won't wait that long. I will be coming back to do my own search. I have to."

Charlie thought hope is a powerful thing. It would have to be for her to be right.

"Good luck. I can post a photo of him as a missing person online and with the authorities and then wait till someone spots him. Let's assume you are right, there are two possibilities. He doesn't want to be found, in which case he will surely contact you, and only you. The other one is just as likely. He's taken a hit to the head and lost his memory. If so, then we don't know if he will get recall at all. If true, then the posting as a missing person might work. We'll send his photo to every hospital in WA because he will surely need some kind of emergency treatment. I have his personal effects back at the station, and I will send them to you when you let me know where. You should go home, and I will be in touch. Is that okay for you?"

"Sounds good, and thanks, Charlie."

"Now, it's getting late, so we should get back to camp and rustle up some dinner. We haven't eaten since breakfast."

Campfire, barbecued rib eye and potatoes in the ashes washed down with a Margaret River Shiraz from Ferngrove followed by billy tea made the perfect ending to a stressful day. Hanna watched Charlie move from one job to the next with what looked to her as elegance born of familiarity, even intimacy. The fire leapt to life under his hand, the steak was grilled to perfection, and he knew exactly when to pull the spuds from the ashes. Then, the wine. She was familiar with the best of Margaret River, and this Shiraz was right up there, the perfect companion for the rib-eye. OK, they were drinking from metal tumblers, but that didn't dull the pleasure. The conversation was easy, mostly about Kenny. Charlie didn't know about his stint at the top gun outfit in the U.S. Nor had he any way of knowing about Siobahn's terrible murder, the only woman Kenny had ever really connected to. When they had met most recently, Charlie didn't notice signs of the black dog in Kenny's behaviour.

"Honestly, Hanna, trouble has stalked him his whole life. You are clearly the one bright spot amongst it all."

"True, Charlie, but I get a sense the two of you have something special as well. If and when he comes to his senses, you will definitely hear from him. You don't know this, but he found a way of coping with his issues by writing a movie script about four old guys who find a way to strike back at fate before they die of ailments contracted as a result of their occupations. They all die happy, having struck a blow for what they knew to be right. I'll get a copy to you."

"You're kidding. You know, he could do anything, hey? The wrong people get cursed just as the wrong people end up being in charge. Life sucks sometimes."

It was getting late, the fire was dying and the chill invasive when they called it a day and headed for the sleeping bags in their one-man tents. Charlie loaded the fire with enough fuel to keep it burning for hours. Its flickering light and crackling would extend the pleasure of the evening and deter local nocturnal wildlife. He showed Hanna the shovel, torch, and a toilet roll she would need to take for a walk between then and the morning.

Morning, hot tea and toast helped warm them before breaking camp and heading back to headquarters. Conversation on the way back was as warm as the noise of the craft would allow, but it was clear Hanna had grasped a shred of hope and had convinced herself Kenny was alive. Hanna would enjoy one more night at the homestead before Charlie drove her back to Alice Springs and her flight to Melbourne. The two-hour drive back was more interactive than the drive out. Hanna was chirpy and inquisitive about Charlie's background and experiences. She had him surrounded, and he was an open book to her. His father was of this country, a career drover, and his mother raised four boys while cooking for the station in the Kimberly where they lived. Charlie was the youngest and probably got the best care of them all with access to schooling and serious consideration when it came time for work training. He gained a scholarship for the station he came later to manage and learned quickly enough to be selected for the last years of secondary schooling, where he met Kenny. He went on to tell her all he knew of Kenny, stuff Hanna couldn't possibly know.

"How come you're not married, Charlie?"

That one came out of the blue. He gripped the steering wheel.

"Get yourself ready to answer the same question when I'm finished with yours. I could tell you all the predictable things like how isolation is a factor, or I've not seen marriages that would encourage me to consider it as a choice, but I would be dodging the issue. Really, Hanna, I've been a bit selfish. I've gone out with three different girls for a good while, and with each one, I've felt something missing. I didn't really connect with the dreams they had for their futures. I never really connected dating with being 'serious'. I don't know how being serious has got anything to do with having a girlfriend. People often say, 'Oh, they are really serious,' or 'Do you think they are serious about each other?' It sounds a bit scary to me. I'm very serious about my responsibilities at the station, the colleagues and all the workers and then the animals we look after. I'm serious about maintaining working relationships and about having the best tools for every job. I love planning the future of the organisation. You know, it's a full-time job doing those things. I don't want to be 'serious' about my personal life. What about you?"

"Thanks, Charlie. I'll take my turn now. You can't know what it's like to be a target for unwanted attention from the age of 12 onwards because that's what it's like being a girl. It's so hard to find the core of individual boys or men. They are so obsessively motivated by the need to jump and hump I don't think they even know how to make sound judgements about who they should spend time with. They know and understand one another and build true and lasting connections. Truth is, I stopped bothering a long time ago and concentrated on developing my interests, professional and musical and physical health. You're right, time slips by. Like every other creature, we are built for breeding and are programmed to do it. People too often end up in the rip-tide of biological imperatives and lose themselves in the process. I've been watching my business partner. His wife died, leaving him with two daughters. He's a good lawyer and partner with a good moral compass, and for once in my life, I'm dealing with a man who has more things to think about apart from himself. I like he can do that. Even then, I'm not sure. I like his kids, and they often have sleep-overs, but my space is not mine when they're around, and I love it when they go home."

Charlie listened with full attention, ready for any detail he might read as interest. There was none, but neither was there a sign of her having a firm commitment to this man. He would wait and see. At the airport, Hanna removed the hat he had given her.

"Here, Charlie, hold this for me because I'm coming back, that's for sure."

He took it, and it sat on the seat next to him all the way home. It then found a home in his bedroom. He had hope after all.

She headed for home, encouraged her trip had achieved something. She felt sure Kenny would re-surface, and she was pleased in a big way to have spent time with Charlie, a very impressive man. She also knew she would not stop looking for Kenny until the mystery was solved.

KENNY RETURNED TO HIS TENT to gather what little was there, a sleeping bag, boots and rucksack. Then he stepped outside to dismantle the tent and found an envelope stuck to it which he hadn't seen in the dim light of early morning.

"Jack, I apologise. Trust me. Meet me in two weeks at the cafeteria in King's Park in Perth. I don't know which day yet. You can call me on the following number. I will meet you there at midday on one of those days when I have completed business. You can ring me on my mobile. 004 424 424 to tell me which day. Sue"

The note was obviously hasty, and the ideas scrambled, but he got it. Dilemma. The first thing was to get back to bitumen, 5km, he guessed. The second thing was to decide on a path. Perth? Maybe, but something was telling him to turn east. Did he want to see Sue? No doubt she would have sold the 'Coolgardie Drop', and she would possibly want to offer him money. In his eyes, the ledger was in balance, so he could happily choose not to see her. He decided to get to Kalgoorlie and check his new bank account for social security funds he hadn't accessed for a while. He would need cash no matter which path he took. First stop, Coolgardie. He picked up his pack and slung it over his right shoulder, and took the first step, not knowing what would happen next. It was still early, and being winter, he wouldn't have to face extreme heat. In fact, he would have to move to get warm. An hour into his trek following the fresh tyre marks, he could see occasional trucks and other vehicles maybe a kilometre ahead. He was energised, knowing he would be able to hitch a ride once he reached the bitumen. Out west, drivers will still sometimes stop for a hitchhiker because they don't share the paranoia of city folk. So, it wasn't long before a ute from a mining company stopped for him.

"Let me guess, mate. You're goin' to the big Kal. Jump in. I'm goin' as far as Coolgardie."

The driver didn't even consider Coolgardie as Kenny's destination. Not worth it in his mind. Most people drive through on their way somewhere else. Used to be a gold rush town, but that was a hundred years ago. You can see what it was in the solid style of the buildings, but there's not much happening anymore. Kenny thanked the man, hoiked his pack in the tray and climbed in. It was a short drive to Coolgardie, so the conversation didn't get too invasive. Kenny got away with generalities while not sounding rude. The driver understood. People like to keep to themselves, and that was okay with him. Suffice it to say, he admitted to being curious about the giant pit and having been on the road for a while. The driver acceded to his request to stop in Coolgardie and dropped him at the "Denver City Hotel" on the edge of town.

"Be careful how you go in there, mate, she's a bit of a dragon. But they cook a good counter meal."

That spiked Kenny's curiosity, so he crossed the street and walked into the main bar. It was lunchtime, and the bar was empty. He dropped his pack beside him at the bar and waited. The publican was a woman in her fifties, maybe late forties, blonde and fit. She came from out the back carrying an arm full of logs for the fading fire. She dropped her load on the hearth, chucked a couple of logs on, brushed her hands on her jeans, looked Kenny in the eye and spoke with an edge of authority in her voice.

"And what can I get for you, young fella?"

"Kitchen open missus?"

"Yep, and it's Kate, nobody's missus, ok, and yes, it is. The menu's on the wall behind you."

Reprimanded in the first word spoken.

"Yes, that's okay, Kate."

He turned to check the list and thought he might like the parma.

"You have an ATM Kate?"

"Down the end of the room."

She pointed while dipping into a carton of liquor and setting bottles on a shelf above her while keeping a cautious eye on him. He came back to his stool.

"OK, I'll have the parma, please and a pint of draught. Is the dining room open?"

"Yes, but you'll have to pay extra to sit in there."

"I'll have my meal here then, thank you."

"As you wish."

She was already halfway to the kitchen and speaking over her shoulder. It looked like she was running the place by herself. She was back in a minute with cutlery for him and returned to the taps behind the bar and poured his beer. By this time, a couple of locals had walked in and were looking at the lucky dip machine against the wall.

"Hey, you guys, off you go. Until I get my phone back, you're all banned."

They left without arguing but were clearly not happy. Obviously, they knew the rules. Kenny had to ask.

"What was that about, Kate?"

"I don't mind 'em most of the time, but the other night one of 'em stole my phone. I had it right here, and then it was gone. Don't worry, it'll come back. They won't get any drinking done here until they return it."

And off she went to the kitchen before he could say anything or query her about her attitude to indigenous people. She returned with his lunch. He was hungry, so he forgot about his questions, his appetite was sharp, and he dug right in. The first tick was the hot plate. How often is that not the case? Then, to his surprise, the chicken was tender and covered the plate. It was fresh-cooked, and the sauce was from fresh tomatoes. The cheese had a bite to it, and the chips were crisp and plentiful. He attacked it with vigour, all the while keeping an eye on the hyperactive publican. Wiping the last of it all from his mouth and onto his sleeve, he finished off the pot, a perfect drink with parma and called her attention to his enjoyment. He was about to pick up his pack and leave when she stopped him.

"Are you looking for a bit of work, mister?"

"Jack, Kate. I wasn't really, but what do you have in mind?"

"Well, if you can pull a beer, I reckon you might be able to keep the peace here in the bar. You'll get a room and board and a couple of hundred for a week's work. What do you say to that?"

"Hmmm. Tell you what. I'll give you a week to see how I go, and then if we're both happy, I might just stay awhile. I've only been here for a couple of days, but Coolgardie's my kind of town, I think. I am a bit doubtful about excluding people on the basis of their colour. Their beef is with you, so you'll have to deal with that one, OK?"

For the first time, she smiled just a little, having no idea what he meant about it being his kind of town. Clearly, he was his own kind of man as well.

"That's okay Jack. I know it's not all of them, but they will flush out the culprit without me having to do it. Follow me. I'll show you your room, then you can start."

He was thinking it might be a good place where he wouldn't have to answer questions about himself and his background. Still had little idea, his mind still blank. Western Australia has often provided refuge for runaways. It's a long way from the east coast and the big cities where too many bodies are buried in the concrete, where lives can get complicated. That's not to suggest life in the west is simple, it's not necessarily so. Even so, it's the wild west to everyone who doesn't live there and a good place to stay anonymous.

His room was upstairs facing the main street, directly above the public bar. A bed, a wardrobe, a table and one chair – basic. But the room had good light and a high ceiling, it would do, he thought. Looking out the window, he scanned nearby rooftops and thought he could pick the best places for snipers when the bad guys rode into town. Looking directly down, he didn't fancy being the stuntman who had to somersault into a horse trough when the bullets were flying. Kate reefed his attention back to her.

"The bathroom is down the hall, but there aren't any other guests, so it's all yours."

"Thanks, Kate. I'll just clean up and unpack a couple of things. I'll be down to start work."

She left him to it.

The first thing he did when he returned to the bar was to nick out to the kitchen to introduce himself to the cook. She was cleaning up after a quiet lunch trade when he walked through the door.

"Hello there, you're the cook, I take it. Thanks for the best parma I've had in a long time. Jack's the name, and Kate has asked me to work behind the bar starting now. Will be looking forward to meals, that's for sure."

"Hello, Jack. Sandra. Yeah, people are often surprised by the meals. We do our best. Kate makes sure we have the best supplies, so that helps a lot."

"So, you and Kate have worked together for a while?"

"Funny that. We were both hooked up with no-hopers who only wanted to scrounge around in the bush looking for gold, and drink was their other hobby, the one they were really good at. They're long gone, and we are better off running things by ourselves. It was hard to get money from the bank, but they eventually relented. Kate is persistent once she's decided what she wants."

"Good on you for having a go. Tough game, hospitality, hey. Better get to work, talk later. Nice meeting you."

"Same here, Jack."

Gold was on his mind for the rest of the day. He still hadn't decided to meet with Sue in Perth. He'd shelve the issue for the next week and then decide. Then he chuckled to himself, thinking what Sandra might say if he told her the story of the "Drop".

It didn't take long for him to work out the bar, and it was lucky that trade was quiet for the first couple of hours. He was ready when things picked up late in the afternoon. Denver City is the last pub in Coolgardie, the last of 26! The price of gold is on the march, and there are still big mines in the district. That's a guarantee of a steady flow of beer, at least. What Kenny didn't know was the current owners' marketing strategy. He would soon find out. Miners wear an unofficial badge, look rugged, talk rough, take crap from nobody, always stand up for themselves and revel in a superficial camaraderie, and take the piss out of everyone. It has always been thus.

"Hey, Kate, you promised us fresh meat, and all we get is a parboiled blow-in. Where are the backpackers? Fresh meat, fresh meat, fresh meat."

The chant went up with increasing intensity. It began to look ugly then Kenny jumped onto the bar, grabbing everyone's attention. He said nothing, stepped onto their side of the floor and elbowed his way to the jukebox, curious, judging eyes on him. He slipped a coin and chose the raunchiest tune he could find, something called "All Night Long". He then marched back to the bar, pushing his way through the bullies, all eyes on him at this point, hauled himself onto the bar, and began a very poor impersonation of a stripper, gyrating while unbuttoning his shirt, sliding out one arm then the other and simulating a pelvic thrust that sent the crowd wild. They got more fresh meat than they bargained for, and some of it was charred. Kenny was a hit, and Kate had to help pour the beer because the orders went wild. She cornered him when it was all over, and they were cleaning up.

"You saved my bacon tonight, Jack. I hate seeing the yahoos ogle and grope at the bar girls when I can get them. Imagine what it was like in the gold rush days. It would have been horrible for the women."

"But they said you promised them backpackers, Kate."

"I've given in to them too often, Jack. It's no excuse and an even worse explanation. But Sandra and I are into the banks for half a million, and they want their money. You know, rock and a hard place and all that. I hired you today, fearing it was the last roll of the dice. But the dice were good for a change. What you did was blow the issue away with a bit of humour, going on the front foot with the bogans and winning them over. They're a rough lot, but most of them are OK underneath the filth. They'll be calling for you now. Hope you're up for it."

"I don't mind Kate. Let's see how it works out. What happens to you and Sandra if the bank forecloses?"

"Shattered dreams, Jack. Don't know what we'll do. Too old and too broke to start again. No regrets, though. You make decisions and do the best you can. No good crying if things don't work out."

Kenny liked something about her attitude. He had an idea.

"Kate, can I use your phone for one call?"

"You've earned that tonight. Wait, I'll have to get Sandra's, mine's in a paddock somewhere."

Sandra came back with Kate and the phone. Kenny rang Sue's number, his fingers crossed. She answered.

"Hi Sue, it's Jack. Got a bit quiet at the digging when you left. You OK?"

'Digging?' The women looked at each other, questions framed their faces. Kenny walked away from them, continuing.

"Yes, Jack and I'm sorry about that. It's a bit complicated, and I couldn't involve you."

"OK, Sue. Tell me, do you still have the Drop?"

"I do, Jack. Are you worried I'm going to cheat you?"

"It's a bit hard to not think you might have Sue, but really I'm not sure."

"Well, rest easy, sonny. I have an appointment with brokers at the Gold Exchange, and even over the phone, they were excited. But, yes, I still have it."

Kenny then explained what had happened at the Denver City hotel and the trouble the owners were in. He asked Sue not to risk the actual nugget by bringing it back to Coolgardie but to send a photo of it to the phone he was using. He would like to help the owners of the pub through their tough spot.

"Sure, Jack. I'll do it right now. Come to think of it, why don't we do something special for them. You show them the photo tomorrow, and on the day you can organise it, I'll turn up with an armoured escort, and we'll show the people of Coolgardie something to help your friends. I owe you at least that, Jack, and when you think about it, we would be rude to strike it lucky and run away without sharing with the locals. I'll hire a helicopter for the day. We can afford it, you know. It would be safer than driving and give a great entrance."

Kenny's reaction to her enthusiasm swung between humiliating guilt and excitement.

"Sue, I'll go to hell for the sin of misjudging. Your idea is brilliant and a wonderful gift for a struggling town. If you need to call me, you can use this number. Let me know your timing when you have it. Bye."

He held the phone for a few minutes waiting for the ping. To his very pleasant surprise, it came. The photo was good.

"Kate, can I ask you if you can project photos from your phone to the tv in the bar?"

"Yes, my phone's the same as this, yes we can. Why?"

"I want to show you something. Come with me."

Kate rigged the phone to the television and then selected the photo that Kenny had just received. There, on the 72" screen in full colour, was the precious nugget. Kate stared open-mouthed. She then turned to Kenny, still gaping with questions all over her face. Sandra held on to the bar up on her toes, also gaping.

"Whaaaat the Fuuuuck is thaaaat!"

Two voices not exactly in harmony.

"Ladies, it is a pretty thing, hey. Sue and I found it out in the bush a couple of days ago. Now, let me offer you an idea. What do you say we show your rowdy ruffians this photo tomorrow night, and I'll tell them a story. Then on Saturday week, you can put on a street party, invite your friends from here and from Kalgoorlie, and I will have this nugget on display for all to see. We'll call it the "Long Drop" Fiesta. When the word gets around, I think you'll be paying the bank a visit in the not too distant future. I also think you better get ready for accommodation bookings and caravan camping sites because people will come. The toughest bit will be dealing with the media when they get a sniff of a gold strike. Would this help you?"

The two women hugged each other, bawling. Kenny made to leave the room, but they jumped him.

"No, you don't Jack. Is this some kind of scam or set-up? Who the hell are you?"

"So you want me to cancel?"

"Just tell us it's real? We've had our fill of men who do us over. This must be the biggest nugget ever. How heavy is it? Jack, did you find it? Where did you find it? Come on, Jack, out with it. Why did you come here? What's your plan, the real plan?"

"No fisherman ever tells where he caught the big fish. No fossicker ever tells where he found the nugget. You know that. I will not tell you. But what I will do is give you the chance to solve a few of your problems. If you do, then I will leave town a happy man. I need nothing more. That's the extent of my plan."

"So, you walk into a pub for a meal with the biggest lump of gold ever found in your pocket and offer to put it on show and brag about it to everyone. Is that your game? You just want to show off?"

"It could be that, I suppose. You don't know me from Adam. Believe what you want but also consider you might be judging too quickly. Let's continue. I'll tell your patrons tomorrow night how the nugget was found. That I will do. The word will spread overnight. You can make the arrangements for the exhibition to be held on Saturday week. And I think you should get the boys to build you a stage out the front so everyone will get a good look at the prize. If my guess is right, I'll be leaving town on that Saturday at the end of the fiesta and the beginning of a gold strike fever with you at the centre of it. But I promise you I'll be back after a few days in Perth where there is business to be done. When I come back, I might be able to answer more of your questions. Is that OK Kate?"

The two women looked at each other, uncertainty all over their body language.

"I will suspend judgement for now. You can do it, Jack, but only if you leave your stuff in your room."

"OK, and only if you keep the room for me."

"OK."

"How much is this going to cost us? It is going to cost us, yes?"

"Just like you told me, Kate, a couple of hundred a week. Still sounds like a good deal to me."

Kate found him difficult to read and even more difficult to believe. But there was something about him. She wondered, in spite of herself, if it could be possible he was the real deal. A spark of belief, maybe the last spark in her, shot through her soul. She would take the punt.

"That's the biggest lump of gold we've ever seen, and it might be you are as well."

They hugged and laughed. Kenny broke free, said goodnight and left the room.

"Sandra, it's going to be a monster weekend, and you've got 9 days to get ready. You better do some shopping for the kitchen, and you can get some people to help out as well. I'm going to get our rooms cleaned and prepped and call in what few friends we have to help in the bar. I don't know who this Jack Foster is, but he couldn't have come at a better time. If he's right, there'll be a gold rush like the old days, and it could go on for a couple of years if fossickers find more gold. You and I are going to have to decide if we ride the wave or sell into a mania, take the money and run."

"Kate, you're getting ahead of yourself. We've been just getting by, we know the town is slowly dying. Looking past the rush of people, we will own the pub outright and still be able to offer locals and tourists a good experience. I mean, what else are we going to do? Do you want to retire? And do what? We'll talk more, but we can do something good here, Kate. You know, I think Jack is the real deal. He's had a bit of luck and wants to spread the honey. What do you reckon?"

"In my experience, apart from you, I don't have much love left for people generally. And that includes myself. I've done some really wrong stuff. I don't often do much for others because of disappointments when I've tried. I don't know about this Jack character. He sounds too good to be true, and you know what that usually means. You're right. Let's ride this thing and make decisions later. Right now, I'm going to bed. See you for a morning cuppa at 6 tomorrow."

Thursday morning onwards, the phones ran hot, and questions flew around the town. Bush telegraph is a splendid thing. What, people wondered, was going on at the pub? They were hiring staff and buying in heaps of supplies. A big order went out to the Kalgoorlie pubs for access to kegs of beer. Woollies was raided for soft drinks and nibbles. The local butchers and bakers were stretched with orders. Then, Kate talked to every motel and accommodation house in town, warning them to be ready for a big weekend. The funny thing and unusual for her was she had no strings attached. She was being inclusive purely and simply. If Jack came through as he promised, there was going to be plenty for everyone. People noticed the change in her because they expected her to be looking for kickbacks. Terry, the local builder, was running around getting timber and helpers to do something structural outside the pub. He was Albanian originally and boasted when asked that he came to Australia as a nine-year-old with one shoe. He lost his other shoe off the gangplank. He reckoned that if he could make it in this country with a start like that, then there was no excuse for anyone born here. Kate liked his energy and often called on him for little jobs. She knew he would do something solid. With all this happening, she didn't have to do any advertising, people were picking up the vibe from one another.

So, Thursday evening. Enough of a stir had erupted to ignite interest. By 5:30, locals began arriving in numbers, all of them hungry for information. Utes from the mining camps, town locals and a few carloads from Kalgoorlie were all headed for Denver City pub. The pub was ready for them. Kenny was one of four barmen. Kate didn't want barmaids for this job. She had been down that road and learned her lesson. The kitchen, however, was a different matter. Sandra had half a dozen local women flat-out with preparations.

The normal Denver City crowd was raucous once lubricated, and it was the kind of energy most people shunned. An outback beer hall is a wild thing. Not this night. A kind of calm expectation settled over the room, sages and prophets offering their reasons for the occasion over hands full of chips and hamburgers. One old digger who drank at the pub most nights and sat at his usual spot confided to the drinker next to him.

"You know Les, I can smell it. There's been a strike, it's in the air."

"Ya reckon, mate? Be a surprise, but ya can only hope. Pass the sauce."

At 8pm, Kate grabbed a cordless microphone they used for karaoke and called for attention. She asked for quiet so that Jack could tell them a story. A buzz followed. Most of them had never seen Jack. He had only worked one night at the bar. Those who had seen his performance quietly shared what they had seen. Kenny stepped forward and took the mike from Kate. He ignored a couple of miners from the previous night calling for him to take off his shirt.

"Coolgardie people, thank you for these few minutes and thank you, Kate, for your permission. A few days ago, my good friend, a lady named Sue, was with me when we called in for camping supplies. Sue is a fossicker. I give her some help."

"I'll bet you do, mate. Hope she's worth it."

A few of the boys laughed, hoping to set up a hijack. Kenny fixed his gaze on the big mouth but showed no aggression in his reprimand.

"The woman I refer to, gentlemen, actually saved my life out the back of Alice Springs. It's a story worth telling, and I'll be forever grateful to her. To me, she is a saint. So you, young man, are out of line, OK? Now, back to the story."

He had their attention and their respect. Anticipation shot skyward.

"We headed into the bush about 5kms off the road. Let's say somewhere between 10k's west of here and about the same distance towards Kalgoorlie. We set up camp, including my one-man tent and a fire. (He stared at the big mouth). Sue is her name, and she travels in an old Patrol with a pop-up van. As it turned out, we were only there for one night. By the time I woke in the morning, alone in my one-man tent, she had already left, but not because of any kind of disagreement. It was what happened while we were setting up I want to tell you about. She asked me to dig a hole for our toilet. Look at this poor savaged left arm of mine. It's not as good with a shovel or crowbar as it used to be."

They were onto him.

"Go on, tell us what you found in the hole."

Kenny laughed.

"I can't even tell a good yarn. You're ahead of me. Anyway, I'll just show you. Turn your attention to the television."

Kate flashed the photo. The room was in stunned silence for a full 30 seconds. Kenny added.

"It was a dunny hole, so we called the nugget The Long Drop. We were pretty excited and forgot our manners. When we came to our senses, Sue said that we should acknowledge the place it was found, and we changed the name to "The Coolgardie Drop.""

Laughter and applause were followed by screams. One wag suggested:

"Yeah, Coolgardie, the shit hole!"

The retort was good.

"It takes a genius to turn a shit hole into a gold mine."

Another burst of laughter. The bigmouth, who embarrassed himself earlier, stepped forward and held out his hand to Kenny.

"Sorry mate, for being an arse before. Won't happen again."

Others in the crowd voiced what everyone was thinking.

"How much does it weigh?"

Silence returned to the room. All eyes were on Kenny.

"We only had Sue's bathroom scales. Oh, yeah, they weigh 2kgs light because she likes that."

More laughter.

"OK, here's the thing. After we cleaned it up. I mean, after she cleaned it up, we carefully laid it on the scales, and it read……. 44.5 kgs. There that's it."

"Where did you dig? Where did you dig?"

The crowd turned in on itself, such was their amazement at the size of the thing. This was major, and the buzz of excitement made hearing difficult. Kenny had lost their attention, and even if he could have told them, they wouldn't have heard. In the absence of an answer, the crowd eventually turned back to him.

"I know what you're thinking, and good luck to you if you run into the bush looking. But I want to suggest something else. You people are this town, all locals. When the news gets out, you're going to see a tidal wave of visitors keen to try their luck. They're going to pester you for information, and they're going to need equipment of all kinds to go gold hunting, even guides. Many will need accommodation. You were not here in the original gold rush over a hundred years ago, but you are about to be in the middle of one. You have also seen what happens when the big guys take over. Just look at Kalgoorlie. There probably is more gold out there, but the real money is going to be in the services you can offer the starry-eyed romantics who will stream into your town. I can't tell you where we found it, and we are not going back there anyway. The thing is, you can benefit from the find if you choose to. What I can do is show the nugget to you. It's in the possession of professional gold assessors in Perth right now. They will bring it here on Saturday next week at midday to show it to you. Do you want to see it?"

The noise of approval was deafening.

"You may not like the intrusion, but you should prepare yourselves to be on international news. Coolgardie is back in business, and good luck to you. You'll probably see a bit of a run on your real estate. When there is mania, anything can happen. You may not care, but I kind of do. I'll be working behind the bar for a while to keep an eye on you all. So, all of you, have a good night, you've got a lot to talk about and plan for."

More shouts of approval. Best trading night for a long time. Kate and Sandra shone with affirmation through a veil of perspiration and fatigue. Eventually, the crowd melted away, chattering about their ideas for exploiting a gold rush. The chatter was about hardware shops, bush clothing, groceries, everything.

"Thank you, Jack. I didn't know what you were up to at first, but you've done well for us. Thank you. I'm starting to get what you're doing. You are one sneaky and honourable son of a gun."

"I am, Kate. Hope it all works out for you and Sandra. Just be ready for Saturday, it'll be huge."

Back in Perth, Sue hired two security guards for the trip and a helicopter for the day. It would be too risky to stay overnight in Coolgardie after everyone had seen the nugget. The Perth Gold Exchange wanted to send a minder with her to guarantee the arrangement they had with her about the future of the find but reluctantly settled on the idea that the hired guards would be enough. She booked a chopper big enough for five passengers. The cost of the jaunt, it was agreed, would be underwritten by the Gold Exchange. She also called Kenny to make sure it would be okay for the helicopter to land on the main street of Coolgardie. In turn, he visited the local police in Coolgardie to get that clearance. Interest in the weekend was surging.

The photo was on permanent display for the next week, and people from all over the district and beyond came to see it. The rest of the world saw it on their news bulletins. Opportunists from Perth were already trickling in, looking for every kind of accommodation. Business was so brisk Kate had trouble getting all the ordering done for the big event. Swan Brewery promised a truckload by midweek, and she had back up from a couple of Kalgoorlie pubs if she needed more. In fact, traders in Kalgoorlie were making their own preparations for the spill-over that would certainly come their way. Of course, the media had their broadcast vans on site by the middle of the week, wandering journos quizzing locals about their thoughts and feelings, the lifeblood of mass media. They toured the many recently sprouted fossicker camps and interviewed dozens of diggers. Coolgardie was a national hot spot and an international curiosity. Kenny gave only one interview, footage shared amongst local and international outlets. He told the story just as it had happened, and together with the photo of the nugget, the headlines went viral.

Saturday came, and at 10am, the main street was closed to traffic. Sue had confirmed her arrival by helicopter at midday. A range of pop-up food stalls began business, and Terry Memett, the local builder, had erected a stage at the front of the pub. Coolgardie was ready to welcome its most famous nugget. Local band 'Bricks of Gold' played for an hour, warming the enthusiasm of the building crowd. 'Party' is the word for the ambience, and it wasn't adults only. Kids and oldies helped generate a family atmosphere, and buffoonery was unlikely. National media cameras were perched on top of vans to get a bird's eye view of the exhibition. Big names in news media circulated.

Approaching midday, all eyes turned to the sky. The clatter of a helicopter signalled its approach. A buzz whizzed around the crowd. Kenny looked up and thought,

"Hmm, Sikorsky S-76C, she's coming in style."

And then he stopped himself. How did he know that? Too late to wonder, the craft was just setting down about 100 metres away from the crowd. By the time its blades stopped whirling, and the doors opened, Kenny was there. A burly security guard held up his hand, warning Kenny to stand back. Sue defused and threw her arms around him.

"Thanks for this, Jack, it will mean a lot to locals and to my dad."

"What? Oh, I get it. He was the first person you thought of when we lifted the rock out of its resting place. I didn't know he was still with us, let alone accessible. Good on you. I would've done the same thing, though probably without the mystery."

"He's in care in Freemantle, where he retired. I had to bring him."

"Of course, let me help with him. I'll get him a seat on the stage. Bet he's excited hey."

"Here, Dad. This is Jack. I told you he's the one who really found it. He'll show you to the display area, okay?"

Blinking in the strong light, the old man held out his hand for help getting out of the helicopter. Kenny was surprised by the strength of his grip.

"Thanks, Jack. I'm Lou. Glad to meet you."

Nobody took any notice of Kenny ushering the old gentleman towards the pub. Their eyes were on the box being carried between two security guards while the pilot helped clear a path for them through the crowd.

Terry had built two sets of steps to the stage. Kenny wanted to allow people to walk one way past the exhibition for a close look. The ceremony began with Kate.

"OK, everybody. Let's get this started. There's no need to push and shove because you will all get a good look at the nugget once we finish with the speeches. Our mayor, Wynter Parsons, is first. Wynter, they're all yours."

"Thanks, Kate. People of Coolgardie are pretty much all here, and so we should be. Today is special because the people who found the magnificent nugget we are about to unveil have thought of us before doing anything else with their treasure. And it is theirs. Good luck to them. But thanks to them for arranging this assembly. Before we hear from them, let me add this find could signal a return to the prosperity of the last gold rush more than a hundred years ago. Let's hope so. Are you ready?"

A roar of approval erupted, viewed by millions across the country and the world. She held up her hands and added.

"Let's hear from the two people who have struck the first blow. Jack Foster and Sue Whittaker, we salute you."

Another roar. Sue stepped up, and a hush fell over the street.

"It gets in your blood, you know. I was a little girl just 10 yrs old, when my dear father, who is with us today, first took me fossicking. I have a biscuit tin of about twenty-five small pieces and a phial of dust. I take them with me everywhere I travel, looking for more. I have to thank my dad Lou for that, and I'm so proud to be able to show him the end result. Jack might have told you I left him stranded in the bush the night we found the nugget. He was not to know I was thinking only of my dad, and he probably thought he wouldn't see me again. Anyway, here we are, and while it's easy to say we love Coolgardie, I really hope this discovery brings you great prosperity. As they say, it's been a long time between drinks."

Loud and genuine applause.

Kenny took the mike.

"Let's do it now. Boys, would you open the box and show us the Coolgardie Drop."

The guards opened the container and lifted the nugget carefully into view and onto the table. The midday sun struck the nugget, it flashed a great smile at them. Gasps were everywhere as if they were witnessing a miracle. Kenny asked two of the pub workers to stand at the steps.

"Now, we welcome you to walk calmly up the steps and past the table. Have a close look, and then proceed down the other steps to your place."

It was like being in church. God couldn't have commanded more respect. It took thirty minutes to complete the viewing. 'God.' 'Gold.' Only one letter different. Kenny whispered to Sue's father.

"By the way, Lou, I've been out fossicking with Sue for a while. She tells me you got her started."

Lou, late eighties, but his eyes signalled alertness. In looks, he could have been taken for Willie Nelson, straggly long silver hair tied back in a ponytail and old broad-rimmed bush hat. His hearing was still sharp, and his voice was the gravel of Kristofferson.

"Reckon so, sonny. You seem to have had in one day the luck I've been looking for all my life."

Kenny nodded and smiled. He was right on the money there.

"That could piss a man off, Lou. Is that what you're feeling?"

"C'mon, Jack. Not at all. You have the look of a man who won't spoil easily. I got nothin' to cry over, son. Not many have had the luck we've had today. Y'know it's worth more than the weight of the gold, don't you?"

"No idea, Lou."

"Put it this way, this'll help you figure it. That giant pit they've got there in Kalgoorlie. How much does it take for them to get 45 kilos of gold out of the ground, hey? Probably a month, with all that machinery and men. They only get a fraction of an ounce out of ten tons of excavation. To find a lump like you have is a damn miracle."

"Yes, it is, and clearly, everyone here understands that."

"You think some jokers'll have a go to knock it off today?"

That jolted Kenny. Had not expected that question, and it forced him to sit up straight and scan the crowd for signs. Not sure what the signs might be, but he scanned for them.

"The guards are armed and ready, so I hope no one is silly enough to try."

"They better be careful on the way back to the chopper. It could happen. I've seen what gold fever can do to a sane man."

"There are a few cops, journos and photographers here, Lou. We better get a couple of shots with you, Sue and the nugget. You can show your friends."

"Friends? Got no friends in that bloody death camp."

"Whoa."

Kenny was taken aback.

"Sounds like you have a story to tell, Lou. Do you have to be there?"

"That's the worst part. I do. This dying caper is a pain in the neck. People who drop dead are the lucky ones. Hanging about and decaying is too slow. Not that I want to die either, I don't. When you define ecstasy as the absence of pain, you know you're on the slide. But I'll take that. A day without pain is a special day. This day, for example, is out of the box and is one worth waiting for. Not only is it without pain, but it also has the icing on the cake, real, undiluted pleasure. I'm not even thinking about going back. I'm sitting here with you and Sue and on national TV, how's that for a good day?"

"Got to admire the way you've thought it out. Can I talk to Sue about your choices for the next couple of weeks at least?"

"Nice of you to offer what you're about to offer, Jack, but no way am I going to be carted around. Gotta be fair to people, y'know."

"Look, the procession has just about finished. I'll have to wrap it up. Talk to you later. Might come back to Perth with you for a couple of days. Stay in a good hotel. What about it?"

"Don't ask me twice. Great idea. At least that's on the way back to Freo. Don't want to cramp your style, hey."

"Ha, yeah, all style and no class."

Old eyes sparkled while Kenny lined up the media throng for close-ups of the nugget with Lou and Sue. The pictures would go round the world in a matter of minutes and be on every news service over the next 24 hours.

The crowd started to disperse, moving to the food vans or the pub, time to eat and drink. The security guards packed the nugget and headed back to the chopper. Interviewers, microphones in hand, scoured the crowd for instant feedback. Kenny scanned for trouble. Sue guided her dad back to the chopper. But the pilot was not ready, in fact, he didn't appear to be close by. Then one of the locals yelled for help.

"Someone get me a belt quick, this bloke's just been bitten by a brown snake. He's already down."

Help was immediate, and first aid was applied. People in the bush know how quickly to move on snake bites. But there was no way he could fly the helicopter, he was in a swoon and needed a hospital.

Kenny assessed the situation.

"Get him on the chopper and belt him in."

"Why, Jack, what are you doing."

"No time to argue Sue. I'm qualified to fly this thing. Let's get going, we have to get this man back to Perth."

He spoke with such authority that nobody challenged him. He slid into the pilot's seat and automatically ran through all the pre-flight checks. He didn't know how he knew these things, he just knew he did. Within a couple of minutes, he had ignited the machine and was scanning to make sure he was clear to take off. Lou was in the seat next to him, aware he was watching something special. He had sat with Kenny for the best part of an hour at the exhibition and had a strange but good feeling about him. The two burly security guys were not so sure and showed it, frozen in their seats.

"Anything I can do to help, Jack?"

There was a sparkle of mischief in the old man's eyes. They smiled at each other. That was enough distraction, and Lou kept quiet after that. Sue was in charge of watching the pilot, and he couldn't have been in better hands. She knew about pressure bandaging and how to manage releasing and reapplying pressure. The flight took an hour, Kenny pushing it as much as he safely could. He radioed ahead for an ambulance to meet them and informed emergency services what the ailment was. He also alerted the Perth Gold Exchange to have an armoured vehicle waiting to take the Coolgardie Drop to safety. Not one official challenged the pilot.

On the ground, and once all was taken care of, Kenny, Sue, and Lou felt a need to debrief and found a coffee shop inside the terminal where they could sit for a while.

"Jack, who are you really?"

"Sorry, Sue, I don't really know. But I am getting intermittent flashes. No idea how I knew about the flying. Anyway, the pilot is in good hands. He'll be okay. What are we going to do with this old bandit?"

"I'm taking him back to Freemantle."

"Lou, if Sue thinks it possible, would you like a little holiday back in Coolgardie, staying at the Denver City Hotel? I'll look after what you need. Sue has a few things to do, and we could have a bit of a rest and some fun while we wait for her. OK with you?"

"I brought my meds, there's enough for two weeks. As you say, Sue's got a few things to do in Perth, but she doesn't need us, do you, Sue? And the walking corpses at hell's waiting room won't miss me. I'm up for it Jack. Thanks for the offer."

"Oh no, you don't know what you're setting yourself up for, Jack. He'll be holding court all day long as long as his glass is full."

She stopped herself from being a killjoy, saw her dad's shoulders sag and reconsidered.

"On second thought, what's the downside? What do you think, Dad?"

"C'mon, Lou. I know you're dying to get back to your little room and your favourite bathtime nurse, but what's the hurry?"

"Haha. Let me see. A road trip, free booze, good food, a willing audience, country air or straight back to the death camp. Hmmmm. OK, you win, let's play."

"Now, down to business, Jack. The Gold Exchange will give us the going price for gold which is around $1500 U.S. an ounce, and on top of that, 20% for the nugget. So on Wednesday, I can pick up a cheque for more than $3m. They will also throw in the expenses for today's trip to Coolgardie. I have to ask Jack. How much do I get? Remember, you found the nugget, and you've let the light shine on me so far."

"Sue, I was going to ask you the same question. I reckon the ledger between us is even now. I was worried I'd never be able to repay you for saving my life and monitoring my recovery. So, I think 50/50 works, you do the business, OK?"

"Won't say no to that. I'll deposit the money in your new account. Then I'm going to come back and spend a few days with you guys before taking Dad back to Freemantle. The next question, Jack, after all this is done, are you coming with me? We could plan a trip that suits us both. Promise I'll get a big supply of all-day suckers."

"Yeah, Sue, let's do that. I didn't think you noticed about the chupas. Now, a good hotel and dinner. Tomorrow, Lou, you and I are going shopping for a vehicle for your daughter. The old Patrol has done its job. OK with you Sue?"

"Why not. I've been looking at twin cab utes, they look versatile. Can I trust you to get me a good one?"

"Darlin', we can do that, can't we, Jack?"

"Yep, and you're paying, Lou. No, don't fall over, just kidding. Sue, you can pick it up when you've finished the business. But you can't see the vehicle until then. After we get the car organised, I think it might be a good idea if your dad and I jump on the Indian Pacific train on Tuesday to get back to Coolgardie. I don't need a vehicle, and afterwards, I'll be travelling with you for a while."

"Haven't had so much fun in years. Now, where are we going to eat?"

EXHAUSTED AFTER THE FLIGHTS and the worry, Hanna was happy to get home. You can travel in comfort, but there's nothing like your own space, your own room and definitely your own bed. She didn't even feel like talking to Mark, dropped her bag and fell onto the bed, kicking off her shoes in the same movement. Then, nothing. Nothing until woken by the aroma of fresh-brewed coffee. Orientation moment, and then she padded to the kitchen where she found Mark deep in breakfast preparation.

"Oh, there you are. I opened your door, so the aromas would reach you. Welcome home."

Mark had his own key, and Hanna's next thought was a little concern that she had allowed things to develop too far. She checked herself for being ungrateful and allowed her face to show she was pleased to see him and thankful for breakfast.

"Morning, Mark, thanks for this. Good to be home."

"The girls are fine, and we've held things together in the office though it'll be good to have your input on a few things the developers are up to."

Hanna sensed rebuke and thought, "Oh, oh. If this is domestic bliss, it's short on bliss."

"Tell you what, Mark. When we've finished here, you better get to the office. I'll need a little time to get myself in order. And don't worry about the developers, we know the game they're up to, and there's no way we're going to let them sign contracts for sub-standard materials with false compliance paperwork. More about that later, let's tuck into this lovely breakfast. This girl could eat a rabbit on the run."

Forehand, backhand, down the line passing shot. That's how long term relationships manage conversation. Either that or total silence. Mischievous sniping is more entertaining. Mark fussed around the cooking area while Hanna enjoyed her scrambled eggs. She stood up, sipped the last of her coffee and returned to her bedroom. A few moments later, she heard the front door click closed. She looked in the mirror. "Lucky you've held back on that one girl."

An hour later, showered, refreshed and dressed for work, she was ready to face the day. Mark had asked her nothing about Kenny, he was clearly more interested in his own situation. Just as clearly, he was still disturbed by the overshadowing spectre Kenny represented. And just as one finishes a sentence with a full stop, she knew the significance of his key to her apartment on the kitchen bench. She would have asked for it, but this gesture made it easy. "Don't get your meat where you earn your bread." Wise words often ignored. Then, she surprisingly thought of Charlie. No warning, nor real reason, but there he was, front and centre. Then the thought disappeared, and she focussed on the day ahead of her.

After work the same day, Hanna wanted to check on Kenny's place. She didn't see Mark because he had to take his daughters to his mother before leaving for Singapore. He was scheduled to meet with the principals of the developing consortium doing the massive

Prince's highway job. They were eighteen months into the job, and he was under pressure to allow Chinese-made cladding to be ordered. Mark knew Hanna's stand on the issue, but she had been absent while the issue needed settlement. Next morning, Melbourne time, he called her.

"I've held the line, but it's no good. They don't listen. It's not negotiable for them, and they don't care about our objections. They say their documentation proves the material satisfies standards, it is economical, and every major builder in Australia uses the material. They then reminded me subtly that they owe us three months' fees, more than $700,000, which they are still holding. They are prepared to cut us loose from the project if we don't give them what they want. What do you think?"

"It's a tough one Mark. Take all the important stuff into account when you make the decision. It's easy for me here to take the moral high ground, but the practical issues are important. I think we'll consider the relationship with these people when you come home. If you come home with their debt to us cleared, it might help us make the right decision."

"I hear you. See you in a few days, and then we'll lay down some plans, clean up our act and put these people behind us."

She had a good day in the office without having to deal with Mark and the elephant in the room, their relationship intentions for each other. She began thinking about how the business might evolve without the internationals. At the end of the day, she headed straight to Richmond with Kenny still on her mind. It felt eerie opening the door to Kenny's cave, like walking into a burial chamber. She shivered and then noticed an envelope just inside the door. It was a note from Wolvie. "Hello Bobby. Hope you're good. Things are a mess under the bridge, and I'm going bush busking. See you. Wolvie." Hanna had met Wolvie and remembered his story about Kenny visiting him and his homeless friends under the Swanston St. bridge and listening to their impromptu concerts. Might be homeless, but still an interesting character. She could tell why Kenny would be accepting of him. The switchboard was on the wall near the door, and she flicked on the power. Otherwise, everything was as Kenny had left it, dusty perhaps but no disturbance.

The first thing to do was to tidy things. She flipped his computer, took out Charlie's email address and fired off a greeting email and asked him to send Kenny's things to her address. She wanted to see what Kenny had taken with him when he left Melbourne. Not much, she found. He travelled light. While waiting for Charlie's reply, she checked out the fridge. It was turned off, and the door jarred open. He had thought of everything. The workshop was as neat as a pin, and 'Javelin' was on stands. What a classic. Holden lovers would kill for this specimen. From there, she heard the computer 'ping'. Charlie.

Hanna, glad you are home safely. Kenny's things will be in your hands as soon as possible. I say that because, in a way, we are worlds apart. Should only take a week. Amongst his things was a USB with his movie script on it. What a great story. You promised to get the film made. Good luck with that. I was thinking it would make a good novel. I'd love to help. If you are interested, I would like to write it off the script. Let me know. It might be easier to get the story published than to get a film made. The owners of the station have decided to let me do a Masters Degree in Management through Monash University. There is a twelve-week residential element in the first year, so I will be in Melbourne for that time. That will be in mid-May. Be great to catch up on all these things.

Cheers

Charlie.

Sitting at Kenny's living room bench, Hanna had raided his coffee supply and was sipping a steaming brew, black without milk, while thinking about her next moves. Then there was Charlie. It had been only a couple of days, but she thought softly of him. Putting those thoughts aside, her mind switched to Kenny. She didn't want to be passive, sitting for god knows how long, waiting. Clearly, he would be injured though a search of hospitals had not found him. What, she thought, were the possibilities? Then she thought of the fire remains she found half a kilometre from the crash site. Someone had camped there. Kenny could have stumbled though injured and found the camper. Or else the camper found him. Clearly, the hypothetical camper would have sought help had he or she seen the remains of the helicopter. Maybe Kenny had dragged himself and found the camper, far enough away from the site that the camper didn't even know of the crash. What condition might he have been in? Dazed for sure. Maybe lost memory. He would have contacted her had he been compos mentis. OK, he's probably amnesiac. Probably with a camper. So, if I start looking, where to start because this camper is definitely not on the bitumen? Burdened with an invalid, where would this camper go? I don't know where to start. Throw a dart into a map, maybe. They were in the vicinity southwest of Alice, on Charlie's station. They could've headed south and possibly to Coober Pedy or Finke and Oodnadatta if they were heading to SA. More likely, they'd head west towards Warburton and then south towards Kalgoorlie and from there to Perth, perhaps. I'm going to Kalgoorlie. I'm looking for a vehicle with an off-road trailer/camper. But first, I better square things away with Mark. So, it was going to be a long shot, but a calculated one. They have to come out of the bush at some point, she thought.

No way she could just head out on a possible wild goose chase based on a dozen different 'what ifs'. First, she'd have to work things out with Mark, help get them both out of the contract with the Chinese, now that it had soured. Then she could and would go.

KENNY AND LOU HEADED OUT on Monday morning after their big weekend. They were off to find a new vehicle for Sue.

"What do you think, Lou. Toyota or Nissan?"

"Jap is Jap, Jack. What say we take the first dealership we see."

It happened to be Nissan. They parked Sue's Patrol and wandered inside. Nobody approached immediately, so they sauntered around the vehicles on display.

"Morning gentlemen, Jet Jolly. I see you're looking at the Navara. Just tyre kicking today, or are you more advanced in your decision making?"

"Jack and my good friend here is Lou. Actually, Jet, we're ready to buy. Are you ready to sell?"

They shook hands.

"Hell yes. Navara, yes?"

"Yes."

"Next question probably is about configuration, yes?"

"Well, let's not mess around. Top of the line is this one?"

"STX-550 Diesel, 3 litres, turbo. Like a test drive?"

Lou stepped up.

"Why not? You got one ready to go?"

Jet led them to the demonstration vehicle, allowing Kenny to slip into the driver's seat and Lou beside him. Jet sat in the back. He took them on a short tour of the port and then onto some open road where they might let the beast loose. Lou was bamboozled by the gadgetry while Kenny got a sense of the handling, driver vision, the convenience of controls and the comfort of seating, thinking all the while about Sue since it was going to be her car.

"Now, Jet, let's talk about the package. What can you add?"

"Depends how far you want to go. Let's see, bullbar hugging the shape of the front, driving lights, towing package, tinted glass, wind deflectors on the windows, bin liner and your choice of bin cover, tonneau or hardcover with remote control. Then there are the side steps and mats for the front and back to protect the carpet. The total package would come close to $70000, but I reckon if you are a cash buyer, you could expect to pay about $64000 drive away. Say, How come I know your face?"

Lou stepped up again.

"You've probably seen his face in the news. This, young man, is the fella who tripped over a 45 kg lump of gold up in Coolgardie."

"You're right. Saw it on the news. Congratulations Jack. Tell you what. Let me go talk to my boss. I reckon he'd like to meet you. And don't say anything to him, but he sneaks into the bush himself sometimes with a metal detector, and a dog he believes can smell gold. It probably can't, but he reckons, so we have to let him have it. May I get him to meet you?"

Lou again.

"Yeah, Jet, go and find him. We might get a better deal, hey, Jack."

Jet, grinning ear to ear, raced up the stairs to his boss's office.

"What is it Jet? I see you working those guys over. Did the test drive get them over the line? Hope so, or it was a waste of time?"

"Mr Duke, you won't believe it. That guy, the younger one, is the man who found the big nugget in Coolgardie. You were talking about it the other day. Would you like to meet him? And yes, he's ready to buy a Navara, top of the line and all the extras."

"Hmmm, good boy, Jet. Yes, I'll come down to meet him in just a minute. I've got an idea."

Richard Duke made a quick call to his photographer and then hurried downstairs to meet the celebrity.

"Richard Duke, Mr Foster." He reached to shake Lou's hand.

"Not me, Dick, he's the genius," pointing to Kenny.

"Look, boys. My staff have told me what you're after. Let me help you."

"Richard, you're not going to hijack this man's commission, are you?"

"Haha, of course not, Jack. But if you allow us to photograph the two of you in front of one of our Navaras and use it with the published photo of the nugget for our marketing, I will make it worth your while. How about that? And if I can persuade the other WA dealers to join the campaign, we can do even better, much better."

"Richard, it sounds like a generous offer and let me confer with my senior partner here."

Kenny took Lou aside.

"Lou, it looks like we're on a winning streak, what do you think?"

"Put the lot on black."

"Richard, can you get specific if we wait for you to ask your colleagues?"

He was like a white pointer with the scent of fresh food in his nostrils.

"Give me fifteen minutes, Jack. Jet, take these gentlemen to the board room and open the bar. I'll join you in a few minutes."

"Yes, Mr Duke."

When he joined them in the board room, he was smiling broadly.

"Well, boys, I have six dealerships lined up to use a photo of you photo-shopped with the nugget in an advertising campaign. We think it'll be a winner. You OK with that? The photographer is only a few minutes away."

He didn't add that the promotion was going to be taken national.

"And the final price for the vehicle?"

"Oh, sorry, of course. We will take responsibility for the total price of the vehicle with all the extras. It will be our pleasure."

"We accept your offer on two conditions. Your salesman here has been most helpful. My partner will pick up the car next Monday and will pay Mr Jolly here $5000 for his work, and you can have the value of our trade-in vehicle. Is that OK with you?"

"Of course, Jack, of course. What's the other condition?"

"You give us a letter now, signed by you, detailing the exact terms of the agreement you offered us and that it will be valid for a twelve-month period, not beyond. OK?"

"To be truthful, Jack, twelve months gives us plenty of time to make this deal worthwhile to us. I'll activate the letter right now."

"Jack, what are you doing. I was happy enough selling you the vehicle. You didn't have to offer me money. But I will take it, of course."

"That's all right, Jet. We're getting a good deal, so should you."

They gave the dealer Sue's phone number, and when they spoke to her, she confirmed she would be in to pick up the vehicle in a week's time. With a bank cheque for the agreed commission for the salesman. Lou stepped forward.

"Thank you, Richard, we've enjoyed buying a car from your organisation."

They shook hands again and left with other things on their minds.

"Lou. Now we should book our train ticket for tomorrow, we'll take Sue's car back to her and then go to lunch."

"Then I'll need a nap, Jack. So much excitement. Never bought a new car before, never been so close to money before, never been a celebrity before. I'm bloody near tuckered out. I mean, I started out life poor, and I've ended up broke. And just for the record, good deal with the car. Like it."

"Good on you Lou. As they say on tv…with the best yet to come."

Kenny was on his way to retiring after a big day with his new old friend. Sue came running after him before he reached the lift.

"Jack, phone for you."

"Hello, oh, hi, Kevin. How are you? Snakebite can give you a fright. Did you see what bit you? Yes, a good thing someone spotted you quickly. No, Kevin, that's fine. I'm glad I could help. Yeah, heading back to Coolgardie tomorrow. Thanks for the call, and good luck. Oh, by the way. Sikorsky's a dream machine. I enjoyed it. Yes, bye."

"You all right, Jack?"

"Sure, Sue. That was Kevin, the pilot. He's feeling better."

"You saved his life, Jack."

"Yes, Sue, but someone else would've stepped in. Glad it worked out well."

"And thanks for looking after Dad. He's having a great time."

"Sue, my pleasure. He's fascinating, but you know that. Tomorrow will be easy, just a train ride."

"Dad told me about the new Navara. Nice deal."

"Really, I didn't do anything. The dealer came and suggested it. We just said yes."

"For a man who does nothing, takes no credit, plenty seems to get done."

The next morning, the Indian Pacific left Perth at 10am. Sue waved the two boys off, and they settled in quickly, a nice cabin with a big window and only one carriage away from the dining car. They both snoozed a bit with the motion of the train. But when they stopped for a few minutes at Ghooli with only an hour to go, Kenny was leaning on his elbows, nose on the glass, Lou had gone to the bathroom. The train line was beside the great northern highway opposite a BP servo. He was just staring, with no particular focus, and he saw a Kawasaki sports bike and a silver BMW R1200 RT slide-in for fuel. Both bikes were rigged for touring, with side panniers and top box. The Kawasaki rider was unmistakeably female in the way she strode to the kiosk. Her companion on the Beemer, tall, athletic, glided after her. Kenny felt nostalgic and couldn't understand why. He made no connection, but he might have seen the two most important people in his life. The train began to move, and he watched them sit astride their bikes and look his way at the train moving away. So close.

Kalgoorlie mid-afternoon. The amnesiac and the geriatric, one bag each, seeing the train off into the distance and Kenny thinking for the second time he should be heading east without knowing why. He didn't know it was better he stayed where he was.

"No, Lou, we're not going to the red lights of Hay street. You won't have the energy. Anyway, your memories are probably sweeter."

"Damn it, Jack, but you're right. Can't help the occasional reminder, though, and I have to say they were a lovely distraction. You know they say if a man isn't thinking about them, then he's not concentrating. Guess I've had my share of concentration. But we can have a couple of beers before we leave, how does that appeal?"

"Of course, we can, and there are quite a few pubs to choose from."

"There you go, the Palace Hotel. Let's go and have a beer on the veranda upstairs and get a good view of the main street. Looks nice and sunny too."

"You're full of good ideas, Bandana Bob. Why not."

"Can I tell you a little story Jack, a true story?"

"Sure, Lou, thou I smell a rat."

"No rat Jack. It happened at the death camp a little while ago. It was about 6:30 one morning, change of shift for the nurses, and one of them did a walk around. She saw one lady's door open and looked in. She rocked back on her heels because that old lady had a visitor, and they were having a nice time if you know what I mean. The nurse gathered her wits and coughed to announce her presence, but it made no difference, the two oldies were hard of hearing. So she spoke up a bit louder. 'Excuse me, Reg, I know you are grown-ups and can do what grown-ups often do, but I hope you know that Emily there has acute angina. Reg heard her vaguely and, looking up, said to her. 'You're damn right she has.'"

Kenny had never heard that one, and he laughed from the belly. It would have been easy to settle in for the rest of the afternoon, Lou was in top form, but Coolgardie was calling, and after a 'couple', they walked back to the street looking for a taxi, Kenny was still chuckling at the image stuck in his head. Maybe the story was really about Lou, not Reg. He was certainly cheeky enough to be the one.

Big Bill, the taxi driver, was happy for the fare to Coolgardie.

"You two look familiar. Have you lived here a long time?"

"Yeah, mate. I'm all about a long time. Some would say I've had too much time, hey."

"Denver City hotel, please, Bill."

"That's it. The Coolgardie Drop what a great name for a nugget. Pretty happy guys, hey? I dug out the metal detector yesterday. Like everyone else, I'm going bush every chance I get. Wish me luck."

"Eyes on the road, Bill. I wish you all the luck that is good for you, Bill."

"That could be a two-edged sword. But I know what you mean. My life is probably full of luck I don't even see. Is that what you mean?"

"Pretty much, Bill, but it's good to have an interest, and the bush is a great place to spend time.

Late afternoon and the bar was busy when Kenny and Lou helped each other through the door.

A mid-afternoon chill was driven back by the ferocity of the fire, and Kenny found a table close to it. Lou felt the cold these days but not in this room, it was ablaze with warmth.

"Beer, Lou?"

"Only if there's no champagne. Kidding, Jack. Swan draught if you please."

The amazing thing was Kenny had spent only a handful of days in the pub, and he was being treated like royalty.

"Keep your money in your pocket, Jack. Kate's house is your house, same for your old friend."

"You can call him Bandana Bob."

The photo of the nugget was still on display, right above where they sat. Many of the drinkers were visitors, wave riders looking for a thrill. Couldn't help themselves and had to try their luck with Kenny.

"Hi there, I'm nobody from somewhere. You're the man who found the gold. Do you remember where you found it? Only want to know so we can see the place. The same question was asked differently a thousand times. Strangely, Kenny had a way with these people, as if each one had an image of the holy grail in his mind and was looking for guidance.

"Yes, I am. And you are on a pilgrimage to see the spot where God touched the earth and left his footprint. Your precious time, your normal life, a holy quest. What is it you seek?"

And that is all he would say before returning to his conversation with Bandana Bob as he was now called.

"You been out in the sun too much, Jack. They don't know what you're saying to them."

"Maybe that's important, Lou. They should be careful about what they want."

"Jack, you're trying to enlighten ignorance. Take it from me if you try to tell an ignorant man something, he won't be grateful. He'll turn a gun on you."

"You have just made this whole trip mean something. Thanks, Lou, I'm going to think long and hard about that one. And I still can't get the image of Reg out of my head."

A few beers, a warm room, a wholesome dinner, and a few more beers and Kenny had to guide Lou to the bedroom he had organised for him and gently lay him on his bed. It was closing time, so he stood to return to the bar to help with the clean-up.

"Jack, can I tell you about Reg and Emily?"

"You already did, Lou."

"No, Jack, they were going to get married. Reg thought he might as well get the important stuff on the table, and he asked Emily what she thought about sex. Emily thought about the question and then replied that she liked it infrequently. Reg asked quickly. Emily, is that one word or two?"

"Go to sleep Lou. You are a sick man."

That's where Kate found him.

"There you are. I'm sorry I didn't have a chance to chat, been helping Sandra in the kitchen all night. Welcome home Jack. Got a minute?"

"Sure, Kate. Pardon my laughing. Bandana Bob is on a role. Hello, and glad to be back. As you can see, I've brought Sue's dad with me. He'll be here till Sue arrives middle of next week. Is that okay with you?"

"C'mon, Jack, what do you think I am? Don't answer. I just wanted to bring you up to date. Everything you talked about last week is happening. No details, but the town has come to life. Every business is surging, and it's all down to you getting stuck in a shit hole in the bush. How's that for a joke. The pub has never been so busy, and we've picked up some really good workers. Sandra and I have been beating back offers from people who want to buy the pub, they've been coming in from all over. Don't think there's anyone in the whole country who hasn't heard the news. So we're going to be all right, again thanks to you. Would you believe it, people are actually stopping here instead of driving through to Kal, which is what they never used to do. And after everything else, you go and save the chopper pilot by flying the thing back to Perth. I didn't know you could do that."

Kate was right about the news reaching everywhere. It might have been better for it not to have happened, but Kate, Kenny, all of them couldn't know.

"That's all right Kate. I didn't know it either."

"You are one dark horse, Jack Foster. The world could do with a few more of you."

With that, she threw her arms around his neck and hugged him. It was real, full-bodied hard loving, and eye to eye. She then let go and left the room. Rattled by the intimacy, he went back to cleaning out the fireplace and then to bed. The importance of her hold wasn't lost on him. He knew what she thought of men generally, and it was big she could get past the mindset. A man doesn't miss an invitation like that because it happens so rarely. Kenny didn't know when or how, but coming back to Coolgardie became top of the list of things to do.

For the next week, the food, the beer, and the story-telling continued. Bandana Bob was a celebrity. His stories, carefully embellished so as not to make people doubt them flowed as freely as the beer. Kenny worked the bar with the new barmen while keeping an eye on the raconteur, made sure he had regular breaks for short walks outside the pub and put him to bed each night. Lou had found a reason to live, it had been missing since his wife died and he installed himself in the retirement village euphemistically called "Big Sky Village". No way was he going to happily return to that place. He was having the time of his life.

Sue arrived on Wednesday the following week, having completed all her business with the Gold Exchange and the vehicle swap. She was permanently smiling.

"Have you checked your bank account, Jack?"

"Sorry Sue, haven't thought of it. Everything went as planned?"

"Smooth as silk. Man, I love the Navara, its got some toe and all mod cons. It's going to take me a while to figure out all the gimmicks. Hope I'll have you to help. Have to take Dad back to Freemantle next, and then we should maybe plan another trip. Do you feel like fossicking?"

"Done that, Sue. Lost interest. It was too easy. We should do something with a bit more of a challenge."

He laughed before Sue saw the irony, and she joined in. Kate caught up with Sue and Kenny.

"There you are. Now we've got the three of you together, could we organise a banquet morning brunch for tomorrow. Our way of telling you stuff. Can't do it later because you can see how crazy the place is."

"No, Kate. Let's do lunch in the dining room tomorrow. Normal menu, normal routine. Sandra's got enough women in the kitchen to keep things going for an hour or so, and you can also stop for an hour. You've got plenty of help. Word them up and let them do it."

Kate hesitated, scratched her head, and her eyes lit with acceptance. She had an idea.

"You haven't been wrong yet, so that's what we'll do. Tomorrow, 12pm, great."

Kenny and Sue moved off, leaving Kate and Lou together.

"So, Bandana Bob, you'll be heading off soon. You've been a big help with the entertainment. I've heard the laughing coming from your corner, it has been a real pleasure."

"Loved the opportunity to chat, Kate. It's all I'm good for these days."

"Dunno about that, Lou. There's a sparkle in your eye. I've seen it."

"I've watched you too, Kate. You're far too smart and young for someone like me. Even if I was a bit younger, I can tell you've learned too much. What makes me glad is you've had all the disappointments life throws at you, and you're now free and young enough to take advantage of it. I can see where you're headed, probably knew before you did. But you know now, don't you? And you can have this for nothing. You couldn't pick better than you have, and good luck to you. Wow! Did I say all that?"

"Yes, you did, Lou, but why don't we keep it all between us for now. He's nibbled the lure but hasn't swallowed it yet. You seem to have picked up a few smarts along the way. Love your style."

"Yeah, older and smarter, hey? But not many people listen."

They giggled.

He had enjoyed the notoriety, but Kenny had watched him sag a bit over a few days. He could see the old fellow needed rest. But he was happy, so the price was acceptable. The old theory at work again.

The love feast lunch was a triumph. The dining room was busy, but most eyes were on table one. Kate and Sandra were forced to sit tight no matter what the demands might have been. It worked. Kate allowed herself to trust the staff to do their best. The main course was wheeled in on a portable barbeque, a full lamb on the spit which had been rotating over hot coals for four hours. Kenny jumped up to do the carving, and Kate stopped him.

"No, you don't, let the cook do it. Take your own medicine."

He did what he was told, and everyone laughed. Roast vegetables and two loaves of homemade crusty bread, and the diners dived in. Kate then instructed the carver to offer other diners the chance to share the lamb. She got a standing ovation, and twenty of them enjoyed a generous slab of hot, roast lamb. To finish off the feast, Sandra had the kitchen prepare a bread and butter custard served with whipped fresh cream, tea and coffee all around. Poor Lou had gorged on the lamb and fresh bread smeared with butter and had to force himself to tackle the custard. He had to, it was one of his all-time favourites. He was of an age to still remember Depression food. He could hardly speak after but grinned from ear to ear. He stood to get attention.

"Dear folks, a toast to your generosity."

All around the table raised their glasses.

"One last thing. You've all been talking about my friends Reg and Emily at the retirement village where I live. I want to tell you that the wedding has been called off."

There was a hush. They had come to know that it was hard to guess what Lou would say next. But someone always falls for the line. It was Kenny.

"Why, Lou, from what I've heard, they were made for each other even if they were 90."

"Sorry, Jack, there's been a hiccup. They can't agree on how to raise the children."

Lou had set up the best joke for last. He was a consummate performer. But that was it. He asked if he might nap for the afternoon so he could go the distance in his corner spot for the evening session. Everyone in the room was still laughing, and they waved his exit. Hugs all around, and Sue ushered him to his room. He sat on the edge of his bed, fatigue and satisfaction oozing from him. He patted the bed to get her to sit beside him.

"Sue, when your mum passed, and you were busy with your career, I couldn't look after myself, and I found that retirement place to go to. It's not so bad there, even if I make it sound bad. It's not, really. The last two weeks have been a real highlight. I am so proud of you. Not just for finding gold but for being gold. You saved Jack's life by taking him in. That's not an easy thing to do. Then when you found the nugget, the first thing you did was bring it to show me. Remember the looks on those old faces in the village dining room. First time in my life, I was ten foot tall. And I've been ten foot tall ever since, thanks to you. Honey, give me a big hug and let me go to sleep. I'm tired. Sue, darlin', what do you think happens when the lights go out?"

She thought, "The room goes dark, Dad, that's all."

She hugged him and helped him into bed, walked to the door and felt the chill of the hairs on her neck as she looked back at her father.

She would find out when she went to rouse him that the chill she felt was his spirit leaving the room. She hadn't answered his question aloud, but it didn't matter. Now, he had his answer.

Kate, Sandra, Sue and Kenny, arms around each other and tears streaming, stood silently around Lou's bed, him lying at peace and gone.

"Sue, your dad was a fossicker all his life, as you well know. How about we lay him to rest in the Coolgardie cemetery? Kind of a nice spot for him. He did like the place in the end. And if anyone in town hears noises coming from the cemetery, it will most likely be Lou telling some of his stories. That is unless you have another idea."

"Well, my only thought would have been to rest him beside Mum. But she was cremated, so I think your idea is the one. He would like it too."

"Then that's what we'll do. Sue, leave all the arrangements to me, and after the service, we'll put on a wake fit to bring joy to any Irishman's heart."

"Was he Irish?"

"Don't know, but I do know the Irish have the best wakes ever."

Tears and smiles all around.

"BOSS, HERE'S TODAY'S PAPER. Great story there about a multi-million dollar nugget in WA."

The boss moved his breakfast plate aside to look at the paper. Something strange about the story and the bloke at the centre of it. The hair stood erect on his neck. He knew that face. Of course, it was older, but he knew it, knew the smile too. The article said his name was Jack Foster. But Chook knew him by another name. He could still see his face as a young boarder at Chook's secondary school. He could still see that boy bowling two of the hardest to play spinners he had ever faced in the nets or in a game. No, that is no Jack Foster, that is none other than Kenny, fucking Burgess, that's who it is. That is the boy who humiliated me in front of my friends, and that is the boy who killed my uncle, the headmaster. He's the one who forced the school to close and me to end up in a shit high school for the rest of my final year. I have two reasons for wanting to see Jack Foster. It's time to pay the tillerman, Kenny Burgess.

"Sammy, come in here."

Sammy always waited outside his boss's office. He didn't need to hear his conversations with visitors or on the phone, but he needed to be close for when he was called. Chook had found him five years earlier in the middle of a football crowd barracking madly and loudly for Carlton, who were playing against Collingwood. Chook liked his energy, and they finished the day in a local pub with other rabid Collingwood fans, drinking pints and watching a replay on the pub television. At the end of the night, they shared a taxi, and Chook told Sammy to look him up at the Orrong Hotel in Prahran if he wanted a job doing security work. They parted the best of friends, and the friendship continued to firm over five years in question.

"Yeah, boss?"

"I want you to go see Spotty Cooper at his office in Chapel Street. Bring him here, I've got a job for him. On the way back, bring half a dozen pies from Wilkie's."

Sammy didn't need to know any more, and he didn't need to question his boss about why he wanted to see a private investigator. He had seen other spivs disappear for asking the wrong question at the wrong time. Chook Fowler could be a benevolent dictator when it suited him, but his dark side was deadly unforgiving.

HANNA AND MARK HAD A BOARD meeting as soon as he returned from Singapore.

"They think we are on board with them, Hanna, but I would like us to get out of the contract. I'm uncomfortable with this whole vertical integration thing they're doing. They must have their hooks into the bureaucracy because everyone knows their documentation for the products they bring in is fiction. They've set the bar, and all competitors here have to follow their lead, or they don't get the plum jobs. We have enough local developers to look after. We don't need the corporate gangsters from another country. What do you think?"

"Totally agree, Mark. Do what you have to, and we'll move on. Actually, you did well to get what they owed us. Makes our move a lot easier. I've worked out a way to shake this contract, but it's going to take a bit of time to do. A bit like getting out of a riptide by swimming with it rather than against it. Our best shot is to keep them thinking we are compliant. They've paid their last account, and we haven't closed them out. They'll think everything is normal. But by the time they pay their next account, we will be ready. You good with hanging on for a while?"

"Good plan Hanna. I'm okay with the strategy."

"Now about our other business. I know it upsets you to be caught up in my difficulties with Kenny, and if you want to cut me loose, I'd understand. Regardless, I have to try and find him before accepting the real possibility he's dead."

"Yes, let's do that. In the meantime, let's put everything else on the shelf. I need time to untangle my feelings, and I am happy to go solo, at least until you resolve those issues with Kenny. You will always be able to take the time you need and leave me to run a streamlined arrangement here. That way, you are funded for what you need to do, and your mortgage is covered. I will run the business until the day you walk back in."

"That's fair, Mark. I can concentrate on what I have to do now. And thanks for your patience and support. But first things first."

The desk and the air were cleared, and Hanna felt a weight lifted. One weight at a time was as much as she wanted to carry.

Back on the computer at home, she fired off an email to Charlie.

Charlie,

Got the package, thanks. Now preparing for a big ride. Going to ride to the West and see if I can pick up Kenny's trail. Will keep in touch along the way. Call me any time.

Cheers.

Hanna.

Within minutes she had his reply.

Hanna,

OK, good idea. Maybe two heads better than one, two sets of eyes and all that. I have plenty of leave due and could meet you. I want to be the one to find him if he's out there or at least with you when you do it. Didn't show you my Beemer when you were here. Could meet in Perth and work out a strategy there. Your thoughts?

Charlie.

Hanna mused for a while over his email. She thought, hmmm, Charlie rides a bike and can cover ground fast. Good. She continued, admitting to herself. Hmmm, Charlie and Hanna on a road trip. Should be pleasant. Why not?"

> Charlie,
>
> *Happy to do the ride together. Just need a few weeks to put business matters to bed then I'll be free. Have already looked at some maps. If you can head towards Warburton and then to Kalgoorlie, we could time it close enough to meet there. Then we could head to Perth and work out a plan from there. The idea of riding alongside you on this perhaps futile quest allows for some positives. Let's do it.*
>
> *Hanna.*

And finally.

> Hanna,
>
> *Done. Give me two weeks' notice, and I'm in.*
>
> *Cheers.*
>
> *Charlie.*

IT TOOK KATE ONLY A DAY to organise a plot for Lou. Plenty to choose from. Space is not an issue in big country. A small gathering but touching and simple service in the catholic church. They are experts in death. Kenny couldn't put his finger on the feelings he had in the church. He couldn't remember his upbringing.

It was a short drive to the burial ground. The entrance is some of the best stonework in town, and the gates, though huge, are welcoming. A tree-lined driveway guides visitors and new arrivals to the selected plot. Sue, Kenny, Kate, Sandra and a dozen or so patrons of the hotel witnessed the event. It felt a bit like a boot hill funeral in an old-time western movie. Funny thing, there were a lot more people at the wake.

"You know, Jack, Dad lived more in the last couple of weeks than he had in many years. I'm sad to lose him but am so happy at the same time. He sat in his corner in the pub surrounded by eager listeners, and he could really tell a story. He had a glass in his hand all day long, good wholesome food, and a warm bed, but mostly he was appreciated. Does it get any better?"

"No, Sue, it doesn't. It was an honour to know him even for a short time. He would have been a handful for the retirement village managers. I'll bet they breathe a sigh of relief he won't be returning. I'm not sure about his girlfriend, she might miss him."

"Yeah, I'll have to deal with them now because he paid a lot to go in. He'll have left a few things, so we'll have to go there first when we leave here."

"Sure, Sue. We can leave tomorrow straight after breakfast if you like."

"You're going to miss this place, Jack. You found a spot behind the bar. You fitted in nicely and seemed to enjoy the banter with roughnecks."

"You know, Sue, if you listen with your eyes, you can avoid making mistakes communicating with aggression or ignorance. Yeah, I enjoyed it. But it's time to go and leave it to the locals to prosper in the wake of the Coolgardie Drop. I can always come back."

Sue headed to her room for a final check, and Kate, who had twigged what they had discussed, stepped in and shot Jack a little bait.

"Jack, I think I've said it all, except for this. I want you back here, anytime and for any time. I think you understand."

"Kate, the collision we are headed for will not be a train wreck, I promise you. I don't know what happens next, but I'm so happy to know when I walk through the door, you might see how right it is going to be. How about that?"

"I'm lickin' my chops. Never thought I'd pull those feelings off the shelf again, but you cut through. Now get going before I let your tyres down. Oh, here comes Sandra with your lunch."

"Jack, would you throw this on the back seat? It should get you to Perth with the lingering taste of Coolgardie in your senses."

She was struggling with a big sized Esky, and Kenny had to help her get it to the car.

They drove out of town, still waving as they passed the cemetery and off on the next adventure. An hour and a half later, Sue realised she needed to top up with fuel, and they glided into the BP servo in Ghooli. Kenny got out to stretch, walked around the car and stood there looking at the train station. An image of two bikies passed across his memory. He was standing on the same spot where they fuelled their bikes, and he watched them do it from the train.

THINGS WERE WORKING OUT between Hanna and Mark. A close working relationship sounded good to each of them. No need to complicate things. They had only brushed up against possibly divisive issues, but their solidarity held. They worked with great focus, exited their deal with the Chinese developers with minimum financial trouble and set Mark to run the business as a sole director while Hanna was away. She alerted Charlie and agreed on a day to start their search for Kenny.

With the road trip upon her, Hanna could breathe deep and easy. She could concentrate on the big issue. Even if he was alive, and she felt strongly that he was, she could have no idea of his condition until she found him. Studying her maps, the route to Perth was a practised run, the same as when she headed north from Port Augusta on the ride to Darwin. So the first stop would be Nuriootpa, some caravan park. On the second day, she figured she could comfortably get to Ceduna. Play by ear from there. Of special concern were grey nomads. She had to look at everyone carefully. It'd be a disaster to ride right past him somewhere on the way to Perth. She would be alert, looking at campsites and fuel stops for signs.

As always, when riding, she liked to leave at first light. The first stop would be at the big servo and Macca's close to Calder Raceway. Walking amongst resting travellers took time because she wanted to show Kenny's photo around in case someone recognised him. Because older travellers can be keen on conversation, she could get held up, so it was a bit of a dance. Polite, engaging, but unable to stop and chat for too long. It was a bit like hawking a manuscript to potential publishers, you have to get used to knock-backs.

The only thing she could do was to let the Kwaka loose where she was sure it was safe. She remembered one of her father's sayings. 'Rules are a guide for other people's behaviour.' It is okay to be naughty as long as nobody gets hurt. Hard always to guarantee when you roll the dice. Hanna was cautiously daring if there was such a thing. Anyway, she was able to make Nuriootpa in time to check-in before the office closed for the day. Her cabin backed onto open paddocks, and she saw a gathering of wallabies nonchalantly enjoying themselves in the long grass. A couple of kookaburras let everyone know it was bedtime and ever-present screeching rosellas took a break for the night. Her last duty for the day was to stroll and chat with as many travellers as she could. No result, again. She heard a lot about the price of fuel, the challenge of coping with huge road trains, ungrateful children and the cost of being on the road, especially if dependent on pension payments. And illness, there was so much illness. Busy day, restful sleep.

Refreshed and caffeine loaded by first light, Hanna knew it would be a big day. Stops would gradually be further apart as she left big centres behind but to make Ceduna would be an achievement. The road west of Port Augusta is a gift to bikers. Traffic is scarce, light is strong, the road is well maintained, and wildlife is prevalent only at night. She made Ceduna by evening, and the caravan park manager had a cabin for her. She had rung ahead from Port Augusta. A walk on the beach, toes in the low-tide ripples and feeling of fatigue slipped away. Back to the cabin, with a long, hot shower and clean clothes, she was ready for dinner. The pub is next door. It's a modern building, with lots of glass giving views of the sheltered water of Murat Bay and offers a broad menu. Oysters are locally harvested and a joy to behold. Hanna didn't have any, but she did have a serving of the best fish and chips with a glass of crisp white wine. She was ready for bed not long after the sun slid out of view.

An early morning walk around the park offered no information about mystery campers. Hanna fuelled up on the way out of town and set her sights on Cocklebiddy for the next major stop. It broke her heart to see so much roadkill. Road trains don't slow for anything, and she saw heavy carnage from one night, counting 34 dead kangaroos in the first fifteen kms. The highway should be called 'Death Road'. She could do the 760kms easily but had to allow for a couple of stops to check out vehicles along the way. Most tourists stop at designated look-outs to the Great Australian Bight in the hope of seeing pods of migrating whales.

Cocklebiddy is an oasis. Fuel stop, dining and motel rooms or parking space for trucks and vans. She was in her room, showered and refreshed an hour before the dining room opened for dinner, so, with a cold beer in hand, she sat in the scarce shade outside the office and called Charlie's number. Same time of day, and he was also relaxing. Only, he was already in Kalgoorlie.

"Charlie, where are you today?"

"Hi, Hanna. I'm in Kalgoorlie, and guess what? I asked a few questions in Warburton yesterday and found out a bloke in the general store recognised your brother from the photo I showed him. He's with an older woman. They came through here a couple of months ago, bought some clothes and a one-man tent. By now, they'll be in Perth. The woman said they were heading for Freemantle. You can stop looking at nomads, catch up with me here tomorrow, and the next day we can make it to Perth."

"Oh, great news, Charlie. He's alive. Thank God. See you tomorrow, can't wait."

"You already sensed it, your instincts are good. Yeah, see you then. Ride safe."

What a restful sleep she had in Cocklebiddy. Big country goes quiet at night. It goes black too, and the air chills. OK, there are occasional road trains skimming past, and the station generator runs some of the time, but mostly quiet. And it rained heavily, which made her feel cocooned under the doona, warm in certainty.

She rose at first light and opened her door to crisp, damp fresh air cleansed by overnight rain. Her bike needed a good wipe-down, and then she packed and loaded panniers before taking a bouncing walk around the property. Behind the main buildings, she found a 1000sq metre, two-storey high cage where three recuperating wedge-tail eagles entertained themselves and occasional visitors with their strutting and spreading of giant wings. She was struck with awe at the majesty of alpha creatures and wondered at them as one must. She was the first of all the travellers to be ready to roll. Then all loosened and refreshed, she headed back to the bitumen and a much easier day's ride, stopping only once at the giant servo at Norseman to top up with fuel and to alert Charlie to be ready to meet her in the main street of Kalgoorlie in two hours. She intended to have lunch with Charlie and talk with him about the great news.

Hanna spotted the BMW backed into the kerb outside the Palace Hotel. Or rather, she spotted Charlie, leather jacket unzipped and riding jeans over boots. He had all the right gear, a good sign and one she expected. She didn't exactly jump off the bike, but as best she could after two more hours in the saddle climbed off and threw her arms around his neck.

"He's alive, Charlie, he's alive."

She shuddered, weeping with relief. He held her too, stirred by her emotion and her understanding of his own pleasure at the news.

"Come with me, I've found this quirky café down the laneway opposite. Good coffee, great food."

After two hours, meatloaf, a salad sandwich and several coffees, they had caught up.

"I've booked a couple of rooms in a clean motel further down the main street just opposite Woolworths supermarket. What say we check in, rest up for a couple of hours, then there's a pub just across the road. They cook for miners and serve great homestyle meals. Should be fun."

"Great idea."

It was, but Hanna was keen to get back on the road, clearly anxious for the following day. She was closing in and needed to find out what had happened to Kenny. The next morning, they walked the full length of the main street and back, got their blood flowing and body loosened. It would be a full day's ride to Perth. Hanna's bike started but coughed and spluttered. It needed attention. Charlie would have had a go at the problem had he been at home with all the tools at hand. Better to find a repair shop here. They found Ray Moore's repair shop prominent on a secondary main street. The owner saw they were well equipped as riders, and being a rider himself, he was keen to help them. He listened to the gasping engine and confirmed their own assessment the problem was clearly a fuel blockage.

"Tell you what, kids. Go for a walk, have a coffee and in about an hour, come back with a regular cappuccino for me, no sugar, and we'll be done. You right with that?"

They smiled at his cheek and agreed.

It always takes longer than expected, so anticipating this, they thought breakfast would be a good idea. The café they found previously was bustling with morning business. Charlie could see the impatience in Hanna, and she was annoyed her bike had misbehaved. She was keen to get to Perth.

"Hanna, how's the scrambled egg?"

"Oh, good. Sorry, Charlie, you noticed. Tell you what, this fresh-squeezed orange and pineapple has a bite to it. What about your 'big breakfast'?"

"Country cooking in the right place is a treat. I'm ready for today. What say we take a bacon and egg toasted sandwich and coffee back to Ray?"

They did, and the mechanic appreciated the gift. He still charged them, but he didn't take advantage of their situation. Happy all around as it should be. Goodbyes all said they were on their way at last.

As it turned out, they rolled through Coolgardie at about 11am. There seemed to be a fair energy in the town, with more caravans and Land Cruisers than one would expect to see in a secondary town. There was a lot of activity outside the Denver City Hotel, with people chatting and drinking in small groups. They might have kept going, but Charlie signalled Hanna to pull over. He lifted his visor.

"Looks unusual, Hanna. Do you mind if we stop for a minute and check it out?"

They hooked their helmets on their bikes and wandered over to the pub. They overheard people talking about fossicking and finding nuggets and about the one they saw in the pub. Walking through the door of the pub and up to the bar, they stopped and looked at the television screen and saw the huge photo everyone was talking about. A most stunning giant nugget.

"Can I help you, ma'am?"

"Yes, you can. Two lemon squashes, please."

The woman behind the bar hesitated, staring at Charlie.

"You're not local, are you, mate."

He was taken aback by the undertones in her comment.

"No, is that a problem for you?"

"Not for me sonny. One of your mob nicked my phone, and I'm still waiting to get it back, and I've banned them until I do."

He might have been insulted, she wasn't talking about him being a bikie, but this was a dance he'd done a thousand times.

"I know, missus, it's a surprise they know how to use them, hey. Bloody primitives. Not like us from the Kimberly at all."

Kate didn't know whether to froth at the mouth or go with the humour. But looking them both up and down, she thought better of continuing.

"You're OK, I reckon."

Hanna stood silent, poised. Couldn't help but be impressed with her companion. She turned the conversation to the nugget.

"Somebody had a bit of luck, I see."

"Yes, luv. The town's gone crazy since it was dug up close by."

Kate's attention was diverted to other customers. Hanna and Charlie had their drink and went their way. An hour and a half later, they rolled into a little town called Ghooli and used the opportunity to top up with fuel. Charlie noticed the Indian Pacific train was about to leave the station opposite where they were standing. He couldn't help but be impressed with the length of the thing. It was huge.

"We should be right now, all the way to Perth?"

"Yes, but probably a good idea for a break and refuel at Northam."

They flipped their visors, lit up the bikes and moved off in loose formation.

KENNY TRAVELLED WITH SUE to Freemantle. They took a cabin in a caravan park there, and while Sue was busy negotiating the extraction of Lou's equity in the retirement village, Kenny busied himself mastering the intricacies of satellite navigation system and hard-drive music storage. He was quietly amused at the simplicity of those systems, blissfully still unaware of his own history in the RAAF.

"Well, can't say it was a lot of fun, but job done, Jack. We can go. I was thinking we could take a contract on a cattle station. They're always looking for nurses, cooks and roustabouts. Fancy a stint as a general hand on a big station, Jack?"

"Truthfully, Sue never thought about it, but it could be interesting work. Where do they advertise?"

"On the internet, where everything else is done these days. What say we take our time while we're here and head down to Margaret River, across to Albany and Esperance, before getting back to the Nullabor? It's pretty country, and it might jolt your memory. If not, we can still have a good time."

"Well, there's nothing holding us here, so let's do it."

Before setting off, Sue took Kenny to an internet café and searched for jobs in the outback, leaving their details and contact number with four different stations looking for general hands, cooks and nurses. Sitting at the terminal, Sue had a look of triumph about her, couldn't help herself and whispered to Kenny.

"Got you for a bit longer. Think we're both lucky."

Job done, they got up, left the room and on the way back to the ute and trailer, walked past a huge billboard with Kenny and Lou smiling down at them. They headed for Margaret River, surf coast and wine region, cheap camping and fine weather. They were on holidays. A perfect rehab thing to do. Sue was happy for Kenny to do a share of the driving. It allowed her to free-range chat on any subject she chose. She kept her chupa chups stored.

"This money is a godsend, Jack. I can get nearly twenty years on the road with my pension thrown in. That will surely see me out. Did I tell you how smart I was sending you out with a shovel?"

"Given the result, Sue, it has to be one of the smartest things, for sure."

"What will you do with your share, Jack?"

"No big decisions, I'd like to find out who the hell I am first. I don't know if I have a family, am married, a felon or anything. Don't know where I live or what I do for a living. I mean, what was I doing out there in the desert and what was the accident? My memory starts when I opened my eyes, and you were there. Once I figure out all those other things, I suppose the money will be handy enough. I can't even be sure I'll find out all that stuff. Would I even recognise people who were close to me? I assume they would recognise me. Anyway, I can cover half the expenses of our trip, and I feel good about that."

"Was going to ask you about that. Thanks for bringing it up. The thing is, you'll go one day, I know it, and you know I'm not looking forward to it. I like your company and the fact you can chip in on our costs. To be fair, though, you did get me this fantastic new vehicle for a knock-down price. What say we aim for lunch at Margaret River and sort out where we'll camp for a couple of days."

"You happy to stay in cabins in caravan parks and have all the mod cons on hand?"

"Why not? We'll save the pop-up and your tent for when we leave the bitumen. Got to say, the cabins are roomy and comfortable. And if we want, we can get supplies and do our own cooking using their barbecue. Makes cleaning up a lot easier. I don't mind the idea at all."

"Careful, Sue, you'll talk yourself out of camping."

"No way, Jack. I still have a yearning to kick the dirt off more gold, and you can't do that in a village, hey."

"I've only ever found one lump of gold, and you know, I think that'll do me."

"Haha. Fair enough."

A couple of weeks in the south passed. While they enjoyed their holiday, Sue was getting a few messages on her phone to make contact with a number of big stations looking for their kind of help. This meant when they left Esperance, they could think about taking up one of several offers. On the way out, they first picked up a half dozen fried local scallops, the biggest and freshest they had ever seen and were driving past The Harbour View Hotel. Sue was driving. Kenny was checking the neighbourhood, and he noticed a sign outside the hotel. "Thursday Night Live, Wolvie and the Wailers"

"Stop, Sue."

She did, and Kenny left the car and walked fifty metres back to the sign. He stood and stared at it for a few minutes.

"I don't know, Sue. Something sent a shiver up my spine. Would you keep the pub's phone number in your phone in case the flash comes back?"

By end of the day, they were back in Coolgardie. Kenny walked into the bar while Sue refuelled. It was nearing dinner time, and the pub was as busy as he remembered it being over a month ago. The television still displayed the magnificent nugget. Kate, as usual, was hurrying from one job to another. She saw him, stopped in her tracks, put down the plates she was taking to the kitchen and tentatively approached him. His eyes gave away nothing, but his heart thumped a welcome. She stepped close.

"Are you back?"

It was just a whisper, but there was intensity behind it. He caved.

"I reckon I am."

"Follow me."

He did. She led him to her office down the corridor from the bar. He followed her into the room, and she closed the door, holding it closed with her back. He turned to her and walked into the second most intimate hug he had ever enjoyed. They were silent. It was all said much more clearly than with words.

"Now get behind the bar while I see if I can concentrate on my jobs. Oh, is Sue with you?"

"Yes. Would you arrange something for her dinner, and I'll pour beer."

They left the office to do their jobs.

Sue came into the bar and sat at the same table where her father had held court. She watched the ease with which Kenny had slipped into 'barman' mode. Dinner arrived for her, and it was a treat. Kate spared no effort in making her feel welcome. She even took time to sit and catch up with what had been happening. The three of them were ready for the conversation they knew must happen after closing time. For Sue, the time had come much sooner than she had hoped, but she had nothing but good feelings for what Kenny was going through.

"I answered the people from Annabella Creek Station, Jack. But the job is for one person, a nurse. That's me, of course. Would you mind if we said our farewells here? I'm not kicking you out. Our time has been life-changing, but, like I said to you, it was always going to be temporary. On the other hand, it's not hard to see how welcome you are here."

"Good on you Sue. You won't be going till tomorrow. We'll have a farewell breakfast in the morning."

Kate was silent while they sorted themselves out. But she wanted to add her bit.

"Talk about life-changing! You two blew into town and completely disrupted its roll to oblivion, submission to defeat. Look how lively this old pub has become. And did you notice all the vans and interstate cars? Coolgardie is like a bear shaking off the effects of hibernation, hungry for action. Everyone in the town is feeling it. I'm feeling it too. I don't know where you found Jack, Sue. But thank God you did, and thanks too for bringing him to us. In all your travels, remember there's always a place here for you. There. Now, I'm buggered and need to sleep. See you both at breakfast."

HANNA AND CHARLIE FELT the effects of renewed energy in their search for Kenny. They knew he was alive. They arrived in Perth and set up base in a comfortable hotel in Scarborough, across the road from the beach, with underground parking for the bikes. The next day they hit the road and visited twelve caravan parks and camping sites north and east of the city without any luck. There were four more in Freemantle, and they decided to leave them for the next day. Riding through the centre of the city on their way back to the hotel, Charlie noticed signs to King's Park and signalled Hanna to follow him. It was his first visit to Perth, and he had heard about King's Park and thought on impulse they might take a look at it.

"What made you dive in here, Charlie?"

"It's been fantastic to find out more or less where Kenny is, so I feel the pressure is off for a while. I know we still have to actually catch up with him, but we're closing in. It's early afternoon, and a stroll around this huge park might be a good thing. OK with you?"

"I wouldn't have thought of it, but you're right. Yeah, let's stroll. Looks like they have a cafeteria too, we might even have a Devonshire tea and scones, just like an old married couple on holiday."

"What a funny thought. It's a deal."

More than 4 square kms of rolling lawns, expansive garden plantings teeming native bird life and sculpture features including fountains, architectural paving and shelters offering broad views of the lower Swan River and the city itself.

But more interestingly was the comfort they were finding in each other's company. No holding hands or any other overt display of affection but there were unmistakable signs of magnetism.

"We haven't had much luck today, and there are only a few more sites to cover. You confident?"

"He's definitely close, Hanna. Can you feel it?"

"Ask me tomorrow after we complete our sweep. I won't be certain until I can hug him. Then I'll know."

"You know, I was so happy he and I would be working together at the station. I had so much to show him, and I knew he had a lot he needed to tell me about his life beyond that shocking school we attended. Top Gun pilot, hey?"

"Not only that but top of his class and selected to go to the States to manage the implementation of the super FA-18s into the RAAF. But you know what it's like with him. Disaster is never far away. After the mid-air incident, he was lucky to survive, he was two years in recovery, much of it unhappy. Now, this. He deserves a break, you know."

"I know you and I used the Richardson helicopter, and it was incident-free, but I've done a bit of research. The original concept was to offer something for the bottom end of the market. That's why you see them on most big stations. Easy to fly, small and good for helping with musters. It turns out they've been involved in a scary number of accidents. A major problem is what they call fuselage slap, where the rotor blade smacks the fuselage. The company tries to lay blame on human error and poorly trained pilots. Truth is more complicated. When I get back to our station, I'm going to look into options. I hope Kenny will be able to help me sort it out. He certainly has first-hand knowledge of what can happen. We have to come up with a strategy safer for our workers."

"How's your scone, Charlie?"

"Yeah, sorry, shop talk. The scone is delicious but don't fill up on them because I was thinking China Town for dinner tonight."

"You're full of ideas today. Yes, maybe Vietnamese would be nice. Time to move, so let's go."

Re-energised after the pleasantries of the previous day, they returned to their mounts and set off to Freemantle to continue their quest. At the first caravan park they visited, they booked a cabin. While checking out the next morning, Hanna showed the owner her photo of Kenny and asked the question. He hesitated for a minute before an 'aha' moment struck.

"Your brother hasn't stayed with us, Hanna, but I know where I've seen his face. Tell you what, when you leave here, turn left, and about 200 metres down the road, you'll come to a Nissan dealership. They've got a huge poster advertising their Navara utes. I'm pretty sure your brother features on that poster."

Hanna nearly leapt the counter to hug the man, ignoring the obvious question about Kenny being involved in advertising cars, thanked him and left to follow his instructions. Charlie was sitting astride his bike, waiting for her to return with more disappointment, but he could tell there was good news when she came flying out of the office to him.

"Just follow me, Charlie. Get ready for a surprise."

She led him out of the park and eased along the road. She came to a stop outside the Nissan dealership she had been told about. They parked their bikes, and Hanna signalled to Charlie he should remove his helmet. They stood on the footpath across the road from the car yard and faced the billboard. Charlie followed Hanna's eyes. And there he was, large as life. Kenny standing with an old digger in front of a giant gold nugget. She was dumbstruck, as was Charlie. They looked at each other sharing a light bulb moment.

"That's the nugget they were talking about in Coolgardie. Kenny was there. We were there and didn't see him. Somehow he's been involved in finding that nugget."

They convulsed with laughter and relief. They knew where he was, and if he wasn't still there by the time they got to the place, then the woman publican surely knew. Only a day away. They hurried across the road, anxious to find out more.

The sharply dressed and gelled shortish blond-haired young man approached them, a little unsure of himself, unusual for such a tall, strong-looking boy.

"I would like to think I can help you but forgive me, you don't look like you're interested in cars. Am I right? Sorry, Jet Jolly."

They shook hands, all smiling.

"You're right Jet. I'm Charlie, and this is Hanna. We were looking at your billboard and have a couple of questions. My best friend and Hanna's brother has been missing through no fault of his own. But we were passing by and noticed you've used him for your advertisement. Here, look at this photo."

Charlie showed Jet his photo of Kenny.

"Wow! How cool is this? Yeah, he was here with his old friend Lou. His name is Jack Foster, and he found the gold nugget in Coolgardie. He came in here to buy a ute for his travelling partner, Sue. My boss did a deal with him. Would you like to meet the boss?"

"That would be great, Jet."

"I'll get him for you. We've been selling a few Navaras since he was here. He's been good luck for us."

Another interesting day for the young car salesman.

"Good morning, Richard Duke. You are relatives of Jack Foster?"

"Hello Richard, I'm Hanna, and this is Charlie. We've come a long way looking for my brother, and today, a miracle. Up there on your billboard, there he is."

"Your family seems to be blessed with more than one miracle, Hanna. Your brother found that nugget you see on the poster, and he came here to buy a vehicle for his partner Sue Whittaker. Is he missing on purpose or by accident?"

"Long story, Richard, but in short, it's by accident. It seems he was injured in a helicopter accident and has amnesia. Doesn't know who he is. He came to work with me on a station in the King Valley area. He was out surveying cattle numbers when the chopper malfunctioned and crashed. He saved the co-pilot's life and went down with the helicopter. Evidently, he was able to wander away from the scene and was taken in by the woman you have met, Sue. We believe she nursed him back to health. If he knew who he was, we are certain he would make contact, but he hasn't. So here we are on his trail."

"That's some story, Charlie. I can tell you only they were headed back to Coolgardie. There was some talk about working on cattle stations as general hands. At least that's what Sue told us. Your best tip would be to go there."

"Thanks, Richard. We'll be heading there tomorrow, for sure. Nice photo, by the way."

Back at the bikes, they chatted about what to do.

"It's only 10am. Would you like to take a shot at it today? We'd have to go back to the cabin, pack and check out. Then it's a 6hr ride. Or we could have a good look at Freemantle while we're here, lunch on the pier early night and ride tomorrow."

"Charlie, I'd really like to get going now, but I see your point. I can wait one more day. Let's do a seafood lunch on the pier and then sit on the beach at Scarborough, make a day of it."

The next morning they were out of Perth by 7am, fully intending to be in Coolgardie by lunchtime. There was a new purpose in their riding. True to their intention, they pulled into the curb outside Denver City Hotel at 1pm. They hesitated, helmets in hand and butterflies in their stomachs. They had no idea how it would work out.

"You ready for this? Let's get an idea of how things stand before we say anything."

"Sure, Hanna, I'll take your lead. Cars indicate they're doing a fair lunch trade."

They swung the door open and stepped into the bar, scanning. No sign of Kenny, but the owner spotted them immediately.

"You two again. And you, young man, my apologies for my attitude last time. Let me treat you to lunch today, your choice."

"That's okay, Kate, isn't it? Thanks. We will have lunch, but you don't really have to cover it, just do your best."

"Had a delivery of fresh fish from Perth this morning if you'd like to go that path. The calamari is Australian, and the cook grills it on a very tasty salad. Goes well with a serve of hot chips."

"I'll go with it, thanks."

Hanna had been studying the menu on the wall.

"Could I have grilled chicken thigh pieces on salad with chips, please, Kate?"

"Take a seat, it's on the way. You drink lemon squash, don't you?"

"Usually, but we hope to stay in town for the night, so we might share a bottle of something white and Margaret River, maybe a Verdelho if you have one."

Kate raised her eyebrows at the request. That wine happened to be one she stocked only for herself and Sandra.

"If you're staying in town, we have a couple of rooms or a double room if you like. Take your time, try our meals before you decide."

"Thanks, Kate, will do."

They didn't know Kenny was in the kitchen running meals and dishes to and from the bar and the dining room. They sat at a table and poured the wine.

"This wine has some age on it. Nice to see. What do you think, Charlie?"

"Not a big fan, Hanna. Usually have meat with meals, and I drink a bit of red. But this one's delightful. Straw coloured, glistening and with a hint of fruit sugar. Nice."

A few minutes later, their meals arrived. Kenny stood before them.

"Let me guess. The calamari is for you, sir, and the chicken is yours."

Hanna could hardly restrain herself but managed to not leap at him.

"Thanks, you're Jack, aren't you? Charlie, Jack, and Hanna."

Kenny froze. He half-turned away, then turned back. Blood drained from his face, and tears welled and then coursed down his cheeks. He would have fallen except Charlie slid a chair under him. Nothing was said. They stared and waited and waited.

Kate was at the bar and knew something looked wrong. She hurried around to the table.

"Jack, Jack. What's the matter? Tell me what is it?"

Still crying and shaking all over, he stared into her face.

"Kate I… I… this is my sister, Hanna, and this is my lifelong best friend, Charlie."

He slid out of the chair, dropped to his knees and embraced his sister, convulsing beyond control.

"Mac, Mac, oh Mac. You found me. Thank God you found me."

The curtain lifted. A new light shone in his drowning eyes. The convulsions stopped, and a grin appeared on his face. Hanna clung to him like a limpet to a rock. Her tears mixed with Kenny's on the floor, a puddle of recognition, affection and relief all swirling. Charlie was the first to speak.

"Kate, you are now part of a huge story. Let me introduce you to Captain Robert Stephen Daniels, formerly of the RAAF, survivor of two major aviation mid-air events and my dearest friend in the world. Hanna, his sister, the love of each other's life."

He held back on the rest of it because he wasn't yet fully aware of the relationship Kenny had with her. He would spill the beans a little later. Kate stared at him, then at Kenny and Hanna, picked up one of the glasses and took a big draught of the wine. She was not the kind of person to show emotion other than annoyance or sarcasm. This one was beyond her, unsettled her. She was feeling things totally unfamiliar. So, she stood.

"Jack, I mean Robert, you stay here, I'll bring you a drink and pick up what you were doing. Then I'll be back. You OK? I'll bring another glass… and another bottle."

He turned his head to her with a look that unsettled her even more.

"Thanks, Kate."

He loosened his hold on Hanna and turned back to his chair. The three of them were stunned and wrung out with emotion. Hanna was the first to giggle. The other two started. The giggles turned to laughter, arms linking, bodies leaning back in ecstasy. Together, alive and together.

"The police said you were dragged off and eaten by wild dogs. This is a miracle."

Laughter erupted again, celebrating the realisation of the moment.

"Charlie, what happened to Ben? There was thick scrub beneath us, but we were a bit high. Has he recovered?"

"You remember, wow! Your training kicks in when you need it, Kenny. Yes, he's OK. He had a few minor fractures in his legs, but he's fine. He's going to be a whole lot better when I tell him we've found you."

"Would you two mind if I nicked off and had a shower. There's a lot of downloading going on in my head right now, and emotional surges are almost disabling. Make sure Kate brings the next bottle because we have a bit to talk about. Sweet sister, what a revelation you are. And you, Charlie…. I don't deserve this."

"No, brother, you do deserve this, at least this."

Unsteady on his feet, he made his way out of the room. Charlie pulled his chair close to Hanna, beside her. He whispered.

"How did that go, do you think, Hanna?"

She swung her face away from looking at Kenny walking away and looked directly into Charlie's eyes.

"Charlie, I am alive with electrifying intensity right now."

Her intensity rattled his bones all the way to the source of his manhood, but he held his look of calm.

"Let's have a quiet toast. To a quest fulfilled."

"Clink."

Kate walked into the room. She scanned the room to no avail.

"Needed a shower. It's been overwhelming. Too much information crashing his hard drive. Kate, you seem to have taken a shine to him."

"You know him, it doesn't matter what his name is, it's still him. How could I not? He won us over with his innate goodness. No fuss, no ego, just goodness pure and simple. How often do you get to see that in someone? He walked out of the bush with a rucksack over his shoulder, believing Sue, his fossicking partner, had abandoned ship with the gold nugget he found. No fuss, no anger. Disappointment in the face of ignorance, but that was it. He walked in here, had lunch and even in that short time, I couldn't help myself. I asked him to stay and work behind the bar. When he learned this business is held together by willpower alone between Sandra and me, his first thought was to do something about it. The next thing I know, the whole district has gone crazy with gold fever. He, singlehandedly, was engineering a way to save the town from complete demise. He doesn't even know how much money the nugget sent into his bank account, he's too busy looking after us. Men aren't supposed to be like that. He's the best I've seen, and I've been around a while. So yes, Charlie, I've taken a shine to him, and I'm petrified about what might happen next. Is someone going to tell me the whole story? Is he married, got kids? I'm completely in the dark, and I don't want to find myself in a wasp's nest of trouble."

Hanna understood. Kate was trembling with apprehension and on the verge of declaring something that excited her and scared her at the same time. She deserved to know. So while Kenny was out of the room, Hanna gave a thumbnail sketch of his story from the beginning. Kate got to see the teenage boy kneeling before the crumpled bodies of his two classmates, breathing their last as he cradled them. She got to see him sink his boot into the face of the paedophile headmaster and stand before a court convicted of manslaughter. She was with Hanna when she met him as a RAAF top gun graduate and shivered at the story of the mid-air destruction of the FA-18 he was flying. Then just as Hanna finished telling Kate about his depression managing tactic of writing a film script and that he was and had always been single, Kenny came back into the room looking much more settled than when he left.

"I'll get that bottle of wine, we are going to need it. Hi Robert."

Kate jumped up to do that and bring two more glasses. There was a bounce in her step.

"Robert? Is that who I am again after everything?"

"Didn't know whether to go all the way, Kenny. I've given her the rest of the story so far."

Kate returned after farewelling the last of the lunch guests. She was armed with wine and glasses, and she brought her friend Sandra with her.

"OK, Sandra is my business partner and house cook. Sandra, Hanna here is Jack's sister, only he's not Jack, but Robert. This is Charlie, Robert's best friend from school days."

"And one more thing, Kate. My real name Is Kenny. The government gave me 'Robert' when it saved me from jail and sent me into the

RAAF. No more name changes. You can all call me Kenny from now on."

The wine flowed, and tongues loosened until late afternoon. Kate brought the session to a close.

"Sorry, you lot. I've got to prepare for tonight. Hanna and Charlie, you've got to get your things from your bikes and settle in. Do you need two rooms, or do you want one double room?"

Charlie dived in.

"We want one room, but we need to have two. We haven't decided on visiting rights."

Kenny leapt, Hanna raised her brows.

"I'm so glad I don't have to defend my sister's honour at this very early stage in the relationship."

They laughed, and the issue was settled. Two rooms!

Kate looked burdened during the evening shift, and Kenny picked up on it. He took a moment as she passed by to grab her hand, spin her towards him and say.

"You and I have started something nice, Kate. I know I'm not Jack anymore, but Kenny and Jack are pretty much alike. I will not leave without you. One thing more. I am single with no baggage other than my damaged mind."

"Let's talk later, but you have a finely tuned knack for knowing what's going on without being told. Jack was like that too."

She smiled at him and went back to work, somewhat comforted but didn't know Kenny had no idea how it was all going to work out. He was confident the group would come up with something. No doubt breakfast would be interesting. Meanwhile, he would visit Kate after closing time and after she'd had a chance to shower and wind down. Charlie and Hanna had gone for a walk, no place good enough nearby, so they decided Kalgoorlie might be the place to go for a Chinese meal. They doubled up on the Beemer and headed off for the evening. She didn't have to hold on to him as tightly as she did, but she did, and he pushed back into her letting her know he was aware. They found a reasonable looking Chinese restaurant, not too busy and settled for that.

"Charlie, we've found Kenny, but what do we do now?"

"Doesn't really matter. We couldn't really have a better result. Kenny's alive, he's in good shape, he's clearly knocked down Kate's resistance, and it's basically up to him. He might want to stay, he might want to try my place again, or he might want to head back to Melbourne. Let's wait. I'm still on a high just seeing the man. So are you, I know it."

"Hmm, you're right. I am over the moon. See the look on his face when he brought our meals? The sight of us brought him back pretty smartly, hey? There's something else, young man, and it's now the elephant in the room. What's happening with us? Don't answer me, I'm asking myself, really. You should know I'm very comfortable with you. I don't care about the fact you're outback and I'm city-bound, I've maintained a love affair with my absent brother for many years. On the other hand, I've enjoyed riding with you, and I don't want to wait until May to see you again. There, it's on the table."

Charlie had watched her open up to him. He smiled to himself about her ability and willingness to broach any subject important to her, especially this subject. He felt encouraged to crystallise his own feelings and tell her. He rested his hands under his chin and watched her unfold, waiting for his turn.

"You've read the situation pretty much spot on, Hanna. I've been looking forward to this conversation from the moment I first saw you. You've beaten me to the punch. You have stepped into my space on three occasions and hugged me because of Kenny. Next time will be different. Can't see the long term, but I sure as hell can see the next few hours, I hope."

The look between them was intense, and four feet under the table were busy making their acquaintance, searching, feeling, as much as limitations allowed and promising more and closer intimacy later. It would be a short meal and a quick ride back to the hotel. Probably just wave to Kenny and Kate if they saw them on their way past.

All was quiet at the Denver City Hotel after another busy session. Kenny finished his clean-up and then headed for the kitchen. Sandra was finishing as well.

"Sandra, you've heard about today. I wanted to say hello to you as the real me. Hello, Sandra, I'm Kenny."

"Ha, ha, so I hear. Come here, hugging time, don't be scared."

They embraced.

"You've been through quite a lot lately. You seem to be OK about smashing through the amnesia thing. Clear head at last, hey. Good on you. I take it you're happy about seeing Hanna and Charlie too. They did a great job looking for you. She wouldn't give up on you, that's some sister."

"Yeah, she's had my back when I should've been looking after her. She's a helluva human being."

"Pardon me for saying it, but I reckon it runs in the family. You know Kate is ready to throw caution to the wind, don't you?"

"Hope I can handle the attention. She's unique in my experience too. Not too many women like you two, running a pub in a goldfield town with more roughnecks than grains of sand, busy as sharks in a shipwreck. But, truthfully, I'm flattered. Anyway, Sandra, I bid you good night and see you at breakfast."

Sandra returned the greeting with a huge smile, free of charge.

Kenny knocked timidly on Kate's door. He guessed the time was right. The door opened. Kate knew it could only be him. Her short blond hair was still damp and unbrushed, giving a stunning backdrop to her suntanned face and ice blue eyes that shone a piercing challenge in his direction. A white T-shirt and pyjama bottoms over short ugh boots completed the vision. Impressed was the reaction written all over his face. Not a word was spoken, but everything was duly noted. She read it, liked it, then stepped back, holding the door open for him to enter. He did.

Four relaxed, smiling adults around the breakfast table. It must have been the clean country air and 8 hours of well-earned reward in two comfortable beds. Sandra was doing her best to add to the idyll by preparing a breakfast fit for royalty. She had an inkling they would come with an appetite. Looking at her partner and friend, Sandra reflected she had never seen Kate as comfortable as she was with these three people. She didn't have to play the tough guy with them. They, in return, respected her purely and simply. She could see how good it was for Kate but felt unease at what might happen to their business partnership. She knew Kate should not have to surrender either her business or her developing relationship with Kenny. But she also felt Kenny wouldn't be staying too long. Being a barman wouldn't hold him for too long. If he went, would she go too? If so, then Sandra would be in a bit of a pickle. She would wait and see but prepare herself with options.

Hanna placed Kenny's wallet and keys on the table.

"You'll need these to help extinguish the existence of Jack Foster. Your bank cards are there so you can transfer funds. The keys are for Richmond. I presume you'll check in at some point. I was there recently and picked up a note from your friend Wolvie. He let you know he was heading bush, too much trouble under the bridge in Melbourne and needed to clear his head."

"Hanna, he's in Esperance. Saw an A-frame outside a hotel. "Wolvie and the Wailers" Shame I wasn't myself. Would have said hello. Thanks for all that. Yeah, had better tidy up the banking. Be silly to lose the hard-earned, hey?"

They laughed. Kenny rang Sue later that day to put her in the picture.

"Sue, where are you?"

"On the road to the Kimberley Jack. Taking one of those jobs, we looked at. Are you still at the pub?"

"Yes, I am. Things have happened, Sue. My memory is back. My sister and my best friend turned up at the pub. They'd been out looking for me. Didn't believe I was dead. Turns out that I was flying a helicopter, and it crashed near where you found me. Only you can call me Jack, Sue. I am Robert Steven Daniels to the world."

"Oh, Jack, that's great news. Where are you from?"

From Melbourne, Sue and at some stage, I'll probably go back there, at least for a time. While I've got you, have you still got that phone number of the Harbour View Hotel in Esperance? A guy who is or was playing music there is someone I know."

She gave him the number, wished him well and hung up. She pulled into a rest stop and parked the car, held her forearms on the top of the steering wheel and rested her chin on her knuckles and stared into the distance. It all flashed before her mind from the moment she first saw him fall to the ground in front of her, broken. She saw the light come back to his face and strength to his body, and she saw him beckon her to the hole he had dug, revealing the nugget. She saw him offer a bag of chupa chups to her, not realising she knew exactly why he did. She saw him sitting with her father in the pub, both chuckling away and sipping beer, and she loved him for his generosity with the old man. She always knew it couldn't last, and she decided there and then that the story could not have ended better than this. He had been found, and he remembered. She would remember too, always.

He went back to the table, only halfway through his meal.

"Have to ask, what do we do now?"

"I'll have to get back to the station, take me a couple of days."

Charlie was looking at Hanna while speaking.

"I'll have to get back to Melbourne, but I'm thinking of a career change. Fancy having a shot at becoming a Jillaroo. Wish I knew someone in charge of a ranch somewhere."

They laughed. Clearly, they would work out something. Kate looked at Kenny. He read the challenge.

"I've got a fairly good job at this pub. Don't want to be anywhere else for the moment. There's so much happening here with drilling crews and drones and satellite dishes, you'd think there was gold to be found. I have to fend off offers to guide fossickers on a daily basis, and all of them want to hear about the Coolgardie Drop. Every time somebody discovers a good sign or traces, they come here to share the news. At the moment, I'm an asset to the business, and that's good for Kate and Sandra. Then, I've got a few personal matters to sort out, and I can do that in Kalgoorlie or Perth if necessary. Will have to make decisions soon, but not just yet."

"No strings, Kenny. But if you think you're gonna leave here without me, you better sleep light."

They laughed but were pretty sure she meant it. Blue eyes on fire can be particularly ferocious.

Bikes packed and riders back in leathers, Charlie and Hanna were ready to head home. Kenny, Kate and Sandra gathered to wish them safe travelling. Charlie had decided to ride with Hanna as far as Port Augusta and then head homewards up the Stuart Highway while she would continue to Victoria via the Barossa. They would have two nights together, one at Cocklebiddy and one at Ceduna. They would be memorable nights. Hell and high water would not prevent them from seeing each other again. It was mid-afternoon on the third day when they reluctantly parted, her stationary, astride, watching him disappear into the distance, one last wave to her as he did so.

Hanna had time to think and much to think about. Charlie had been a revelation. She wasn't looking for anybody, focused solely on her need to find Kenny. But she discovered Charlie to be magnetic. Not least of all, he genuinely loved Kenny like a brother. All the time they were looking for Kenny, there was no hint of another agenda. But when they found him and embraced, she had felt something. It was like he'd been waiting for her to discover him. His excitement was in her response to him at that moment. Finally, she knew he was there, with her, for her. It was an awakening. Had she not seen it, then he would never have made any gesture. As it was, he would never forget having her as his pillion on the ride back to the pub after dinner at Kalgoorlie, and he had thought he was the one driving. She locked onto him with vigour and anticipation, ready for him for the first time, a time of powerful electricity, trembling, coupling with the intensity and ecstasy that took their embrace to the ragged edges of life itself. And that was in the knowledge of what was about to happen before they got back to the pub. Sometime later, lying, wrung out bathing in satisfaction, both personal and mutual, they could only wonder if that moment could ever be recaptured. Was it possible to be as alive as that a second time? As they fell into the most pleasant sleep of their lives, the answer came to them. *Maybe not,* it said. *But they sure as hell would give it a try.*

Charlie's sense of being complete lasted all the way to Woomera, where he decided to stop for the night. He glided into the settlement and past the display of rockets and missiles that had been tattooed on the ancient landscape, western civilisation's reminder that man has not come far from the days of caves, clubs and useless exhibitions of his deeply embedded suicidal tendencies. On other days visitors to unfamiliar territory might be confronted with skulls wedged on sticks as a warning to not proceed. In modern times tourists flock to see the marvellous technological achievements typified in the discarded and obsolete prototypes of today's war toys and celebrate their very existence. Are we not completely mad? The poet within us would say with poignant and undeniable clarity, we are. But the poet within is dulled by the overwhelming white noise of our distracted lives. We do not listen to the poet.

He easily found the hotel, welcoming a soul-refreshing hot shower, clean clothes, and a walk to the bistro. He felt like a beer and a moment of reflection on the decking. Regular customers were happy with their routine in the dining room. Still, he couldn't waste the chance of juxtaposing a multi-coloured western horizon sliding back the curtain on a spectacular cosmic show with the lingering taste of a beautiful woman caressing his soul. Dinner, in a way, was an anti-climax after that. While enjoying the Thai beef salad, his mind was drawn to work,

Ben, and the myriad of issues he would face back at the station. There's dreaming, and there's life. Sometimes one impinges on the other, and sometimes one gives meaning to the other. He wasn't sure which way it was working for him.

It was touch and go for Hanna. She wanted to get to Nuriootpa before dark but found it necessary to ease back on the throttle as the light gave way to evening. She made it safely, picked up her key at the assigned place and threw herself under a hot shower, drenching in the delicious memories of the last couple of days. The trip had been a stunning success because she had found her brother. Her heart danced for two reasons. Charlie had been remotely in her life since the boys' school days, and now he was colouring her existence in the most exquisite way. She was now keen to get home, sort out the business issues and work on adjustments to her lifestyle that would allow her to pursue new interests, one in particular.

MARK TOOK HANNA'S CALL announcing her imminent arrival back in town and her keenness to catch him up with all developments, well, most of them. He couldn't wait to tell her how they had dodged a bullet with the Chinese developers and their shonky ways. A major fire had broken out on one of their properties. The cheap and flammable cladding turned a moderate fire into an inferno in which eight lives were lost. The value of the surviving units plummeted to zero. Many unhappy people.

"That's a thumbnail sketch of the incident. But more to the point, Hanna, are you happy with the trip?"

"Got loads to tell you. I'll be at the office first thing, we'll have a good catch-up."

Back in her living room, first coffee of the day in hand, standing at the big window overlooking the city, Hanna caressed her recent memories and steeled herself for the reality check of the coming days. There is something comforting when life is in order, even predictable when one can glide through routines. Doesn't mean you become numb to life, just comfortable. Hanna could do with a predictable routine, disruption had run its course for a while. It might settle a gnawing that had begun to eat at her. She tidied up and left for the office. Breezing past Mark's desk, she pointed to the staff room and signalled five. He got the message and nodded. She was at the table with a cup in hand when he arrived. Big smile on his face.

"Well, I've been on edge all morning. Give it to me, all of it. And welcome home, by the way."

"Thanks, Mark. Good to be home."

By that time, he was beside her with his cup in hand.

"Got home last night, long ride. Have to tell you the trip was just perfect. I arranged with Charlie, Kenny's best friend from school who manages a cattle and camel station southwest of Alice Springs, to meet me in Kalgoorlie because I guessed if Kenny had been picked up by a camper, they would probably head for Perth for medical assistance."

"Does he ride or travel in a 4WD?"

"I didn't know he has a BMW tourer, so he rode. By the time I was halfway across the Nullabor, he rang me to say Kenny had been sighted in a place called Warburton. When I heard that, I knew we would eventually find him, and I upped the pace, full of confidence. We got to Perth and visited all the caravan parks looking for him. He was travelling with a woman who had found him injured. She's a nurse and was able to manage his recovery. When we got to Freemantle, we saw his face on a big advertising poster for Nissan Navara. It was such a great moment. And get this. While he and his friend Sue were fossicking near Coolgardie, they found a huge gold nugget, the biggest ever found in the area, 45 kgs."

"That was in the news here. Something about digging a long drop and finding the nugget in the hole. The same poster you mentioned was used to announce the big find, truthfully, I didn't recognise Kenny on that. How does that happen, hey?"

"Charlie and I were actually in the pub on our way to Perth. Kenny was there, and we didn't see him. We didn't find him there until we came all the way back. You should have seen it, Mark. Charlie and I ordered lunch, and Kenny actually brought the plates to the table and didn't recognise us until I spoke to him. It was fantastic. There he was in front of us. He nearly collapsed when he realised, and I was frozen to my chair. Once in a lifetime moment. So, there you have it. Kenny, alias Robert Stephen Daniels, alias Jack Foster is now working in a pub in Coolgardie. I'm sure he'll be coming home but don't know when."

Mark showed nothing of his reaction. He had secretly hoped for a different story. But he was happy for Hanna. It seemed if you had one of them, you had the other as well. He knew he couldn't come between them and really didn't want to try. He had put the other dream to bed.

"Hanna, that's a great story. You could have searched many wrong directions, but you picked the right one."

"OK, enough about my adventures. How are things here, Mark?"

"We made the right decision to cut the Chinese loose. There's been nothing but crisis in the industry here because of the way they operate. There are a dozen high-rise projects planned for the inner city. We're in a good position with three of them, negotiating with the local establishment. The State government is rolling out some big infrastructure programmes, so things look good for us. In the meantime, we are looking after a couple of high volume home builders with their own network of sub-contractors. They're not as lucrative or complex, but they pay the bills. It's good to have you back, and when you're up to speed, I'd like a couple of weeks to take the girls away camping."

"Of course, Mark. Is that really something they'd enjoy?"

"I've found this great camping ground in Twofold Bay, Eden. It's right on the beach and not real busy. We can do campfires, swim in safe waters, go fishing and take whale spotting cruises. I think they'll be OK with that."

"And they'll have your undivided attention, hey."

The meeting finished on a good note, and Hanna slipped back into work mode quickly and easily.

SAMMY OPENED THE DOOR and announced to his boss that Spotty Cooper was waiting to see him.

"Send him in, Sammy."

Chook looked up from his desk as the diminutive Cooper walked into the room and thought to himself: *"Thank Christ this guy is a genius hacker because you couldn't believe he could do anything else."* Spotty Cooper was thrown out of Telstra years ago for using their systems to travel the digital world for his own purposes. He thereafter put his skills up for hire and learned to make a living out of them. He stood before his employer, and his voice squeaked.

"Morning, Mr Fowler, it's been a while, what do you have for me?"

"Don't know if you saw this photo in the paper, Spotty, but I want you to look at this bloke in the photo. I want you to find him for me and anything he's done over the last twenty years. Can you do that?"

Cooper looked at the photo and straight away knew where he would start looking.

"Sure Mr Fowler. I'll get back to you as soon as I've found him. I'll need…"

He didn't get to finish because Fowler reached into a drawer and pulled out a wad of fifties, and slid it across the desk.

"I know, Spotty, this should keep you happy for a while. Now don't keep me waiting too long. I want to find this guy quickly."

The meeting was over, and Spotty Cooper headed back to his apartment, which hid behind a former dairy on Williams Rd in Prahran. The stables had been refurbished and divided into four bedsits. He didn't need or even want more room than he had there, after all, most of his waking hours were in front of screens.

"HARBOUR VIEW HOTEL? GOOD. Do you still employ Wolvie and the Wailers as part of your entertainment? Yeah, good. If I give you a number, would you please ask Wolvie to give me a call? Thank you, the number is 456 67 321. Thanks."

Kenny was in his room after closing time. He put the phone down and felt a presence that disturbed him. His skin was suddenly clammy, and he broke out in a sweat. Everything about being Kenny had been fine for him for more than a week. Now, other memories were stirring. He should have been knocking on Kate's door, and instead, she was knocking on his. He hesitated to answer before forcing himself to do so.

"Kenny, you look unwell, what's going on?"

"Not sure, Kate, but it's not comfortable whatever it is. I smell death in the room, death that I've caused, and I know the faces I'm seeing. They're coming and going, and I'm hearing the sounds of screaming jets and getting waves of vertigo. Then it all stops for a while. I'm remembering everything that's happened. I'm sorry you have to see this, but it's part of the package, I'm afraid."

"But you didn't have this experience before you got your memory back, did you?"

"You're right, but they're back now, damn it. I will manage it, but my behaviour might be unsettling for you. Nothing violent or weird, I just disappear into a dark place from time to time. But if it's too much for you, I will push on, OK?"

"You think running this place I haven't seen weird? Your weird is more likely to be a blessing compared to some of the things that have happened here. I'll be okay with you, don't you worry about it. Not only that, but I'll find a way to drag you away from the black dog whenever it appears."

"Come here, could do with one of your hugs."

She stepped into his space, up on her toes, arms around his neck and took away his breath with a voluptuous mouthing that drove everything else from his mind.

"I better sleep alone tonight, Kate, if you don't mind."

"You're not sleeping now, are you?"

Nothing more needed to be said. He slept later, exhausted, and Kate tiptoed out of the room feeling like a parent who had calmed a traumatised child, though not in the way she had calmed Kenny, of course. Whatever her remedy, it worked. He slept in peace, swathed in her lingering aura. The next morning, after his personal routine, he stepped outside for a walk in the brisk air. His phone rang, strange, it was only 8:00.

"Hello, Kenny."

"Kenny? This is Wolvie, I had a message to call this number."

"Wolvie, you old larrikin, my midnight friend from under the bridges of inner Melbourne. How the hell are you?"

"Don't know any Kenny, man. You sure you've got the right guy?"

"Westbank Terrace, coffee on the steps of my place, RAAF greatcoat, should I go on?"

"Yeah, hey, it's you, Bobby. How'd you find me, man? You didn't jump in the Yarra after all. Good on you."

"It's not over yet, Wolvie. Long story, and love to tell you. Now, you tell me. Is there a chance you will finish your gig in Esperance any time soon?"

"Good timing, Bobby. This is our last weekend as a group. I was thinking of heading up to Freemantle, but nothing's in concrete except a few of my old friends, haha."

"Tell you what. If you can get yourself up here to Coolgardie, the pub where I'm working is flat out coping with a gold rush, and there's a few spots for you and that dancing harpoon of yours if you want it. I'm sure I can fix accommodation and meals as part of the deal if you want. Then we can catch up on the stories. I reckon you've got a few to tell as well."

"I'm not gonna ask why you're doin' that, man, sounds cool to me. You can tell me when I see you. Few truckies drink here, and I'm pretty sure of getting a ride your way. Great talkin' to you, Bobby. See you next week, as soon as I can get there. And I've got a little surprise for you, brother."

"Surprise? Wolvie, this is the land of surprises, can't wait to see yours. See you then."

A tingling sensation and a smiling feeling made his morning special. He'd tell Kate over breakfast and felt sure she'd back his call. He turned and headed for the kitchen and board meeting over the best meal of the day.

"Morning Sandra, Kate, hope you slept like I did."

Kate smirked, looked down at her toast, and Sandra walked into the invitation.

"Sure did, Kenny, good thing about hard work is the sleepin' that follows."

"Ladies got some news for you, hope it's good. Before all the recent adventures, I met a group of homeless people under the bridge at Southbank in Melbourne, some good musos amongst them. The unofficial leader was a bloke called Wolvie, who plays a mean harmonica and sings a bit. He's been busking from Melbourne to Esperance, and I spoke to him this morning. I like what he does and think he'd be good entertainment in the bar for a while if you're prepared to give him a shot."

"Where is he now?"

"Just finishing a gig at the Harbour View Hotel in Esperance. Will be here after the weekend."

"Our last band has gone gold prospecting. If you say his music's good, then we trust your judgement, don't we, Sandra."

"Hmmm, track record a bit dodgy, but we could give him one more chance."

Kenny nearly choked on his cereal before chuckling.

By lunchtime, the bar and dining room were showing signs of another busy session, and Kenny busied himself making sure beer kegs were tapped and ready. He had just returned from the cellar, and two men, newcomers, walked through the door and headed straight for him at the bar.

"G'day, Jack. Heard a bit about your luck. Didn't think we'd see ya workin' the bar, all that money ya got, hey. Names Gavin and this here's me mate Gallagher, Guts for short."

"Hmmm, Gavin and Guts. Nice combination. What will you have, gents?"

"Well, nice of you to offer Jack. We'll have anything that's on the house. Ain't that right Guts?"

"Yeah, Gav. That's about right, whatever's on the house. Thanks Jack. Haha."

Kenny looked the two men up and down. They had seen better days, both wiry and their ragged clothes hung loose. Two men with nothing to lose, the most dangerous of all people. They needed a drink, Kenny could see that, and he grabbed the opportunity to divert their attention. He picked up two glasses without taking his eye off them. He reached for the tap and began to pour a beer. Too much for the desperados, their eyes went straight to the filling glass, surprised that they had not been challenged. What happened next was completely out of the blue. Kate and Sandra appeared behind the two men, armed with heavy pans from the kitchen. Nothing was said. Kenny saw what was coming but pretended to concentrate on the beer. Two almighty thuds of hard steel on soft heads followed, and the two men hit the floor, out cold.

"Give us a hand, Kenny, we're going to drag this filth outside and chain them to the verandah post and call the cops. Then we're going to tell you about these two mongrels."

After Kenny stopped laughing, he did as directed.

"OK, ladies, time to fess up. What just happened?"

"Hate to admit it to you, but those two bastards are what's left of two men who nearly ruined our lives. They've obviously heard about recent events and got up the courage to try their luck."

"Well, lucky I was here to help you, otherwise, anything might have happened."

They laughed, and then other customers who had been riveted to the spot while it all happened laughed too.

"Any chance I'll have to throw them out again later?"

"Funny, Kenny. No, the boys in blue will take them back to their camp in the bush, and that will probably be that."

CHARLIE SETTLED BACK INTO his routine at the station. His job was to monitor the bores, maintain infrastructure, distribute licks for the cattle, keep track of where the animals were, monitor the movement of camels and organise mustering and transport to markets or abattoirs. The station covered close to a million acres, so managing distance was a major issue. He had access to a team of skilled indigenous hands, though he never used that word to define his people. Some of them worked in the maintenance sheds, keeping all machinery in good working order. A couple of his colleagues were trained aviation mechanics, so they looked after the plane and the two helicopters apart from major repairs.

The station owner looked after the politics of marketing products which meant travelling to the Middle East for both beef and camels and lobbying state and federal politicians on behalf of those industries and the development of indigenous participation at all levels of operations. He was chair of the board of directors and was the conduit for day to day management issues one way and management directives the other way. He had guided Charlie's career from the very beginning and had his judgement amply endorsed by the youngster's performance.

"Macca," as he was known to all the workers, had accepted a request to visit from Qatar. His name was Mustaffa, a man who had a lifelong love for the camel business at every level in Arab countries. He had heard about the Australian government policy of culling feral camels and wanted to know how a barbaric policy could be tolerated. It was going to be Charlie's job to show him a wider perspective. Macca's concern was on several levels. Firstly he had dealings with Mustaffa and others of his countrymen and wanted to give assurances that his management of camels was based on a respect for them that the culling programme did not allow. He professed impotence to stop the policy developed to protect beef industry interests. Secondly, he could see the time when investment in a sophisticated camel industry in Australia might come from countries like Qatar. Mustaffa could open doors. Long term vision would be to integrate breeding, husbandry, and processing of a dozen products.

"Charlie, you have seen the itinerary for the proposed visit. I would like you to chaperone Mustaffa and his film crew. You don't have to hide anything. He should see the whole picture. I've arranged for representatives of the culling programme to be available for interview across at Quentin Springs. Our territory and federal members have also agreed to speak with him. You don't have to show any urgency, we all know it takes time to turn the Titanic. The Arabs know that as well. They are also aware that the Australian government listens to them when they speak. The groundwork is done, and the rest is up to you. You okay with that?"

"Yes sir. Glad to be involved. When do you expect him?"

"Ten days from now. A party of four, so you should be able to accommodate them in one vehicle. I suggest the company Landcruiser we use for VIPs. For aerial purposes, you can use the Cessna or the chopper. After recent events, both craft have been thoroughly serviced and examined for structural integrity and are fit to fly."

"Boss, I've done a bit of research into the Robinson range of choppers. It looks like they have design issues that have factored in many of the accidents these craft have suffered. I'm wondering if we should look more closely and perhaps study alternatives."

"I don't mind, Charlie but not just yet. I've also seen some disturbing reports. Let's get through this visit first, and I'll even help you follow up on that matter. There'll be no extreme flying while our visitors are here. If you are unsure, then use the Cessna."

The matter was registered, and Charlie trusted his boss would be good to his word. He didn't want any more problems with aircraft, they were too important to the business.

Then there was Hanna. Charlie had little time to think about her beyond the fact he'd need good contract legal work when the camel business got going. She might not get to be a Jillaroo, but the opportunity would be there for her when it came time to set contracts in place.

How do ten days disappear? Charlie found himself back at Alice Springs airport to welcome the station's guests from the middle east. They were easy to spot, dressed in traditional garb. He signalled to them and spoke to the one who was clearly the one in charge.

"Mustaffa, I am Charlie, welcome to you and your companions to Australia and to Alice Springs."

"Hello Charlie, thank you for meeting us. My friends, Mahommed, Nabil and Rami. They will be our film crew for the duration of this visit. Does that meet with your approval, Charlie?"

"That will be fine, Mustaffa. Come this way, we will collect your luggage and film equipment. Then we have a long drive to the homestead and station."

"Is that your farm where you look after camels?"

"Camels and brahman beef, yes."

The conversation turned to the many differences in managing style in a harsh environment. The Arabs dress heavily in woollen gowns and closely wrapped headdresses. The Australians, of course, do not cover-up. Wells in their country were sacred sites shared, even by normally warring tribes, when their animals needed water. In Australia, each station in the outback has its own water resources tapped from the Great Artesian Basin. Lots of nodding indicating comprehension but not guaranteeing it.

"Charlie, we are concerned that your government has a policy to cull wild camels roaming your country. Can I ask how the government can have such a cruel policy?"

"You can ask, but you must know the beef industry here is historically dominant, and the government listens to it more than any other interest group. The last thing these people want is competition from the camel industry. I think their policy is really counterproductive because the high number of wild camels can no longer be ignored. Some of us see the camel as a resource we should be exploiting. After you've seen what's here, you will be well enough informed to represent your own ideas to the politicians. In the meantime, stations like ours are showing what's possible."

"Yes, I see. But do you see how terrible it is for us to see these beautiful creatures described as vermin?"

"I do, and we are doing our best to show our neighbours how wrong it is, how ignorant. But you must be patient with us even when you see the results of culling. People are slow to change their ways."

"We will do our best, Charlie."

Charlie began to understand this trip would not be all pleasant for his visitors. They love camels the way Australians love horses. He dreaded having to show the results of drop culling of feral camels. The sight of swollen, putrifying carcasses would be offensive to them. He wasn't sure there was a way around the issue. His one strategy was to minimise their shock. They were so deferential, aware of being outsiders. It would have been a mistake to misinterpret deference as weakness, it wasn't at all. These were people from an old and proud civilisation with deep-rooted convictions. They were smart enough to appear gentle, and Charlie, himself from an old culture, could read them.

First off, he wanted to let them see local camels from the air, see them grazing and moving casually through the landscape. After a couple of days of looking from a distance, it would be time to demonstrate a small muster using only vehicles and motorbikes with the station hands worded up about minimising stress on the animals.

Mustaffa was full of questions on handling issues. Outback camels feed well and carry none of the diseases seen in middle eastern camels. The nearest thing to a crisis was one poor creature who damaged a front leg and had to be put down. Charlie made sure the euthanasing was well away from other animals and ordered a truck equipped with a hoist to take the carcass away.

"You know, Charlie, when this happens at home, our people come and butcher the animal. The meat is used for a feast, so don't feel too bad. At least you treat the animal with respect."

Charlie looked surprised. Then he smiled at the rightness of those people. All parts of nature work for the whole.

"Before you go home, I will take you to see an abattoir we use to process camel meat. It is underused at the moment because there is only a small demand locally for the meat. If there was a need to export, I'm sure the facility could be activated to cope. You will see for yourself."

Charlie couldn't avoid confronting supporters of the culling programme. His guests wanted to meet the issue head-on. When Mustaffa asked his question about how culling could be allowed to happen, the operations manager from Quentin Springs was quick to show how intolerant he was to camels because of damage they did to infrastructure designed specifically for cattle. There was no room for compromise, and he told Mustaffa bluntly unless he was prepared to cover the costs of change, then he had no right to an opinion. Charlie sucked air when he heard it, but Mustaffa had to know how far Australia was from a viable camel processing industry. The Arabs left with mixed emotions. Investment from the middle east would be risky in the current environment. They could see the potential for an industry only if changes were made. Mustaffa made this clear to the few politicians he was able to speak to during his visit.

"You did good with the Arabs, Charlie. They went home with plenty to think about. We will continue our commitments, and eventually, they will work with us. So, back to work you go. Show us how we can run camels beside beef."

As professional as he was, Charlie turned his mind to other matters.

WOLVIE WAS PACKED AND READY to leave Esperance. He made a pact with Billy Fingers to travel together in Billy's Kombi all the way to Coolgardie.

"I tell ya, Billy, Bobby is cool, man, and digs good music. I reckon if he's got a spot for me, then there'll be room for you. If not, then we can try the pubs in Kalgoorlie. We've got a bit of travelling dough. It'll be good, yeah?"

"Got a rule, Wolvie. Trust everyone once. This is your once. If it turns to shit, then you're gonna pay."

"Deal Billy, let's hit the road. It's only four hours, we'll be there by lunchtime."

The two musos had met at the Harbour View and hit it off straight away. Billy was from Nashville, Tennessee and had a long career there as a guitarist for hire. Had played on albums by some of the great names, like Kristofferson and Hank Williams Jr., Kenny Rogers, Johnny Cash, Willie Nelson and Merle Haggard. He came to Australia with professional curiosity about the country music scene here. There's no greater place to start than in WA. When he heard Wolvie on the harmonica, it was love at first song. They had a feel for each other's rhythm, and both loved Country and Blues. Billy was the little surprise Wolvie had in store for Kenny.

Norseman was halfway and a good spot for breakfast. The café is set up for quick meals, deep-fried heaven, and they left there with greasy fingers, pardon the pun. By 12:30, the Kombi eased into the gutter outside the Denver.

"What's this, Wolvie? Denver City Hotel. There has to be a story about that."

"C'mon, let's go in and see Bobby."

Pushing through the door, the warmth of the open fire hit them, a good drinking temperature. They walked straight to the bar and confronted Kenny, who had spotted them. He held out his hand in a warm, welcoming gesture.

"Well, what do we have here. G'day Wolvie, great to see you."

"Yeah, good to see you too, Bobby. This guy here is my little surprise, meet Billy Fingers, direct from the USA and one of the best guitar players you're ever likely to see and hear."

"Hello, and welcome, Billy. Kenny."

"What, c'mon, you changed your name?"

"Not really Wolvie. It's a long story, and I'll tell you later. Might as well get off on the right foot from the start. Kenny it is. How'd you get here? You said something about hitching in a truck?"

"Did better than that. Billy drives a Kombi set up for camping. It's a bit of a squeeze with two but better than some places I've been in. He's on his way east to look at the scene in the big cities but is a country boy and wanted to get a look at our own wild west."

"Sit for a minute, beer?"

"Yes please."

"Here you go, straight from the barrel. Give me a minute, want you to meet the boss."

Kenny scooted out to the kitchen, where he found Kate. A nod, a gesture, and they both returned to the bar where introductions were made.

"Tell me, boys, you both sleep in the Kombi? We'll have to do better than that while you're here."

"Music to my ears, Kate. Billy here is not a big man, but he sure can snore."

"OK, Wolvie, you really wanna go there? Shall we talk about the noises you make in the middle of the night? No? Then man, don't poke the bear."

"No domestics, please, fellas. Let's talk about your music instead."

"What say we give you a night on us and see what you think, Kate?"

"Sounds good to me. Do you mind starting tonight at about 6:30? You can have dinner first, and then it's over to you."

"Done. Can we get a shared room while we're here as part of the deal?"

"Dinner and the room and breakfast is on us tonight. Tomorrow we'll talk about how long the gig might last, OK? If your music's any good, you might need a room each."

"Very fair, Kate, thanks."

Kate went back to work, and Kenny showed the boys to their room and left them to get settled. Kenny found her and grabbed her attention for a moment.

"Kate, if you don't mind, I will cover the accommodation and the meals for the boys but don't tell them. You can be good cop with a big heart. I don't know for sure, but they might add something special to the evening. I hope so. The thing is, I don't want this thing to be any kind of burden on the business."

"I know I can't talk you out of it. Let's see how they go."

It was early in the week, but the pub was busy. Kenny asked Sandra for two parmas and brought them to the table in the dining room, where Wolvie and Billy sat waiting, absorbing the ambience. Among the early crowd were grey nomads and a handful of miners, both groups early to rise, early to bed. Music from the jukebox in the bar filtered into the room.

"What do you reckon, we set up here or in the bar?"

"We could do a set of ballads here, not too noisy for diners who want to talk and then maybe move into the bar a bit later hit 'em with some rockin' blues numbers. You nearly finished your meal?"

"Sure, Wolvie, gimme your plate, and I'll go compliment the chef. That parma's damn good. Already better than the slop they served us in Esperance."

Billy shyly walked into the kitchen and stood in the doorway, waiting for the right moment to speak. Sandra looked up, noticed him and raised her eyebrows.

"Can I do something for you, buddy?"

"Names Billy Fingers, ma'am. Just want to thank y'all for the steak and fries. Much appreciated."

Sandra froze for a moment, transfixed by the southern twang and easy politeness.

"Kenny tells me you and your friend are going to play for us tonight. Hope it goes well for you. And you're welcome for the meals."

Billy's turn to be taken by surprise. The chef was in her cooking uniform but projected a warmth he couldn't explain.

"Ma'am."

And he was gone. Sandra went back to work, hairs on the back of her neck still standing. They hadn't done that for a long time, and the feeling brought a smile to her attitude for the rest of the shift. She would keep an ear out for the music. It started shortly after.

The first couple of songs were from the legendary Hank Williams, songs covered by all the great country singers. *Hey Good Lookin'* and *Your Cheatin' Heart* got them going. Kate and Kenny hovered and were impressed with Billy's interpretations and his clever picking. And Wolvie was on fire from the start weaving around the guitar riffs. Billy's whining twanging southern accent gave a level of authenticity the crowd loved. And it was all happening in the Denver City Hotel, not Colorado but Coolgardie. The diners could not help but give their attention and show their appreciation at the end of each song. The boys were off, warmed up and feeling welcomed. The songs flowed. *The Gambler* is everyone's favourite, and when they launched into *Bobby McGee,* people around the room joined in. All this was in the dining room. Drinkers in the bar stopped feeding the jukebox when Billy and Wolvie walked from one room to the other while still playing. Every recognisable song had everyone in the pub joining in choruses. They played without a break for two hours, sipping only from glasses of water on the bar drawing on their wide repertoire. Most of the patrons had never heard Leonard Cohen's *Democracy is Coming* and demanded it be played three times. It was appropriate to go back to Cohen with his stirring song, *It's Closing Time,* to finish the set. When Kenny got the last to leave and closed the doors, he, Kate and Sandra sat down with the troubadours.

"Before we finish, Kenny, we'd like to do one for you, our hosts."

It was a Willie Nelson classic, *Always On My Mind.* Billy's delicate and virtuoso licks and Wolvie's classy and gentle breathing harmonica wove feelings around every heart at the table. The song brings tears every time. Kate felt for Kenny's hand under the table, and Sandra was a goner. The song faded, and Billy slid his guitar into its case, Wolvie shook his harpoon and slipped it into his shirt pocket. They smiled at their audience and accepted their first beer for the night.

"So, how'd it go in Esperance? I don't understand how they'd let you go."

"Put it this way, Kate, the rest of the band held us to their kind of music, and we were happy for that gig to finish. With just the two of us, we can stick to the classics, giving them our own interpretation. Your patrons really connected. It was very satisfying for us tonight."

"OK, the question is would you like to work out a format for, say, three nights a week. I don't want to overexpose you. Like drinking great wine, you don't do it every day, and you guys are great wine. I will offer you your room, your meals and your drinks, as long as you're reasonable with the drinking. On top of that, you tell me how much money would be right for you."

Billy looked at Wolvie, leaving the negotiating up to him.

"You're covering our major expenses, and we love the chance to play, so I reckon if you offer us $500 each for the week, we'd be happy. OK, Billy?"

"Sure is, and just tell us when you've had enough of us, and we'll mosey on. Is that okay with you, Kate?"

"Not really, boys. Tell you what. We'll start with your deal, and my guess is we'll be busier than usual. Let me see how the figures work out, and if I'm right, there'll be more in it for you, not a lot but some."

By this time, Sandra was sitting next to Billy.

"Billy," she started, "I've only heard your southern twang in the movies. I could listen to it all night. Start talking boy."

They laughed, and Billy blushed out of shyness and pleasure for the attention.

Billy and Wolvie shared a room that night. Other arrangements became necessary for the rest of their stay.

Four weeks rocked by, marked by blossoming connections, intense business and great entertainment. Kenny showed the boys how the bar works, and they became busy day and night. The pub was a hub for social contact, and they heard stories of gold discoveries amongst tales of woeful disappointment. It made sense the pub was central because it all started there, and all fossickers needed lubrication and good food. They got it all in spades at the Denver.

Kenny was always going to call time and head back to Melbourne but was having such a good time he didn't mind waiting. Billy Fingers was keen to get to Sydney and Melbourne. He had saved enough travelling money to be thinking about moving on. His only complication was his blossoming relationship with Sandra. It wasn't only his southern accent she liked. The attraction was mutual. She had never travelled outside of WA and was likely to agree to go with him if he asked. She had caveats on the idea, her commitment to the business would have to come first. Her stirred emotions would not lead her to damage her deal with Kate. But a girl could dream, no? Wolvie remained a free spirit. He enjoyed having money in his kick, but he loved what he did and would continue as a roving troubadour.

The business had been buoyant since Kenny's discovery, and it was inevitable entrepreneurs would see opportunity. Brewery interests were amongst them. The one pub in Coolgardie was doing as much business as four of the best in Kalgoorlie. Kate knew the Kalgoorlie publicans and was ready when they came knocking.

"Kenny, would you ask our musos to join us for morning tea in the dining room. We need to get a few things sorted before we open for the day."

With the table set for elevenses and everyone in the room, Kate called the meeting to start.

"A bit nervous about what's happening, but Sandra and I want you all to know. Business has been the best ever, and you have helped make it so. The gold rush has not slowed down, and local businesses are doing well. Sandra and I have been approached by a number of interests who want to buy the pub. We have paid off the bank and can walk away with enough money to follow whatever dream each of us has. Look out, Kenny and Billy. Haha. It will take us up to ninety days to complete the deal we are prepared to take, and by then, all of us should be ready enough to move on. What do you think?"

There followed a lot of tea pouring and buttering of scones while the information was absorbed. Wolvie was the first to speak.

"Kate and Sandra. It took me a lifetime to find you, and I've loved every minute. I travel light, and before leaving the district, I think I'd like to try some of the pubs in Kalgoorlie. After that, I don't know, but am not worried. Look how things can happen. Good luck to you all, and let's continue what we've started till it's over."

"You mean y'all won't be crowdin' my Kombi no more big Wolvie?"

They laughed.

"Stop talking like that, you make me shiver."

Sandra's hands went to her face, but her eyes told the story.

Kenny said nothing, but his mind raced. He and Kate enjoyed the most intensely romantic time either had ever had but had not worked out a post-pub strategy. He knew she would have ideas, but he hadn't yet been told. His own plans certainly included her, but he hesitated to say much because he knew he could be a burden, and he didn't want that. Now she had announced moving out of the business, he would save his thoughts until they got together later. The meeting ended, but there were many conversations to be had.

"Sandra, honey, ah get the impression Kate and y'all are partners."

"You didn't need to know, Billy, but I think it's safe to tell you now. We've been talking about moving on together, and I'm glad it worked out you didn't know something, 'cause it might have made me think twice. I'm happy to travel with you and pay my way. I think it's smart if we keep our money separate. If that bothers you, tell me now."

"Hey, there wild one. Far as ah knew, you were workin' here just like me. Look at the way ah live. Ah go hand to mouth, always have, and it always worked okay for me. Ah have no reason to wanna change. We get along just fine. Ain't no amount of money gonna change it. Sure keep y'all hands on y'own money. That's only right. It's not money ah want with you, honey. You know what it's about, ain't that a fact now?"

"OK, Billy Fingers, you're fine with me. Just thought you ought to know. Let's get back to work. I'll see you later."

Kenny waited until after closing time and didn't have to wait too long before Kate knocked on his door.

"Come in, Kate. It's been a big day for you. It had to happen. I knew they'd come. It makes sense for them. Good business is about seeing opportunity and seizing it. And it's a good opportunity for you to decide how much you like being here. You've proved to everyone you're good at running a busy pub, and it looks like you have a good chance to cash out if you've had enough. The question is, what do you do next?"

"Don't worry about me, young fella. I've a clear idea about what I want to do next. The thing is, I don't know if you'll approve. I'm nervous if you can believe it. Before you waltzed into Coolgardie, my life was totally predictable, slowly going down the gurgler. Kenny, get it into your thick head, I'm with you now and for a hundred good reasons. Firstly, it was all those things you are I've never seen in a man before. And then, Hanna and Charlie turn up, and I find out about all this other stuff. The fact you are hounded by the black dog is a godsend for me. I find out you're not the complete package. Thank God. It means I can actually be useful to you apart from romping in the hay. Don't get me wrong, romping with you is one of the best things, and I hope we make it last for a long time. But other stuff has got to matter too. You might not need me as such, but it would be crazy of you to puddle along through bouts of bad times when I could be with you riding shotgun. You don't scare me, mister. What do you say?"

"Kate, it's complicated. Let me try to explain. I have a track record with people who get close. It might make you change your mind. Two school friends suicided because I didn't step in and help on time. The only real girlfriend I've ever had was murdered because she was with me. Next, on a training flight over Arizona, I was piloting a plane that disintegrated, and my trainer lost his life. I joined a successful flight charter business in Texas, and within 6 months, they went broke. Then I hook up with my best friend after many years, and the first thing that happens is I crash his helicopter and nearly kill one of his pilots. People who get close to me get hurt. Now you come along. Kate, it would be the last straw for something to take you out of my life. It would be safer for you to let me go. On the other hand, it would break me to see you go. See, complicated."

"Pardon me for saying this, but you are an idiot. I can list a dozen things to show how your presence enriches lives and not just in money. I won't do it because you are convinced in your mindset. What say you leave the decision to me about who I spend my time with. You know what? I don't care if I'm rolling the dice in some deadly game you imagine is going on. I choose to roll the dice and to hell with everything else."

There was a long silence hovering like a force field between them. Then Kenny blinked. He could not stand the obvious pain she was in waiting for him to say something.

"Kate, what did you say about romping?

The force field collapsed. Nature took its inevitable course. No more was said until the romping and recovery were complete. Kenny's left arm was under her neck, cradling her. He rolled her towards him and, with his right hand, caressed across her forehead and down her left cheek and across her top lip, tickling her so she had to show her pleasure. His face was right over hers when she opened her eyes.

"Kate, after serious consideration, let me tell you I would be overwhelmed with pleasure if you decide to continue being with me after you have sold the pub. I have a few ideas about what comes next, and I hope you would like to join me in those things."

"Hmmm, don't know. It might get complicated."

Simulated wrestling ensued, and then she pushed him away.

"Tell me more tomorrow. I need to sleep now. And so do you."

THERE WAS SOMETHING MISSING for Hanna. Going to work has lost its appeal, and it wasn't in her character to pretend to be interested. Her clients demanded and deserved her full attention to their interests. What was happening to her was more than post-holiday disconnection. And, to be fair, her trip to find Kenny had not been all holiday. It had been stressful being told by authorities he was gone, and she had ridden thousands of kilometres before discovering the happy truth he had survived. Even then, it took weeks more before she found him. Parallel to this was the gestation of a relationship with Charlie. She had never before given herself as she had to him, and the sense of rightness about it was overpowering. Her mind had never turned this way with such force, and she knew she would find a way to complete the wild ride she had started with him.

To hide her creeping indifference, she worked harder than usual. To all appearances, she was the same as she had always been. She made productivity a priority and set demanding standards for herself and her staff. A huge amount of effort went into research and verification of products and services required for projects and contracts. Assessing quotations and looking for the best providers was intense. She had to meet and greet developers and building contractors as part of due diligence. A nightmare for contract lawyers. She threw herself into every aspect of the business.

Outside of work, there had always been music commitments. She had always loved performing in the string quartet. Still, since she had been away, the group had taken another musician and were now settled. Her recreation was reduced to a few hours of practice a couple of times a week. She loved to liberate 'Chancellor'. Running a dust cloth over the memories of exquisite melodies his glossy curves gave her prepared her for every practice session. They would sit in front of the big window and carouse the city beneath them. These days there was, however, an unusually tense, melancholy undertone.

The highs she had experienced travelling with Charlie and finding Kenny had been disruptive. Not only, but those weeks opened her mind to options she had never considered. Big sky country, Charlie, regional as opposed to metropolitan, Kenny's wanderlust, all these things were now tugging at her. She had always been so practical, almost obsessive/compulsive in her habits. The motorbike was the only nonconformist part of her life. The only wild card in her life had been her brother. Everything else was on rails.

She no longer enjoyed the comfort of certainty. A seismic shift had jolted her. She might have been saddened, but amazingly she wasn't. Uncertainty was almost a thrill for her. She would never be like the Dice Man, who made decisions every day based on options he gave dice before rolling them, but a creeping need for change had its own momentum.

Up to this point, she hadn't been sure how things would work out with Mark, but now the end game was written in. She could no longer see herself partnering at work and sharing parenting duties at home, her home.

He was back from holidays, and they met for the necessary debriefing in the same room where they had made all the big decisions and allowances for each other.

"Come on, Mark, tell me how you handled being fun Daddy, for a couple of weeks."

"Yeah, we had a ball. Safe swimming, the sound of waves caressing the beach every night, trail walks, pier fishing, whale watching, campfires, and shared cooking. The girls and I reconnected. Hardly a cross word amongst us for the whole time. Eden's a funny place, they don't seem to care too much about tourists, but it's a village, and it sits on the cliffs above the Pacific ocean. It's a spectacular place.

One other thing. The girls struck up a friendship with two boys their own age. They played all day together on the beach at the park. And there's more. Their mother runs her own business supplying organic cereals to restaurants and specialty supermarkets. She's able to grab a week or two from time to time because she's so well organised with distributors and suppliers. It's taken her five years to get to this point, and it cost her a marriage along the way. Hanna, I am going to continue to see this woman. Her and her boys live in Mordialloc, the kids get on well, and she seems to think I'm worth an effort. What do you think?"

Suddenly, without doing anything off her own bat, one of the elephants in the room vanished. He showed no sign of regret about slinging his affections in a new direction.

"Whoa, Mark! You have an aura I've not seen. You are smitten, I could tell as soon as I saw you. So, struck by lightning, hey! Good on you. Tell me what she's like."

She was going to soak up this moment.

"I don't know what to say. My age, curly red hair, ivory skin, green eyes and freckles, lots of freckles. She laughs a lot and keeps fit by running. She talks a bit too much, but she's mostly funny. I have half a notion she loves the girls more than me, a change from having only boys herself. She was raised a catholic and still goes to church and drags the boys with her. My girls just wave them off when they go, I don't think they'll catch the habit. She's been divorced for two years and wasn't looking for a boyfriend. The first day on the beach, it's a small beach, the kids met in the water, and it all started there. The girls brought the boys over to say hello. I was reading and didn't even notice. Their mother came over, and the next thing I didn't pick up the book again for the rest of the holiday."

"How are you going to organise a blended family?"

"That's the thing. Too early to tell. I don't want to make a mistake by moving too fast, but I can't stop thinking about her. Does it make sense to run two households and have visiting rights? What do you think?"

"OK, reality check. Who have you told?"

"You're the first. Oh, told my mum a bit of the story, not everything."

"Hmmm. I am so happy to see you this way, and I'm sure you'll work through the logistics and everything. I agree you shouldn't move fast. The chemistry is obviously going wild at the moment and will continue, let's hope for a long time. I might as well not say this, but I can't help it. Remember. There are two points in our emotional cycle when we shouldn't make significant decisions. One is when we are excited, and the other is when we are depressed. You, my friend, are excited. So, enjoy now and for as long as it lasts. The changes you are already thinking about are significant for all six of you. Don't hurry. In these matters, time is your friend. Promise me. Then you have to ask who I am to be giving advice on relationship issues. So!"

"So, let the head rule the heart, hey?"

Hanna wasn't sure if she was advising Mark or herself.

"Your survival depends on it, that's how serious it is. How does your new friend handle all this?"

"Sorry, her name is Deanna, and her boys are Jack and Harry, the same age as my girls. To answer your question, Deanna doesn't need a meal ticket. She is already comfortable."

"I'm not asking about money. What does she think about you, first of all?"

"We speak every day and plan ways for us to meet, sometimes with the kids and sometimes without. I'm sure she wants to see me."

"Sounds good. Love to see you like this. Let what comes next reveal itself to you, to both of you. You don't have to worry. Keep me informed, and good luck."

"Now, what about you, Hanna. You've found Kenny, and you're back at work. Are you happy to be back in the old routine, work, music and bike trips?"

He was deflecting any possibility of talking about his former interest in her. She allowed him the deflection.

"In a way, it's been good to be able to concentrate totally on business. We have built up a dossier of great builders and contractors who do their best work for us and who are able to limit variations they claim on jobs. It's been good for me to be so focused while you've been away."

"I know what you mean. I've enjoyed the break, but I still like to see projects go ahead more easily because of our work. It's good to be back. We have a good portfolio of developers who move smoothly from one project to the next. My question is do we have enough, or should we build a waiting list?"

"Really, Mark, if you look at our overheads, you, I and our six staff are a tight unit. We occupy just enough space, and everyone has the right balance between work and private life. It's a comfortable set up, and I don't want to see balance disrupted. What do you reckon?"

"Before current circumstances arrived, I'd say take more work. Now, I agree with you. Let's not rock the boat. Let's stay high quality, exclusive service and happy workers."

It was time to deal with the other elephant, the one he hadn't even suspected.

"Having said all that, Mark, I have to tell you my motives are mixed. You have to know I will soon want to make some changes. Regional and Outback country have my interest. I have an offer to help build camel farming and related value-added products on a big station near Alice Springs. Kenny's friend, Charlie, needs help with the regulatory side of the project. The whole thing about camels is they are so big, and it costs a fortune to corral them. They are difficult to handle. He has this idea of genetic intervention to breed the size of them down. If he can, then a whole new industry is possible. The Arabs may not like smaller animals for their racing. Still, Charlie's more interested in a domestic value-added industry than racing. There are many more benefits to be had. To be truthful, I'm looking forward to working with him. No details yet, but that's what I want to do next."

Hanna surprised herself with the story she had just told Mark. There was no such plan. It was an impulsive moment in which she wanted to justify her interest in the camel management project Charlie had mentioned in passing. But a light went on in her head. Surely genetics could be the answer. She determined she would start researching possibilities. Mark almost disappeared from the room at that moment.

"Wow, Hanna. You started this business, and you've made it successful. You're saying you want to step away permanently? I smell something else, something you're not telling me. Charlie, hey. Something happen there?"

"You've been frank with me, so here goes. In a word, yes, something has happened, and I'm feeling the same things you are about Deanna. The lecture I gave you was really meant for myself. Maybe the stuff about camels is just rationalising. So, yes, I am going to make a clean break. 'Burgess and Joseph' can become 'Joseph and Associates'. It's all up to you."

"Maybe we should both step back and think before we decide. My impulse is a mixture of grief and excitement, but I think the idea needs some fermentation."

"OK, Mark, let's. Same time, same place, one week."

"Done."

Mark was game enough to consider the proposal, and Hanna was sure he would take the offer as long as the price was right. He was impressed anyway, so object achieved. She couldn't wait to get home and start the conversation with Charlie. He might laugh at the idea, but he might not.

Mark walked away from the meeting with ideas spinning. He could see himself as the principal of the legal firm. If and when he could stamp his own presence on the culture. It would be challenging, but he would be in complete control. He had never been in total control. He smiled at possibilities as he headed back to the day's work. He would confide in Deanna and measure her reaction against all other possibilities in the mix.

Hanna was engulfed by the flash of inspiration. Imagine camels small enough to be managed like cattle. Outback dominance enjoyed by the cattle industry would evolve to include a synergetic partnership with the camel industry. She couldn't wait to get home.

In the meantime, she made contact with three institutions, one of which was the University of New England, within which camels were being studied for their benefits in pharmaceutics, milk, cheese and meat.

After a couple of emails back and forth that night, Hanna picked up the phone. Two reasons. One of them was to talk about camels.

"Hi, you. Wanted to hear you. The texting is effective, but I wanted to hear you too."

"Good idea, Hanna. I've been preoccupied with the camel business now

on my shoulders and haven't been able to talk to you. On the other hand, lots of thoughts flash through my mind every day, so you are with me."

"Sounds good to me, and we can deal with both issues at once now I've got you on the line. I've had a few thoughts about camels since you mentioned it to me a while ago. They are big animals, hey. Even the small breeds are tall compared to cattle."

"That's right. Though the weight of a good brahman can get close to the weight of a camel. It's just that the camel is tall and can run through fences. The cost of infrastructure would be prohibitive to farm them. They need broad territory to roam. It would be cruel to corral them."

"OK, now don't laugh at me for what I say next. Not only am I no expert, but the whole idea is brand new to me. I'm hoping that my naivety is an asset. I've been online today to three universities where they study the camel genome. Their interest is all in medicines and a few food products. Nobody is looking at their size in the context of farming them. Australia is unique in collision with cattle for space. What if there was a camel genetically modified to a size closer to a cow? There, that's my question. And don't tell me about alpaca and llama, they don't fit the bill."

There was silence at Charlie's end. Hanna waited.

"Hanna, this question is now real. Do you want to work with me? I love your question, and it deserves to be researched. What you are suggesting is we can separate the problems we have with feral camels from the camel farming industry. It strikes me. Why haven't we thought of it? So, I ask you again. Do you want to work with me?"

"I'm seriously thinking, you know. We could deal with two birds, so to speak, with the one decision. You think about what we've just touched on, and I'll do a bit more research. Then I'll say a resounding 'yes' to your question. How's that?"

"My first thought is we should talk to the scientists in a confidential way. You know what it's like with good ideas. When the word gets out, it creates a rush. It would be nice for us to control the thing as long as possible. I'm thinking of the owners here who have shown interest enough to get me working on the subject. If the science is good, then we could centralise the delivery of the techniques to a burgeoning industry. See, you've got me going already. Time for sleep for you. Talk to me tomorrow after I've done my own thinking."

Hanna whispered into the phone.

"Good night young man."

DENVER CITY HOTEL VIBRATED with energy the following morning. Billy interrupted Sandra's preps in the kitchen, with two steaming pots and a huge rump of beef on the cutting board about to be sliced. Beads of sweat on Sandra's brow, tears in her eyes. She looked up. There he stood, the man who made her shiver with pleasure. Skinny but wiry, grey beard that used to be red, long hair waiting for attention, grey shining eyes and a huge smile fighting its way through the beard.

"Mornin' darlin'. You left me stranded there in a big ol' bed alone. I missed you, honey."

"Stop it, Billy Fingers, you know you drive me mad with that talk."

She stopped chopping onions and rested both hands on the bench, her face beaming at him.

"Need to know, darlin', how long before we can git on the road again to coin a phrase of a good old pal of mine?"

"Can't answer yet Billy. You know we have to sell the pub first. Get out of here and have a shower before breakfast. Go on, git. And don't worry, Kate is on the job. It could be three months, is my guess. You in a hurry?"

The rest of it was slung over his shoulder as he left the room.

"Ah was before ah saw you. Now nothin' matters more than us."

She called after him, laughing at the same time.

"Don't worry old boy. I can't wait to get on the road and see some more of this country. You've got me now, so hang on for the ride of your life."

"Whoopee. Doggone, gal! Life's a big ol' rodeo."

He left her to her work.

Kate and Kenny sat at a table in the backyard behind the hotel where the morning sun began its daily job, water vapour steaming off empty steel beer kegs and paling fence. Coffee in hand, they were silent for a few minutes. He opened.

"You see what's happening with Sandra? She's a goner for Billy's sweet accent. You think things will work out for them?"

"Don't know. We made a big mistake with those two guys you met the other day. The thing is, you either learn to make better judgements, or you don't. In truth, I think she'll be good to him but look after herself first. If she's smart, she'll have an exit plan. He's a drifter, he's not looking for someone to lean on. Mind you, he doesn't mind having a good time, and you can't blame a man for that, hey."

"Hmm, yeah. Now, let me ask you. Would you like to visit the east coast, specifically Melbourne, for a while? I've got a base there and some good part-time work bringing Tasmanian seafood across the Strait. We could combine work with pleasure until you've had enough and want to do something else. Remember, you need an exit plan."

"I've been thinking about it for a while, as you know. Let me say it one more time. I am with you for the journey. Can't tell the future, but the present has been the best I've had in my adult life. Yes, let's go to Melbourne. Love to see what you've done, and I don't mind being your flight navigator at all. As soon as I can hook the right offer for the pub. Now, if you're warm enough on the inside and outside, it's time to get some work done."

She put down her cup, stood and pushed herself between the table and him, perched herself daringly on his lap and sealed the deal in the most delightful embrace. He was helpless and shuddered with pleasure in the holding. He brought his mouth to her ear and growled contentment that weakened her for a moment. Then they rose and went their separate paths to the day's chores.

Kate was in a strong position with potential buyers. Trading figures were the best of any pub in the district, including Kalgoorlie. The gold rush continued to gain pace, spurred on by finds of other lucky fossickers and the taking up of leases by big speculating companies. Business would be buoyant beyond anyone's ability to see it wane. Even locals began to forget how hard it had been for them. One offer came from a group of executives within the Perth brewery who were looking for a sea change. They knew exactly how well she was doing. The owner of two of the hotels in Kalgoorlie was the other main interest. After a couple of weeks of to and fro, his offer was in her best interests. The bonus was he could settle within 30 days. He didn't mind setting a new record for a pub sale because he had two others in his portfolio. It was good business to pay a premium and lift the price of the other properties. On top of the price he offered, he calculated the estimated profit for the next two years extrapolated from the earnings since the gold rush. He then added it to the buying price. The girls could not deny him, the offer was too good. The signing of the contract gave certainty to the girls' plans and plonked a huge lump into their superannuation.

In the carve-up of assets, Kate got the pub van, a ten-year-old Toyota Hi-Ace. She had a few things to take with her to Melbourne, and the van, while not ideal for long travel, would ideally suit her other purpose. Kenny was flexible. He figured the workshop space could cope with the few pieces of furniture and memorabilia Kate had without compromising the primary purpose of the space.

So, by mid-afternoon of the day, they were leaving Coolgardie, having completed all the hand-shaking and wishing of good things, especially to Wolvie, who would now be travelling alone, the convoy was ready to leave. Sandra in her best of hippie style little white cotton button-up blouse with most of the buttons done up, reaching close to the waistline of a mini skirt she'd been waiting for ages to wear. A pink pair of Adidas runners completed her kit. She looked like the life partner of the Nashville cowboy singer who slid into the driver's seat. Kate, wearing a denim western shirt and well-worn tight-fitting Levi's and an old bush hat, jumped in to drive the van for the first leg. Both vans backed out of their parking spots at the front of the pub, paused for one last wave and left Coolgardie headed for the Nullabor, aiming to get to Belladonna in time to book a room for the night. Belladonna is a busy roadhouse, all hours of the day. There was only one room available for the night, so Sandra and Billy agreed to spend the first night on the road in the Kombi as a trial run. The four of them ate an early dinner, a safe steak and chips, in the dining room before adjourning to a table under cover, outside, where they could enjoy a few more drinks before retiring.

"It feels so funny on the other side of the counter. I think I'm going to enjoy this trip."

"Yeah, Kate, welcome to the other side."

"Me too. Someone actually cooked dinner for me. That's a first for a while."

The holiday was off to a good start.

"Good night, lovers in a shoebox, see you at breakfast."

"You'll get yours, Kenny. Good night, enjoy the luxury of a bedroom in a donger."

The next morning they crisscrossed between donger, vehicles and the ablution block before an appetite-arousing walk around the car park and picnic area. They then headed for breakfast in the diner amongst a dozen early travellers with the vans fuelled and packed, ready for a big day on the road.

The two vans continued for the next four days idling their way across the country, drinking in the sights of the Great Bight, where they did some whale watching, ate fresh oysters in Ceduna and made a detour to Port Lincoln before finally getting to Adelaide, where they parted company. Sandra wanted to show Billy the Barossa and Adelaide hills she had heard so much about. Kenny and Kate wanted to get to Melbourne to see Hanna before she left for the red centre.

Kenny didn't want to push the old van too hard and decided one more night on the road wouldn't hurt. Ballarat was worth a look in any case. Having booked their accommodation for the night, they took a 6km walk around Lake Wendouree and dined in the hotel beside the lake. By the time they got back to the hotel, Kenny remembered with clarity where his body had been over the years. He fell with conviction into a cosy chair in the bar while Kate attended to pre-dinner drinks.

"You know Kenny, I can't remember sleeping as well as I have been these last few days. When the pub turns up in my dreams, I get scared because there's no beer and the bar is full of miners. Then I wake up and sigh with relief, reach over to check you're still there and then sleep deeply for the rest of the night. You doing OK?"

He had stopped panting by this time, and his aching joints eased.

"It's funny. Over the years, sleep has been torture, largely. Lately, I'm not even dreaming. When I wake, my foot goes looking for you, and as soon as I feel your leg, I drop off again. It's restful."

Middle of the following day, they cruised into Melbourne, Kate's face stuck to the window taking in the sights of a spectacular city profile from the Bolte Bridge on the way to Richmond. When they pulled the van to a stop outside the garage door of Kenny's place, Kenny sighed. He was home. He hit the button, and the first thing he saw was his beloved 'Javelin' sitting just where he had left it, waiting to be resurrected.

"Oooh! This is nice. I bet you did the refurb. Yeah, it's got you written all over it. Kind of industrial, of course, but big on open space. Let's make our presence felt."

She was off to look into every corner while Kenny liberated cargo from the van and lowered the car off its stands. He connected the battery and started the engine. It was ready for him. When Kate came back, he could see the pleasure on her face.

"A girl could get comfortable in a place like this. That is, of course, if she had the right companion."

She flirted, weaving and eluding his awkward grasping at her, ducking around the car, the benches, the tool racks. But he had a strategy.

"What do you say to a hot shower to wash away dust and the miles?"

She scampered, he lumbered up the stairs, but he knew where he would catch her. He did, and they didn't come up for air until near dinner time.

"Have a treat in mind for this evening. You interested?"

"Of course, why would I want to stay in bed?"

It was almost an offer, one he couldn't possibly accept, for a while anyway.

"We could do a raid on the supermarket, and then I'm going to introduce you to a cuisine I think you'll like, and I don't mean I'm cooking."

He made the call to book a table and then found it hard to get off the phone, promising Pierre the full story later.

"Kate, this is Javelin, a project I loved doing when I first came back to Melbourne."

She walked around the vehicle, looking over its roof at Kenny, who said nothing but whose face said it all.

"How did it get such a name? Are you going to give me the keys?"

They came sailing through the air, landing right in her outstretched hand. He didn't answer her question. She slid into the driver's seat and guided the ignition key home. It came to life on the first try, not noisy, more like hissing but ominously powerful.

"It was my call sign in the airforce."

"Ooooh, deadly in the air, hey? Nice name."

Kate got to drive it before Kenny, in fact, no one else had ever driven it. But he was comfortable having watched her style on the big drive they'd just finished.

Walking through the door and into the dimly lit intimacy, Pierre went straight to him despite the number of tables he was serving. The embrace was heartfelt.

"Don't say a word, Kenny. Hanna has been here since she got back from her trip west. What an amazing story. I know you've written the movie script, but for sure, there's a book in your own story. Come in, hello, you must be Kate. Pierre and you are so welcome, Kate. Mark, come over."

His son was in training to learn the business. He had his degree in international business, but his gregarious nature made him a natural for the restaurant business. Clearly, Pierre had an exit plan.

"Kate, this is Mark, my older boy."

"Hello, Mark, Kate. I can see the resemblance."

"Mark, would you get a banquet prepared for our guests?"

"Sure, Pierre."

He scooted to the kitchen.

"Thanks, Pierre. I think we'll be seeing a bit of you from now on. I'm looking forward to trying your cuisine. It's my first time."

"Say no more, sit here. I hope you like red wine, I've got a wonderful Western Australian Malbec, so good with Lebanese food. And if you prefer white wine, just say so."

"Thanks, Pierre, tonight, we are in your hands, the malbec will be fine."

Within minutes they were surrounded, tasting the wine, scooping dips and tabouli into pita pockets accompanied by the most delicate and tangy pastries and falafel. Kenny smiled, and Kate was in heaven, taste buds singing. She had worked up a good appetite earlier and dived into the banquet.

"Been a fair start to our holiday Kenny, how do you top this?"

"Try sitting beside me in a light aircraft scooting across Bass Strait in search of the best seafood on the planet. That could be good."

She chuckled.

"Yeah, take me to great heights, hey?"

"Yes, right where you have taken me, haha."

Sated and tired, they left Samsara after everyone else and after an hour of deep and meaningful with Pierre. Mark had left earlier when his jobs were done. Social life calls the young. Kenny drove home, loving the car and familiarity of his old self, now home in his own place and the elevation of being connected to a woman who had an uncanny knack of reading him. Significantly, what she read did not scare her. She had perspective and had already shown the strength of conviction. She wanted to be with him. *How often does it happen,* he thought.

The next morning Kenny took Kate for a stroll around the neighbourhood. She loved the style of tiny workers' cottages in Bendigo Street and was curious about trees growing out of bitumen on footpaths. They walked as far as the café where Kenny had met Siobhan and where she had lost her life. It was still operating, so they stopped for a coffee. He told Kate nothing.

"This is cute, Kenny. Love the wisteria covering the outside area. So, this is inner-city living? Not like country life, is it?"

"You might say that. This place used to be a lot busier, and had a good feeling about it. You can tell when people don't like what they're doing, hey."

The coffee was unremarkable and the ambience indifferent, but they didn't care. Moving on, he took her for a tram ride as far as the sports precinct. They left the tram and walked around under the railway bridge and as far as the renowned MCG, a silent concrete monument to a nationwide obsession with professional sport. Kate's eyes were transfixed. She didn't seem to tire with all the walking. Kenny, however, had reached his limits by the time they reached Flinders Street, and he was very happy for the tram ride back to Richmond.

"OK, I think it's time to call Hanna and maybe catch up with her for dinner, what do you think?"

"Of course, is she close?"

"Middle of the city, and she'll have a good idea for dinner as well. But first, I need to shower and straighten my body."

"You do that. I'll explore more of your man cave."

"OK, and later, another tram ride to Hanna's, and you'll get a bird's eye view of the city from there. Then I think it will be Chinatown tonight for dinner."

They stood outside the Rialto building, and Kenny pointed to where Hanna lived.

"See what you mean by bird's eye. Let's go, can't wait."

Hanna swung her door open to them and embraces followed.

"This is sooo good. Welcome to Melbourne, Kate. I really hope it works well for you. I won't have to worry about our friend here, never knowing what he's doing or what trouble he's causing. He's your job now."

They laughed. Kate wasn't intimidated at all. Never been as contented. She then walked around the large living area and stood at the floor to ceiling window facing the bay. City lights, the port of Melbourne and traffic movements. She was silent. Coolgardie, Melbourne, the contrast couldn't be greater, but she wasn't dizzy. She always loved the country, its space and clean air and the control she had with her business. But what she was looking at now was unique in her experience and beautiful in its own way.

During the short walk to Chinatown, Hanna filled them in about her plans to help Charlie with his venture into camel breeding. Kenny asked about her business.

"Time to let it go, Kenny. Mark will do well enough without me looking over his shoulder. I'll still be doing legal work at the station, and our international experience will be a great asset. While I'm away, you two can hold the keys to the apartment to use when you want a break from living on the ground. And anyway, you can always fly out to Charlie's place to visit us and do some farm work."

"Sounds like you're ready for a change. Charlie will be happy, I know. But know this, and it's the joke of the week. Make sure you've got an exit plan."

Hanna didn't laugh but saw the other two share an insider moment.

"Well, I'm keeping my apartment, aren't I, and will always have music if I need to make a living. I think I'll be set. Kate, you're the one who'll be looking for something once the pair of you come up for air. You can't live solely on the fruits of love. Oh, on a practical issue, I'm riding the bike and can't take everything I need in panniers. I'll box up the rest, and could I ask you to courier it to me when I call? Thanks, big brother."

"Give us a couple of weeks for a holiday, Mac. After that, we'll work something out for each of us. For the moment, it's all about holiday stuff. Yes, I'll send your boxes."

It was a well-earned holiday, up close and personal on a daily basis. It is the only sure-fire way to find the warts and all view of a new love, often learning more than one wants to. Back in 'shed' as Kate called Kenny's place, she had made herself comfortable setting up the second bedroom for her retreat. Each of them was so used to sleeping alone that neither wanted to give it up. Visiting rights were naturally part of the deal. In the back of Kenny's mind was slight apprehension about the kind of sleep he would have if alone. Fair enough, the demons had haunted him most of his life. He would wing it. Kate thought she might have to sleep with one ear alert to the next room. She would wing it.

HANNA SAT LOW AND FORWARD, nose just above the edge of her windscreen. Once past Coober Pedy with little traffic and a beautifully clear, warm afternoon, she gave the 'Kwaka' licence to run, Charlie on her mind. She had never heard about the danger of the bones of road-killed critters to country travellers, bones made brittle by exposure to the sun and sharp enough to puncture tyres. Even truckies avoid the flattened, almost hard to see remains of rabbits and other small critters. So in the middle of the road, on a broad left-hander, Hanna paid no attention to the skeletal remains she ran over at high speed. In her mind, she was already turning into the Erldunda roadhouse where she had arranged to meet Charlie. Only 50 kms to go when she lost control of the bike's front end, and her world went into slow motion chaos. Then, nothing.

First to the scene was a 'Toll' road train she had shot past about 2 minutes before. The driver, 'Hackles,' to everyone who knew him, could still see the dust settling from his high position. He didn't waste a second and radioed ahead to the Flying Doctor service based in Alice Springs to call out an ambulance plane. He made a second call to Erldunda roadhouse to let them know about salvaging the remains of the bike. His hazard lights gave fair warning to any other travellers. He jumped to the ground and across to the motionless rider. It was a path of destruction that led to her possessions, parts of the bike strewn all over the place. Charlie was in the roadhouse when the call came through from the truck driver and heard the chatter about a disintegrated bike. He was out of there in a flash, panic in his heart. Back at the scene, Hackles knew the drill, knew not to move the body or remove the helmet but to try and detect signs of life. He knelt beside her, lifted the visor to check her mouth and nose were clear and felt her neck under the helmet for a pulse. If there was one, it was faint and intermittent. His phone rang. He had given his number to be able to talk to paramedics on their way to him, maybe get instructions. He was in the middle of relaying that the rider was still alive, but they should hurry when a bike from the other direction came flying towards them. The truckie ran to the road to wave the rider to slow down. No need, it was Charlie. He was off his bike and across the verge, throwing his own helmet aside, he dived to the ground beside the motionless body. He looked up at the truckie, pleading in his eyes.

"Mate, she's alive, but only by a hair. Don't touch her, could kill her if you do. The flying doctor's on the way should be no more than 30 minutes. If there's a chance, they'll know what to do. You might want to get your bike well clear of the road so the plane can land. I've got a blanket in the truck, should keep her warm while we wait. Here, take these flares with you. They'll help the pilot land safely."

"Sure. And thanks for calling them so quick. It will make a difference to her chances."

The plane turned up fifteen minutes later, circled the scene and came in to land on the Stuart Highway from the north, the scene being at the end of a long straight stretch leading to the bend where it all happened. The doctor, Geoff McCallum, was with her immediately and examined her as closely as he could. The most confronting sight Hackles had ever seen was the insertion of a huge adrenalin needle directly into her chest. Dramatic but effective. Signs of life strengthened enough for the doctor to have her moved to the plane and attached to monitors. They were gone in fifteen minutes after arriving. Charlie was unable to go with her. He rode the quickest 200 kms ever and went immediately to the ICU within the Alice Springs hospital, where he stayed until summoned by the operating doctor two hours later. It was time to make the call.

❖

THEY HAD BEEN FUSSING around all afternoon, and Kenny's prime interest was to allow space in the workshop for stuff that wouldn't go into Kate's bedroom. He wanted minimum interference with his set-up and was glad there were only a couple of small items to deal with.

"That's it for the day, Kate. Think I'll grab a shower, and then we'll think about what to do for dinner."

"Sounds good. Want company?"

The look he threw over his shoulder was not encouraging.

"OK, your loss."

"Not at all, I'm thinking nightcap rather than matinee."

He was gone. Within minutes his phone rang. Charlie.

Kenny padded out of the bathroom, jocks only and towelling his wet hair vigorously. He knew immediately something was wrong. Her ashen face warned him the news was not good. He accepted the phone from her.

"Charlie. How bad is it?"

He sat with his elbows on the table, phone glued to his ear, head down, absorbing the information. He paused to speak.

"Kate, we're going to Alice Springs. Would you mind booking a couple of tickets for the next flight?"

Hanna didn't know how long she'd been out to it. She was aware of the smell of disinfectant and then the sound of swishing curtains. There was another smell, one she recognised, her brother. She knew she was on her back, but she had no feeling she could move. She had no memory of the accident happening, only of a sense of flying through the air. She gasped. Before she opened her eyes, she ran a check, head to toe. No pain, feeling in toes and fingers, so far so good, she dared to open her eyes. She knew she was in trouble because the first face she recognised was Kenny's.

"What the fuck, Mac. If you want to fly, then come with me. You are not meant to fly on a motorbike, or more accurately, off a motorbike."

His hands cupped her face. Her smile was a mixture of adoration, helplessness and amusement. At that moment, she realised both arms were immobilised in casts and her left leg below the knee.

"Might as well use me for a boat anchor, hey!"

She turned her head to identify the chuckler.

"Oh, Charlie."

She couldn't help the tears.

"Yeah, couldn't wait to get to me, huh?"

She sobbed.

"I'm so sorry, but you're right, and I was so close. Tell me. What's the deal? Is it just the arms and leg?"

"Mostly, but you hit a big rock pretty hard and ruptured your left kidney. They had to take it. No head injuries and the rest is broken bones. You'll be here for a while. But you're here, and that's all that matters. Nothing more for you to worry about, just get yourself better."

"Oh, by the way, we have a new best friend. Don't know if you remember passing a road train just before it happened. The driver's a bloke called Hackles. He had the flying doctor booked as soon as he saw you hit the dirt. He kept you warm and was smart enough not to touch you. We'll call him in the morning. All your stuff is at the roadhouse, and they'll send it on when I let them know."

"Really. That's a bit lucky. Could have been lying long enough to die."

"It took a big adrenalin shot in the chest to get you going, but yeah, it was close."

The three of them were ushered out of the room and told to leave her for the night and not to return until midday. Hanna spotted Kate.

"Kate, can I speak to you before you go?"

Kate turned and bent to her.

"Sorry about all this, but would you stick close to Kenny. I know he'll find a way to blame himself, and it won't be good for him or us. I did this all by myself, right?"

"Gotcha, Hanna, already on to it. Hurry back to us babe."

She stood and turned to catch up to the others. The morphine kicked in, and Hanna drifted into a wonderful calm world of drug-induced sleep, the kind of ecstasy addicts die for.

"Well, Charlie, we have to decide what comes next. It'll be a long convalesce, it could be tricky."

"No, I've got a room and bathroom for her in the homestead. I hope she'll come."

"OK, but let me arrange for a carer, I have someone in mind, and she's only a couple of days away, and she's a nurse. Let me do that.

The rest of us can come and go, but someone is going to have to be on call. Have you another room for a carer?"

"Sure we do. Always need accommodation for visitors and vets and engineers and mechanics. The bloody place is like a hotel sometimes. So, make the call. Are you and Kate coming back with me to the station? You know you're more than welcome."

"Thanks, old friend, but we'll stay in Alice for a while and ride shottie on Hanna. I'll let you know about Sue Whittaker."

Back at the hotel, he made the call.

"Hello Jack, great to hear from you. Still in Coolgardie?"

"No, Sue, but still with Kate from Coolgardie. A story I must tell you when we catch up."

"Catch up? Great idea. You coming up to the Ord country and bring Kate if you are. She's a fine catch for an ordinary bloke like you, hey?"

"OK, I am a bit lucky, but she reckons she's done worse. Here's the thing, Sue. My sister's in a bit of a mess. Motorbike accident on the way from Melbourne. She's here in Alice Springs with a broken leg and broken arms. Also, minus one kidney."

"Oh my god, Kenny, I'm sorry to hear that. Can I do anything for you?"

"She'll be in hospital for the next two weeks, and then we're taking her to Charlie's station where she'll recover fully."

"Oh, I get it. She needs a carer, and you thought of me."

"Yeah, but I'm sensitive about your commitment up there. Don't know if it will work."

"You wouldn't believe it. I've been filling in for the full-time nurse here, and I'm just moving out of her room. She gets back after the weekend. I was just checking my maps for a place to go fossicking when you rang. Of course, I'm available for you. So what's the deal, digger of giant gold nuggets?"

"Haha, full board, all the gear you want for the job, on-call 24/7 and rehab when she comes out of the casts. $1500 a week. Probably three months for the whole job."

"Hmmm, happy to do the job but a problem with the money."

"Sure, Sue, name your price."

"$500 a week and board and no argument from you. My final offer."

"Hard bargain as usual. All right, you've twisted my arm. Well, if you're on the road, what say we meet in Alice, make any prelim arrangements, go out to the station and look at the set-up there, and have a good catch-up ourselves. OK with you?"

"See you on Wednesday, can't wait to see both of you, I mean the three of you. Oops, the four of you. Sorry, I'm damn stupid."

"Yeah, dumb like a professor. Done, Sue. See you then."

His attention turned to Charlie.

"Charlie, g'day, good news. Sue's on her way, and we'll see her middle of next week. We need to work out a package for Sue and Hanna to stay with you. Remember, you mustn't upset your employers by treating us. We'll cover whatever it costs. And whatever that is, you mustn't confide in Hanna, this is between us."

"You wound up or something, brother? Slow down. You're in the bush now, and we only speed on the roads. Everything else is country casual. You got it?"

"Sorry, Charlie, of course, I'm wound up."

"Kenny, I want Hanna here for several reasons. One of them is to consult with us on setting up a breeding programme for genetically modified camels. It's going to be a big job and take years to complete. The owners want this to happen. As soon as she can use a phone and computer, I'll have her doing as much research as she can handle. She'll be doing more than earning her keep, so don't worry. The more important reason I want her here is personal. You don't have to worry, you know how important she is to me."

"You're right. I should know you'd have everything covered. Once we get her to you, I can relax."

There was nothing more to do. They could see Hanna for an hour or so each day and then do a few touristy things. Kenny wanted to see 'Kangaroo Jack', who ran a sanctuary for injured roos. Kate wanted to do a camel ride into the countryside, there was plenty to do with their time.

While Kate was off riding camels, Kenny called the truckie's number.

"G'day, is that you Hackles?"

"In the flesh, who is this?"

"Hackles, I'm Kenny, Hanna's brother. You saved her life yesterday when she came off her bike. Just want to thank you. Man, you are professional. Hope all truckies are as good as you. She has a broken leg, two broken forearms and has lost a kidney, but she's conscious and will recover. Where are you today?"

"No worries, Kenny. Glad I could help. It looked bad, I have to admit. The flying doctor saved her mate, I was just watching. Real glad she'll be OK. For what it's worth, I think she got a puncture on that bend. The front end just went way off. Before, I had watched her for a while in the rear-view mirror, and it was clear she was no idiot rider. She sat well back, took her time to pick the right moment to pass me and when I signalled the all-clear, she didn't muck around, she accelerated to get past quickly, which is smart, nodded to me in the truck and then I could see her back off a bit almost straight away. No mistake, she was still moving but not crazy like. Yeah, I left Alice early and have just passed Tenant Creek on my way to Darwin. Thanks for the call."

"No, mate, thank you and good truckin'."

Kenny then jumped into the hire car and headed to the flying doctor's office at the airport, window down, feeling the winter warmth and thinking it would be a different heat in summer. He drove across one of the bridges over the dry Todd river bed. He took in the sight of thriving native grasses and dominant old eucalypts, a healthy-looking, classic outback vista. Hard to imagine the watercourse in flood.

"Good morning, sir. Can I help you?"

"I hope so. Yesterday a doctor, Geoff McCallum, attended to my sister on the Stuart Highway. Is he here because I would very much like to thank him."

"He is. Can I have your name, please?"

"Oh, sorry, Robert Daniels."

Kenny sat and waited a couple of minutes before an inner door opened. A 40'ish, fit-looking man with a short beard, George Harrison face and frame walked into the reception area, hand extended to Kenny.

"Good morning, Robert, Geoff. I've spoken to the ICU this morning, good news, hey?"

"Doctor, thanks for your prompt attention to the crisis yesterday, much appreciated. You and that truckie saved her life."

"Thanks, Robert, it means a lot. But not all outcomes are as good as this one as you would realise."

"Did you fly the plane as well?"

"Yes, it makes sense to do it that way when we can. Costs are a big thing with the service, and we are always sensitive that people support us with their hard-earned."

"Tell me, who should I speak to if I was interested in offering to fly one of the planes in your fleet?"

"You fly?"

"Yeah, done a bit and am attracted to what you guys do."

"Sure Robert. Tell you what, if you are happy to wait another few minutes, I'll get Mattie Carmichael to come out to talk to you."

"Thanks, Geoff."

Another few minutes passed. The same door flew open, and a rather jolly-looking, bulky crew-cut 30-year-old burst into the room, with sandals slapping the floor and a billowing khaki shirt over comfortable navy blue shorts.

"Mornin', Mattie Carmichael, you must be Robert. Geoff mentioned you fly, what kind of experience, Robert."

"Few years in the RAAF, Mattie. Mostly FA-18, Boeing 737, C-130 and Blackhawk choppers. Done a fair bit in single and twin-engine turbo props since then and was wondering if you could do with some help with your fleet, not permanently but as a resource on call for temporary assignments."

"Hmm, have to check out all that experience, but we always need good pilots. Do you want to know how much we pay?"

"Mattie, I'd like you to have access to me when you need it, but I'm not looking for a career. I've seen something of what you do, and I'd just like to help out. Probably won't be long term, to be honest, but for the next few months."

"Tell you what, Robert. That's mighty good of you. Would you put a package of documents together for us to look at? I'll speak to the boss, and we'll then get you to do a few hours beside our pilots so they can see what you're like. That okay with you?"

"Sure, Mattie. I'll get back to Melbourne, put the package together for you, and then you can let me know if anything is possible. Thanks for your time."

"Good, Robert, see you."

Sue arrived the following day, and Kenny was keen for her to appraise his sister's progress.

"How things change quickly, you're not Jack anymore, my dad's gone, Kate's not in the pub business, Coolgardie is a thriving country town, we are Australia's most successful fossickers, and sadly, your darling sister is banged up in hospital. It's a lumpy road we travel, master Kenny. What on earth is next?"

"What's next, and it's as far as my predictions go, is we catch up with Kate across the road in the indigenous art gallery, head off to the hospital and have a chat with Hanna and her doctors, what do you think?"

"Good idea, let's go. Does she like the indigenous painting styles, or is she just waiting for us?"

"I think she's just tasting the ambience of the town. It's a bit bigger than Coolgardie."

Hanna was sitting up, still in bed, of course, but looking more cheerful than the previous few days. Her face lit up at the sight of the three visitors. It would have lit up equally had it been Charlie, but she understood how much work he had to do. He would be there if he could, she knew. The hours are long when you're laid flat. The mind wanders creatively through all one's relationships, and imagination uses facts as ammunition for creations. Anyway, he was getting things ready at the homestead to accommodate her after hospital. They would see a great deal of each other before long. Waiting might have been hard for her. It was agony for him.

"Hanna, I'm Sue. There's been a fair bit said about both of us, and our paths have crossed a couple of times. It's nice to meet you at last. Jack here, I mean Kenny has asked me to …"

Kenny cut her off.

"I want Sue to give me an idea of your rehabilitation, she's had a career in nursing and saved my life in the desert. I know she'll be good for you too."

A pregnant pause followed while Hanna connected the dots. It didn't take her long.

"You know, Kenny, I don't want to be a burden on Charlie while I'm getting better. Sue, has my brother engaged you?"

"Ooops, sorry kids, sometimes my mouth just has a mind of its own, chattering away before I can think. But, yes, Hanna, he has asked me to spend some time with you. Tell me does Charlie's station have any dried river beds where a girl can fossick for nuggets?"

Kate was the only one enjoying the awkward silence that followed. She defused the apparent intensity at the moment.

"Yeah, and when you've finished with her, he wants you to bathe me."

"Don't think so Kate?"

"OK big brother, I see what you're up to. Logically it makes sense. Look at my arms, I can't even use crutches, let alone take care of other matters. Thanks, Sue, it's generous of you to give us your time. I graciously accept the idea. As for bathing you, Kate, I don't think you really need Sue for that, hey?"

For the second time, they all laughed. In the course of the conversation, Kenny told them he would have to fly to Melbourne and back for some business. Kate already knew what he was thinking of doing but said nothing. Sue, helpful as always, offered Kate a week in the bush, fossicking while he was away, and Kate jumped at the idea. While Kenny stayed to chat with Hanna, they decided to head off on their adventure. Sue was bubbling away as they left the room.

"You won't need a tent, Kate, there's enough room for two in the van. We'll just grab a few provisions, and we can head off. That's the beauty of the van. It shortens the time between making a decision and hitting the road."

"Mac, I'll only be gone for two days, I hope you don't mind."

"Mind? Every other time you've left, it was for years. Of course, two days is fine, as long as my nose doesn't itch."

When Kenny returned to Alice two days later, the first thing he did was drive straight to the hospital. Hanna was pleasantly surprised, looked at him and twitched her nose.

"Kenny, please."

To her surprise, he pulled a back scratcher out of his jacket and presented it to her.

"There you are. Now you can reach your nose."

He bent down and embraced her chuckling broken body.

"I'll be back later, got a little job to do."

He rang the number Mattie Carmichael had given him on the way to the car.

"Robert, got the email yesterday and have had a good look at it. Glad you're back so quickly. If you come out here this morning, I'd like to introduce you to some of our pilots. Our chief pilot is Ryall Wainscott, he'd especially like to meet you, and he's here this morning."

"Thanks, Mattie. I'm just leaving the hospital, see you if twenty minutes."

Mattie and Ryall met Kenny at the door.

"Robert, Ryall, nice to meet you. I've had a look at your records. Top shelf flying Robert, no doubt you worked hard to manage all the stuff I've just read about. Now, come with me, I want to show you our Pilatus PC-12 workhorse, go for a short flight and then meet some of the other flyers at happy hour after work. They're all busy doing maintenance or studying for endorsements but will be free later."

"Ryall, thank you. Sure, let's have a look."

Ryall and Kenny walked around the demo plane doing a visual check, Ryall probing all the time to get an idea of Kenny's competence. For Kenny, it was like being a champion jockey doing a visual inspection of a thoroughbred before leaping aboard. Ryall couldn't fault his observations and comments on things like tyre pressures, condition of wing surfaces, door seals and especially the tail rudder. Top of the list of the important stuff was his question about maintenance routines.

"A pilot is only as good as the plane he's given, you know what I mean."

"Certainly do, Robert. Let's go for a ride."

Kenny sat in the co-pilot seat and ran his eyes over all the switches and dials, nodding and clipping into his belt, looked at Ryall and said.

"OK, skipper over to you. I'll help with the checklist as we taxi, tell me if I miss anything."

He didn't miss a thing. Ryall lined up at the end of the runway and asked Kenny.

"How much tarmac do you reckon for take-off, Rob?"

"Well, this four-blade Canadian Pratt and Whitney is a powerful little beast, I reckon you should be airborne in 600 metres."

"Not bad, Rob. 558 by the book, so you're spot on. Now I'm taking us on a run to a couple of sections where we use the highways."

On the way, Ryall handed over the controls to Kenny and asked him to do a couple of manoeuvres, climbs, turns and even a stall and start. Kenny was in his element, and Ryall soon understood that his new flyer was as good as any he'd ever seen. So, having spotted a landing strip on the Stuart Highway north of Tenant Creek, he asked Kenny to put the plane on the ground in as short a distance as he could safely manage. The book allows just over 800 metres, and Kenny brought the plane to a stop at the 700 metre mark without causing any stress. Ryall hadn't said anything, but it was a cross-wind landing, and it was so pleasing for him to feel the plane time its alignment with the road at the last moment.

"There. You happy with that, Ryall? Don't worry, this plane is a dream to handle, I just let it do its thing, really."

"Very happy, Rob. Now just to confirm what I already think, we'll do a couple of stop and go runs on unsealed strips, you right with that?"

The rest of the flight confirmed for Ryall that he had just met one of the best pilots in his long and varied career. He had not confided anything of his own background, but the truth was it matched Kenny's in much of its detail. Back at base, he introduced Kenny to office staff and other pilots who had gathered for happy hour. Kenny worked the room for a while but didn't stay long because he wanted to check in with Hanna before the end of the day. Ryall concluded the interview process with him before he left.

"There's some paper shuffling to do, Rob, but I would love to have you with us under any circumstances. Next time we meet, I'll show you how we roster, and we'll see how you can fit into the system. We'll have you start as a second officer and let the guys get used to you. I'm sure you'll fit nicely with the others. We must share call signs when I next see you."

"Talk then, Ryall and thanks for today."

Kenny had said nothing before, but he had recognised Ryall's style at the controls. Each had pretty much sussed the other without saying too much but showed appropriate respect.

While Hanna progressed, Kenny stayed in Alice, spending his time between the hospital and the aerodrome, adjusting to his colleagues in trips to emergency scenes at road accidents and workplace trauma on stations, mines and rushing sick children to hospital from a wide catchment area. Kate was away with Sue playing in the bush, taking the opportunity while Hanna was still in the hospital. Kate was having a good time with Sue working their way from one potential site to another, scratching around in dry watercourses, camping, cooking, and enjoying the isolation.

Hanna was so ready when it came time to check out of the hospital. The fossickers were summoned, and Charlie assumed the role of convoy leader. Together, they fussed Hanna into the vehicle and made her comfortable for the bumpy ride ahead. Kenny brought up the rear in the hire car he and Kate had been using. It would be a slow drive, but it didn't matter, spirits were high. Hanna's arms were out of plaster, but she wasn't ready for crutches, the wheelchair was her mobility and would be so for a couple of more weeks. Kenny knew she was in good hands, and he could make arrangements to return to Melbourne with Kate. It was time to go home.

SPOTTY COOPER WENT TO WORK using the fragments of information Chook Fowler had given him. He was looking for Kenny Burgess, but it was Jack Foster who had found the 'Coolgardie Drop'. He would have to start there. It was a short search because there was no information about Jack Foster except for a recent driver's licence and social security ID. Because he was good at his job, Cooper relished the challenge of a difficult case. This case would be difficult unless he had some luck. Kenny Burgess disappeared from all databases immediately after his trial for the manslaughter of the school principal, including prison records and search of death records, all proved futile. He would start with the pub in Coolgardie and the Nissan dealership in Freemantle. Jack Foster must have been someone else, and that person would lead to Kenny Burgess. Cooper didn't have contacts outside of capital cities, so his nearest contact would be in Perth. He pressed that button, and his agent headed out to Coolgardie to do a little excavating.

It wasn't hard for the agent, sitting in the pub, chatting to all and sundry about the former owners and staff. He heard about the great gold discovery, the helicopter and the regular entertainment in the pub.

"Yeah, mate, thanks for the beer. You're new here, passing through or looking for gold? They're the only options at the moment."

"You say this Jack character worked behind the bar?"

"That's right until he left after the girls sold the pub. They all left. The two owners, Jack and the musos."

"Musicians?"

"Yeah, Billy Fingers the yank and Wolvie. They were good too, real country."

"If they were good, I reckon I'd like to catch up with them if they're still in the district. Are they, do you know?"

"Dunno, mate, gee glass is empty, hey!"

"Let me get you one."

"Ta, you're all right, I reckon."

The agent got no more leverage and retired with more questions than answers. He'd have to take a punt on what to do next. He couldn't go back to Perth until he had something worthwhile for Spotty. Might be a waste of time, he thought, but he might as well have a look in Kalgoorlie. Maybe the musos would be still around.

"Hi, Kenny, it's Wolvie, how are you?"

"Good to hear from you, old boy. Anything happen for you In Kalgoorlie?"

"Not as good as the Denver City pub, that's for sure. No, mate, I'm on the way to Alice Springs, hitching in trucks mostly. I want to tell you something. It might be nothing, but it might be something you should know. There's been a bloke asking questions about me in Kalgoorlie but not for me, for Jack Foster. A lady I had a drink with called me this morning. Don't know any more than that but thought you should know."

"Yeah, the story of the gold nugget hangs around my neck like a millstone. It's too big to take off and chuck into a pond. Glad I'm far enough away, even though it was a great thing to experience. But thanks for the nod, Wolvie and happy busking. Talk to me any time."

"Will do, buddy, bye."

Kenny was fussing around in his workshop. After the call from Wolvie, he stopped work and went upstairs to join Kate for a 'smoko' without the smoke. He needed to ponder. Had the inquirer been interested in the gold discovery, or was it something else? He needed to think.

"Coffee's ready, Kate."

Kate was getting herself used to casual starts. For years she had needed to crack the day open early. Not now.

"Be there in a minute."

SPOTTY'S AGENT, FRUSTRATED at not being able to unearth anything at all, headed back to Perth. On the way in, he noticed one of the big posters advertising Nissan Navaras around a photo of two happy faces and a huge gold nugget. The penny dropped, and the agent was able to find out the dealership where the campaign started.

Jet was on the job as usual when Colin Spriggs walked into the showroom.

"Morning, Jet Jolly."

"Colin, Jet. Thought you might be able to help me find the guy who's on your billboard. I've been to Coolgardie but just missed him."

"You wouldn't be the first, Colin. Can I ask why?"

"Of course. He bought a Navara from you, right?"

"He did, but it wasn't for him, it was for his travelling partner, Sue."

"Right, good. I thought I'd have to find him to find her because it's her I need to speak to. Look, I shouldn't pester you. After all, I could be anybody or a scammer of some kind. I'm not, but you don't know that. Hey, thanks for even speaking to me. I can find her in a way that doesn't look suspect. Thanks, Jet."

With that, he left. He had enough now to go on. At least he could tell Spotty Jack Foster is travelling with a woman called Sue who recently bought a Navara in Freemantle. He should be able to get her name and number from car registration files with a bit of digging. The next option would be to search real estate records for information about the owner or owners. He'd shake the tree and see what falls.

SUE WHITTAKER'S NAME floated to the top of the pond, and Spotty soon had her number.

"Morning Sue, how's it going with the patient?"

"Yes, good, Kenny. She's pushing herself as you knew she would. She's scooting around on crutches. She won't need me for much longer. But I called for another reason. Out of the blue, I had a call from a Mr Cooper who was asking questions about Jack Foster. He gave some cock and bull story about why he needs to find him, but it sounded dodgy to me. If he keeps looking for Jack, then he won't find Kenny, but he gave me a phone number where he can be reached."

"Thanks, Sue. Don't worry, it'll be some kind of treasure hunt. Jack's quite famous these days."

"And rightly so. How's it going with Kate?"

"Great, Sue. She's enjoying being free of the pub, and she likes Melbourne so far. Don't know about the long term but so far, so good. Sue, thanks for letting me know about that other business. Will talk to you soon. Bye"

This time he thought more deeply about the interest someone had in finding Jack. Or were they really looking for Bobby or even Kenny? It was time to do something about it but not by ringing the number Sue had given him. If it was trouble of some kind, he didn't want Kate to be swept up in it. Then it occurred to him that if someone was serious about finding him, they would eventually find Kate O'Connell through real estate sales records. He would have to tell her something. He would also have to ring Sandra to make sure of group solidarity. It was like trying to contain a virus that threatened to get out of control. His conversation with Sandra was delightful. She was somewhere in the Barossa with Billy having the time of her life and totally in love. He laughed at her joy. When he told her of recent inquiries, she had heard nothing. That was good because now she'd be prepared if and when the call came. She promised to let Kenny know.

It was only twenty-four hours later that Kate's phone rang. Kenny listened.

"Mr Cooper, is it? Yes, sir, Jack Foster was at the Denver City Hotel until he got his windfall from the gold nugget you no doubt know about. He was off to the big city pretty fast. That's where all the big rollers go, isn't it? Why do you want to know? Oh, yes, OK, hmmm. Mr Cooper, I hope you find him. Where am I? Mr Cooper, please. Jack did say something about visiting his home city of Port Moresby. That's all I know. Hope it helps. Bye."

"Good work, Kate. You've made it harder for them to find anything. I'm quite sure Sandra will get the same call. This guy is serious and will keep digging. The thing is, I've got no idea what it could be about, but at least we have his cell number. Now about your phone. You need a new one."

"Why?"

"It's called radio-location. We can't have a character like this one knowing where you are. It's not safe. We'll sort this out tomorrow."

"Hmmm, this is getting serious."

Jack Foster, unknown to the people looking for him, had disappeared. No ongoing bank transactions and social security payments stopped, no phone number. Kenny had paid a good lawyer to sort out the identity issues. He was back to being Robert Stephen Daniels, visible only to those who knew. Spotty Cooper and Chook Fowler certainly did not know.

Fowler wasn't impressed with Cooper's report. The photo of Jack Foster in the newspapers was the only lead, and now he had disappeared. Spotty was intrigued, Fowler was frustrated. This identity dance he was following had him puzzled but not beaten. Fowler wanted results and had no patience. Cooper needed patience while he thought about what to do next.

Reading over the report he got from Perth, there was a story about Jack Foster saving a helicopter pilot by flying the craft himself. What, he thought, could it mean? This phantom walks out of the bush with a huge nugget. He then takes over the controls of a commercial helicopter. Next thing, he is gone. He knew there had to be a story. A voice inside his head told him to go back to the beginning, the answer was somewhere there. Boarding school, a paedophile nest, dual suicide, murder and then nothing. A search of prison records told him Kenny Burgess only spent a short time in remand at the time of his trial. He was found guilty but was never jailed. Cooper sat back in his chair, smiling with self-satisfaction at his ability to scrounge around in protected databases. Smarter minds had been at work. Cooper knew, but he wasn't beaten yet.

Almost grasping at straws at this stage, Spotty Cooper rang Kate O'Connell's partner.

Sandra and Billy were in the Adelaide Hills about to dine in a tiny historic hotel where winemakers and vineyard owners played. Billy sat sipping a delightful Riesling, and Sandra was in the restroom. Her phone rang. Billy picked up.

"Hello, could I speak to Sandra, please?"

Cooper was surprised at the accent he heard.

"Y'all hold on now. She'll be here presently, man. OK?"

Cooper saw the opportunity and jumped.

"Maybe you could help. I've been trying to reach Jack Foster. I believe you know him."

"Surely do mister. Wonderful man, if I say so mah self. Y'all call him Jack now?"

Billy saw Sandra heading back to the table just as Cooper pursued, his curiosity now sharpened.

"Why, does he go by another name?"

"Man, Sandra is here. Y'all can talk now. Bye."

Cooper thought: 'Damnation, two more seconds and I would've had it."

"Hello, Sandra here, who is this?"

"Sandra, I'm O'Brien, a journalist for 'The Australian'. I'm doing a follow-up story about the 'Coolgardie Drop'. You know Jack Foster, and I wonder if we might chat about how it all worked out. Do you have a couple of minutes?"

Alarm bells. Sandra remembered being warned by Kenny that something like this might happen.

"Sorry, Mr O'Brien, that story is not mine to tell. You'll have to talk to Jack. Bye."

"SUE, I HAVE TO THANK YOU for being my carer but forgive me for being excited I can look after myself from here on in. You can continue to use the homestead as your base for as long as you like, but I'm now strong enough to be OK."

"In record time, if might say, you have been a model rehab patient. I agree, my job here is done. Let's talk with Charlie today and I will make preparation for moving on. I enjoyed the Kimberly and think I might head that way again and eventually down the west coast."

"Sounds like a plan, Sue."

Hanna found Charlie in the compound. He was working on a fence design he wanted to test on camels. He was thinking of a kind of collapsible fence from pressure outside the perimeter but be resolutely resistant the other way. They could get in okay but couldn't get out. Hanna had news from the New England research lab they were consulting. They had successfully identified genes that control the size of the animal. Progress was happening. He saw her coming toward him.

"Wow, look at you, walking stick only. Fantastic. I'll soon have to run to keep ahead of you."

"Like they say, young man, you can run, but hiding is out of the question."

"Have you heard from the insurance company?"

"Still shiver at the thought. A violent jerk and bucked into the air is the only memory, but it has not dimmed. I'll get the replacement and will ride it, but I am in no hurry just yet. Oh, you should know Sue's heading off, job done. I've been spoiled and will miss her."

"C'mon, let's go and see her. She doesn't have to go today, does she? We should put on a dinner at least."

"I'll talk to the kitchen, we could do it tonight. I might even bake a cake."

"You do that, and while you're at it, make sure we give her some takeaway packs."

"SPOTTY, YOU SPOKE TO a Sue Whittaker. Do we know what she looks like?"

"Yeah, Mr Fowler, I got her driver's licence photo."

"Do you know where she is?"

"Her phone puts her in the middle of Northern Territory and moving north, why?"

"Get on a plane and go find her. She knows more than she's telling. And Spotty, don't be squeamish. Do what it takes to get her to talk. And when you're finished with her, I don't want to see her turn up somewhere with a story to tell. Get my drift? I'm sending the Ferret with you, he'll finish the job, you just get her to talk."

Sue enjoyed the farewell party, and loaded with plenty of provisions, she set off back to Alice Springs and then north. Every time she used her phone, the forces of evil knew where she was. She would get as far as Litchfield National Park before she was spotted by her pursuers. She had no idea and took no notice of the tail she had acquired. Ferret used his nefarious skills to jack a Landcruiser from a supermarket car park in Alice Springs. He and Spotty were well past the reach of local police before the vehicle was reported stolen. In the meantime, they had nicked different rego plates from another vehicle in Tenant Creek. Sue decided to set up camp in the caravan park just inside the park, her every move scrutinised. It was off-season, so she had plenty of room to herself. There were a few like her, but they were fifty metres from her camp.

They waited until dark before making their move.

"Ferret, you stay out of sight. I'll try a soft approach, see how I go."

"Whatever you say, Spotty."

Ferret had his own orders, and he didn't need to alert his companion at this point. Spotty wandered towards Sue, who sat by her open fire with a cup in hand, staring hypnotically into the flames.

"Hello, missus. Nice night for camping."

His voice roused her but didn't startle her. Campers are generally affable and often looking for someone to talk to.

"You're right, the sky is coming to life. You camping here too, I suppose."

"Yeah, I am, I'm just over there and was thinking of going to bed, and I saw your fire. Too good to ignore."

"Sure, step in. Would you like a cuppa. Billy's hot and loaded?"

"Thanks, names Johnno."

"Hi, Johnno, I'm Sue. Where you from?"

"Been on the road so long I don't remember, really. But headed to Darwin, think I'll get some work on a prawning boat. The season starts soon. What about you?"

Sue passed him the same chipped mug Kenny had used and offered the same chair Kenny had sat in, saying she thought safely, "Here, Johnno, sit in Kenny's chair." He settled in quickly and amicably, chatting about lots of nothing. That was Sue's last cup of tea and her last campfire.

"Come on, Spotty, let's get out of here. We'll take the old girl's ute and leave the Landcruiser here looking like it's her car, and she'll be in it when it goes up. The stupid old bitch didn't tell you much, did she?"

As they drove out of the park, Spotty saw in the rear-view mirror a ball of flame gutting the silhouette of Sue's makeshift coffin.

"Just one word. 'Kenny'. Don't know if that's enough for Chook, but she had nothing else. We better call him."

"You call him, it's your problem, not mine. He doesn't take bad news well. I've had to take out a few blokes who'd upset him."

"OK, but it's all we've got. Let's head on to Darwin, we'll dump the vehicle in the city somewhere and jack another to get to the airport."

"No hurry, Spot. I like a big drive, and this ute is crazy. Let's head south and fly out of Alice."

"Road trip, hey. I'm in."

"Hi, Mr Fowler, we're on our way home."

"What do you have?"

"Only one word, I'm afraid. Hope it helps."

"What word and this better be good."

"Kenny"

Silence at the other end.

"Mr Fowler, does that help?"

"Yeah, it helps, get back here straight away."

"We're on the way."

They were invisible, all tracks covered, so they thought. They were in Katherine by midnight and parked off the road to sleep for a while, intending to get to Mataranka for breakfast. They were not to know the police from Darwin got Sue's registration from the park office and had radioed Katherine to ask if the ute had been seen. The police in Katherine went straight to the two service stations to look at CCTV footage, and sure enough, the vehicle was seen filling up at about midnight. The boys' road trip was not going to get too far. The word was out all the way down the line, and road patrol vehicles were on alert to let the vehicle get to Alice before stopping it.

Ferret was driving when they slowed down to drive into the town limits of Alice Springs. He was stunned when the police car lit up directly behind him. Spotty woke from his doze, the two idiots looked at each other with the question in the air between them. Before they could decide to try and outrun the pursuit vehicle, another appeared in front of them, barricading their approach. They were done.

Charlie made Hanna stop working an hour before dinner. There was no immediate urgency, and she was still tired by the end of the day. He sat her in the recreation room at the homestead, flicked on the tv for the evening news and poured a glass of wine for each of them. He sat beside her, they clinked glasses with a 'cheers' just as the headlines were broadcast.

"Police arrested two men from Melbourne today in connection with the brutal slaying of a grey nomad at her campsite in Litchfield National Park. The victim, Sue Whittaker, was shot and her body incinerated. The alleged murderers took her Nissan Navara and headed south before being cornered and arrested as they drove into Alice Springs. What appears to be the murder weapon was found in the vehicle."

Hanna dropped her glass as the information smashed into her.

"Oh, my God, Charlie, Sue's been murdered. It looks like they just wanted her car. I must call Kenny."

"Hanna, it's Kate, good to talk. How's it going?"

"Oh, Kate, we've just seen the news. Sue's been murdered in a caravan park up near Darwin. The two guys who did it are from Melbourne, they got caught in Alice, driving Sue's ute with her gold nugget collection in their pockets. Kate, I know what happens now, so be ready. Kenny knows it's about him. We know someone's been trying to find him, and they've found Sue. That poor woman. Kate, Kenny won't take this well, none of us have, but he'll blame himself, and it'll kick start the depression he's been managing."

"That's horrible, Hanna. I'll have to tell him, and I'll do the best I can. Leave it to me, and I'll get him to call you."

Kate walked down to the workshop where Kenny was mucking around, as she called it.

"Hey, I've brought you a hot drink, got a moment?"

"Not for anyone else, but you had me from the moment you stepped into the room. Yeah, cuppa sounds good."

They sat at the workbench and sipped tea. He sensed something was coming.

"Kenny, your phone rang, it was Hanna. I spoke to her, and she'll want you to call back as soon as you can."

"Yes, and?"

"She was watching the news we won't get till tomorrow, but the police have arrested two guys who they say murdered Sue Whittaker."

It took no time for Kenny to connect the dots.

"Someone's looking for me, and they got to her, yeah?"

"It looks that way."

She made no move to approach him, just watched him put down his mug, get up and walk to the stair before turning and coming back to her.

"You know what this means, my dearest friend? It means you could be next. Whoever is looking, he's looking hard. I have to find out who it is, or you might be next. I'll have to get to him first."

Kenny's phone rang again. This time he got to it first. It was Charlie.

"Hello, Charlie. Terrible about Sue. Are the guys responsible in the lock-up in Alice?"

"Yes, Kenny, they are."

"They are working for someone, Charlie. We need to know who their boss is. Do you know anyone in the department up there?"

"The boss at Alice is a bloke called Martin Somerville. We go back a while, all the way back to primary school. We catch up now and then. Why?"

"My guess is there'll be a phone number on one of their phones. They will have spoken to their boss after the deed was done. It would be a great help if we can stop this thing from getting worse, which it will do if we don't find out who's pulling the strings."

"Do I have your permission to be honest with him about you?"

"Anything you like."

"The cops might have the same idea, we could be interfering."

"On the other hand, we might be able to save the state a lot of expense and time if we can solve the problem."

"Kenny, I love you, brother, like no other. Are you sure you want to go this path?"

"If he's not stopped, Sue's death might only be the first of a number, all people close to me and all of them important to me. Do you get my meaning?"

The reference to Hanna was not lost on Charlie. Immediately he was on board.

"Got you. We both now have the same reason to find this bastard."

"All we need is the phone number. Knowing you're on the job will keep me focused. Thanks, Charlie."

Charlie arranged to meet with his old school buddy the following day over lunch at the steak house.

"Good to see you, Charlie. Something's up, I can tell."

"You're right, Marty. It's about the two idiots you picked up the day before yesterday. How's that going?"

"What can I say? It wasn't just random."

"I know it wasn't. Can I fill you in a little?"

"Wow, Charlie! What's going on?"

"All I can say is, it's a great story, lots of players. Did you run into Bobby Daniels recently, at the Flying Doctor?"

"Didn't meet him but heard about him walking in there and offering to fly jobs for them because they looked after his sister. Is he the one?"

"Yeah. I'm going to spend the rest of my life with his sister. She was on her way up to see me when she came off her bike just south of here."

"Yeah, our boys attended. How's the girl going?"

"Back on her feet and working for us at the station. She's the link between us and the future of a great industry for the territory. I'll tell you more about that at another time."

"Family trait, hey?"

"You can't know the half of it, but yes, Marty. Someone with bad intentions is looking for my friend Bobby Daniels. The guy must be bad because Bobby has done nothing but good things for anyone who has ever met him."

Charlie passed over a drinks coaster.

"Marty, if you can write down the phone number of the last call made by these two idiots, I can make the big problem go away and perhaps save the lives of other people who are in between Bobby and the bastard who's chasing him."

"Hmm, I'm going to need a bit more than what you've given me, Charlie, to do what you've asked."

They continued their meal, and Charlie told his friend the whole story of Kenny Burgess, aka Robert Stephen Daniels, aka Jack Foster.

"My god, Charlie. I see why you have asked. All those years ago, he would have upset a large organisation with a long reach. It's a wonder he's lasted this long."

Martin consulted his notebook, wrote a number on the coaster and slid it across the table.

"I take it we won't have to worry about finding this man. We'll just make sure the two we've got take the fall for what they did to your friend."

"It's funny how justice and the law can appear to be on different sides of the street, hey?"

"What do you want for dessert? They've got a good bread and butter custard here."

"Couldn't think of anything better. Thanks, Marty."

Chook Fowler knew he was far enough away from recent events in the Northern Territory. They wouldn't be able to pin anything on him. The upside was confirmation Kenny Burgess was in play. His phone rang. It was another busy working day, he answered.

"Morning, Fowler Waste Management. Can I help you?"

The penny dropped for Kenny. 'Fowler', Chook Fowler, it all made sense. Boarding school Fowler. The same Fowler who was persuaded to accept Kenny as a member of a cricket team after the embarrassing incident in practice nets bowled twice in two balls. Him the best batsman in the school. It was obvious he didn't like Kenny and did nothing to make him feel welcome. All these years and the antipathy was still raw. Kenny didn't know the second reason. The pervert principal whose face he caved, 'Glider', was, in fact, Fowler's uncle. Blood, water and all that. Kenny didn't need to talk to Fowler just yet, he hung up and was now one up. He would use his advantage at the right moment.

The fact that Fowler's minions had squeezed 'Kenny' from Sue before they killed her meant anyone at the Denver City Hotel at the time knew more than they had so far offered. And the bullshit about him heading to New Guinea made him focus on Kate O'Connell. The trouble is Spotty Cooper was off the grid and not likely to be available to him for quite a while. He needed another hacker. The word went out, there was always a gun for hire. Cyber-crime, worth more than $2 billion a year in Australia, was a thriving industry, operatives were legion. Fowler's 'men' lined up their suggestions, and he interviewed five before finding the one he wanted. Had to be someone who was already a customer for the 'ice' or coke Fowler supplied to a wide customer base that covered Prahran and South Yarra, and young Casey O'Rourke fit the bill. The joke was that the police were already using him for their own purposes. Casey had no problem working for both sides.

"Casey, can I call you Jonesy as in Casey Jones, the great locomotive driver?"

"Sure, Mr Fowler, what do you need?"

"Ex-girlfriend I'd like to catch up with. Her name is Kate O'Connell, former owner of the Denver City Hotel in Coolgardie up to a couple of months ago. I want to know where she is today. Can you do that?"

"'Course, Mr Fowler. Just need a couple of days."

Tap and go purchases are so convenient, and most users don't even care that the information generated at the point of sale goes into the supercomputer networks that provide the raw material for targeted marketing across the whole retail landscape. Any part of information can be harvested by those who know how. Jonesy O'Rourke was one of those who knew how.

"Mr Fowler, this is a photo of your friend taken by the authorities in WA for her driver's licence. The other records show where she's been using her plastic cards. You can see what she spent on her way across the country. Funny thing, though, she stopped using her card the day she got to Adelaide. Can't tell why. But the phone number you gave me is active, and I can tell you she spends a lot of time in Warnambool. I can give you the coordinates."

"Good work, Jonesy. Here have this bag of good stuff and this little wad of cash. You've earned it."

"Thanks Mr Fowler."

It took another two days for another minion to discover the owner of the phone in question was a remote rural fence post, and the phone was attached to a mini solar panel. When told, Fowler realised it was game on. Kenny knew he was a target. But he had lost his advantage because he still didn't know Kenny's alias or where he was. Fowler could see another wildly spinning ball headed in his direction, and he had no idea which way it was going to bounce. His hatred for Kenny went up a notch.

KENNY'S NEXT JOB WAS to locate the business headquarters of Fowler Waste Management. Public domain, so no trouble there. Time for a stakeout. For once, he was glad of the old Hi-Ace van. It was the perfect choice for the job. Over the next week, he was able to follow Fowler from his preferred office in the back of the Orrong Hotel to his depot in Oakleigh near the now-defunct but once popular drive-in theatre, where he had a factory and ample parking for his trucks. It must have been more than an acre because there were large piles of scrap metal, tyres, and old machinery. He had a car crushing machine and a huge crane. Well organised, Kenny thought for the type of work

Fowler did or had done for him. Between the pub and the factory, Fowler travelled in a chauffeur-driven customised Chrysler 'mafia' limousine. Like everything about this thug, Kenny thought as the limo passed him, it was cliché. It made him predictable, and that suited Kenny.

He hatched a plan to re-establish his relationship with Josh at Moorabbin airport and with his former customers if they would engage with him after a long absence. But every former customer remembered the quality of the service he had provided and was happy to renew business with him. His contacts in Tasmania and on Flinders Island were also happy to supply. So, he began his regular deliveries. This time, though, he took Kate with him for two reasons. He wanted her close as often as possible. He wanted to please her with the venues he visited and to see the quality of seafood Tasmania offered. He also wanted Josh to become accustomed to seeing a second person in the aircraft.

"Hello, Charlie, all well at your end?"

"Yes, you've got news, I hope."

"Go back in your mind, old buddy. You and I walking back to the shower block, and you saved my scone by catching a whizzing cricket ball aimed at my head. Remember?"

"I do, what are you getting at?"

"Get this. Our target is none other than Chook Fowler. Medium size gangster, waste management business and wholesale drug dealer. He knows I'm on to him, but he doesn't know my alias or where I am. He's tried to find out, but if it wasn't for bad luck, he'd be having no luck at all. Wanted to let you know our business with him will be concluded soon. Will let you know when the sun shines on a slightly better world."

"Yeah, a better world for five minutes till someone else moves in on the same territory."

"True, Charlie, but all we can do is let the sun shine happily on our own patch. No way we can reach the whole paddock. Evil is too entrenched. My love to Mac and I will talk again soon. Bye, mate."

"Bye Kenny."

Something happened to encourage Fowler, call it coincidence, you can't really call it karma. Karma would be later.

"What are you doing here, Jonesy? I didn't call you."

"True, Mr Fowler, but I want to tell you I've seen Kate O'Connell in Prahran. I was leaving the movie theatres in Toorak Rd, across the street from a fishmonger. I saw her carrying a box of seafood into the shop. I couldn't believe it."

Fowler was stunned and impressed but showed nothing. Can't afford to gush in front of hired help. In fact, he went straight on the front foot.

"Thanks, Jonesy, but I know about it. But good on you, I'm grateful you're thinking about the job all the time. Here, take this."

He passed him his reward in a one-gram bag of the nightmare crystal all the kids on the streets hungered for.

"Gee, thanks, Mr Fowler, see you later."

No sooner had he gone than Fowler called his driver. There was work to do.

From outside the shop, Fowler could see what he thought would be the owner in his white plastic apron. He was not a big man, neither tall nor bulky. Fowler was empowered and stepped out of the car and confidently into the shop. There were no other customers. The man looked up from a blue grenadier he was filleting.

"With you in a minute, sir."

The accent was heavy with Greek and surprisingly baritone for a small man.

"Nice shop you have here, eh, your name is .. is..?"

"You want my name? Is it not enough that you want my fish, but you want my name? Who is it who wants my name, my very proud name?"

He continued with the fish. Fowler thought he might have to tilt the balance. He half-opened his jacket to reveal his weapon. The fishmonger saw it, put down the fish and picked up his sharpening stone and began to caress it with the evil-looking thin blade.

"Let me help you, sir."

He turned to face the room at the back.

"Con, you got a minute, my brother?"

Fowler was getting impatient. He didn't expect another worker. Neither did he expect to see such a giant of a man step into the room. He carried a cleaver he was using to cut chops from a huge tuna, splattered blood on his white apron.

"What for you want, brother? Oh, you have customer, good."

He turned his attention to Fowler, who had suddenly lost all sense of managing the situation.

"You want some fish? What you like? We got everything, what you think?"

Fowler half recovered his poise.

"Yes, the fish looks fresh. I was wondering who supplies your fish because I've got a few friends at the market. Maybe we could do business?"

The smaller brother was not intimidated, so he pushed back a little.

"So, you want our name first, and now you want to find fish for us, you very interesting."

"Okay, okay, off on the wrong foot. I apologise to you and your brother. Thing is I saw a woman delivering fish to you yesterday from a van, an old van and no sign on it. I would like to meet this woman."

"Ho Kay, who are you to ask questions like this hay? You man from tax office or you health man from council? Oh, oh, you saw woman, you looka her and like huh? "

His big brother was getting edgy.

"Might be you should go now, buy your fish in other place, not this shop. If you want woman, you find her yourself."

With his spare hand, he picked up his phone and before Fowler could move, the big guy had taken his photo. He walked to the window and took another snap of Fowler's car and registration. On this occasion, Fowler was outgunned. He would leave, but he wouldn't forget. He was too exposed to try and intimidate. These peasants weren't smart enough to be scared. As soon as he left, Nick, the smaller of the two, called Kenny.

"Bobby, what you doing. You upset somebody. What you thinking. Me, I'ma thinking you got trouble. I send you photo, you tell me who this man is."

He recounted the incident and thanked Nick for warning him.

"Nick, thanks for letting me know. This man is not a good man. I tell you this because he might send other men to cause trouble. I will be speaking to him soon and will ask him to not bother you."

"Bobby, we like you, you find good fish, you funny man and you not charge us too much. We will help you talk to this man. You think Greek people are easy to scare? Bobby, we have many friends, and you know, some of them are, you know, they drop their problems in concrete, you know what I'm saying? Bobby, get rid of that old van. He has seen it. He will look for it for sure."

Kenny laughed, encouraged that these boys could look after themselves. He didn't need to be told about the van.

Two days later, a courier arrived at the Fowler yard and factory in Oakleigh. Chook was there plotting what to do next when a parcel arrived addressed to him. Not unusual, and in front of the men who were with him, he opened the chiller box. It was a message in the shape of an octopus chopped, garnished and ready to cook. The note read. "Mr Fowler. Make sure your hot plate is hot. Cook the octopus for three minutes, no longer." It was signed, 'The Lesbians of Toorak'. The brothers were from the island of Lesbos and had a finely tuned sense of mischief. Fowler didn't show his friends the note. First of all, he smiled, thinking the stupid Greeks were sucking up to him. Then the second thought arrived hot on the heels of the first. He looked at the octopus all chopped up. The Greeks knew his name and place of business. They weren't worried about him at all. He had done business with Greeks and knew their ways. He would leave the fishmongers alone. But Kenny was in town, he was now sure. It was only a matter of time. Kenny had already cost him two men, and his heart was even more hardened. Kenny Burgess would not end well.

With Sue gone, Kenny knew he had to act soon. The last thing he wanted was news of others being attacked. He needed to isolate Fowler.

"Mr Fowler, there's a man on your cell phone, he wants a quote on a special salvage job."

"Yes?... What kind of plane? ...Is it still able to fly?... Yes, yes, I get it. I think I can help you. And you are?... OK, Mr Young, I'll be there in an hour to have a look at the job. Bye. You'll land at Essendon? ... That'll be fine."

"I've always wanted a corporate jet. But a Cessna will do to start with. It could be a great help for us moving stuff interstate or bringing stuff back from Queensland. Come on, Bugsy, we're off to Tooradin aerodrome. You'll drop me off and then come back to Essendon airport. I'll be flying back with the pilot. How would you like to get your pilot's licence Bugsy? Another string to your bow."

"Sure boss, love to."

Kenny picked up his usual ride at Moorabbin, telling Josh he was off to Flinders Island. He would be going there as usual, but first, he had a quick stop at Tooradin to keep an appointment, a detail he didn't share with Josh. Tooradin, close to Westernport, was a quiet airstrip with no control tower and little traffic during the week. He got there early and scoped the place for the best spot for the business he had in mind. He didn't need to be watched or interrupted.

The limo turned into the parking area, and there was a man in overalls, sunnies and a beanie limping towards the car. Fowler stepped out.

"You Dennis Young, mate?"

"Yeah, you, Fowler?"

"I am. You going to show me this plane you want recycled? Wait here, Mugsy, till I sort this out."

They walked over to the Cessna.

"Doesn't seem too much wrong with the plane, Dennis. What's the story?"

"It's still airworthy, Mr Fowler, but not for too much longer. I can't afford to do an overhaul, and I can't sell it without doing it. Want to know what it would be worth for you to scrap."

"Really don't have much call for aeroplane parts in my game Dennis. What would the overhaul cost to keep it airworthy?"

"I've had a quote for $8,500, money I don't have."

"Will you take me up to check how it flies?"

"I reckon that'll be OK. Do you want to tell your driver to pick you up at Essendon airport? It'll only take us twenty minutes to get there."

Fowler was hooked. He instructed Bugsy and came back to the plane. The limo headed off. Kenny walked with Fowler the 200 metres to where he had secluded the plane, he ushered Fowler to the passenger side and showed him how to get in. As Fowler sat, Kenny tapped him hard enough on the side of his head to stun him and then snapped a pair of handcuffs on him before he could react. He then lashed his feet together with gaffer tape, secured the seatbelt and casually walked around to the other side, climbed in, belted up and got ready for take-off. They were in the air before Fowler came to.

"What the fuck do you think you're doing. Who's paying for this? Whatever it is, I'll double it. Who the fuck are you?"

Kenny removed the beanie and glasses and looked straight at Fowler.

"You heard about karma, Chook? Today is the day you find out."

"You'll never get away with this, you bastard. Where have you been hiding, you dumb little fuck!"

"Yes, Chook, dumb like a rat."

Kenny had nothing he wanted to add. To him, Fowler was already dead. On the way to Flinders Island at five thousand feet above Bass Strait, Fowler got to find out about terminal velocity and how hard water is when you hit it at speed. The rest of the trip went as planned, and Kenny returned to Moorabbin on schedule with a cargo of fresh seafood for the usual customers.

In the absence of any verifiable information, Fowler Waste Management did not dissolve in chaos. Chook Fowler was the only one to dissolve. He was at the bottom of Bass Strait, and all Bugsy knew was his boss jumped in a light plane he hadn't seen at Tooradin and was headed to Essendon. Exit one villain. One can speculate the world would be better off with one evil bastard eliminated. Truth is, there was a short power struggle at Fowler Waste Management, resulting in the next bad bastard in charge. Business continued as usual, as it always does.

Hanna picked up her buzzing phone.

"Kenny, it's you. I'm so glad. Everything okay down there?"

"Hi, Mac. Yeah, it couldn't be better. I guess your healing is complete?"

"Pretty much, and I'm enjoying country life even if Chancellor cello isn't with me for now. We're making good progress on the mini camel front. Charlie's here, want to say hello?"

"I certainly do…. Hello Charlie. All is well, I hear."

"I take it everything is good with you too."

"The sun shines a little more brightly these days. I am devastated by what happened to Sue. I owed her so much. Hope those two rats get what's coming."

"I'll pass on the good news and keep you informed, but the two in hand will be inside for a long time, for sure. Kate enjoying the holiday?"

"Doesn't miss the pub at all. Cheerful and busy with me supplying seafood to a few pubs and restaurants. I think she wants her pilot's licence, so I'll have to find someone to teach her. Okay, we'll talk soon. Bye"

"Bye Kenny."

In truth, Sue's murder had been avenged, but Kenny wasn't at peace. His curse had struck again. The demons were back. Kate had noticed the change in his sleeping and those times during the day when he was clearly absent and intense. No way she could have known how deeply he was damaged.

"I know trouble is brewing, Kenny. Tell me about the visions."

"They vary a bit. Often it's faces of the dead I've known. They come rushing at me out of the night, horrible looks on their faces. There are terrifying noises in my head, and the fear slashes at my nerves. There is a new one. I'm standing beside a lake. It's night with only a sliver of a moon and streaky cloud. The surface of the lake is black and oily. I think it's deep. Standing a little way from me are people who are or have been important to me. I saw the twins who jumped from the bell tower at the boarding school. They stared out across the lake, and then each one picked up a stone, a flat stone, and the stones glowed in their hands. First one and then the other stepped up to the edge of the water, bent low and threw the stone so that it would skip across the lake's surface. I watched the glowing stones skip half a dozen times across the surface before sinking into the depths. There was a hissing sound as each one sank. At the same time as the stone sank, the boy who threw it looked in my direction, a look that seared my soul, then disappeared in a puff of smoke, gone. A terrible pain gripped my gut, and I slumped to the ground. I dragged myself to my feet with a stone in my hand. It began to glow. I stepped to the edge of the water. I turned to look behind me. On a raised grassy knoll, you were standing with your hands on your hips and fire in your eyes as if daring me to throw the stone. I didn't do it."

His eyes bored into her, helplessness and fear apparent in his pallid skin.

"Shit, Kenny, sit down here. I'll get you a hot drink. If you can, have a look at this brochure from the flying school at Moorabbin. I want your help in picking the right one. On the other hand, don't look now, just try and relax while I put the kettle on."

She allowed the kettle to simmer, went to Kenny and held out her hands to get him to stand. He looked up at her, not sure if he wanted to respond. Her gesture encouraged him, so he stood, she led him to the shower and, fully clothed, she pulled him into the confined space and under the stream of hot water. The hot drink had to wait till the therapy was over. When they returned to the living area, they were warm, conscious, and recovered in terri-towelling dressing gowns and soft slippers.

"Maybe you should open a clinic for people like me. You sure have a good system."

"Ha, ha. I've barely got the energy for one. That'll do me."

"But, you have to see, Kate, how dangerous this beautiful thing between us is. There is a real fear that it could be taken just as has happened too often before."

"You've had other therapists?"

"No, not like you, except for one who didn't even get to the first session. But people who matter to me have been taken."

"Well, my big boofhead, at least if I'm taken from you, I'll still know what we've had between us. I am too into what we've got to be worried about losing it. So, don't worry. I am with you for as long as it lasts, and that's it. Here, take your mug."

"Ta. Now, about the flying school…."

"You could teach me."

"Could, but won't. It'd be the best way to ruin our affection for each other. No, let another instructor teach you, then you can learn a few other things by watching me."

BLURB

KENNY DOESN'T DIE in the helicopter. He miraculously survives, but his life continues under another pseudonym. He is now Jack Foster, a fossicker in the care of his saviour, retired nurse Sue, and completely oblivious of his former life. Fate, it seems, has other plans for him. His sister is devastated at his disappearance but is never convinced that he is dead. In fact, she mounts a search of her own, giving up her successful legal practice to do so, alongside Kenny's only long-lasting friend, Charlie, who manages a cattle station in central outback country. They travel on their motorbikes across large sections of WA looking for him, sometimes coming agonisingly close to finding him. Wherever Kenny goes, he takes his innate goodness with him. He spreads light in dark places, warding off every appearance of evil and empowering all who come near him. Like a stone skipping across the water, he brings joy to his surroundings. The thing is, the stone must inevitably sink to the bottom when it runs out of its momentum. The black dog stalks him to the end. The best he can do is manage its surprise assaults. He is lucky, in the end, he has the intrepid Kate in his corner. Maybe that will be good enough. And maybe it won't.

Shawline Publishing Group Pty Ltd

www.shawlinepublishing.com.au

SHAWLINE
PUBLISHING
GROUP

Lightning Source UK Ltd.
Milton Keynes UK
UKHW020745200722
406119UK00009B/1113